Dirt Tracks and

Shrapnel Scars

Helen Charlesworth   2017

Cover and illustration courtesy of Michael Foreman.

CHAPTER ONE

It was a last-minute decision to go and stay with Gran and Grandad. It was mid-way through the school summer holidays and Joel was already bored. His best friend Marley, (real name Marlon, which he hated. He'd apparently been named after some famous actor) had gone to visit some relatives in Scotland and from the postcard Joel had received this morning, looked likely he wouldn't be back until near the start of the new school year. Marley, his siblings, dogs and parents had all crowded into their 4-wheel drive and gone to stay in a crofter's cottage on a farm, somewhere near Aberdeen, and so the friends were separated by nearly as far as you could be without leaving the United Kingdom. Actually, it was 581 miles – Joel had checked it out. They could text and phone each other, but it wasn't the same as doing things together. Saying that, there was no internet at the cottage and Marley had to walk to the end of a long road to get a phone signal.

Joel had other friends of course, but he enjoyed the company of Marley more than any of them. Marley seemed to be on the same wavelength, they understood each other. Where other boys would be talking about the latest PS4 or Xbox game, sport or TV programme, he and Marley would be planning day long adventure trips, sending each other secret coded messages that only they could decipher. They read 'boys adventure' comics and spent hours poring over old books and internet sites. They enjoyed discussing UFO's, unsolved mysteries, espionage and crime. They had notebooks filled with information on the comings and goings of their neighbours and the local neighbourhood. They observed people's habits and routines and anything out of the ordinary would be highlighted in red or *starred* as carrying around an assortment of coloured pens wasn't always practical. They also had a computer file of photograph's they had taken with their mobile phones of suspicious looking characters, or people just looking shifty. The Police was always asking for information regarding crimes and they felt that by keeping track of the local area they were providing an important public service. Only a few months previously Joe and Marley had both been presented with a 'Young Citizen's' award by the Chief Constable, after they had noticed a shoplifter stealing bacon, cheese and a number of other items from their local Spar. They had followed him home and once he had entered the address, they phoned 999 and gave the call handler his details. They then waited for the Police to come and arrest him.

The presentation was attended by a photographer from the local free paper; in which their picture appeared a week later. They also had a write up (penned by Marley) and picture of them receiving their award in the school newsletter, which made them feel like minor celebrities for a few days.

Joel's proudest moment though had been a little closer to home and it was down to his detective work that his family were saved from losing everything; their home, their car and dad's job. Well, Dad had said, "we could have lost everything," but he was probably saying it out of relief more than anything. Joel's dad had been 'head hunted' for a job in Milton Keynes. It came with a much higher salary and lots of perks including use of the company's nine holiday villas scattered across France, Spain and Italy. Membership to an exclusive gym and golf club (not that his dad had the slightest interest in golf) and a generous holiday allowance. Mum had started looking up properties near to where Dad would be working and found a very nice four bedroomed house which on his new salary would be affordable. Joel admitted it looked nice, but he really didn't want to leave his friends. He'd been to Milton Keynes before when he visited Bletchley Park and thought it quite a nice place to live, but without Marley it wouldn't be much fun. Mum and Dad would try and convince him of the benefits of the move; bigger house, more pocket money – also he'd be near a number of speedway tracks and they'd be able to attend on a regular basis as his dad's working hours were to be eight till four, five days a week, with flexibility.

This was the clincher for Joel – the prospect of getting to see speedway on a regular basis. Marley could always come and stay for the weekend or during the school holidays. He'd make new friends.

He started looking at the Ofsted reports for the local school and pinned it down to the two he'd prefer. It was then he decided to look at where his Dad would be working. He typed in the company name and it showed it as being based in a terraced street in an out of town suburb. He then started doing a little more research and began to see that all was not well. The company only had three employees and had been running just over a year. They didn't have the portfolio his dad had been lead to believe and had assets of less than 5K.

After a little more detective work, Joel printed out his 'evidence' and gave it to his dad, who in turn did a little more digging himself. It turned out that the job was nothing like as good as it seemed – it was legitimate, the post was anyway. The salary wasn't possible though based on the company's portfolio. It was all false promises, luring him in to hand over his present companies' contacts and, contract information, before suddenly pulling out of the deal.

Dad gave Joel a £25 pocket money tip and his employer, gave Joel a £50 'Game' voucher as thanks for his ingenious detective work.

Joel texted Marley saying he was off to spend some time with the 'olds' and would update him when he arrived in Plymouth. An hour or so later, when Marley's phone picked up a signal, he sarcastically texted back that they both were living the dream and that their friend Jez who had been updating his social media posts with poolside pictures from Italy, was seriously missing out.

He laid out his belongings on the bed to check he had everything he needed, before putting them into his back pack and Sainsbury's life-time carrier bag: Mobile fully charged, charger, torch, notebooks x 2. Pens and pencils. His Nintendo DS, Mars bar, Aero. A pack of chicken and mayo sandwiches, crisps, comics, bottle of flavoured water, clothes and toiletries.

Once everything was packed he scanned his bedroom to see if there was anything else it might be worth taking. He picked up a small pair of binoculars from a shelf, sending the books they were holding in place tumbling to the floor. Momentarily he stopped to pick them up, then decide against it; hopefully Mum would do it when she came to put his laundry away, otherwise he's do it when he came home. Slipping on his trainers and pulling his Jason Doyle racing snapback on his head, he left his bedroom door slightly ajar and headed down the stairs. Mum and sister Tabby, which was short for Tabitha, but no one ever called her that, were busy in the kitchen making alphabet biscuits using cookie cutters. Tabby, or 'Tabbycat' as he often called her, for no other reason than to annoy her, was seven and a bit of a madam. Tabby liked to copy everything her mum did and would sometimes scold Joel as if she were an adult. He would flick her curly hair when she did so and off she would go, running to her parents crying. There was six years between Joel and Tabby and although he was protective of his little sister, they didn't have all that much in common. They lived in the same house, had the same parents and ate tea at the same table, but that was about it. Sometimes they would snuggle up on the sofa together or go out on trips with their parents, but now that Joel was getting older they were drifting apart. Tabby had her own little friends and his friends certainly didn't want her hanging around with them when they came over. His friends talked adult stuff, and anyway and some of his friends were fourteen.

Joel watched as fields, hedges, trees, valleys, sheep and cattle flashed by. Suddenly a tunnel – darkness, then fields and hedges and sheep and cattle.

This was his first real grown up adventure. Okay, it was only going to stay with Gran and Grandad, but it was the first time he had taken a train ride alone and was going to be away from home without mum and dad for more than a few nights. He'd been on a few trips when he was in the cubs, but they were only from Friday to Sunday. Oh, and he'd gone on a school trip to Cambridgeshire the previous year which was from Monday to Thursday - three nights. They'd visited Bletchley Park, the home of the British codebreakers during World War II. They also went to a theme park where he'd been sick after eating too much food and going on too many rides.

This time he was going to be away for at least five nights – which seemed quite a long time, especially when it was staying with his grandparents and with no plans for anything exciting to do and no-one his own age to talk to.

A small part of him wanted to text his mum and say "I'm getting off at the next station, come and pick me up." Another part of him thought, 'you great big wuss!' His dad had always told him to enjoy the time he had with his grandparents, because when they were gone all he would have was memories and he would regret not having spent more time with them. His dad had often spoken of his grandad Armstrong – a Geordie, a man renowned for yarns about 'the good old days,' whenever they had visited him. He and his sisters would listen for hours as their grandad told them colourful and long drawn out stories of his childhood on Tyneside.

They only got to see him twice a year as he lived in Northumberland, but apparently, the long car journeys were worth it; for his stories and Grandma's cooking.

The train pulled into Totnes station, Joel watched as people got on and off – holiday makers, shoppers, people going to work, people coming from work. Some with suitcases, buggies, shopping bags. Others carrying cardboard coffee cups and staring down at their mobile phones. Everyone seemed busy, pre-occupied, only concerned with their own business.

Mum had driven him to Exeter and put him on the train there with words of advice not to speak to anyone, other the train conductor and on arrival at Plymouth station, not to speak to anyone other than those in Great South Western rail uniform; until he saw Gran.

'I'm thirteen for goodness sake, not five.' He thought to himself. He hated being treat like a child. His friend Sam who was fourteen, could do whatever he liked. He had a Moto-x bike and took part in competitions. He was allowed to go to late showings at the cinema and his dad would let him drink lager shandy when they had barbecues.

As the train pulled away from the station, Joel slipped his headphones on and began listening to some music. He noticed an elderly chap who had just boarded the train and was looking at the seat numbers as he made his way along the carriage. He stopped to check his ticket, and then looked intently at Joel. His gaze had made Joel slightly uncomfortable, so he deliberately began looking out of the window and away from the old man's stare. Moments later he felt someone sit down in the vacant seat next to him. Still looking out of the window he moved his Sainsbury's for life carrier bag so they would have more leg room. He then took a sly sideways look to see who it was; it was the old man.

"I've not been on one of these in over forty years," said the elderly gentleman, determined to have a conversation. "When I was young we used to have these noisy old steam train." He chuckled at the memory. "They had these big heavy doors that you had to slam shut and turn the handle; nothing like this thing. You sat in little carriages, like tiny rooms." He used his hands to demonstrate the layout, forcing Joel turned to look at him. The gentleman smiled and carried on his story. "There was a passage way that ran down the side of the carriage and each little booth had its own door. Unless you had a newspaper or book to read you sat staring at the person opposite," he chuckled.

"I bet that was awkward," replied Joel. Feeling obliged to have to join in the conversation, he laid his headphones on top of an empty crisp packet on the small lap table in front of him. He remembered going on a steam train trip when he was younger. It was somewhere near a beach, they had been on holiday and he had sat on his dad's lap because he kept sliding off the shiny wooden bench that ran the length of the carriage. His legs being too short to reach the floor. He recalled the rhythmic clickety-clack sound of the wheels on the track and the loud whistle that made him jump.

"They poured out a mountain of steam and smoke; huge plumes of it." The gentleman demonstrated by waving his hands in the air, exaggerating the plumes of steam. "They were noisy too – clackety-clack, clackety-clack. Used to have a train track run past the back of my house when I was a boy." He paused for a while, deep in thought. Joel was just about to pick up his headphones and put them back on when the old man began chatting again.

"Only used for pleasure trips now, steam trains are. The cost I suppose and the pollution. They ran on coal you see. All that pollution filling the atmosphere – mind you it never harmed us. All this electricity and microwaves and what have you, surely must be more dangerous?" Joel looked at his mobile phone and thought of the signal pinging from it to the nearest network tower and then to a satellite somewhere in space orbiting the earth, and back then again. The microwaves passing through his and everybody else's bodies all day long and everyone being blissfully unaware.

"I used to sit for hours on our back wall, watching the coal and goods trains go by when I was young," reminisced the old man. "Ah, it was different when I was a young'un though. The corner shops have all disappeared and its' all big out of town supermarkets now. I don't think you even get milkmen now delivering the milk – it's all in plastic cartons....." He stopped and pondered for a few seconds. "All the little villages around have been eaten up by the city expansion," he sighed to himself and muttered, "progress."

They both then sat in silence, neither knowing what to say next. Joel didn't really want to converse with the old man, although he seemed harmless enough. He wondered if his great-grandad Armstrong were still alive, he would be talking to strangers he met on trains, telling them stories about when he was a lad? His mother had specifically instructed him not to talk to anyone and he was well aware of the 'stranger danger' strategies he had been taught at school. The silence between them carried on for a few minutes longer and Joel hoped that they could now carry on the journey in peace. He was just about to attempt again to put his headphones back on when the old man noticed them.

"May I?" he said, holding out a wizened hand towards them. Joel looked at the him a little surprised. The old man nodded towards the headphones. Joel hesitated, but thought it was probably okay. The gentleman looked quite smartly dressed – not the sort who would steal them from him and sell them on for drugs money. Anyway, there were other people in the carriage and he could always shout for help if needed.

The old man smiled as Joel handed them over to him. He caressed them gently, and still smiling he put them on his head and closed his eyes as he listened to the music. He sat there for what must have been about a minute, maybe more - eyes closed and grinning away to himself. Taking them off he handed them back to Joel and said "Thank you for that. I always wondered what they sounded like." Joel slipped them back around his neck and giggled to himself thinking of the old man listening to 'Major Lazer.'

"Didn't have things like that when I was a lad you know. If you wanted to listen to a particular piece of music you had to put a record on the gramophone player to hear it. I bet you've never even seen a record?"

Joel hadn't actually seen a 'real' record but he had seen pictures of them on the internet. He remembered his gran saying she used to have a record player and she'd take it to her friend's house and they would play records and dance to the music.

"And I bet you've never listened to that sort of music before?" said Joel. They both laughed.

"So, where you off to then eh? On an adventure?" the old man nodded towards Joel's open carrier bag. His Nintendo, sweets, four copies of 'Commando' comics, his binoculars and other random items on show.

"I'm going to stay with my gran for a while," said Joel. "You?" enquiring as to the old man's journey. There was a slight pause and then the old gentleman pulled himself upright in his seat and took a deep breath before speaking.

"I'm seeing a very dear friend of mine; someone I haven't seen for a very long time." He looked at Joel and smiled. His blue eyes appeared a little watery. Joel smiled back.

"Does your friend know you're coming?" enquired Joel.

"No….." The old man paused again. "No, he doesn't." He gave a sigh and a wistful look. Joel said he hoped the old man's friend was at home and that his journey wasn't wasted.

They then chatted about everyday things. The old man kept on about when he was a boy and how things had changed. He mostly spoke and Joel mostly listened. They then sat in silence for a while longer, both watching as the passing countryside turn into city and gradually the train began to slow down as it neared Plymouth station. Joel began gathering his possessions from the lap tray and packed them into his carrier bag. The old man noticed his cap.

"Jason Doyle." He said it reflectively, rather than questioningly.

"Do you like speedway?" queried Joel, sensing recognition in the old man's voice.

"Used to go watch it when I was young. It was very popular back then." He smiled wistfully and his eyes became watery again. Joel suspected he might have an eye infection.

"Got my boy to take me to Somerset a few years back. Took me to see Jason ride. I remember it was Baltic. Middle of June it was too." He chuckled and then sighed. The old man dabbed his eyes with a cotton handkerchief, he pulled from his pocket. He then looked at Joel intently and said, "I hope you have a lovely time, make some new friends, maybe have a few adventures too?"

'Not likely' thought Joel, Gran and Grandad weren't exactly the most exciting of grandparents – they weren't bad though, they could be worse. One of his class mates, Chelsea Johnson. Her grandad was in prison for fraud. He'd faked some building company in Spain, where he'd set up home and made thousands of pounds from the scam. If anything, he thought he'd probably be heading home sooner rather than later, especially if the weather wasn't very good. If he wanted to go to speedway though, he'd have to stick it out until at least Saturday. The deal breaker in him going to stay with his grandparents was when Gran said Grandad had promised to take him to speedway on Friday.

"I hope you have a nice time with your friend," said Joel, as he put on his Jason Doyle Racing snapback.

Once the train had come to a standstill, the old man got to his feet and slowly made his way along the carriageway. Joel picked up his carrier bag from the floor, took down his back pack from the overhead luggage rack and followed behind along the carriage. He helped the old man, who was having trouble stepping off the train, to disembark. Once on the platform he followed the other passengers as they made their way into the station foyer and through the ticket barriers. He stopped to wait on the other side, just outside W.H. Smiths and looked around for his gran, who was due to meet him there. The old man shuffled by, it had taken him much longer to get to the ticket barrier. He stopped in front of Joel and held out his hand. "It was very nice to meet you, young man, very nice."

Joel was a little surprised but offered his hand in reply. The old man shook it firmly putting his right hand across to seal the shake. Joel thrust his mobile phone into his pocket and with his right hand and zipped it up. He felt to check he still had his headphones around his neck. He suddenly had the random thought the old man might be a confidence trickster and whilst appearing genuine, either having sleight of hand or have a 'partner' standing nearby to whisk away the item of choice.

"Take care Joel," said the old man as he turned to walk towards the station coffee shop. He dabbed his eyes again. Joel hoped the old man didn't have conjunctivitis, as he didn't want to catch it. He remembered when Tabby caught it at playgroup and her eyes went all red and puffy and crusty and mum had to put drops in them for a week. He rubbed his hand on his jeans to try and wipe away any infectious germs that might be lingering and then re-checked his belongings, making sure he had everything and hadn't left anything behind on the train, even though he checked before he left the carriage. 'Damn' he thought. He was supposed to text Gran when the train left Ivybridge station, so that she could be at the station on time to collect him. Now he would have to wait around for ages. He went on sat on the uncomfortable metal seats in the waiting area and sent a text message to Gran, stating that he had arrived and forgot to message her sooner as he had been 'distracted by a daft old man sitting next to me who wouldn't stop talking.'

Gran texted back immediately 'on way xx'

Joel sat in the waiting area, watching the automatic doors open and shut – eventually after what seemed like an age but was probably less than ten minutes, Gran came bursting through the doors. She hurried over to where he was sitting and seized him in a bear hug, made Mm-Mm-Mm noises as she kissed and hugged him. Joel adjusted his back pack and again checked his headphones were still in place. He hadn't really minded the wait, he did what he often did – daydream. He imagined he was in Jason Doyle's van, his travel buddy and mechanic. They were on their way to a meeting at Zielona Góra where Jason rode for the Falubaz team. Joel often imagined he was helping Jason out before and after race meetings. They often had long imaginary conversations and sometimes Joel would fall asleep in the middle of them, especially if he was travelling in the back of his dad's car or lying in bed. It didn't matter though, he could always carry on where he left off another day or start a new adventure. When he was worried or upset he often turned to Jason for advice. Jason would always say "You'll be fine mate," or he would just listen. He was never judgmental.

"Come on Grandad's waiting in the carpark and he hasn't got a ticket."

Gran seized the Sainsbury's carrier bag and bundled Joel and his belongings towards the exit doors and Grandad's waiting car.

Joel didn't notice the old man sat in the coffee shop, watch him leave.

Grandad waved from the drivers' seat of the car. He had the engine running and was obviously keen not to hang round. The usual pleasantries about the journey and the weather were discussed on the short journey home, as well as how busy the roads were how many idiots were on them. Every time Joel went out with Grandad in the car it was the same.

Grandad never had anything pleasant to say about other drivers. They all appeared to have a conspiracy against him to make his journey as difficult as possible. Once he was out of the driver's seat and his key hung back on its hook in the kitchen, Grandad was as nice and kind and mild as ever. Joel didn't particularly like going out in the car with him and would always try and make excuses not to go. Not that he went out with Grandad very often or very far, but the few occasions he had gone out with him were awful. He even shook his fist and swore at a seagull once because it dared not to move from the parking bay he wanted.

Back at Gran and Grandad's house, Gran showed Joel to 'his' room. It was the spare bedroom where Gran had previously stored all his Dads' and his Aunts' old toys and books, bric-a-brac and other things she didn't want to throw away. He was quite surprised when he entered it and found it very tidy and devoid of much of the clutter that he enjoyed going through on previous visits. As if reading his thoughts Gran said "If you haven't used it in the last two years and are unlikely to use it in the next two; get rid. I read it in some magazine. I've kept somethings." She got down on her knees and showed the neatly packed boxes under the bed. "The best toys and books." Her tone of voice made it sound as though she had kept them for Joel to play with; but he was too old for toys now. Well, some of them were ok and the books were pretty interesting.

He took his time as he unpacked his backpack and carrier bag. He placed his clothes in an empty drawer that Gran had allocated him. The other drawers in the chest being filled with some of the clutter Gran felt unable to dispose of.

He took his toiletries into the bathroom and placed them next to Grandad's on the windowsill. He then arranged his binoculars, comic books and other small items on the bedside table, next to a small red cased travel clock that said five-past twelve and had done so since he entered the room. He sat down on the bed and set it to the correct time and then wound it up. It wasn't the sort of clock you could buy in shops anymore; it was really old, probably as old as his dad.

After twenty minutes or so making himself comfortable and having played a few games on his phone Joel thought he should really go downstairs. He could hear Grandad making some noise; bangs, drilling and general D.I.Y sounds. Grandad always had a project on the go, whether it be repairing an item of furniture for a neighbour, fixing a radio or simply painting the shed. Today it was something a little more difficult and messy than most of the other jobs he undertook. Joel walked into the dining room and was promptly instructed to 'keep the bloody door shut!'

All the furniture was covered in dustsheets and Grandad, who was not, was covered in dust. Joel could see that the wall where the fireplace used to be was stripped of paper and plaster and the old fireplace ripped out. "Putting an electric flame effect fire on the wall." Said Grandad proudly. Warm as toast in five minutes. These things are dated and too messy." He pointed to the shattered cast iron fireplace lying on the floor. "Look pretty but not practical, not nowadays."

Joel had always thought the real fire lovely. Gran only lit it at Christmas; the rest of the year the room was heated by a radiator under the window and a dried flower arrangement sat in the grate of the fireplace where the coals should go.

 "Here." Grandad took his phone from his pocket and with his grime encrusted hands flicked at the screen until he found the clip he wanted to show Joel. It was Joel admitted, impressive – a framed fire that sat in a recess in the wall and which looked like a real log fire with flickering flames. "You'll have to decorate too Grandad," said Joel, pointing out the state of the torn floral wallpaper around the gaping hole in the wall. "I know son, I know." Grandad looked and sounded a little dejected, but Joel knew he was more than likely relishing in the prospect of another project to work on. Something to keep his hands and mind busy. He'd taken the week off work, as things were usually slack during the school holidays and it gave him time to catch up on some of the jobs he'd been procrastinating over for the past few months.

"Here, look what I found!" Grandad sounded eager, suddenly remembering something he had forgotten. He rummaged in a pile of rubble on the floor and then carried gently in his hand, as though nursing a tiny baby bird – small unrecognisable items covered in years of soot. Looking closer Joel was able to make out what Grandad was holding. An old-fashioned key, a small elliptical lens, likely from old fashioned pair of wire framed glasses and another thing that looked like a hook of some kind. "These have probably sat behind that old fire for donkeys' years," said Grandad. "A bird, likely a magpie; they like stealing shiny things. Probably picked these up and then, when sitting on top of the chimney, stopping for a rest on the way back to its nest, accidentally dropped them down."

Wow, thought Joel. "Is there anything else there?" He imagined a little haul of tiny treasures – shiny twinkling trinkets, concealed behind the fireplace.

"Unfortunately, not" sighed Grandad. "But we'll clean these up and you can show them to your Gran. Here you go." He handing the items to Joel. "I'll finish off in here."

Joel gently took the items from his Grandads' hand and exiting the door, remembered to close it behind him. He went to the kitchen where he placed the items in the sink and let the warm running water rinse away years of soot and dirt. He then patted them dry with a piece of paper kitchen towel and took them to show Gran, who was watering some plant pots in the courtyard.

"What's that you've got there?" she enquired, resting her watering can on a small wooden table. She wiped back her fringe and squinted her eyes from the sun, as Joel held the items towards her to see. "Grandad found them behind the fire place."

Gran picked each one up in turn to examine. "Oh, that looks like the end of an old Edwardian button hook. It would have had a wooden handle on it once upon a time," she said, holding the thing that looked a little like a hook, "and this looks like the key for a cupboard or a wardrobe." This time examining the rusty old key. "Oh, look at this," she said, lifting the lens up towards her eye and trying to look through it. "Oh, someone had bad eyesight," she chucked. She placed the items back into Joel's hand and as he walked back into the house Gran called after him. "Just chuck them in the bin, they're no good to anyone now."

Joel passed the bin and hurried upstairs to his room. He placed the three pieces of treasure on his bedside table, careful not to damage the rusty old corroded hook and key. The lens looked as good as new. He held it up to the window and played around with it until he caught the suns refractive light, which sent a beam of light fringed with all the colours of the spectrum, dance on the wall opposite. He remembered how in 'Toy Story' Sid, the evil child next door, tortured Woody with a magnifying glass, burning his forehead. He sat on the bed and put his hand on the window sill and the lens above it. In no time, once he had caught the suns reflection on the glass, he felt his hand beginning to sting and then burn. He quickly pulled his hand away, realising it had been a rather silly thing to do. He pushed the lens into his trouser pocket and made his way back downstairs; his left hand still smarting.

Grandad was coming out of the dining room with a bag full of rubble and nodding his head towards the door said "We'll be eating on our laps tonight – TV dinners." He struggled along the hallway with the heavy bag. Joel went ahead and opened the front door so Grandad could put the bag outside. "Well, that's that for today." He clapped his hands together and a small plume of white dust escaped into the air. "Right, I'm off for a shower." Grandad then made his way upstairs and Joel headed back to see what Gran was doing in the kitchen.

"Chicken curry, rice and naan bread; how does that sound?" announced Gran as she put a foil covered tray from the oven. "Tikka and a Passanda, your Grandad doesn't like it too spicy, where as I do."

"Yea, sounds great." He would have said that to whatever she had on offer to be honest. Joel decided to watch some television while Gran was busy; there wasn't really anything else to do. He went into the sitting room and picked up the remote control. He flicked through the channels and was going to put on a music station, but then remembered Grandad would probably come in and say 'Oh, you're not watching that rubbish,' tut and to put something 'decent' on. He searched further down the channels and stopped when he came across a programme about spies in the second world war - it looked interesting. He loved anything about spies; he remembered recently reading about the French Resistance and how they helped trapped Allied airmen escape from Nazi occupied French territory.

The documentary was about a man called William Joyce, otherwise known as Lord Haw Haw. Joyce had been the main German broadcaster in English for most of the war. His distinctive pronunciation of "Jarmany calling, Jarmany calling on Radio Hamburg had many British listeners glued to their wireless sets, awaiting news of what the Germans had planned for Britain, be it true or not. Although it was illegal to listen to his broadcasts in Britain, they had apparently become very popular with listeners. During his peak, Joyce had almost as many listeners as the BBC. He caused alarm with his tales of a Fifth Column in Britain and talks on how to treat bombing wounds. He caused mass panic with his seemingly accurate descriptions of Town Hall clocks that had stopped and how many steps there were in a particular church steeple. Joel found it fascinating.

Gran came into the room with a tray of food. "Clear the coffee table can you dear, were going to have eat in here tonight."

When she came back into the room with plates and cutlery, the tray was still balanced at the end of the coffee table and nothing had been moved. Joel was still engrossed in the TV.

"Come on, clear the table or I'll switch the TV off," sighed Gran. She stood waiting while Joel moved the magazines and other bits and pieces from the table into a neat pile on the floor. Grandad soon after came in wearing clean shirt and trousers. The scented aroma of perfumed shower gel followed him. Not the manly sort that Joel or his dad used, but more the sort mum would use.

"With undertones of sandalwood and jasmine that help you unwind." Joel said it in an exaggerated voice and began to giggle. Grandad seemed oblivious but Gran gave a knowing smile in Joel's direction. Joel then proceeded to ask his grandad about the spies of World War two, but Grandad said as it was before he was born he had little knowledge of them really but did know more about the Cold War spies. How agents would work for the Government; Military and British Intelligence in respectable positions, but trade secrets with the Russians. There was the KGB, MI5, MI6. The Cambridge Spies; Kim Philby, Guy Burgess, Donald Maclean. There were double agents, murders, espionage, the selling of secrets, the list went on.

Joel was picturing in his mind, fine-looking men with bryl-creemed hair, smart suits, trilby hats and long macs; meeting in secret, a few brief words passed between them or a top-secret file concealed in a copy of the 'Times' newspaper left on a park bench. The sort who would have worked at Bletchley Park. Maybe a James Bond like character, smart and smooth, confidently swanning around in luxury cars, and smoking endless cigarettes.

What did a spy really look like?

Gran and Grandad sat with their plates balanced on a lap tray. Joel chose to sit on the floor an eat from the coffee table. The TV programme soon ended, much to Joel's disappointment. As the credits rolled he said "Grandad?" dragging out the word as he said it.

"Mmm," replied Grandad who was multi-tasking; watching television, playing with his slipper that had fallen off and was desperately trying to get back it back on his foot before Muffin the dog made off with it; and also eating.

"Did you Know, If I wanted to, I could find out everywhere you had been and everything you had done in the last 24 hours – without even having to leave the house? "He paused and thought for a few seconds. "To be honest, spying's a bit boring now isn't it? I mean, you'd have to source all the information and codes, CCTV footage and things like that and get the mobile phone companies to cooperate and release certain information and you'd probably need a Police warrant to do that and then trawl though everything. If you didn't have the person's computer to hand you'd need to get the I.P address and their providers assistance again to go through that." He looked a little dejected at the thought of modern spying. There were hackers who would spy on your internet activity and break into your account and steal your details. People who could somehow remotely spy at you through your computers camera. Social media sites where people actually freely would give out information about themselves, where they'd been, who with, what they'd had for breakfast and all with full colour pictures. It just didn't seem at all as exciting as the 'good old days.'

"Here save yourself some time," Grandad tossed his mobile phone towards Joel. "You'll have to 'break the code' first." Joel picked it up from the floor and typed in a random four number sequence. The phone buzzed and vibrated. He tried again another three times, but the same thing happened. The phone buzzed and vibrated but wouldn't unlock.

"Not as easy as you think son, is it?" Grandad slipped his phone back into the pocket he had taken it from. "I agree spying today is 'possibly' easier, if you have the right tools. There's drones, mobile network signals, all sorts of stuff, but it's different and more technical. It's done remotely nowadays." Joel agreed, he didn't like the thought of doing his spying from behind a computer screen – tapping in codes and number sequences or watching an unseen drone or PC computer camera hundreds or thousands of miles away.

"Anyone for ice cream?" Gran's words brought Joel back to the reality of now, the empty plate in front of him and the theme tune of Grandad's

favourite programme which was just about to start.

"Maybe later" said Joel, feeling rather full from his 'man sized' portion of food.

The evening wore on. Joel phoned his Mum to let her know how he was, what he'd had to eat, watch on TV and no, he wouldn't stay up too late or play on his Nintendo DS until after midnight.

By 9.30 pm there was still no room for the ice cream and Joel was feeling a little tired. He bade his grandparents good night and headed upstairs to bed. Once settled in to the unfamiliar surroundings he soon fell asleep.

CHAPTER TWO

Will Roberts walked along the road, kicking up dust. It had been a long hot summer and hadn't rained in ages. The metal bins in the street reeked of fermenting scraps of food. Hungry dogs would come along and try to knock the lids off to see what they could scavenge from inside.

He hoped the suns warmth would continue through to October and ripen the blackberries and gooseberries ready for picking and also bring a bountiful crop of apples.

Sauntering along, his gas mask swinging lazily across his body and a damp towel slung over his shoulder. Will thought back to the idyllic afternoon he'd spent swimming in the nearby river Plym with some boys from school; Alec, Malcolm and Andy Gray. As he neared Stitson's 'Newsagent, Confectioner and Tobacconist,' he remembered it was Thursday; comic day. The tinkling bell chimed as h entered the shop and picked up, this weeks' copy of 'Champion' from the counter.

"Hello Mrs Honeybun" he said to the lady serving and handed her the money. She always gave him a funny look when he called her by her name. He couldn't fathom why, as when his dad called her Mrs Honeybun she always smiled and chatted.

Will loved the stories of Trapper Pete and his Racing Huskies, Ginger Nutt; the boy who takes the biscuit, Rockfist Rogan. Granfer would hopefully have a copy of the 'Wizard' waiting for him when he got home. Granfer, as he always referred to his grandad, said he bought it for Will, but he always insisted on reading it first. He'd collect it whilst Will was still at school so that he could ensure he got to read it in peace before Will arrived home.

Will's favourite story to follow, was the escapades of 'The wolf of Kabul' - Second Lieutenant Bill Sampson, an agent of the British Intelligence Corps, who took on the Nazi's armed only with two knives which he used with unequalled skill. His sidekick, Chung was able to make devastating use of a cricket bat, which he called "clicky-ba."

Will flicked through the comic as he strolled along, narrowly missing walking into a lamp post – his attention distracted by the most recent escapades of Dart Dixon, Speedway avenger. Will loved speedway, his favourite rider was Cordy Milne. He'd first seen speedway in 1936 when his dad had taken him to see the Plymouth Panthers at Pennycross stadium. Plymouth had been in the Provincial league along with Southampton, Bristol, Liverpool and Nottingham. He'd gone to a few meetings in 1936 and 1937 before the track sadly closed down. He loved the roar of the engines and the thrills and spills of the racing, but his dad thought him too young to attend, especially as he couldn't really see much of the on-track action, being so short. It wasn't until 1938 when he was eleven (and much taller) when his family went to stay with Auntie Betty and Uncle Norman near Bristol, that he really got into speedway properly. Mum's other brother, Uncle Jack, and his family, had travelled up from Eastleigh near Southampton and insisted he and Uncle Norman took the youngsters to see the thrill that was dirt track racing. The excited entourage, which included Will's Dad Ed and a multitude of cousins, en-masse made their way to Knowle stadium, to watch the Bristol Bulldogs versus Uncle Jack's home side; the Southampton Saints.

It was the most exciting and exhilarating spectacle Will had ever seen. The crowds filled the stadium to bursting. He was overcome with of excitement and anticipation when he saw the leather clad riders emerge onto the track for the pre-meeting parade. The roar of the engines was blotted out by the whoops and cheers from the grandstands, as the motorbikes and riders made their way around the track. Once at the start line, the riders were paraded and introduced to the fans individually. As each name was announced loud cheers and whistles went up from the enthusiastic crowd and wooden rattles clicked away.

Cordy Milne, a glamorous American from Passadena, rode for the Bristol Bulldogs and had ridden in all the World Finals at Wembley stadium.

What a night it was, the most thrilling Will had ever known; the sound of the engines, the smell of the pies, chips and sausages from the hot food stalls. The chatter and cheers from the hordes of fans, and the sight of the cinders being thrown high into the air as the riders broadsided around the bends. To top it all the home team Bristol, led by their American Captain Cordy Milne had wiped the floor with Uncle Jack's Saints, 64-20.

The following summer, 1939 - as well as a trip to Bristol, Will's family made the pilgrimage to Eastleigh for a few days to visit Uncle Jack and

Aunt Mary. Uncle Jack was a railway engineer at the main depot there. Cordy Milne had now transferred to allegiances to Uncle Jack's team – much to his and Will's delight. Cordy had been joined at Bannister Court, by his brother Jack. Jack had been World Champion in 1937, beating Cordy to second place. The year previously in 1936, Jack had lost a thumb in an horrendous track crash but had been back racing within a month. These men certainly were daredevil hero's, devoid of any fear.

Uncle Jack had given Will a Cordy Milne cigarette card as well as a number of other ones, of which he had multiples; including Cordy's brother Jack. It didn't matter that Cordy was wearing his Hackney Wick race bib and Jack a New Cross one. Will wasn't particularly a Southampton fan, he just loved the racing. Uncle Jack had collected the John Player speedway rider collection of cards and had four copies of Cordy Milne, along with many others including, Gordon Byers, Dicky Case, Stan Greatrex, Morian Hansen, and Vic Huxley. Will's disappointment was in never getting a Bluey Wilkinson card before the collection was withdrawn. His collection book had several empty spaces, destined never to be filled. His dad said he remembered seeing Bluey when he raced at Plymouth in 1932, as part of the visiting West Ham team.

On Will's subsequent visit to Southampton, during the long hot school summer holidays of '39, Uncle Jack had taken him into the pits to get riders autograph's after the meeting. Jostled along by fans all holding out autograph books and pencils, Will thought he wouldn't get any signatures – but he did, including his absolute hero.

"Howdy Kid, how's it going?" Cordy's greased back fringe flopped on his brow. Dirt from the track stuck to his face and his hands and his fingernails were ingrained with oil and grime. Will could smell the warm leather of his race suit and the mixture of oil and sweat, permeating from his adrenalin fuelled body. It was a heady mixture that left Will feeling slightly euphoric. Overcome with elation he simply replied "Great," to his hero's question. His one big moment; his opportunity to ask his hero anything – and all he could think of was to say 'great.'

Cordy handed back the autograph book and pencil. He grinned at Will, acknowledging his adulation, and ruffling Will's hair with his left hand said, "Be good kid."

On the bus ride, back to his Uncle's house, Will settled down into his own little world. He imagined himself riding on the dirt tracks, waving to the throng of fans from his motorcycle, before blasting around the track, leaving his opponents trailing far in the distance as he crossed the finish line.

During his stay at Eastleigh Will adopted an American accent and greeted everyone with 'Howdy' or 'Hey buddy.' But by the time the holiday was over and he'd returned to Plymouth, his American drawl had all but left and his Devonshire accent returned. The memories of those wonderful nights at Bannister Court though were still fresh in his memory.

 Little did he realise that within days of his departure from Southampton, speedway there would be no more, or at least for the duration of the war. The papers professed that Cordy Milne should be declared 1939 Speedway World Champion, the final having been programmed in for 7th September 1939 – three days after the declaration of hostilities. Where was his hero now he wondered?

Plymouth had been granted 'neutral zone status' in 1939, because the government decided that it was too far to the south west for the German bombers to reach, but since the fall of France in May 1940, the war had moved much closer to Devon. Hitler's Luftwaffe now able to reach the sleepy town and villages of the western peninsula, from their air stations in occupied France. A few of Will's pals had recently been evacuated by their worried parents to the safety of outlying villages and towns or further afield. His best friend Eddie, had gone to Redruth in Cornwall to stay with a relation. His Mum had wanted him and his younger brother Ned, as far away from the war as possible. They'd packed up and headed west, leaving their flat under the watchful eye of a neighbour. Eddie's dad was now in the Navy, as was Will's own father. He had other friends of course, but Eddie was his best friend. Maybe if the war escalated he would never come back? Will had received two letters from him, and life seemed pretty idyllic in the quiet countryside of Cornwall. Though Will guessed he would likely be back in time for the new school term starting in September.

He'd heard Winston Churchill's speech on the wireless, where he stated; "We shall fight on the beaches, we shall fight on the landing grounds, we shall fight in the fields and in the streets, we shall fight in the hills, we shall never surrender." The quote had been repeated a number of times in the newspapers and the reality of his 'never surrender' speech was already coming true. The large Naval dockyard at Devonport and the presence of the Air Force and Army in the city had made it a prime target for attacks; experiencing its first air raid alert at 12.45 a.m. on 30th June 1940. The first bombs fell on Plymouth a week later on the 6th July - claiming the city's first civilian casualties. The lone bomber had dropped his bombs on the opposite side of the city, claiming two lives on the day and a young boy who died in hospital a few days later. The Luftwaffe's target most likely being the nearby dockyard. The following day, another lone bomber – probably the same pilot as the day previously; flew back over Plymouth. On this visit, he had a different target in mind; the gasometers at Coxside. He swept in low over the Saltram Estate and river Plym and was all set to drop his bombs, but in his eagerness, he released them a second too soon and they fell short, landing in streets a few hundred yards' short of his target.

The house on the corner of Will's the road was damaged and the occupier, an elderly gentleman died a week later in hospital due to the injuries he sustained when part of the house collapsed. Further along, on Cattedown Road, three people, including the postmaster were killed. The flat above the Post Office taking a direct hit. Another bomb was dropped yards away, killing a householder just around the corner. The same blast also took the life of a policeman and a soldier who were in the street, helping shepherd people to the communal air raid shelters. Many properties were damaged in the raid. It had truly shaken the whole community as they hadn't expected 'they' would be a target. Until only a few months previously, the threat of an air strike on the city was far from people's minds. The 'under stairs' shelters were no longer an option and people were getting used to taking refuge in either an Anderson shelter in their back garden or courtyards, their indoor Morrison shelters, or the communal shelters if they had neither of the afore mentioned.

Will still felt the aftershock of the raid. His mum had been friends with one of the women who had her house damaged. Her husband was away in the services and she and her children had been moved to temporary accommodation until it was repaired. Will just felt blessed that his house was still standing.

It had all been quite exciting at first, hearing about the bombing raids on other cities and wondering when it would be 'our turn.' Playing soldiers and pretending to capture German spies. The old Cowboy and Indian games got forgotten, but after a few months of war and nothing really happening, the period called the 'phoney war;' the stetsons, holsters and feathered headdresses adorned the children at play once more.

In the summer of 1939 a Corporation lorry had come along Will's street and at each house, offered a delivery of a number of heavy, shining corrugated steel sheets, some straight, others curved, together with steel channel bars and a bag of heavy duty nuts, bolts, washers and a spanner, along with an instruction sheet on installation. The choice of whether to install the cumbersome shelter in case the German invaders did come, was up to the individual householder. Some saw it as extra storage space, others as spoiling their pretty gardens and courtyards. Some people, mainly elderly who had no one to do the digging for them turned down the offer and opted for the indoor Morrison shelter instead.

Will's dad had borrowed a couple of pick axes and a shovel from the rail yard where he worked and he and Granfer had hammered away tirelessly all afternoon and into the evening to get down to the required three feet deep hole. Uncle Lennie had come along and helped wheel away some of the innumerable barrows of rubble and soil. Once in place the shelter stood three feet above ground level, three feet below, six-foot-long and five feet wide.

So much had happened since then and Will's dad, like most other men of his age had been conscripted in to the Military and was serving on a ship, somewhere at sea. The only contact they had was by way of the occasional letter. His mum had gone up to Liverpool in April to see him, when his ship docked there for a few days.

Andy Gray, his school pal, had felt the effects war much sooner than most people in Plymouth. On the moonless night of 13th October, a German U-boat slipped un-noticed into the sheltered harbour at Scapa Flow in the Orkney Islands, just after 1 a.m. The 'Royal Oak' was hit by a torpedo. The crew believed it was a small explosion on board and that it could be dealt with. Many men simply went back to their hammocks convinced that nothing was amiss. Fifteen minutes later, three more torpedoes hit the 'Royal Oak.' All electrical power was knocked out and a cordite magazine ignited. The attack was so sudden that there was no time to send out a distress call or fire distress flares. The explosion ripped through the ship and caused it to list. Water started being taken on-board and at 1.29 a.m. she turned over and sunk. Eight hundred and eighty-three men died, including Andy Gray's father.

Will stopped outside number fifty-two, the gate was wide open; that meant Granfer had been along to collect this weeks' copy of 'Wizard.' Granfer had a habit of always leaving the gate open behind him. The front door stood open and the vestibule door closed – to stop unwanted eyes prying in. Will entered and called out. Cousin Sylvie called back a greeting from the parlour. She popped her head around the door frame – her blonde curls hidden behind a turban like headscarf, a cigarette hanging from her lips.

"Just about to head out on the late shift." She pointed to her greasy overalls in a basket by the door. "Don't get time off enough to wash those things, I don't. Granfer's out watering his veg." She bobbed her head towards the back door as she rummaged in her handbag. She then puckered her lips in front of the hallway mirror and applied some bright red lipstick. Taking another drag on her cigarette she picked up the basket, called out "too-da-loo" and blew a mouthful smoke in Wills' face as she walked past. He squinted his eyes and held his breath. "That's horrible it stinks."

"No, it doesn't; its alluring." She dragged out the final word as she said it and pouted her lips. "Anyway, all the girls at work are doing it." She winked, turned and sauntered out the front door. The gate clicked shut behind her.

Will went out into the backyard to see Granfer. His flower pots of yesteryear were now all filled with herbs and tomatoes – interspersed with the odd sunflower and red geranium for colour. Even though he had an allotment garden, he still felt it necessary to grow what he could within the confines of their small courtyard. He was carefully nipping back the leaves on the tomato plants. "Decent crop here don't yer think bey?" Granfer always called him 'bey' – he called all boys 'bey.' "Yea Granfer they look good."

That evening Will and Granfer sat down to a tea of bread and butter, a hand-picked tomato and two sausages each. They listened to the wireless, the BBC carried a report on the ongoing 'Battle of Britain'; having got its name from a speech by Winston Churchill, delivered to the House of Commons two months earlier in June, 1940 in which he stated "The Battle of France is over. I expect the Battle of Britain is about to begin."

Maggie Roberts returned home soon after eight o'clock and ate the tea they had left out for her. She then said she was going to bed to read and have an early night – she had an early start on the buses in the morning.

Will sketched some pictures and Granfer read some comics, until the light began to fade. They closed the curtains, ensuring no light could escape and therefore incurring the wrath of the air raid warden and a fine. They then sat and played cards on a small green baize covered table, by lamp light for another hour or so, until Gran returned from visiting Aunt Ellen who lived a few doors up the road. Every Thursday evening the two of them, Gran and Ellen, would go to the Palladium Cinema on Ebrington Street, whilst Uncle Des looked after the children.

"What you see tonight m'dear?" enquired Granfer, hearing the front door open.

"The Grapes of Wrath, with Henry Fonda." Gran took off her hat and looking at her reflection in the hallway mirror, saw to her hair. "It was 'elluva good. All about a family who lost everything in the depression in America and had to go on the road to try and find work and to survive."

CHAPTER THREE

Joel woke with a start – where was he? Why was the room so light….and the noise outside? He then gathered his senses and remembered he was at his gran's house and not his own. Gran's spare bedroom didn't have blackout curtains and the noise outside was the traffic trundling along the road in the culvert that ran along behind her courtyard. He sat up and pulled back the curtains; kneeling on the bed he watched the traffic go by. There were lorries, cars, delivery and workmen's vans. The traffic was very heavy and much noisier than it had been yesterday evening. He looked at his phone to see the time – it was 8.03 a.m. - rush hour. On the other side of the culvert he could see into the courtyards of the houses opposite. There was a lady hanging washing, a cat sat on a wall watching the world go by. A boy repairing a bicycle tyre. Houses with rear extensions; sheds, garden furniture, toys and plant pots. A whole terrace of houses, but each courtyard completely different to the one next door. The high dividing walls meant that neighbours' never saw or communicated with each other whilst being only feet apart.

After a while of people and traffic watching, Joel got bored and decided to go downstairs, Gran was already in the kitchen. The sweet smell of Jasmine wafted in through the open back door and the familiar voice of Chris Evans crooned from the radio.

"Hello Love," said Gran, looking up from buttering her toast. "Want some?"

"Have you got cereal Gran." Joel preferred cereal for breakfast. Gran went to the cupboard and brought out a box of Weetabix. Joel preferred a granola type cereal, but Weetabix would do. "Thanks Gran," he said "but when we go shopping can we buy granola?"

"I suppose so" she sighed. "Don't want you saying I don't feed you properly." Gran sat at the table in her dressing gown and slippers. Her hair un-brushed and her face bare of make-up. She looked different, probably the lack of make-up he thought. He hadn't really noticed that she wore make-up until now.

"Your grandad won't be home till around 5.30, he's had to go into work today – typical; he's on leave and two people have gone off sick. I thought we could go out together and do something interesting; how does that sound?" Joel didn't mind doing 'something interesting' with Gran, but not spending the whole day with her. He wanted to go out on his own and get to know the area; sit in the local park and people watch, or just go for a walk on his own.

"I know," said Gran "we'll go along to the Barbican, it's lovely there. All the old buildings and quaint little shops and cafés. I'll take you for lunch and we can have a stroll along the seafront and watch the boats in the harbour."

It did sound like a reasonably nice idea, but he still wanted to do some exploring on his own.

"Sounds great - I'll walk back on my own though. I want to take some pictures to send to Marley and have a proper look round. I want to sit at the harbour and watch all the boats and people."

"But you don't know the way Joel!" exclaimed Gran.

"I've been before with Mum and Dad and I've got a app on my phone with maps and I can always ask," replied Joel – instantaneously, as though foreknowing her response.

Gran groaned. "I'll phone and ask your mother, you know she'll only worry." Joel rolled his eyes. His mother would be fine with him going off on his own, it was only Gran who would worry. Why were old people such worriers? He surmised they spent too much time watching crime dramas' and Soaps on TV and assumed that the streets were now filled with murderers, muggers and paedophiles. For goodness sake; these were the people who happily let their children play outside all day or let them wander the streets, uncontactable and out of sigh. Then, encouraging them to write to the BBC in hope of getting on some TV show where they could meet Jimmy Savile, Rolf Harris or the strangely named Garry Glitter.

He'd heard old people going on about 'in my day,' of how hard life was and how they had to walk miles to school when they were five years old, but then contradicting themselves and saying how they played out in the street or in the fields all day, only coming home when they were hungry, or it was nearly dark. He was thirteen for goodness sake. At his age, they were all probably working down some coal mine twelve hours a day.

He could hear Gran in the front room on the phone talking to his mum. "Yes, there's crossings….yes… yes….of course…. No I'll make sure he knows…Alright, alright sweetie. Bye, bye." Gran came back into the kitchen after having made a drama out of nothing at all. "Well, your mum says it's fine; as long as you call me if you get lost and you text her once you get back."

Joel was just finishing his breakfast, when he felt his phone in his pocket vibrate. It was Mum. 'Your Gran is a worrier, just let her know where you are if you go off on your own. Enjoy your day. Love you xx.'

After rinsing his dishes and placing them on the draining board, he went back upstairs to get ready. It was a hot day and deciding what to wear was easy – shorts and t-shirt. After a brisk shower, he slipped on his clothes and before heading back downstairs, picked up the small spectacle lens from the bedside table, the one his grandad had found behind the dining room fireplace yesterday. He put it in his pocket and thought it might come in useful later on when he was out. Maybe he'd try sending signals to boats out at sea or make a small fire with some dried grass – though that possibly could get out of hand so he decided it best to just stick to trying to send signals to boats on the water.

Flopping onto the sofa he began to browse through his phone – social media sites – same stuff different day. The weather – all good. A map of the local area – interesting. He glanced at the ticking clock on the wall, it wasn't yet 9.30 – it was going to be a long day.

When Gran came downstairs she was wearing a long flowing dress. Her hair was tied back with long scarf like ribbon and she wore dangly bright earrings. She rather reminded Joel of a 1960's hippy; all she needed now a flower in her hair. She liked to call herself 'bohemian' – whatever that was. Grandad said it meant she liked to be eccentric and fill the house with clutter, bright paintings and books, be avant-garde and not bend to convention.

"Now, would you like to make yourself useful this morning young man?" without waiting for an answer, Gran went to the kitchen and came back moments later carrying a dish, covered with a chequered tea towel. "Would you be a dear and take this to Mrs Stanfield; she lives on the next street along, over the road bridge; first right - number fifty-two. I promised I would make a quiche for her and drop it round yesterday. I made it Saturday, but clean forgot to take it. Go on, be a love." Without being given much of an option Joel was sent forth to make his delivery. He first went upstairs to put his socks and plimsolls on, and as an afterthought he slipped on his headphones and turned the volume up.

He first of all started off heading left, but then remembered there was a road bridge at both ends of the street, but the one at the top was much quicker than the one at the bottom. He headed back in the direction he had originally come from, turning right at the top of the road and crossing the bridge he looked down onto the busy road below. In the distance, he saw the other bridge at the far end of Gran's street.

Opening the creaky iron gate of number fifty-two he registered the hinges needed oiling. He was just about to lift his hand to knock on the door when he noticed it was standing slightly ajar. Maybe Gran had called ahead to say he was on his way. He slipped his headphones off and placed them around his neck. He pushed the door open and called out 'Hello.'

There was a shuffling sound in the hallway beyond and the vestibule door, separating the front entrance, from the house; it was opened by an older man with a sun weathered face – someone who had spent a lifetime working outdoors assumed Joel. The gentleman had a quizzical look. He was wearing a collarless shirt and waistcoat and held a pipe, clenched between his teeth.

"A'right bey, where you be to?"

Not understanding a word the old man said Joel replied; "My gran sent this along." He held up the plate for the old man to view. The gentleman lifted the corner of the tea towel, gave a wide-eyed look, turned around and started to make his way back along the hallway. "You best come on in son."

Joel followed him into the house; it smelled strongly of pipe smoke and paraffin. Joel recognised the paraffin smell from heater he had in his bedroom when the central heating system broke down last winter. They both passed along the narrow hallway towards the kitchen. By the backdoor the old man stopped and sat down on a wooden chair. "She won't let me in the kitchen wi' me pipe." He rolled his eye and nodded to the closed door that led to the kitchen. "Go on bey, she won't bite."

Joel turned the handle and entered the room – it was very different to Gran's kitchen. It was clean and bright, but rather old fashioned. It didn't have built in units like Gran's or his own house. There was a big cupboard painted green and cream, and the storage space under the sink was covered with a chequered curtain. There was a sort of stove thing, like a range. The room reminded him of one of those old-fashioned posters advertising soap or butter. A kindly looking lady wearing a wrap-around apron and her hair hidden under a headscarf looked up from a small table in the centre of the room, where she was kneading dough. "Hello sonny, can I help you? Are you a friend of Will's?" She noticed the plate he was carrying, "'Ere sit down, he's only nipped out, be back in a minute."

"Err, actually my gran sent me, to give you this," said Joel as he held out the plate. The old lady removed the tea towel.

"Ooh a savoury flan!" Her face lit up. "All those eggs! Does your Gran keep chickens?" With floured hands, she grabbed the dish and slipped past Joel into the hallway to show the old man, who sat puffing away by the open back door.

"It's a quiche" said Joel.

"A Keesh!" chuckled the old man.

"It looks like a flan to me," said the old lady looking rather puzzled. "It does look 'ansome though!" She was rather over reacting to the gift of a simple quiche, thought Joel.

"Stay for a cup of tea an' a slice of cake," she said, ushering Joel back into the kitchen. "Our Will won't be long." Joel insisted he'd already had breakfast and Gran would be expecting him back, but the old lady refused to take no for an answer. She pulled out a chair and summoned him to sit down. From the cream coloured cupboard, she brought out teacups and saucers and gently carried from the funny looking stove, a teapot that had been kept warm; possibly in anticipation of her visitor.

"Does your gran do much baking then?" she enquired, as way of making conversation.

"Sometimes," replied Joel. "I think she just finds it easier to go to Iceland and buy frozen stuff. Load it in the freezer and then takes out what she wants when she needs it. She does a big shop there about once a month."

Mrs Stanfield burst out laughing, spluttering her tea; the boy was funny. Joel felt rather flattered. Mrs Stanfield imagined an old lady hauling a huge wooden sleigh piled high with frozen goods, through the deeps snows of Iceland; boating it across the Arctic and Atlantic Oceans' back to Plymouth, before storing it all in some deep underground ice cellar. She fussed about and offered Joel a slice from a caraway seed cake she said she'd made yesterday. Feeling obliged rather than hungry, Joel thanked her.

"So, your gran 'erm, who is she again?" enquired Mrs Stanfield; pouring them both a second cup of tea. Joel wasn't sure if they knew her as Anna or Mrs Armstrong so he said, "she lives just over the back there." He pointed towards the houses on the other side of the culvert, behind Mrs Stanfield. She in turn furrowed her brow in thought. "Well, it's certainly very kind of her I'm sure and much appreciated."

  Just as Mrs Stanfield was about to top up his teacup for the third time, Joel said he had better go, his gran would wonder where he was. He got up from the table and headed towards the door. The old man lifted his head up from the newspaper he was reading and nodded to Joel as he passed by him in the hallway. Clamping his pipe between his teeth, he checked the timepiece which hung on a chain and which he pulled from the pocket of his waistcoat. He winked and said in a strong Devon dialect "A'right my luvver. Oi be letting our Will know you been an' called."

Outside, Joel replaced his headphones and turned up the volume. He hurried back along the street and across the bridge to Gran's house – she was probably wondering where he was. The smell of pipe tobacco lingered in his nostrils. He'd never seen anyone smoke a pipe before; only in old films on TV. He thought it rather odd and somewhat eccentric.

"Sorry I was so long Gran," he called as he opened the front door. "Mrs Stanfield made me a cup of tea and insisted I had some cake she'd made."

  "Away with you," she laughed. "You've only been gone long enough to walk there and back."

Joel looked at the clock in the front room; it had only moved forward ten or so minutes. 'Probably just slow' he thought. A little while later, after Gran had done her daily chores and hoovered the house, then decided to change her outfit whilst Joel had flicked through all the TV channels at least twice; they were ready to go out.

They took a bus into town and walked down towards the charming harbour and olde-worlde buildings at the Barbican. It was a place his parents had often brought him to when visiting Gran and Grandad. The Barbican was vibrant; full of cafés and restaurants, quaint little gift shops and with bunting draped across cobbled side streets and narrow lanes. There were numerous Tudor and Jacobean buildings too. It was rather like stepping back in time. Joel imagined the sights and sounds of horses and carts that once trundled along the narrow lanes. The brown-masted fishing boats in the harbour and the fishwives lining the quayside selling their husbands catch for the best price available. The fast sailing three-masted 'Clippers' making their way past the breakwater, leaving a trail of white foam behind them as they headed for land, laden with goods from the East – spices herbs, tea.

Gran said they should stop for lunch, as she had a surprise in store for him in the afternoon. They found a quiet little café on a side street, away from the main tourist route, and sat at a small table adorned with a chequered plastic table cloth. There were five tables in the room, which was rather small. The main wall was taken up by a huge fireplace; which was no longer used and had a pine cone arrangement placed where once a glowing fire would have warmed the room and its inhabitants on a cold winters day. An imitation ormolu clock sat on the mantle.

A family of five sat at a large table near the door, each having a Devon cream tea. Joel reasoned they must be on holiday, though they didn't have accents so it was hard to tell. The youngest child, a boy of about four, didn't appear to like the thick clotted cream and was scraping it from his scone onto the side of his plate. A couple of elderly women sat at the table in front of the window. They chatted away like long lost friends who hadn't seen each other in years and who were oblivious to everything and everyone around them. Joel thought it a shame they had chosen the window seat, as he would have liked to have sat there, watching the people passing by and going in and out of the shops and buildings nearby.

Gran had chosen the table at the back of the room, furthest from the window and in a corner. It was though next to the great fireplace. Joel sat opposite Gran who had her back to the room. A young waitress dressed in black and wearing a small white apron, came over and handed them a menu and asked if they wanted any drinks. Joel opted for a coke and Gran a cup of tea. They both studied the menu; well, Gran did - Joel thought how embarrassed he'd be if one of his friends from school saw him now –

sitting in a quaint little tea shop with his gran. They'd probably be out skateboarding, playing on their Xbox or abroad on holiday.

He let Gran choose from the menu; she ordered a selection of mixed sandwiches and a desert of black forest gateau for Joel. They ate in relative silence other than for the odd moment of conversation. Gran said she remembered when she was small that the café they were in now had been a fishing tackle shop. The great fireplace had stood relatively un-noticed behind a large display of rods and lines. It had likely once in years gone by, have been someone's front room.

Joel found history fascinating and was intrigued by how things changed or stayed the same over time. How many people had had been and lived in one place at various times. The different clothing, they would have worn, the world they would have lived in during their time. For instance, the café he and Gran were sitting in was likely built in Tudor times. The builders would have used wooden scaffolding; they wouldn't have listened to the radio while they worked. Everything would have been 'of the clock' and the church bells would have dictated the time, or the rising or waning of the sun. He imagined the first people to live in the house when it was brand new and modern. The floorboards newly laid, cut from a tree that would now be well over 700 years old. Maybe the floorboards beneath him were that old? He looked down and although they looked old, they didn't look quite that old.

Who was on the throne? Was it Henry VII, His son Henry VIII. Maybe one of his daughters Mary or Elizabeth. He'd learned about the Tudor's at school and it seemed rather an exciting time of change and reform. He wondered if this building had interior walls of wattle and daub and if the people who had lived there were rich or poor? From the size of the fireplace he presumed them to have some wealth, though certainly not rich merchants.

"Everything alright?" Enquired Gran, a quizzical look on her face. Joel had obviously been in a world of his own for longer than he had thought.

"Just thinking about this building, you know, being old." Gran smiled, she acknowledged Joel was a bit of a dreamer. "When we're finished here I'm taking you for your surprise. They soon finished up and Gran called the waitress over and asked for the bill.

The early afternoon breeze had picked up they stopped by a bench whilst Gran sorted herself out. Undoing the large scarf like ribbon that she had worn around the ponytail in her hair, she shook free her mane of brown curls and then tied the scarf over her head, securing it under her chin. She took her sunglasses from the pouch in which she carried them in her bag and slipped them on.

"Right let's go see what's instore!" Joel hoped it was something more entertaining than going to look around the aquarium or a trip to the cinema. The aquarium was for kids and the cinema for rainy days with your mates.

"Follow me young man," said Gran, "this is a first for both of us."

Puzzled and excited, Joel followed Gran's purposeful stride towards the water's edge. She pointed out the Mayflower steps, near to where the Pilgrim Fathers had set sail in 1620 on the ship *'Mayflower.'* "Hence the name of the steps," she said. "Having no idea what would lie ahead of them in the 'New Land' that we now know as America."

They carried on past the steps and down a sloping path to a small ticket booth. Joel carried on walking ahead towards the landing stage, keen to have a look at a catamaran tied up. He hadn't noticed Gran stop to speak to the man at the ticket office. Catching up with Joel she said in a Pirate like kind of voice said; "Let's cast anchor and hit the high seas me' hearties."

"But where are we going!" he exclaimed, envisaging Gran had done something silly like hired them a small motorised fishing boat and they would head out to sea, unprepared and uneducated in the laws of maritime and harbour regulations. He wasn't even sure of his port from his starboard side for goodness sake! Luckily as he hurried along behind Gran, who was already making her way down the twisting jetty, he saw a number of small cruise boats lined up at the landing stage. His fear lessened as he saw people boarding and alighting from the boats, all advertising 'luxury cruises.'

They boarded a small blue and white vessel which bobbed lazily in the water, making small splashing sounds. Gran confided to the boats Captain as she clambered aboard, that she had never been on a small boat before and hoped the journey wouldn't be too rough as she had only just had lunch. He teasingly replied that he had only just sluiced it out from the previous trip, pointing to a brush stowed under the wooden seats in the middle of the boat, and that the forecast was for no more than a sea state of moderate to rough, with a north-easterly wind of 7 to 8; but she should be fine. He winked at Joel. Gran thanked him for his advice and she and Joel made themselves comfortable outside of the covered cabin area.

A few more tourists climbed aboard; some English, some foreign. Gran took out a small digital camera and began clicking away. The engine started up and the Pilot or Captain or whatever he called himself as there was two of them, untied the rope that had secured the boat to the landing stage and the boat pulled away from the jetty and made its way out into the gently lapping waters of Plymouth Sound.

As the boat made its way past the Hoe, Joel could see the Citadel, a dramatic 17th century fortress built to defend the Devon coastline from the Dutch. After a query from one of the other passengers, the Pilot explained how legend has it that Sir Francis Drake played bowls on Plymouth Hoe, before defeating the Spanish Armada. Also, how the Hoe as we know it today began to take shape in the 1880's, when the formal gardens were first established, and by the 1920's, it had become a place of theatre with concerts and plays being performed in marquees on the lawned areas.

Gran pointed out Tinside lido, an outdoor swimming pool that was a 1930's masterpiece of art deco design. Joel had gone swimming there with Mum Dad and Tabby the previous summer. They watched as numerous small vessels of varying speeds criss-crossed their path. Joel took a keen interest as they passed the deserted Drakes Island as they sailed by. He hoped he might spot some activity; a trespasser or fugitive hiding out – but there was none.

As the Rame Peninsula, of Cawsand and Kingsand on the Cornish border came closer into view, Gran put away here camera and zipped up her bag. At Cawsand beach the pilot jumped overboard into the shallow waters and pulled a trolley like ladder alongside the boat so that they could alight. As they walked up the beach Gran took off her headscarf and let her hair fall free.

They spent an hour or so walking around the villages, amongst the winding narrow streets with pretty pastel painted houses. They visited a couple a gift shop. Gran bought some postcards and stamps and later gave one to Joel, to write out to his parents and Tabby, whilst they sat outside a pub where they stopped off for a drink She reminisced that when she was a girl, her parents had once taken her there for a daytrip and she remembered having a lemonade in the same pub they had just been in; called the 'Halfway House' because it was in the middle of the two villages. Reading from a leaflet she had picked up in the pub she told Joel how in olden times when smuggling was rife, thousands of casks of spirits were landed in the bay every year by a fleet of over 50 smuggling vessels which operated out of Cawsand Bay.

They then sat on the beach for a while and Joel had a paddle in the water, whilst they waited for the next boat to arrive to take them back to the Barbican, just visible in the far distance. A large Brittany Ferries vessel the 'Amorique' heading for Roscoff in France sailed by. Joel looked at it longingly wishing he was on it, travelling abroad. Maybe driving down to the Loire, the Dordogne or even Spain. When he was six his parents had taken him on a ferry to France. He was poorly most of the journey across, which had been unfortunately in rather choppy seas. They'd had a nightmare trying to persuade him to get on the ferry on the return from their holiday. He couldn't remember if he'd been poorly or not on that journey but assumed he'd been fine.

There was a continual and colourful moving spectacle of different vessels in the water, from gigs and yachts, oil tankers to rowing boats and naval vessels exercising out at sea in the far distance.

The boat for the return journey soon came into view and Joel tried drying the water and sand from his feet with his socks but without much luck. Gran gave him her headscarf to use instead and that worked rather well and he was able to put his socks and trainers back on without them being filled with sand.

The boat trip back seemed a lot quicker than the journey there, but that was likely only because he knew exactly where he was going this time. Gran sat under the shelter on the boat but the wind was still able to catch her there and it whipped her hair about like a yapping dogs tail. Joel felt a little guilty having used her headscarf for a towel for his feel - but she had offered.

Walking back up the landing jetty, Gran said it had been a wonderful trip and she really had enjoyed it. It had been rather like a 'holiday day.' Joel agreed it had been rather nice. He decided that now was probably a good time to ask Gran if he could go off on his own – like they'd agreed. Gran said "Ok but call me if you get lost or aren't sure of anything, oh and be back by six." She checked her watch, it read 4.10pm. "That's plenty of time for you to have a wander and be home."

They walked up to jetty together and at the top Gran gave Joel verbal directions as to the way home and pointed out which way to go and what buses he could get if he decided not to walk back. Joel said he would be fine and had a map on his mobile phone anyway. Gran got him to double check that he did have enough battery on his phone and enough money if needed. She then delved into her handbag and handed him a first-class stamp from her purse, advising he post his postcard on the way home, as his parents would be expecting one. Only once she was fully satisfied was Joel able to bid her farewell. He even offered to walk her to the bus stop to make sure she didn't actually stay behind and follow him surreptitiously, just 'in-case.'

He watched her disappear into the hordes of tourists that filled the area. Once satisfied she had gone, he backtracked on himself and headed back along the Hoe, to get a closer up view of what he had seen from the boat. He took some photos with his mobile phone and forwarded a couple of them to Marley in Scotland – one being a 'selfie' of himself with the 'Smeaton's Tower' lighthouse behind him. A few seconds later he received a picture back in reply. It was Marley wearing a jacket with the hood up and pulling a face.

Joel took a few more pictures, then opened up his map app. He wanted to know what was nearby and what was worth seeing. He quite fancied going down the rocks to the water's edge, but he didn't really think he had time – he could do it another day anyway. Looking on his app there were two routes back to Gran's. One going past the aquarium and the other around Sutton Harbour. He decided to follow the footpath around the harbour to where all the yachts were berthed. He could people watch there too, maybe spot a boat offloading contraband or arms. It was very unlikely though and he knew he had to stop supposing such silly notions. He would keep an eye out though, just in case.

The restaurants and bars were all busy. The smell of cooking floated through the air – fish and chips, doughnuts, spicy Mexican. Joel decided to buy himself an ice-lolly from an old-fashioned ice-cream van which was parked up. Once purchased, he sat on a bench next to a German couple.

He knew they were German because he recognized their accent – and he'd earlier seen them and a number of other tourist disembark from a German registered tour bus. An American group came over and started speaking to the German's in English. The German's responded in English. It appeared they were all travelling together on the same tour bus. Joel wondered why the American's were on a German tour bus and after some thought deducted that they were probably on a European tour and likely started their trip in Germany, possibly being the country of their heritage. He listened for a while, but the conversation was just about some vase or 'vayze' as an American lady called it, that she had seen in a shop but wasn't sure if to buy due to the risk of it getting broken in transportation.

Ice-lolly finished Joel decided it was time to move on. Gran had mentioned a *wonderful little second-hand book shop'* that he went in search of. Eventually finding the shop he went inside; it was rather like how Gran had described – dark, overcrowded and everything in it infused with the glorious smell of time, paper, old ink and grubby hands – the connoisseurs perfume of old books. It was a sort of damp, dusty, leathery smell; Slightly acidic at times. He looked along the rows of shelves, not for anything in particular – simply just for the sake of it. His attention was caught by box saying 'Everything 20p.' He rummaged through and found five copies of the Commando comic dated 1985. He took them to the till and handed over £1.00 to the gentleman serving, who slipped them into a brown paper bag. Rather pleased with his purchases Joel planned on reading them in bed that night. He hoped they were as good as the modern copy he had bought in Exmouth a week earlier.

He got back to Gran' house without any problem. He'd enjoyed the saunter, looking at buildings; old and modern. He'd passed some boys fishing in the harbour and thought it would be a good idea to ask Grandad if they could do that one day; maybe Saturday when Grandad was off work.

"What house did you drop the quiche off at this morning love?" Gran's first words as she opened the door were not of thankfulness that Joel had made it back safely, but of the final destination of her homemade quiche.

"Number fifty-two."

"You sure?"

"Yes."

"What colour was the front door?"

"I can't remember. Mr Stanfield said to come in and I took it to his wife in the kitchen."

Gran sighed "There isn't a Mr Stanfield. Oh Joel, you must have taken it to the wrong house. Oh well," she shrugged her shoulders "that's likely the last I'll see of that dish."

"I'm sure it was number fifty-two, I remember seeing the number." Joel tried to think back, but now wasn't so certain.

"Oh, don't worry about it," said Gran. "At least someone had a nice surprise. Old couple did you say?" Gran thought about it for a while but couldn't think who it could be as neither of Mrs Stanfield's direct next door neighbours were elderly. Mrs Stanfield had been divorced years and had recently become partially housebound after breaking her leg in a skiing incident whilst on holiday in Switzerland. Gran had phoned to ask what she thought of the quiche, but Mrs Stanfield said she hadn't received one and no young lad had called around either.

"How odd," said Gran out loud.

'How odd,' thought Joel to himself. "Tell you what Gran, I'll pop back around and explain. I'll say it was a mistake and I'll get your dish back."

"Oh, alright then, but don't make a fuss, just ask if they've finished with the dish."

Just as he was about to leave, Gran reminded him to message his mum and let her know he had arrived back safely. He took his mobile phone from his pocket and texted 'bk now x'

Joel trotted off up the road. Gran stood at the front door and watched him; she saw him turn right at the corner and satisfied he was heading the right way she went back in-doors.

Joel stood at the door, it was the same house he had visited earlier in the day. The same old man who had answered the door that morning, answered his knock. "Hullo bey, come in, come in."

Joel followed him along the same passage way he had followed him along only hours earlier and into the same small kitchen. A boy, of around Joel's age was sat at the table with a small palette of paints, three brushes and some paper. He had a bright freckled sun-tanned face and blonde hair. He was wearing a plain short-sleeved shirt, shorts, and plimsolls similar to Joel's, only plain black.

"Howdy" Said the boy.

"Hi" said Joel.

"It's your friend who brought along the egg, ham and broccoli flan." Said the old man, before he retreated out into the hallway and to his chair by

the backdoor, where he was allowed to sit whilst smoking his pipe.

"Was tasty, thanks." said the boy. "Mighty tasty." He said it with an American accent as he rubbed his tummy. They both laughed.

"Yea, Gran's not a bad cook," laughed Joel. Both boys appeared a little awkward, unsure of what to say next. The boy seated, shuffled and said, "Have you been bombed out? I don't recognise you from 'round here?"

What a strange saying 'bombed out' thought Joel. What did he mean? Did he mean had his parents got on his nerves so he'd 'bombed out' and gone to stay with his gran?

"Yea, something like that." Joel shrugged his shoulders nonchalantly, as if to say 'it happens.'

There was a silence while both thought of something to say next. The boy spoke first "I'm Will by the way."

"I'm Joel," said Joel. They shook hands.

"What's that you're painting?" asked Joel, seeing the half-finished watercolour on the table.

"Oh, Just a picture. I like painting and drawing. I might be a famous artist one day."

They both laughed. Joel did have to admit though his work was good, especially as it appeared to be done from memory.

"I've an idea," said Will, pushing his chair away from the table. "Do you want to call by tomorrow; we could do something together. My pal Eddie, he's down in Cornwall and it gets a bit boring round here at times."

Joel knew the feeling of 'abandonment' when friends went away on holiday and you were left like Billy no mates trying to amuse yourself. "Sure, what time?"

"Any time," said Will, shrugging his shoulders. If I'm not in Gran will tell you where to find me. If it's nice, we could go for a swim down by the river or if you fancy it take a trip along the pier – do some fishing?"

"I didn't bring any swimming trunks with me." Joel wondered if his gran might buy him some, though he did have two decent pairs at home. To be honest, he doubted Gran would let him go swimming in a river. Maybe the local pool, but not an open river.

"No matter, nor have I, just wear your shorts or pants," said Will indifferently.

Joel was just about to leave when he remembered what he'd come for; the dish. "Oh, do you mind if I take Gran's dish back; that's if you've finished the quiche, er flan."

"I'll go find it," said Will as he got up from his seat. "To be honest I thought you would have been back for it ages ago. I would have brought it round but Gran couldn't remember what number you said you lived at."

Will rummaged in a cupboard in the cream coloured dresser and brought out the dish and the chequered tea towel, washed and pressed. Joel thanked him and said he'd see him tomorrow. Leaving the house, he double checked the door number. It was fifty-two; definitely number fifty-two. He was even tempted to take a photograph with his mobile phone to show Gran, but she might think it rather petty, so he didn't.

"Here's your dish, and the tea towel." Joel handed them to Gran, "and it definitely was number fifty-two. There's a boy lives there, called Will; about my age – he's asked me to call round and see him tomorrow."

Gran looked puzzled but didn't say anything. She put the plate and laundered tea towel away.

"Can I go and see him - please?"

Gran was *sure* Mrs Stanfield lived at number fifty-two. Maybe she had got it wrong and it was actually fifty-four. She'd pop around herself next time.

The following morning Joel told Gran over breakfast, that she didn't need to make any arrangement for him today as he was going along to see his new friend Will and would text her his plans. Gran agreed without much fuss, although did say he would need to let her know where he was going if they went out anywhere.

He trotted off up the road hoping Will would be home and not out somewhere with some of his other friends. He now wished he'd asked him for his mobile number.

The front door was open, but Joel still knocked. A young woman answered the door this time. She wore bright lipstick and had a shock of blonde curly hair. She looked Joel up and down and started to giggle. "What's so amusing?" He queried.

"Oh nothing, you're just dressed 'funny' that's all. What can I do for you. If it's rag and bones you're after, we haven't any?"

Joel thought she could talk; in her flowery old-fashioned dress and funny hairstyle. "I've come to see Will. I'm Joel, I'm staying with my gran." He pointed in the direction of Gran's house.

"Oh, so you're Joel. Will mentioned you the other day, he wondered where you'd got to. Come in, he'll be pleased to see you. He said he thought you might have been re-housed."

Joel was totally confused, but at least she knew who he was and that he was at the right house.

"I'm Sylvia by the way, Sylvie to my friends." Sylvia took a cigarette from a packet on a dresser in the hallway and watched her reflection in the mirror as she lit it. "Will," she called up the stairs, still concentrating on her reflection in the mirror. Joel watched as she took a drag from the cigarette, leaving a red lipstick stain on the tip.

There was a muffled response, and then a few second later Will appeared at the top of the stairs.

"I thought you must have gone home or got moved on," said Will as he clattered down the staircase in his hurry to greet Joel.

"I said yesterday that I'd be round this morning?" replied Joel.

"But it was nearly a week ago you were here," said Will looking confused.

"But I wasn't even here a week ago!" responded Joel.

Both boys looked confused – Sylvia shrugged her shoulders, said "Oh well" and left a haze of cigarette smoke behind her as she made her way back up the stairs that Will had just come down. Will lead the way to the kitchen.

Something isn't right about this thought Joel. Was this one of those weird situations where everyone is in on it? Gran, Grandad, Mrs Stanfield. Was he being used as part of some strange experiment? Were there secret cameras recording his every reaction? He'd heard of that type of thing happening, mind games and manipulation. Maybe it was just a dream? Possibly he would wake up soon either in his own bed or at Gran's.

Will spoke first. "Do you read comics, I've just got this weeks' Wizard." He picked up the magazine from the table in the kitchen. "Want a look?"

"Thanks." Joel sat down and flicked through the pages. It was all war stories of daring deeds, the foiling of enemy plans and subterfuge.

"I've some copies of Commando at my gran's house. I can bring them over for you to read if you want?" said Joel. He looked towards the kitchen window, with its decorative white criss-cross pattern of tape on the window. Rather like mock Tudor leaded windows but in white and on a much tackier scale. The skies were dark and it was raining quite hard. It had been a little overcast when he arrived, but certainly hadn't looked like it was going to rain. Will too looked out the window, he didn't like the idea of getting soaked and less the idea of the comics turning to papier-mâché in the rain.

"Yea, bring them next time, we can read them together. Come on, let's sit in the parlour until the rain stops. We can play cards or build Meccano or something."

Joel followed Will into the front-room, which was rather antiquated but attractive. The wallpaper was pretty and the ornaments decorative rather than bold. There was a small table covered by a heavy cloth and in the centre sat an ornately painted bowl – the sort that would hold fruit; but it was empty. Will went to a glass fronted display cabinet and brought out three sets of cards; Snap, Pit and a Countries of the Empire game. Joel had played snap when he was younger, he still had some sets of cards at home; though likely Tabby had taken ownership of them now. The 'Countries of the Empire set' caught his eye. He picked up the box and read the detail, it looked quite interesting. It was a game comprising of reproductions of famous Empire Marketing Board Posters with descriptive details of the principle industries of each Country. The object of the game being for a player to collect the greatest number of completed sets. The Countries included were: Great Britain, Canada, Australia, New Zealand, South Africa, Southern Rhodesia, East African Dependencies, Malaya, British West Africa, British West Indies, India Burma & Ceylon and the Irish Free State. Some of them he'd never even heard of. Will showed him how to play – "It's about buying goods from the 'Empire' home and abroad."

All the card games seemed rather dated. They followed the card game with 'pick up sticks' and a few games of Domino's. Joel thought it all a little childish, but at the same time he was quite enjoying himself.

Will's Granfer preceded by his pipe and who apparently wasn't Mr Stanfield, popped his head around the door. "Hullo beys, just been diggin' up some potatoes and swede from the allotment. Potato soup an' pasty for tea I think." His eye then caught the Champion comic. He crept into the room pretending to go un-noticed. "Go on then Granfer," said Will laughing.

'Granfer' fitted in to the character of the house, he wore a collarless shirt and braces on his trousers. His slicked back hair and ever-present pipe clenched between his teeth. Everything about the place was slightly odd; but somehow right.

"You been away bey?" Said the old man to Joel.

"No, just at Gran's," he replied.

"Arr." Grunted the old man, looking up from the copy of the Champion. "Who be your gran then?" The pipe in his mouth waggled up and down as he spoke.

"Mrs Armstrong, Anna. She lives; over the back." The old man thought for a few seconds. The pipe went into action again. "What she look like, your gran?"

"Well, she's got shoulder length brown curly hair. She's fairly slim. She's bohemian, you must have seen her around?" Joel thought of Gran with her colourful flamboyant clothes. "What should I tell her your name is? I'll ask if she knows you or your wife."

"I'm Charlie Roberts, the wife's Eadie." He then looked at Joel with a slightly confused expression on his face. "What's it with your clothes?" he queried, changing the subject and peering at Joel's t-shirt. Joel was wearing a cream cotton top with the wording 'Mercer &Co' General Suppliers. Est 1897, printed on in faded ink.

"Looks like you're Ma's cut up an old flour sack!" Both Will and his grandad began laughing.

"It's just a normal t-shirt," retorted Joel. "I've got lots with writing on." This only made Will and his grandad laugh even more. Will, with tears streaming down his face said "One for each season; flour sack, sugar sack, potato sack, coal sack." They laughed even more and even Joel joined in although he didn't know what he was laughing at other than being caught up in the contagion. As the laughing died down Charlie Roberts keen eye noticed Joel didn't have a respirator with him. "Where's yer gas mask bey?"

Joel burst out laughing, but on his own this time. "Why, because you smell?"

Their laughter stopped and the room fell silent; Joel felt silly.

"You wouldn't be laughing if they dropped a gas bomb would you eh? Don't be gettin' too laid-back 'bout it bey. Our lads suffered in the trenches in the last war they did. My Billy, he died at thirty- three 'cos o' the chlorine gas 'e did." Mr Roberts became agitated. "You young un's 'ave no idea what it's like you don't. I nearly lost three beys in the Great War, one at sea an' two in France an' Flanders; one of them I did lose fourteen years later. Our Billy's life was never the same after Passchendaele. Just nineteen when he got gassed he was. Never was right again, never."

"Sorry Granfer," said Will.

"Sorry Mr Roberts," said Joel.

Mr Roberts' features softened. "Arr well, just don't go leaving it at 'ome and thinkin' you'll be 'aright." He shook his head. "If you go gettin' caught without it by the A.R.P you'll be in trouble." He shook his head again. "Any o' these bombs they're dropping could be gas bombs. The sirens going off more 'an more. We're getting' used to it now bey, but you weren't 'ere when the first one sounded, one o'clock of the mornin' it was too, a Saturday mornin'. We was all a panic an' rushed outside to see what was goin' on. There were no bombs dropped that night, but you've seen the damage wi' your own eyes what they did up the road there." He pointed in the direction of the road bridge Joel had crossed earlier. "God be thankful they missed us. Those ones a couple 'o streets back could've easily o' landed 'ere. Bloomin' lucky we was, bloomin' lucky. People killed and dozens of 'ouses destroyed. Do you know how many raids there's been so far bey, eh? Ten; one zero – ten. Three times' we've been bombed 'ere. They be after the gasometers." He took his pipe from his mouth and waved it in the air. "Bleddy Jerry swines."

"I won't forget to bring it next time, I'm sorry." Joel said solemnly.

The old man continued. "People be gettin' out the city at night. Many a family gettin' in the back of a lorry or journeying on foot, pushing bicycles an' prams laden wi' food an' bedding. Going to the moors; gettin' away from the bombs."

What on earth is the old man going on thought Joel. Has he gone crackers? Has he got dementia – going on about bombs and gas masks and war damage. He'd read that people with dementia tend to remember the past and not really be aware of the present. Maybe Mr Roberts was doing that; remembering when he was a boy. Though it wasn't helpful that Will, appeared to be encouraging him.

Mr Roberts then starting questioning him on his grandmother's thoughts on Germany's invasion of Czechoslovakia – 'her being a Bohemian.' Joel couldn't understand why her choice of dressing style should play any part in her opinion on Germany's occupation of Czechoslovakia, but Mr Roberts certainly did. He appeared to have a lot of empathy with the 'Bohemians,' which Joel found bizarre. He truly was a crack-pot. To top it off he put on a pair of gold rimmed, owl like glasses and began reading aloud an article from a newspaper which he picked up from a small table beside him …..*"The great air battle which has been in progress over this island for the last few weeks has recently attained a high intensity. It is too soon to attempt to assign limits either to its scale or to its duration. We must certainly expect that greater efforts will be made by the enemy than any he has so far put forth. Hostile air-fields are still being developed in France and the Low Countries. It is quite plain that Herr Hitler could not admit defeat in his air attack on Great Britain without sustaining more serious injury."*

The boys continued with their games whilst the old man read. Once he'd satisfied himself with reading from the paper, he sat back and got on with reading the heroics in this week's edition of the Champion. Will and Joel then entertained themselves making model aircraft from the Mecanno set Will had. It was nothing like as good as the set Marley had, but it was still fun.

Will asked Joel if he liked to paint, but Joel said that other when he was younger at school, he hadn't really done any painting. He did like art, but mostly drawing. Will showed Joel some of his art work. One of the pictures was in a frame on the sitting room wall. He'd painted it for his parents the previous Christmas. He said he's sketched it down by the wharves then painted it in oils at school, by memory. Joel studied the picture – he didn't know where the wharves were, but it certainly looked pretty. Joel said he had been working with oils, watercolours and pencil drawings. Mr Reynolds his art teacher gave him extra lessons and said he was an A1 student.

Joel asked what he wanted to do when he left school. Will said he wasn't sure, but he'd like to be a speedway rider one day. When Will asked Joel what his plans were, he said he hoped to go to University and study law or forensics or maybe engineering. Will gave his Granfer a surprised look and they both smirked. Mr Roberts shook his head.

The morning passed quickly and it was soon lunch-time. Will told Joel he would have to go home now as they were about to have dinner, but he could come back afterwards if he wanted to.

Joel stepped out into the street; his eyes seemed blinded for a second and then he realised the sun was shining very brightly from a clear sky. The ground was dry – but as it was a hot day the sun had probably dried it up very quickly. He hadn't even noticed it had stopped raining.

Gran answered the door to his ringing the bell. "Back already? I was just about to go shopping thinking you would be at least a couple of hours.

"I've come back for lunch." Joel stepped into the house, he was pretty hungry to be honest.

"But you've only been gone quarter of an hour!" exclaimed Gran. "How can you be hungry already?" Joel looked at the clock in the hallway, it did only read just after half past ten and he remembered it saying nearly quarter past ten when he left the house.

"Has your friend other plans?" enquired Gran, puzzled at Joel hasty return. Joel equally puzzled cried out "He was in and we played cards and his grandad's called Charlie Roberts, but Will calls him Granfer. His gran, she's called Eadie and they all live at number fifty-two. They said I could go back after lunch and bring my Commando comics with me." Joel said it so convincingly that Gran didn't really feel she could disbelieve him. She shrugged her shoulders and simply said "Ok." She didn't know Charlie or Eadie. Mind you, not many people knew their neighbours nowadays, so she may well have passed them in the street numerous times. "Well, I'm off to the shops, do you want to come with me or stay behind?"

Joel chose to stay behind – he had some thinking to do. He went to his room and got out his notepad and pen. He jotted down the time and date he had arrived. Also, a note of the approximate time he had gone to the 'house' where Will lived and the time he had 'apparently' arrived home. Things really weren't adding up. All this talk of gas masks and bombs. He came to the conclusion that for every hour he 'appeared' to spent in Will's house, he was only away for 10 minutes of Gran's house time. Also, Will's house was different somehow, old fashioned. Was Mr Roberts really bonkers and living in the past and everyone in his family going along with the story – or was there more to it. Was he; and he thought this ludicrous even for his overactive imagination – venturing through a time warp, that had somehow opened up. Joel decided to head straight back – if he was right in his theory that he had stumbled across a time warp - a distortion of time where things could move from one-time period to another, then the Roberts would likely have just finished dinner and he could stay for around half an hour there at least and be back well before Gran would even know he was missing.

He ran up-stairs and snatched three copies of 'Commando,' ones he'd already read. He took the spare key from the key-hide and locked himself out. He hurried up the road, across the bridge and without knocking entered the unlocked door of number fifty-two. "Hullo" he called. No one answered. He knocked on the front room door but there was no sound from within. He did the same with the next door, a room he had never been in, and then the kitchen door; but again, no answer. He decided to leave the copies on the kitchen table and call back later on. They couldn't have gone far. Leaving the house, he pulled the front door to a half open position behind him, leaving it as he had found it.

Back at Gran's he couldn't really tell how long he'd been away as the clock had only really moved the distance and length of time it would have taken him to get there and back anyway. He sat down and tried to work out what was going on. His hunger had now subsided, but not his appetite for answers. He took out his mobile phone and typed 'time travel' into a search engine, but the answers he came up with were more science fiction than science fact and it all seemed to be a big joke. To be honest, he did think he was probably over reacting, reading too much into things and his parents were always telling him he had a 'vivid' imagination – like the time he called the Police from school to tell them he thought there was a terrorist in the building and he had barricaded a number of pupils the boys changing room. What had actually happened was that when the boys had gone into the changing rooms, a netball post propped behind the door, fell over. It made a terrible clattering noise, but also left the boys unable to open the door. No one knew what had happened, but in the hysteria, that followed, it was decided someone had fired gunshots and they had been locked in; likely to stop them from overpowering the lone gunman. The rest of the school knew nothing about it until they realised they were surrounded by armed police units. By this time the P.E. teacher had come along and released the boys from their 'prison.'

There were a number of other occasions when it had worked against him, but his English teacher said it was 'a good thing to have a vivid imagination, a hundred times better than having no imagination at all'.

Joel sat around the house till after it really was lunch time. He tried phoning Marley, but the call just went straight to answerphone. There was no mobile signal where Marley was staying, so he sent couple of text messages instead, hoping that Marley would be able to pick them up sometime soon. He told him that he thought he had found doorway into the past. He gave a brief description of what had happened and closed his texts with the hashtag #notjoking.

When Gran arrived home, he helped her put away the groceries, including the granola he had asked for, and over a bowl of soup they chatted about gas masks.

"Gas masks?" exclaimed Gran. "Why on earth are you interested in gas mask? I remember my Mum saying she had one as a girl during the war, red I think it was. She used to have to take it everywhere with her, though she never used it for real. I remember her saying sometimes when they were in the air raid shelter at school the teachers would make then put their masks on and recite their times tables. They had to practice getting them on and off you see."

Joel thought about what Mr Roberts had said about the gas bombs and how they had suffered 'in the trenches in the last war' – but the only time Joel could recall there being trench warfare was in the First World War. Either the Roberts were a bunch of harmless eccentrics living in a time-warp – or there really was something strange going on.

"The German's never did drop any gas bombs," said Gran deep in thought, as she sipped on a spoonful of cream of chicken soup that Joel had heated up for them both in the microwave. "They dropped so many bombs on Plymouth, my gran said the city centre was totally unrecognisable after the war, and then they pulled it all down and rebuilt it as it is today. I remember there still being bomb sites when I was a girl and I remember us moving into a brand-new house on one of the out of town estates, when I was about five."

"Did your mum's house get bombed?" Joel's curiosity grew. He'd seen a lot of footage on YouTube and television of bombed out buildings, but he'd never really thought of it so close up. His own home town Exmouth had been bombed during the war; he'd done a project about it at school.

"I remember my mum saying her street got hit and a few houses all along her road were completely destroyed during the Blitz. Their house was damaged and they had to go and stay with an aunt nearby while they waited for it to be repaired. Her aunt's street had been bombed too I remember. There were so many families bombed out that there was nowhere for the people to go."

Here Joel heard that phrase again 'bombed out' Will had asked him if he had been bombed out.

Gran continued "They lived in Devonport, near the dockyard. When she was about ten, in 1940 I think it was, my mum remembered one particular day when there had been a number of alerts during the morning, but no bombers had appeared – all false alarms. Anyway, that afternoon she was playing outside in the street with a friend, when the alert sounded again. At first, they didn't do anything, there having been so many false alarms that morning. Suddenly, they heard heavy gunfire and people started running out of the houses and towards the public shelter nearby. They only just made it in time and no sooner had they got inside the loud crump of falling bombs could be heard landing near the shelter. They were terrified and clung on to each other."

Gran paused and dipped some bread into her bowl of soup ate a few mouthfuls and then continued. Joel sat engrossed, imagining the scene.

"Anyway, she found her Mum and baby sister in the shelter. Her mum was worried as she'd left the gas oven on in her hurry to leave. When the all clear sounded and they came to leave the shelter, found it to be on the edge of a deep bomb crater. Her little friends' house - and neighbouring ones had been completely destroyed, as well as lots of other houses in the neighbouring streets. They had to climb over rubble to get out of the shelter. Her little friend was crying as she thought her family had all been killed. Luckily, they had gone to another shelter and were safe. My gran's house was damaged, but repairable."

In Joel's mind, he was playing out the scene – he imagined the sirens wailing their dreadful sound calling everyone to 'get down the shelter.' The ground shaking beneath his feet, as the loud droning of the bombers engines could be heard, as they passed overhead. The whoops and crumps of the bombs as they fell, desecrating the buildings they hit. The whining sound as the bombers changed direction, turning around and coming back to bomb the city once again. The searchlights tracking them and the anti-aircraft guns firing upon them – rat-a-tat-tat, rat-a-tat-tat. Once the all clear sounded, he would order calm and help the women and children from the shelter; then go in search of dead and injured......

"My Mum said she grew up that day, she never felt a child again. Her childhood had been taken away by the Luftwaffe. In one afternoon, she had gone from being a child to an adult. "

Again, picturing the scene of destruction; Joel saw himself standing amid a collapsed building. A picture hung crookedly from a wall that had been left standing. Ornaments upright and undamaged, precariously balanced on a mantelpiece whilst everything else around lies in rubble on the floor. A child's doll; it's face smashed and pretty dress in tatters.

 "Didn't your Mum get evacuated" he asked "I thought all children were evacuated?"

"Plymouth wasn't in an evacuation zone. After the first lot of bombs she and her brother were sent away with their school, to Bodmin in Cornwall - but she was only away for a short time. Their little sister died you see; meningitis, nothing to do with the war. It was not that long after their street had been bombed. When her little sister died, my gran wanted her other two children back home, understandably. My mother came home but her brother chose to stay in Cornwall until the end of the war. My mum and gran went down to visit him a couple of times.

"Why didn't he want to come home?" Joel couldn't even contemplate having to leave his parents for that length of time. Having to live with strangers, far from home.

 "Well, he was staying with a family who lived on a farm. There were no shortages of food, they had plenty to eat in the countryside. There were rabbits to be snared, eggs and milk aplenty and the occasional chicken to eat. He was taught how to find the right sort of mushrooms, how to make a whistle out of a Hazel twig. He would help out at harvest time and his weekends and holidays were spent running wild on in the fields and climbing trees. He had an idyllic time of it, nothing like living in the city. I remember him once telling me that he always felt guilty, as the war years had been the best years of his life. He never really settled back into living back in the city."

When they'd finished lunch, Gran took the dishes to the kitchen and began washing up but continued her story.

"My uncle Max, my mum's brother; he moved to Australia when I was sixteen. He got a job on a farm out there – loved it; never came back. Well, he did but only a couple of times for holidays to visit family. He took his wife and children out there. They went over on the 'assisted passage migration scheme.' I still keep in touch with my cousins over there but I've never seen them since I was a girl."

Joel thought it sad having family so far away that you would likely never see them again; ever. "Did your uncle Max still have to carry a gas mask, even in the middle of the countryside?" he asked.

"I've no idea" replied Gran. "I suppose so... I really don't know." She stopped and thought for a moment, then continued washing the dishes, gesturing to Joel to pick up the tea-towel and start drying them.

"You know," said Gran looking thoughtful. "I'm sure your Grandad still has a gas mask from his Army days."

Joel recalled seeing a few photos of his Grandad in Army uniform, but they were really old, taken in the mid 1970's and Grandad didn't really look like that anymore.

"Why did Grandad have a gas mask?" asked Joel. "Was there still the threat of gas bombs when he was in the Army?"

"Oh, there was all sorts going on back then Joel, but no not the threat of gas bombs per se. I think everyone in the Military has a gas mask, it's just one of those things. An 'in-case' measure I suppose." She shrugged her shoulders.

Joel wondered; "Gran" he said, "Could I have a look at his gas mask and maybe borrow it and show it to Will?"

"Oh, I don't know where it is love. It could be anywhere." She emptied the bowl of dish water down the sink and dried her hands on a floral towel hanging from a hook on the back of the kitchen door. "I have a feeling some of his old stuff is under the stairs. I remember a box with old football and speedway programmes in and a few of his Trials riding trophies."

Joel remembered seeing some photographs of Grandad with his various motorbikes, he was quite a talented rider and he and his Bultaco 325 Trials bike had been inseparable for a number of years.

Joel smiled at Gran a with a look of mischief handed her the tea towel he had been drying the dishes with and headed to the cupboard under the stairs.

"Hang on young man. There's other things under there." Gran hurried after Joel and opened the two odd shaped doors that 'hid' the under-stair area. He knew it was where she kept her vacuum cleaner and ironing board, some old coats and a few other things; but he hadn't ever really thought of what other treasure may be hidden within its cavernous depths.

Gran fumbled for the light switch and when the light came on, Joel could see a number of boxes piled up. Some had labels on saying what was inside, others devoid of any mention as to their contents. Gran carefully took a few of the nearest small boxes out and Joel took as peek inside each one. Some he replaced the lid straightaway, when he saw they contained nothing of importance to him at this moment in time. He made a mental note though of some of the contents as it was likely at a future date he may want to investigate them further.

The fourth box, a slightly tattered waxed cardboard box brought forward treasures that made Joel's eyes widen and his heart rate hasten. There were newspaper cuttings, photograph's, documents, letters; a host of ephemera, all relating to the Second World War era.

"What's this?" asked Joel, showing the box to Gran.

Gran leafed through a few items and then took a handful of photograph's and went through them silently. After a few moments, she looked up and said "These were my grandma's papers, I'd forgotten all about them." She sounded slightly choked up but excited too. "These pictures are of your great-great gran and grandad Endacott, my mother, uncle Max, aunt Lily who died; look." She pointed out the unfamiliar smiling faces on a black and white photograph. "This was probably taken before the war; you see my grandad was conscripted into the Navy. He was away for most of the war"

Joel took the faded and creased at the corner photograph and examined the faces. He then looked through the other snaps, identifying the same faces but at varying stages in their lives. There were documents; an identity card belonging to Mrs Elinor Endacott. Various school reports – some from Bodmin. Some tarnished buttons with A.R.P embossed on them as well as a silver A.R.P pin badge.

Joel remembered Mr Roberts going on about the A.R.P and the gas masks, but he had no idea what the initials meant.

"Gran, what's the A.R.P?"

Gran held the silver badge in her hand and smiled. "You know I remember my mum telling me stories about how, when she stayed with her aunt, her mother, my gran - your great gran, would go out at night, one night a week; and ensure the blackout was observed. That was to make sure no one had any light showing through their curtains, as the German bombers might see it from the sky." Joel thought it unlikely one or two households showing a bit of light would attract a German bomber from 20,000 feet – but what did he know.

"My gran would sound the air raid sirens and guide people into public air raid shelters. She wore a dark blue uniform and beret - like the Army, but blue. During a raid, she wore a tin hat of course. She had a torch and a whistle"

Joel tried to imagine his own gran in blue battledress, directing terrified families in the middle of the night towards the nearest shelter. Blowing a whistle and keeping calm whilst bombs could be heard dropping on the distance. Only as the 'crumps' got nearer would she herself disappear into the safety of the shelter.

"What does A.R.P actually stand for then?" He now realised it was something to do with air raids, but the P didn't make sense.

"Air Raid Precaution." Said Gran. "Both men and women could be wardens. Men who were too old to go to war or who had reserved occupations served. Women who were able to leave children in the care of someone else in the family or who didn't have children. All sorts of people were A.R.P wardens. There were fire guards, first aid parties, stretcher parties, ambulance drivers...."

"What about gas masks?" interrupted Joel. "I thought they had something to do with gas masks." Keen to find out why Mr Roberts was so insistent he had a gas mask if ever he came across an A.R.P warden.

Gran thought for a moment. "I assume they were the ones who checked people had their gas masks with them, I'm really not sure. I suppose people got lackadaisical, because no gas bombs were ever dropped and they got fed up carrying around this cumbersome thing everywhere they went. Of course, they never knew that there wouldn't be any gas bombs dropped and therefore couldn't take the risk."

Joel decided that although the box was fascinating, it was probably time to put it aside and have a thorough look through it later on – there was a gas mask to be found. Gran said Joel could look on his own as long as he was careful – as she wanted to reminisce with the items in waxed cardboard box. Items she hadn't seen for at least thirty-five years; maybe longer. She and Grandad had moved in to that house thirty-five years ago, when their children had been small and she couldn't ever remember showing any of the items to them.

He took a few more boxes out and gave them a cursory glance over. The last box; much bigger than any of the other boxes, was Joel's last hope; at least under the stairs. He pulled it forward and with trepidation lifted the lid. It looked promising. There was Grandad's beret – the one he'd seen him wearing in photographs. There was a belt, buttons, random bits and of kit that must have meant something to grandad at one time. There was a green bag, it looked promising.

Opening it cautiously, Joel slowly pulled the treasured item from within its confines. The ugly rubber mask with two googly glass eye pieces and tin screw on canister; presumably to filter the impurities from the air – was far from attractive. He picked it up and took it over to the table where his Gran was still perusing through her box of forgotten memoires.

"Can I take this to show Will?" He asked excitedly. Showing Gran what he had found.

"Well let's get the rest of it tidied away first and we'll see. You really should ask your grandad though." She added as an afterthought.

"But Gran, if Grandad hasn't looked at it for thirty-five years at least I can't see him missing it for a few minutes." Joel pleaded his case.

Gran reluctantly agreed, but still insisted everything else was tidied away first and that it was taken in its protective bag and only shown to his friend – not used as a toy. She warned of the possibility of 'dangerous toxins in the canister – it being so old' - but Joel was sure she was just saying it to scare him. After tidying everything else away and making a mental note of what other boxes were of particular interest, Joel called goodbye to his gran, who was for some reason getting weepy over some old letters she'd found in the box. Gran waved back without looking up and told him to be careful.

CHAPTER FOUR

Outside Joel fairly skipped down the street, he couldn't wait to show Mr Roberts his gas mask. He approached number fifty-two and tentatively knocked on the door. He made sure the gas mask bag was on show around his neck. He heard footsteps in the passageway behind and then the door was opened by a woman, probably in her mid-thirties, whom he hadn't seen before. She was wearing a wrap- around apron just as the old lady had done. She wore a headscarf which was tied on top at the front. Her hair seemed rather large and Joel assumed she had some of those 'curler things' in.

"Can I help you?" she enquired.

"Erm, is Will home?" Joel felt a bit awkward. Maybe the 1940's thing was all a trick and Derren Brown or some other TV mentalist bloke would suddenly appear out of nowhere and put his hand upon his shoulder and say *'Sleep,'* whilst numerous TV cameras would emerge from various doorways, followed by people who were all in on the stupid game. Joel would then *'come to'* and find himself sat in front of a studio audience, and have to painstakingly watch, as he's shown footage of him having totally and utterly humiliated himself; all for the amusement of others. Well, if it did happen, he would punch the mentalist in the face and demand to be put into care and never speak to his parents or grandparents again.

"You must be Joel?" The lady smiled and invited him in. She closed the door behind them and gestured him into the kitchen. "I've heard a lot about you, it's nice to finally meet," she said. "I'm Maggie, Maggie Roberts – I'm Will's Mum."

Maggie ushered him into the kitchen and offered him a glass of water and a seat while he waited for Will, who was out running a few errands. Maggie explained it was her 'day off' from the buses where she worked as a clippie. Joel would have laughed if she hadn't come across so serious - he had no idea what a clippie was. Maggie filled a big black kettle from the single tap at the sink before placing the kettle on the range. She made light conversation about the weather and how Sylvie had been out dancing till late the night before, despite the threat of night time raids and having full 12-hour shift ahead of her the following day.

Old Mrs Roberts who was sitting by the range, was busy crocheting. "What you 'avin for tea?" she asked Joel.

"Erm, I'm not sure," he replied. "Gran likes cooking Italian, so it'll probably be Italian something or other."

"What's Italian something-or-other?" Queried Mrs Roberts, leaning forward, as though it was a recipe she hadn't yet come across.

"What are you having?" Joel asked in return, not quite sure what Italian dish his gran would choose to prepare.

"Corned beef hash and broad beans," said Mrs Roberts. Joel nodded his approval.

After a minute or so of silence, Maggie said, "It was you who brought the Commando magazines for our Will wasn't it?" as she began to load dishes into the sink.

"Yea, I picked them up in a second-hand book shop."

"Really?" Said Maggie, pausing mid-movement, as she picked up the kettle from the stove and was about to pour the hot water into the sink. She then continued her course and poured the water into the sink over some detergent. She turned back to look at Joel. "You do realise some of the stuff in there was very controversial. You know, hush-hush." She tapped the side of her nose, pausing for a while, deep in thought; then said. "You don't think they're propaganda, do you?"

"Er, I don't think so" Said Joel puzzled. "Why?"

Maggie left the dishes and went to open drawer on the dresser. She handed one of the magazine to Joel. He flicked through 'In Enemy Territory.' Everything looked fine; yes, the British had got into Germany and were fighting them on their own soil, but of course that's what the reader wanted to see; it certainly wasn't propaganda. Joel couldn't see the problem.

"I can't see anything wrong with it" said Joel placing it back on the table.

"Look" said Maggie, picking up the magazine. She showed Joel the inside front and back covers – The front showed a 'Star of soccer' named Steve

Nichol and the inside rear a 'Star of rugby union' called Rob Andrew. She then showed him the other two copies – both with their 'Locomotion' pictures – beautiful steam engines; the French 'Chapelon's Pacific' and the British 'Mallard.'

"Why would this magazine have pictures of two 'sports stars' who nobody's ever heard of? They should have pictures of film stars, like Ronald Colman, Robert Donat or Clark Gable." She looked a little dreamy eyed and then pointing to Rob Andrew said, "and look at that hairstyle!" She turned away and went back to washing the dishes.

"Tell you what," said Joel. "He pushed the magazines across the table in the direction of where Maggie was standing. "You can keep them – I won't get any more from that shop again."

 He pretended to feel that he had perhaps been naively taken in by the informer or possible spy who had sold them to him; inside he was chuckling at the reality the magazines wouldn't be printed for at least another 40 years and Rob Andrew 'the oddly dressed spy' was in Joel's present day an MBE and Director of Rugby Union.

"You can't trust anyone can you?" said Joel shaking his head. He gave the magazines one final push, as if repulsed.

Will soon returned, he said he'd been out on his pushbike running errands. He's been down to the dockyard, to take Aunt Sylvie an important letter that had arrived from the War Office with the second post, and then to Devonport to pick up a transistor valve for Granfer. He said he hadn't been expecting Joel – but it was always good to see him.

 "But I was here earlier. I came back and dropped the magazines off at lunch time, when no-one was in. That was just a couple of hours ago. You said to come back after lunch …." Confusion swept over them both. "Look, I've brought my gas mask too. Your Grandad said I needed to have it with me all the time." Joel held forth the oilcloth bag housing his Grandad's 1970's Military issue mask.

Will looked a little unsure and then laughingly said "You dropped the magazines off during an air raid; you silly sod! We were down the shelter! That was yesterday and it's not even dinner time yet!"

"Language!" called out Maggie, throwing a stern look.

They both looked at each other and burst out laughing – it was absurd, it was silly, it was funny.

"Come on let's go up to my room for a while, as me ma's busy." The two boys headed off upstairs. Will took Joel into a small room with a single bed, a wardrobe and a folding camp bed in it. They both sat on the single bed.

"Come on, I'll show my fag cards." Will dived under his bed and brought out a tin box with a scratched and faded picture on it. Joel wasn't really listening; he was looking around the room; the green painted door and skirting boards. The floral wallpaper that decorated the walls.

Joel recognised the picture on Will's box, it was a famous painting, but couldn't think of the name. Will caught him studying it. "The boyhood of Raleigh."

"Yea, that's what I was thinking," replied Joel not wanting to show his ignorance. The bed was covered by a funny patterned lumpy throw; not ugly but not particularly nice. The windows had the same white tape on them as on the kitchen window and in the front room. 'This family' he thought; is absolutely cuckoo, or very good actors. He did again wonder if he was taking part in some type of reality TV show, or the other possibility – he really was a time-traveller.

"Who sleeps on the camp bed?" Asked Joel.

"That's just a spare in case we need to put someone up, you know a relative or a visitor come to stay."

"Oh" said Joel. I might as well go along with this he thought, see if I can catch them out, pretend I believe them.

"Uncle Frank stays occasionally. The last war left him a bit well, you know…. nervous. Granfer says he's got neurasthenia. He doesn't like the bombs." Will pulled an awkward face. He only stays when he's on fire duty at work. He needs to be near the wharves you see – he works down at the Tar works. When the siren goes, he can be there in minutes on his bicycle from here. Him and my aunt share a flat near the dockyard with her sister – they got bombed out in the first raid."

Joel didn't really see; he didn't know where the tar works were or the dockyard for that matter. He's certainly never heard of neurasthenia, but hoped it wasn't contagious.

"Who else lives here?" Enquired Joel, taking in the detail of the room and surreptitiously looking for any hidden wiring or cameras.

Will let out a big sigh "Well" he placed his battered tin box on the bed, not yet ready to open it.

"Gran and Granfer, they sleep downstairs in the middle room. Mum and Dad, well, they've got the front bedroom. My Dad's in the Navy now so he's away a lot. Up in Scotland at the minute. Cousin Sylvie, who's Uncle Frank's daughter, she shares with our Violet in the middle bedroom...." He paused. "Our Vi's in the Wrens, she works at the dockyard in an office. Mum was sharing with Vi and Sylvie for a while, at the beginning of the war when Dad went away. Gran rented out the front bedroom to a young couple, a friend of Dad's. He was conscripted into the Navy as well; his wife was pregnant at the time. They stayed here until the baby was about four months old and then they got a ground floor flat of their own nearby." Will remembered the constant crying of the baby and the pram that took up the width of the hall. "Don't think Gran will rent the room out again. Sometimes my cousin's stay over."

"Crikey," said Joel, thinking of his own uncomplicated family. Even Marley's domestic arrangement which consisted of himself, Mum, Dad and siblings; Greta and Toby, the occasional lodger, and not forgetting their three Great Danes; Oberon, Hamlet and Brian Wilson; appeared to have a less complicated household.

Brian Wilson, a rescue dog was so called because he was found leaping about in the surf on the beach at Sandy Bay. Marley's parents – being dog lovers took him home and temporarily named him until the real owner came to lay claim. They put advertisements in the local paper and online, but no owner came forward and so he became a permanent member of the O'Farrell family. Adults laughed whenever they were told the origin of Brian Wilson's name, but Joel didn't understand the joke. There were a lot of things in life that didn't make sense – and that was one of them.

Will opened his box, it was filled with newspaper clippings, pencil sketches and miniature sets of picture cards. He looked through the various sets and picked out one depicting famous actors and actresses. "Right, let's start here."

Will put two cards at the top of the bed - a glamorous young woman with a parasol over her head and long ringlets curls, also a fierce looking older man in pirate clothing and long black hair.

"That's my Gran and Granfer." Both boys laughed.

"Now...." He looked through his cards, choosing carefully. "This one" he placed to the left of the group "Is Jim. He's my eldest uncle. He was born in 1894." The actor on the card had a jovial look, a cigar in hand and a dart board behind him. His name was Gordon Harker. He looked a comedic sort of character. "Uncle Jim died a few years ago, in a construction accident in Australia. He fell off a bridge. He moved out there after the war. "Granfer said he nearly drowned, when his ship HMS RHODODENDRON was torpedoed in the North Sea in 1918."

He thumbed through the cards, deciding who else to use. "Right, here's Aunt's Bertha and Ellen." He placed the cards of two young looking actresses namely; 'Heather Angel' and' Nancy Ruth' on the bed.

"Bertha lives with her husband Herbie and my cousins at Mount Gould – so they're round here all the time; you'll no doubt meet them. Aunt Ellen and Uncle Des live up the road; you probably know them....... Let's see who next." Will thumbed through the cards again.

"Uncle Billy, who I'm named after. He's the one who died due to the effects of being gassed in the Great War."

Uncle Billy was portrayed by a handsome young actor called Robert Donat. Joel knew who Robert Donat was, His Mum loved the film 'The 39 Steps' and he'd watched it a number of times with her. He felt quite pleased with himself, recognising one of the actors.

"Then there's Uncle Frank, he's the one who sleeps here sometimes," Will nodded to the camp bed. "Uncle Frank, he lives near the dockyard, married to Aunt Eve." Will placed a card of Fred Astaire on the bed.

"Dancer?" queried Joel.

"You got it!" They both laughed. "I think he's slightly older than Uncle Billy." Will swapped the cards around to get the family in the right birth order. "Frank's our Sylvie's dad. Next, Uncle Lennie." Will rummaged through his cards again – he chose the card with an actress on called Grete Naztler who looked very sad. "Why choose that one asked Joel."

They both looked at it for a while. "Dunno", said Will. "Just reminds me of him – the sad face." They looked at the actresses' sad expression for a while and Joel imagined; tall and dark with hair styled just like the actress in a severe bob, skulking around all sad and mournful in a long white silky flapper style dress, whilst stroking nervously at a long set of pearls that hung around his neck.

Next Will placed on the bed a picture of a cheery looking man, huge nose and smiling broadly whilst holding onto his shirt collar and puffing a cigar. His name being Jimmy Durante. Joel thought he looked rather like a 1920's Delboy Trotter character from the TV programme 'Only Fools and Horses.'

 "My dad," said Will.

"Has your dad got a big nose?" Asked Joel in all seriousness, whilst looking at the character on the card.

"No" chuckled Will. He's funny and he does smoke a lot, but not cigars, we're not toffs. He's a comedian. You'll know when dad's home. Him and Lennie are twins, but you'd never think it."

Both boys looked at the cards laid out. Joel was starting to put together the piece of Will's family. Uncle Jim who died in Australia. Aunt Bertha who lived nearby with her family. Aunt Ellen who lived up the street. Then uncle Billy, who died due to the effects of being gassed in the Great War. Next came Frank the dancer, Sylvie's father. Then the chalk and cheese twins; Uncle Lennie and Will's Dad.

"What does your Uncle Lennie do?" Joel was genuinely interested now.

"He works on the railways. Most of the family work on the railways. Lennie comes around sometimes, but him and auntie Elsie are both nervous sorts. She's been in and out the Loony bin a few times. He caught her with her head in the gas oven not long ago."

Joel burst out laughing.

"What's so funny?" said Will, taken aback.

"Why put your head in the oven?" asked Joel. "Why on earth would someone put their head in an oven?" He imagined aunt Elsie opening the oven door, checking the temperature and carefully taking out the now hot oven tray whilst wearing oven gloves and then, after cutting a length of tin foil, gently placing her head on the tray; wrapping the tin foil securely around her head, tucking in any loose edges - getting down on her knees with her head still at an angle on the tray and sliding it into the furnace like oven.

"Well, to gas herself," replied Will.

"Was the oven on or off?" asked Joel.

"Well on of course. You can't gas yourself if the oven's off can you!"

Joel was astounded anyone would think to do such a thing. "Surely, you'd get horrible burns and your hair would be on fire and you'd be screaming in pain, long before you could gas yourself – that would take ages?"

"She didn't light the gas, silly, she just turned it on."

Will pondered over the pictures for a while longer. Checking through his card collection to ensure he hadn't go any character wrongly portrayed. "There's my Mum and our Vi too, but I haven't got cards that remind me of them. Our Vi, my sister, she's working in an office at the dockyard; telephonist she is. My cousin Sylvie works there too, but in one of the shed's. Works on a cutting machine."

"What else have you got in there?" asked Joel peering into the box.

Will rummaged through "Fag cards – lots of. Some newspaper cuttings, my drawings, an autograph book, and a few programmes," he said proudly.

"What are fag cards?" Joel looked genuinely bewildered. He picked up one of the neat little groups of picture cards, wrapped in with elastic bands.

"Fag cards, you know – cigarette cards, the sort you play flick with or collect in albums?"

He could have spoken in Arabic and made more sense.

"Want to see my speedway riders?" said Will, with secretive anticipation. From the bottom of the box he slid out a cream coloured booklet. On the front was written 'An album to contain a series of portraits of Speedway Riders' - accompanied by a drawing of two rides throwing up dirt, and beneath inscribed 'Issued by John Player & sons.'

Joel's ears pricked up – he loved speedway and it wasn't often he came across someone else of a similar age who he could talk speedway with. Some of his friends at school were interested, but not to the extent Joel was.

"I love speedway!" exclaimed Joel. He moved closer to look." Have you got any of Jason Doyle?

"Er, I don't think so" said Will. "I haven't heard of him. Will thought he knew quite a bit about speedway, but that name eluded him. "Who did he ride for?" He flicked through the booklet.

"Swindon."

"Swindon weren't riding in 1937," said Will, a little uncomfortably. "This is from 1937." Will knew that Swindon didn't have a team, but he didn't want to upset his new friend.

"Who else do you like?"

"Erm, Emil Sayfutdinov."

Will drew a blank.

"Name me some in your book then," said Joel. He tried hard to think about the riders he'd read about online and the ones his grandad was often reminiscing about from when he was younger.

"Ivan Mauger, Nigel Boocock....." Joel said enthusiastically, reeling off the names he remembered from his grandads' old programmes and photograph collection.

Will appeared not to hear. "My favourite's Cordy Milne," he grinned. He showed Joel picture number 30 – Cordy Milne, sitting astride his machine. It wasn't a photograph, but an artist's impression, drawn presumably from an original photograph.

Joel remembered a name his grandad often mentioned, "Sprouts Elder!" he called out excitedly. He'd never seen a picture of 'Sprouts' but imagined him to have a rather large head, insipid complexion and with bulbous nose and ears.

"Oh, I don't think I've got him." Will flicked through his booklet – sadly there was no Sprouts Elder. "Who else do you like."

Joel struggled to think of other names his grandad had mentioned from years gone by. When he had been young in the 60's and '70's he'd been a huge Newcastle Diamonds' fan – following in the footsteps of his father before him; a fan since 1929. Gran said that he had only joined the Army, because in 1971, there was no racing at Newcastle that season.

"Bluey Wilkinson!" Exclaimed Joel excitedly. It felt a bit like a quiz show. He'd remembered the name Bluey Wilkinson, because his grandad had said when he was younger his dad used to go on about this great rider nicknamed 'Bluey' because of his red hair; which didn't make sense, but that was probably the sort of thing people found funny back then. Joel's great grandad had apparently seen Bluey, crowned World Champion, at Wembley in 1938. He'd travelled down to London by train with hundreds of other speedway supporters.

Joel relayed this story to Will, which made him rather awestruck – the thought of having seen a world final at Wembley. It was his ambition to go to Wembley one day; after the war and see its famous twin towers for himself. He flicked through the booklet again.

"Here we go" he said. "Bluey Wilkinson, arrived in England from New South Wales in 1929, as a mechanic...."

"let me see," said Joel, pulling the book towards himself, hoping to see a picture of the suave flame headed former World Champion – instead there was a blank space where a card could be glued, and underneath a description of the rider.

"Haven't got that card," said Will disappointedly. "I really wanted Bluey. My dad and my uncle Jack smoked as many Player's as they could before the collection ran out - but they never got a Bluey. Uncle Jack got five Colin Watson's and six Fred Strecker's, but never a Bluey. He sent me up all his doubles and every time I hoped there'd be a Bluey, but there never was. I gave some of them to our Vi, she stuck them in a little photo album and said she could pretend they were her sweethearts. Her favourite rider's Tiger Stevenson."

Will showed Joel card number 43, a blonde-haired rider in all black leathers; wearing a West Ham race bib. "She saw some footage of him at the cinema, on the British Pathé News, and she thought him a 'looker.' She's got lots of newspaper clippings about him, especially about him becoming the England Captain, and she says," he paused. "After the war, she says she's going to go to London to see him race."

Will handed the booklet to Joel to peruse. "He's not really got blonde hair you know, it's brown." He shrugged his shoulders. "Suppose the colourist just took a guess and gave him blonde hair in the picture."

Joel thought that quite funny and wondered how many of the other riders the colourist had just taken a guess at.

"I wish you could still get the cards, I only need seven more to fill the book. I've advertised in a few shops windows for swaps but seems everyone's after the same cards or they want too much money for them."

Will then handed Joel a pencil drawing. "That's Bluey, I did it in art class."

Joel thought Will rather quite a good sketcher. He smiled appreciatively and handed it back.

"Mr Reynolds has shown us how to make paper from old scraps. Every Friday after lessons we go along with all the paper scraps we can find around the school and the ones he thinks are worth using we soak and then put in a press. Once it dries out we use it for our art classes."

Joel skimmed through the booklet and wondered what became of the riders. He read their brief descriptions; Jack Dixon, the first of the northern riders to visit the south. That made him smile, thinking of how modern-day riders travelled up and down the country and across Europe on a day to day basis. The ditty also mentioned that 'Bronco' as Jack was known, was a popular rider in Copenhagen and had suffered numerous crashes, one in which he lost the tops of two fingers. 'Bronco' had ridden for Middlesbrough; Joel was sure his great grandad must have watched him race. "Oh yea, Bronco Dixon, he's, good, isn't he?" Said Joel.

Will said he hadn't seen Bronco Dixon ride, but knew that his last club before the war was Bristol. He had though seen 'local boy' Bronco Slade.

"He's brilliant," enthused Will. "We saw him up at Taunton at a speedway event there in, oh, I think it was May '38. We met up with my Uncle Jack and I remember I got hit in the eye with a stone. Bloody hurt it did, meant I couldn't see properly for the last three races. You must have seen him ride? He's from near you, Exeter way." Will began rummaging through his newspaper cuttings.

"Let me see… He competed in the famous 'International Six Day Trials' event in Germany last year. They had to cut it short because of the outbreak of war. It was in the Western Morning News." He stopped talking whilst he concentrated on leafing through numerous newspaper cuttings. He eventually found what he was looking for and handed it to Joel.

"Anyway; the British riders were told to withdraw on the fourth day of the event because of the rapidly deteriorating political situation. The paper said that when they arrived at the starting point in Saltsburg, there were Swastikas everywhere and all the riders were told to greet the officials with a salute of 'Heil Hitler.' He began laughing. "Imagine that, all our riders saluting and saying Heil Hitler!"

"Ich bin Englander. Hun Hitler!" said Joel in a deep voice, which made them both laughed raucously, though Will didn't quite know what it meant, he got the drift.

"On the third day," continued Will, reading from one of the newspaper cuttings he had in his hand. "The riders were told of the impending situation and then the following day, whilst enduring a two-hundred-mile circuit through the thirty-three-hairpin bends, and eight thousand feet climb through the snowy Tyrolian mountains, a message was received at the British Consul telling them to leave the country immediately. They were told to just dump their belongings at their hotel and leave in their leathers and any other warm clothing, immediately. If need be they were to syphon rationed petrol from parked cars along the way. It was imperative that they left straight away."

Joel thought it sounded like a good old wartime adventure film.

Will then picked up another newspaper cutting he had relating to the same story.

"31st August 1939. Mr Bernard 'Bronco' Slade of Exeter was forced to flee Germany. 'The Great Escape, as they called our convoy of bikes,' Bronco told our reporter. 'We, set off en-masse in the middle of the night, enduring a long and stormy passage back across the route we had raced on only the day before. Even though it was summer, it was bitterly cold, our hands almost frozen onto the handlebars. It was a long and arduous journey. We arrived at the border with Liechtenstein twelve hours after setting off. From there we made our way back, by bike and boat, to England, arriving Dover three days later. There were twelve British teams altogether, of which three teams were from the British Army comprising nine of its best motor cyclist. We stayed together throughout the whole journey, fearing what would happen if any of our party got separated.

Those that chose to stay and finish the race, including my good pal Tom Whitton, of Newton Abbot, were guaranteed safe passage home and were escorted to the border by German Military – a chap called Colonel Grimm I believe! The Germans declared themselves winners of the event, as most other competitors had already left. It's a shame as the British boys were well in the lead when we were told to leave.'

Joel seemed unsure of the story, but Will insisted he must have heard of Bronco Slade and his 'escape from Germany.' Joel decided to agree that he had heard of him, rather than look silly.

"Brilliant name 'Bronco Slade' isn't it?" he said, imagining a rider dressed in impressive black cowboy clothing with tassels; rather like the Lone Ranger - riding around on the presentation lap, pulling wheelies singlehandedly and shouting 'yeehaa' to the cheering fans; whilst firing a six-shooter into the air.

"He does loads of speedway and grass-track; Swainswick, Taunton, Kingsbridge; all over the place. He rode for Hackney in '38 and Crystal Palace in '39."

"Yeah," said Joel. "That's right," to place name and teams he'd never heard of before.

Will then changed the subject; he said his Uncle Norman and Uncle Jack, who were 'on the trains,' had both seen Bronco race up at Bristol. Uncle Norman lived just outside Bristol and Uncle Jack in Southampton; Jack was his mum's brother. Will said he had also been to Bristol a few times before the war; as his dad had also worked on the railways then, and they had gone up to see his mum' sister Betty - her husband being Uncle Norman. Will described how Aunt Betty would have a huge bell tent put up in her back garden, so that the family could 'picnic' in it during the day and then the younger members of the family could camp out and sleep in it at night. Every summer the family would gather at Aunt Betty's house for a long weekend, usually at the beginning of July. It typically averaged around eight adults and twenty children and was like Christmas in the summer. Aunt Betty lived in a very large old rambling house with massive gardens. It had no gas or electric, but with running water, fire and candle light the family lived quite happily. Uncle Norman would 'hire in' goats during the early summer months to cut down the grass and then leave it until the following year. Aunt Betty had a beautiful flower garden which she tended to regularly and there were always fresh flowers in a vase in her dining room.

Will smiled wistfully at the memory. He hoped they would get to go and visit her again soon, though Uncle Norman had not long been conscripted into the Royal Engineers.

Last year, in early July they had all gone to the speedway together one Friday night, to watch Bristol Bulldogs take on the 'mighty' Newcastle Diamonds, at Knowle. Will and his numerous cousins had positioned themselves next to the fence which overlooked the pits. On the other side of the fence was one of the opposition riders warming up his bike, he spied Will watching intently as he revved the throttle of his bike; listening to the purr of the engine. Will mimicked his actions. The rider called out "Hey kid."

"Me?" said Will, pointing to himself; amongst the crowded group. "Yea you. D'ya wanna try it?" pointing to his handlebars of his bike. Will nodded.

The rider called over to a chap in a flat cap and white overcoat, manning the pit gate. "Hey, buddy - let the kid through." Next thing, Will found himself surrounded by noisy engines and his nostrils filled with the smell of warm oil and fuel. It was just as exhilarating as the time he had met his all-time hero Cordy Milne.

The rider motioned him to sit astride the motorcycle. He showed Will how to gently pull the clutch in and rev the engine, but not too hard. Will could feel the vibration of the bike beneath him; it made him feel excited, his heart beat faster. His cousins on the other side of the fence shouted words of encouragement.

The rider asked who he was there to support and Will, not as dumbstruck as he had been when he met his all-time hero Cordy Milne; said Newcastle. He said it was because he'd never seen them before and they'd come a long way, just like they had, for the meeting. He told the rider he had travelled all the way from Plymouth. The rider asked how far away Plymouth was and Will said that it was 'more than 2 hours by train' - but he didn't know how far in miles. The rider told him that it had taken him seven hours to drive to Bristol. Will, noticing his accent, asked him where in America he came from. The rider looked indignant and said "Do I sound American? Oh boy!"

 Will felt silly and said "Are you Australian then?" The rider laughed and said he was Canadian, from Belleville, Ontario. Will being a collector of autographs, asked the rider to sign his autograph book, which he kindly obliged to do. He asked Will his name and wrote: 'To Will, the kid with the nice smile. Maybe see you on the dirt tracks one day. Best wishes, George Pepper.'

Will showed the page in his autograph book to Joel. He could just make out the wording through the swirly writing.

 "George Pepper! exclaimed Joel. That's who my grandad told me about. He got chased by tigers or something and then killed in a plane crash. Grandad's dad was a big fan of his – he won all his races didn't he – couldn't be beaten."

"What you on about?" said Will; stunned.

"George Pepper, he died in a plane crash during the war…." Joel stopped, he saw the look of absolute horror on Will's face.

"Oh no, I'm thinking of someone else, stupid me." Joel's face flushed red, he tried to back track as quickly as possible. What was he doing, what was he saying? If this was real, then he was possibly saying things that were yet to happen.

"I mean George Pepper, he was really good wasn't he. Best rider in the league or something. Yea, my grandad, he lived, err lives in Newcastle. He watches the Diamonds every week."

Will gave Joel a disbelieving look. "But there's been no speedway since last summer when the war started; well other than a few of meetings at Belle Vue in Manchester, but that's not near Newcastle is it?"

"Yea, my Grandad goes on about it like he still goes every week. He reads about it in the paper and hears it on the radio. You know what old people are like." Joel tried to act nonchalant.

"Radio, radiogram?" said Will. "That's a funny word to call it. Don't you mean the wireless?"

"Err, yea, the Americans call it a radio." Joel felt uncomfortable, he didn't feel at ease anymore; more like a rabbit caught in the headlights. He felt the conversation was likely to disintegrate and he was going to either have to make a run for the door back to 2017 or shout out 'Okay okay – game over and await the hidden cameras to come rolling out;' but he was starting to feel the escape route was more likely the reality of heading out the door and back to 2017.

"Look," said Will, taking a newspaper cutting from a manila envelope. He handed Joel a picture of a boy sitting astride a speedway bike, watched over by a rider with his left hand on the handlebars and apparently in conversation with the young fan. "That's me with George Pepper."

The Newspaper article was from the Bristol Evening Post and dated 8th July 1939. The heading read *'Speedway leaders win by three.'* Joel read the article and studied the picture even more carefully. The article stated that with only one heat to go the Newcastle side were in the lead 39-38 and so the Bulldogs still had a chance of winning. However, their luck was out and particularly Jack Bibby, whose machine reared at the gate and try as he might, he could not get it down. He crashed out and was therefore unable to ride in the re-run. It went on to describe how the riding of Captain George Pepper was outstanding and his maximum score was only equalled by Diamond's team mate Rol Stobbart.

Joel studied the picture once again and had to admit the boy in the picture looked exactly like Will. The footer underneath said *'Newcastle Captain George Pepper shares some tips with a young fan.'*

What was there to say? If this was a joke it was more elaborate than was possible. The detail was too fine; it must be real.

"Here's some more articles, d'you want a look." Will offered Joel a handful of newspaper cutting – most relating to Cordy Milne. Joel flicked through them. He found it weird, he really wanted to talk to Will about the Grand Prix standings and his favourite riders - but, how could he? They didn't yet exist.

Will sorted through his spare cards – he offered Joel a Frank Goulden cigarette card. "Here, he used to ride for Plymouth."

Of course, Joel had never heard of him but was very thankful all the same.

He put it in his pocket. He slid it in next to his mobile phone. He really wanted to pull it out and call someone or open and app and see Will's reaction; but a sudden feeling of fear ran through him and he knew he mustn't. The last thing he should ever do was to let Will know he was from another time; that he was a time traveller. Someone with the power to change the course of world history. It scared him, terrified him in fact. He needed the loo, he also needed some time to clear his head.

"I just need to use the loo, which door is it." Will headed towards the door that in Gran's house led to the bathroom.

"Same place as your gran's – unless they're posh and got an indoor one!" added Will as an afterthought.

Joel remembered Grandad talking about their kitchen having once been the outhouse where the washtub and toilet had been. There were no indoor toilets when the houses had been built and so former occupants had to go outside and to the back of the yard to use the toilet – which was thought more hygienic. At night Grandad said they would have used a potty or bucket indoors which they kept under the bed and emptied it into the loo outside in the morning. It seemed funny at the time but he would have gladly sat on a potty now if one was offered.

In haste, he made his way downstairs and out the back door and past a tin shed thing buried in the ground. Thankfully, where his Gran now had a kitchen, the Roberts had an outhouse and on opening the door were another two doors. The first led to the toilet, the other he assumed to the wash house. He drew the bolt across behind him and sat down on the cold wooden seat. He took his mobile phone from his pocket – it had power, but no signal. He felt a sense of nausea and fear. His tummy rumbled and his guts opened.

The tin hut thing had to be an Anderson shelter. He really was back in the 1940's. They didn't have mobile phone masts back then. There were no mobile signals bouncing down from satellites floating around the earth – the only signals back then were radio and television masts and cables under the sea.

As he stood up to flush something dropped to the floor. Joel looked down. It was the glass lens his grandad had found in the fireplace in the dining room. He picked it up and examined it. Was that the object that was allowing him to travel through time – a miniature window in space and time? He held it up to his eye. The magnification was very good. He recalled the other day when he had held it up to the light and watched the colours it made dance across the bedroom walls. Had he energised it with the light – did it need recharging like a battery? He had kept in his pocket ever since; he didn't know why – he just liked 'things' and this was one of those 'things' that he liked.

Was this meant to happen, was he chosen to travel in time?

CHAPTER FIVE

Will sat on the bed packing his 'treasures' neatly away in his tin. He never tired of reading the newspaper articles about Cordy Milne or the other great riders of the day. He thought about Joel and how he seemed 'odd'. Even Granfer had said he thought him 'strange in the noggin.' Sometimes he acted normal and then other times as if he had no grasp of reality – like the times he came around without his gas mask and his seemingly lack of understanding of time. The daft headphones he wore that had no wire to plug into the wireless and appeared to serve no purpose at all. The strange clothes and the way he spoke. It's like when he got excited or liked something he would say 'wicked' or 'cool.' It was as though he had a sort of verbal tic. Vi had said he was very 'vague' at times and Granfer said, "More like doolally tap!"

Maybe they were overthinking and always assuming strangers to be spies. Maybe where Joel came from the war didn't really affect people and life carried on pretty much as normal just as it did for folk in parts of the countryside. He was still surprised though at Joel's parents being happy to send him to stay at his grandparents' house in Plymouth, knowing that bombs had only weeks previously been dropped a few hundred yards away for their house, killing people killed.

Will reached across to the carrier in which Joel kept his gas mask. It certainly was smart – members of the public only had carboard boxes to carry their gas masks in, unless they bought a proper carry case for it. Most people had decorated their boxes with wallpaper, stickers or fancy pictures stuck on with paste. It made them individual and protected them somewhat in the rain.

Joel's was made of a sort of waxed canvas; waterproof and it had a Military crows foot arrow symbol stamped on it in black. Will opened the bag and pulled out the mask. It was definitely of better quality and design than the one he had. He tried it on. The smell of rubber was the same and the cumbersome inelegance of it much the same too. J. ARMSTRONG was stamped on it in black writing, followed by a series of numbers. Just as he was taking it off Joel entered the room.

"I was just trying it on... it's err much better than mine," said Will awkwardly. "How come you've got a Military one though?"

Joel was prepared for this question – he'd been going over a lot of things in his mind while he was sat on the loo. He was going to play along – well, not exactly 'play along' as that would be taking the mickey out of the situation. He was going to do his best to not get caught out and to participate in the past as best he could. He suddenly felt very courageous. 'Just think' he said to himself, 'you are very possibly the world's first ever time traveller… though of course there could very well be many others out there too, having found their own window to the past.'

"My dad works for the Military, he's doing some hush hush stuff with the Americans; intelligence related."

"But the American's aren't in the war." Replied Will, furrowing his brow and looking puzzled.

"Not yet, but they're doing a lot of covert work on behalf of the British. There's quite a few American airmen in our RAF already. There's Canadian's, Poles – they'll get involved and help us out soon enough." Joel said just enough, without giving too much of what he actually did know, away. It was apparent to most people that the American's would be involved in helping out their British cousins as the war escalated, just no one was sure of when or on what scale their involvement would be.

"Does your dad get your clothes from the American's; second-hand?" Will asked seriously, looking Joel up and down. Joel was wearing a Stamford University T-shirt, probably some old sports kit no longer wanted he assumed. Joel laughed, at least he could get away with wearing modern clothes if people thought he'd got them second-hand from America.

"I'd love some American stuff." Said Will in awe. "Do you think he could get me something?"

Suddenly there was a loud wailing sound. Joel shrieked "What the…..!" Then immediately realised what it was.

"Come on." Said Will. He quickly closed his box of cards and newspaper snippets and slipped it back under the bed before heading downstairs. Joel had to double back to grab his gas mask. He then followed Will who had by now seized his gasmask from the hallway table and was heading towards the back door. Joel's heart was thumping in his chest; What was about to happen? Were bombs going to start dropping? Was he going to find himself back in 2017?

They stepped out into the courtyard and clambered into the dark and dank Anderson shelter. They kept the door and gas curtain open; waiting for Mr and Mrs Roberts to join them. Just as Mrs Roberts was about to clamber in, the 'all clear' sounded – it had been yet another false alarm. Joel felt a sense of shock but no one else seemed too perturbed, maybe a little shaken but more than likely they were simply relieved.

"That's the second one today." said Will. "We're starting to get more and more day time raids. There were none before the fall of France.

Joel's heart gradually got back to its normal rhythm, but his mind was still racing.

"Just the other day, "said Will. "When there was that air raid about 10 o'clock at night."

Joel listened, but didn't acknowledge.

"A bomb exploded near to where my Auntie Eve was walking. She'd just left the chippie with Uncle Frank's supper. Anyway, the shop was bursting with customers; they all got caught in the blast and were killed. All in bits they were, no-one knew who was who. They had to look for their identity cards to find out who was who and then try and put the bits of bodies back together on the pavement outside. In full view of everyone too!"

Joel didn't know if Will was telling the truth, or just trying to shock him. He felt a little queasy.

"I think I best go check on Gran," he said. Then suddenly realising he couldn't – he was still in 1940 or whatever year it was. Panic rose again in his chest. Would he ever be able to get back home?

"Your Gran'll be fine," said Will flippantly. "She'll be used to it now – false alarms. Come on, let's walk up to town, see what's going on. We could have a walk along the Hoe if you fancy it? We can watch the warships out in the Sound, and if the German's do come back, maybe see a dogfight in the skies?" That thought appealed to both of them. "You want to see the allotments down there, continued Will. "There's nowhere left to play footie there now. Everywhere we used to play footie is now taken up with either allotments or Nissen huts for the Military."

"Can we go and look at the bomb sites first?" asked Joel "I've not seen one yet?"

Will looked puzzled. "You haven't seen any bomb sites? Do you never get out or what?"

"Err, I've just not gone far since I got here, that's all." Joel hoped his answer would suffice.

"You don't have to go far to see a bomb site," replied Will astounded, as they walked down the path. He then realised he couldn't see Joel, there was nobody there. "Joel," he called, and walked back towards the front door to see if Joel had gone back indoors. Just as he was stepping through the door, Joel re-appeared behind him, and tapped him on the shoulder.

"Flippin' heck, where did you disappear to?" cried Will, in surprise.

"Nowhere," replied Joel. He wasn't actually sure what had happened, everything had just sort of gone fuzzy.

"You hid behind the wall, didn't you?" laughed Will. "Nearly got me that time."

As the boys went to leave again Joel took hold of Will's sleeve. This time they both walked down the path and out the gate together. They made their way up the street and crossed the same road bridge that Joel used to get to Will's house. Instead of cars underneath there was the train line, and either end of the bridge was manned by Home Guard armed sentries, it apparently being a vulnerable point in the event of an attack. They stopped at the top of Gran's street. Joel noticed how different it looked. He noticed how all the windows in the street were dark wood; none of them were white UPVC like in his own time. The front room bay windows all had flat roofs; his gran's and just about every other house in 2017 had a sloping roof above the bay. Will seeing the intense puzzled look on his face, asked what was wrong.

"Nothing," said Joel. "Can we just pop down for a minute. "I won't go in."

Will shrugged his shoulders and followed Joel down the road, as he looked in wonderment at all the properties and stopping outside of what was in his own time, his Gran's house. He noted the differences; here and now in Will's time, the front door and window frames were dark blue wood. The window panes themselves had on them the same white criss-cross tape as Will's and every other window in the street. Joel tried peering through the nets but was only able to discern a large mirror on the wall, where Gran now had a picture hanging.

Before Joel could say anything, Will had opened the gate and was knocking on the door. Joel stood on the pavement terrified that his cover was just about to be blown. He was overcome with the same feeling he had in Will's bedroom when he wanted to just run away; but his feet wouldn't move. They felt like they were cemented to the pavement and were slowly becoming at one with it. Will knocked again – they waited, no answer.

"I guess she's gone out - Oh well."

The relief Joel felt was enormous, he had been saved from a huge and ugly embarrassment and his feet were now able to move freely, although heavily; the invisible wet cement having vanished from the pavement. He was actually more than relieved that the occupants weren't home.

It was getting quite chilly and Joel really wanted to go in and grab his hoodie. He knew where it was, it was hanging on the newel post at the bottom of the stairs. But of course, it wasn't really there, not in 1940 anyway. It made him wonder if other times overlapped and if there were a host of items draped over the newel post. Items from the 20's the 50's, the 60's. Did everything that ever got put anywhere, somehow stay there, like a recording or a memory? He remembered how his Great Aunt Emily's house looked. She'd been dead several years now and the new owners would have changed the place drastically; but in his mind, it was still as it was when she lived there. He could picture the faded patterns made by the sun on the front room wallpaper. The crochet cushions and the magazines in a pile beside her chair. However much her front room changed over time, it would always look the same to him.

There was the overwhelming smell of coal. Will pointed out that it was coming from the Plymouth and Stonehouse Gas Company which burned coal, and he pointed to a gantry which carried the small trucks of coal. He said the locals called the 'nose' the 'Cattedown Gin' as opposed to the drink 'Plymouth Gin'. Plymouth Gin was made using sweet juniper berries with the gentle hint of cardamom, coriander, orris and angelica root. Cattedown Gin had the bitterness of coal dust, mixed with the unpleasantness of the boneyard, followed by the aromatics of the tar yard; which bound it all together.

Joel concentrated, he could discern the distinct aroma from a nearby tar distillery. A little further away, the breeze picked up the pungent stench from the boneyard on the foreshore. The mixture was not pleasant and on a hot day with the wind in the right direction, the smell would be quite overpowering.

Two large gasometers stood towering behind a row of houses. An obvious target for the Luftwaffe thought Joel. No wonder the inhabitants of Cattedown were terrified whenever there was a raid. If they went up, the whole area would have to be evacuated – if they weren't incinerated first. What use was a bucket sand or water and a stirrup pump if they got hit? Joel tried to imagined the carnage if they did receive a direct hit. He hadn't noticed them in 2017 so whether they had been disassembled, bombed or just put out of use; he wasn't sure. There were also some huge chimneys in the far distance; much taller or so they seemed than the gasometers. Smoke poured from them in big grey clouds and then dissipated as it floated made its way across the sky.

As if reading his thoughts Will said, that's the power station. Makes the 'lectric.

Joel's mind began to wander, as it often did; he imagined his speedway hero *'The impressive Jason Doyle,'* as the TV pundits called him. Joel's could see Jason the 'Flying Aussie Ace.' He pictured him as a heroic WW2 pilot – the gasometers ablaze; Jason, now based at the nearby Royal Australian Airforce Base at Mount Batten, just across the water from the burning fuel tanks. Here Jason piloted the enormous Short Sunderland flying boats.

Commandeering huge canvas sheets and tents or anything he could find; Jason strapped them beneath his plane with ropes attached through the cockpit. He would then fly out to sea, sweep low and at full throttle dragging the sheets through the water, fill them up and then fly at a safe height over the burning gasometers, and from the cockpit, cut the ropes and let the sea water spill out onto the vast flames, dampening them down. It probably wouldn't do much good, but it would be something. Joel knew the Australians did something similar when there were bushfires; he'd seen it on TV, and Jason knowing all about this would put it into practice. He would continue his mission until there were no tents / sheets/ rope left. Exhausted he would return to base to a hero's welcome. The local newspaper would hear of his heroics and send an interviewer along to speak to him about his gallant act. The headline above the article in the paper the next day would read;

'FLYING AUSSIE AIR ACE DOES IT AGAIN!'

'Australian speedway sensation Jason Doyle, who never knows when he's beaten. Yesterday, helped save the lives of hundreds of people by parachuting thousands of gallons of water on the burning gasometers at Coxside. Having been brought up in Newcastle, New South Wales, Australia; the Hunter Valley racer was no stranger to bush fires and knew exactly what to do when he saw the flames licking around the large flaming metal containers. He jumped in his plane; a Sunderland Flying boat, and with the help of fellow airmen tied a large canvas sheet loosely to the bottom of the plane with rope. He then flew out over Cattewater and made five missions over the fiercely burning flames. He dropped the water by cutting the ropes that held the water filled canvas sheet in place.

The fire service who were tackling the fires from the ground, were unable to get close enough to the flames due to the intense heat. They said without Doyle's help the damage caused would have been much worse and they are putting his name forward for a Victoria Cross.

When interviewed Doyle had this to say; "Yea, it's just what anyone would do, you know. I've seen the devastation these fires can do back home in Australia." He joked he found the winters here too cold and 'just wanted to get warm.'

"Yea, I just like to give 110% all the time and if it's not racing then it's in whatever I do. The guys here at the base are great and the locals are really friendly. You know, for us boys who fly, it's just another day at the office. I want to give as much to the war effort as I do to my racing. I've heard they've put my name forward for the Victoria cross; that's amazing, but I'm just doing my job."

They hadn't gone more than a hundred yards when Joel saw the reality of war for himself. They passed a few houses that had obvious damage but were in the process of being repaired. Corporation workmen and soldiers on wooden ladders were repairing windows and replacing lost roof tiles.

"Everyone goes down the shelters now either their own or the public ones," sighed Will. "Your gran got an Anderson as well?" he asked. "Grandad, me and my dad built ours. We broke up the concrete in the courtyard and put it in. A right old job it was and no mistake. Cost us £8 as well it did!"

Joel pictured his own dad and grandad breaking up the patio and erecting a corrugated Anderson shelter – ensuring they had it buried up to the right depth so to safeguard it from filling up with water when it rained. Joel would read the instructions and take the measurements whilst his grandad and dad did the physical work. Grandad would be swearing and getting irate and saying the instructions were all wrong. He'd be just like he was when he was driving. Once erected they would then cover it in the soil and Gran would sprinkle seeds on top, so when the flowers grew, the courtyard still looked pretty. Joel and Grandad would then fill sandbags and place them around the entrance.

"Maybe when things get worse we'll go to the main shelter, you know for a bit of morale boosting," said Joel. He remembered seeing pictures of people crowding into the London underground stations bedding down for the night.

"Gets worse!" Cried Will. "Worse, how can it get any bleddy worse?"

"I didn't mean like that" said Joel back tracking, already in the knowledge that it would get worse; much worse in fact. The 'Plymouth Blitz' as it was to be known, hadn't yet begun. "I meant if Gran's nerves get worse. You know, for a bit of company or whatever."

Joel pictured Gran, Grandad, Muffin and himself all lying under a corrugated shelter in the garden, along with a flask of tea, some sandwiches and a few dog biscuits for Muffin. Joel would have his headphones on to drown out the din of the bombs raining overhead and Gran would be clinging on to Grandad and crying. Grandad would be swearing profusely and threatening any German pilot who dared bomb his *bloody house or scratch 'me car.'* Sweet peas would adorn the top of the shelter, along with a few carrots and potatoes for sustenance. Possibly a couple of hens would be squawking wildly and fluttering around in a cage – breaking eggs recently laid.

They walked a few yards further on.

"There you go – a proper bomb site," said Will, even he looked on it in wonder although he had walked past it many times. He didn't like it, it gave him the creeps; especially knowing three people had been killed in the blast and a good few others in adjoining properties had been injured. Everyone locally had known them, it was the postmaster, his wife and brother-in-law. When his mum heard the Post Office had been hit she flew into a panic. Maggie's sister lived above the Post Office at St Jude's and had thought it was that one that had been hit. There were other people killed too. Just around the corner a civilian, a soldier and a policeman in the street directing people towards the public shelters. The bombings on Plymouth were a new thing, people had previously become complacent and didn't expect bombs to be dropped on Plymouth, especially not right at their door. People had been naïve; they had learned a harsh lesson.

 The boys were confronted by a row of houses; their exterior walls reduced to piles of rubble and bricks, the downstairs interior rooms very much exposed. Upstairs Joel could see tattered bits of bedding, flapping on a broken bedstead. Scattered bits of furniture thrown about like toys that had suffered from a child's temper tantrum. The roofs he thought, looked as though a giant hand had just swept along, scooping off roof tiles and timbers and sending them flying across the road and through the windows of neighbouring houses. The dividing walls had been left intact, though some leaning precariously. The downstairs rooms, where accessible had been cleared of what undamaged items were salvageable and taken to a place of storage or taken by the former occupants to a temporary or new house. There was a strong smell in the air, rather like damp plaster. Joel allowed himself time to let the depressing scene to sink in - the once unimportant details. Things such as the dying flowers in a small vase on a bedroom mantelpiece. Curtain still drawn, hanging from a pole that no longer had a window to shade. He was tempted to clamber over the rubble and see what he could find, but the 'danger do not enter' signs put him off.

"You couldn't get along here when it first happened" said Will. "The rubble went right across the road and we found loads of shrapnel." Three of 'em bought it– found 'em cowering under the kitchen table. The old 'uns, thinking they'd risk it. Granfer said when there's a raid on you need to open the back and the front doors and some window's if you can – it lets the blast go through and lessens the damage."

That remark sent a chill up Joel's spine. He imagined people scrambling into their Anderson shelter or scurrying along the street in their pyjamas and nightgowns to the main shelters. Leaving their homes open and valuables accessible to anyone who might have less than desirable ideas of safety of a possible direct hit. Those less mobile already sleeping beneath or clambering under a Morrison shelter in their front room and praying there wasn't a direct hit, all doors and windows shut. Likely many up until that point 'risked it' assuming the chances of a direct hit were minimal.

After a minute or two of taking in the devastation, the boys went on their way. It wasn't good to stare, especially not at someone else's misfortune. "Just think," said Will. "Half a second, maybe not even that. If the pilot had released the bomb just that fraction earlier, it could have been your gran's house, my house, someone else's house, just happens it was these people's houses."

The walk into town was a distraction from thoughts of bombs and bodies. For one Joel didn't recognise the way at all. There were houses where he knew there were no longer houses. The footbridge over the busy road was no longer there, nor was the busy road – instead there was a row of houses and running in a slightly different orientation. The route was mostly unrecognisable. A couple of the buildings were familiar from 2017, but the rest was different, so very different in fact. So many of the houses they passed were no longer there in Joel's time. They had been replaced by industrial units, modern flats, retail outlets and grassland. Had they been lost in the war, or been part of a later modernisation plan? He didn't know.

He noticed the white lines painted on kerb stones and on lamp posts. He didn't dare ask Will why but was sure he'd read somewhere it was to give people some sense of direction in the blackouts. There were 'swill' bins on every street. He saw a woman emptying her vegetable peelings into one and assumed it was to be used for animal feed.

"Hullo Mrs Northmore," called Will and waved to the lady, who was wearing the 'uniform of the day' – a floral wrap around apron. She had a small boy in her arms, probably around a year old, he waved too and began giggling. "Aunt Ellen's friend Edna," said Will, assuming Joel would want to know who she was. She made her way back towards her front door where another boy about four years old was waiting. "Mummy I need a wee," he cried and was frantically jumping up and down, holding his shorts.

Joel noticed there were no green and brown plastic refuse or recycling bins to be seen, at the front of properties or in the back lanes. In their place were metal 'ash bins' as Will called them.

Shops had canopies on the front that shaded the goods on display from the sun. On the corner of one street they passed was a piano shop. He was sure that was the same shop he'd been in previously with Grandad to buy a lottery ticket and a newspaper. Groups of children played in the streets, unworried by traffic. He passed a group playing hopscotch on the road, the grid marked out in chalk. One of the strangest things though, was seeing people sitting outside of their houses on kitchen chairs, sitting on walls or leaning on their gates. They couldn't walk along a street without seeing at least a couple of people sat outside watching the world go by. He wondered if that's what they did for entertainment in the evenings, not having television or the internet?

A wholesale ironmonger stood where a modern-day garage now stood. The cars, the people – it was like being in dream. There was a row of houses and a railway goods station where in Joel's day stood a retail park. It was so very different. The little cobbled side streets that were in 2017 alleyways between big office blocks, hotels and industrial units, were busy streets, brimming with life, houses, people. They were real, as real as anything he had ever seen. Probably even more real, because it was the first time that he had 'really' thought about what it was like to be alive.

Nets blew in the breeze in open windows. Horse drawn carts made clackety noises as they trundled along the cobbles and the hooves of the horse clip clopped. A car horn tooted to warn a cyclist it was near. He was fascinated by the cars; huge and ornate by 2017 standards. Glamorous even would be a good way of describing them.

People were dressed differently too, smarter somehow. All men wore a hat or a flat cap – a lot of the smarter men looked how he imagined spies to dress, pork pie hats and long overcoats over suits. Quite a few of the men, mostly middle aged or older, smoked pipes – he'd never seen anyone smoking a pipe before he met old Mr Roberts.

He also noticed none of the streets had road names on them or if they had they did, they had been painted over. Joel remembered learning in school it was because if the Germans invaded they would not know where they were. He found it funny to think that they would be suspected of specifically looking for some random street in a town. He imagined a gunner calling to the pilot of a Heinkel 1-11.

"Ve are looking for Meester Jones. He lives at 37 Hawthorn Terrace. 'Eee is a bad man; 'ee called us 'bratwurst eating 'uns. Ve are going to blow 'ees 'ouse up. Get closer – closer! I vant to see the street names." The plane bearing down in a dive towards the rooftops; people below fleeing for their lives as the engines deep growl gets closer to them. The plane skimming across the chimney tops whilst the gunner anxiously looks out for street names and tries to tie in the scene beneath him with the map in his hands. Chimney pots tumbling to the ground below as the planes' undercarriage sends them along with roof tiles crashing down.

"That's where my cousin Vinnie got married last month," said Will. "Charles Church. He's off to sea now. No idea when we'll see him again. Granfer said it was a shotgun wedding 'cos it happened so quick, but Gran says it's likely just 'cos he was being sent to sea…."

Joel stopped listening. There in front of him was the 'bombed out' church; as it was known as in his day. Charles church stood proud – not in the middle of a major traffic roundabout, as he knew it, but surrounded by a pretty graveyard and squeezed in between a multitude houses. It was intact, it had a roof, windows – it was alive!

They carried on past more unfamiliar buildings, ornate and splendid. All the windows had the familiar white criss-cross of tape across them. There were signs pointing to public air raid shelters and A.R.P warden stations. Shops had signs up mentioning 'coupons.' It seemed everything purchasable needed coupons – clothes, food. He needed to find out more about rationing and coupons. Joel felt it best to make a mental note of everything he saw. He was going to write it all down when he got home – he dared not take his mobile phone out and take a picture, though it was tempting.

They came to a large department store 'Spooners' said the signage across the store front. It looked very grand but was very likely more austere than it had been before the war. He noticed a sign on the window saying that the Spooners staff were raising money to buy a Spitfire for the war effort. Joel insisted they go in and have a look around, he was keen to see what a 1940's department store sold. He read the 'department' signs – drapery, furs..... furs made him imagine a department full of bear skins, deer heads with antlers. Tiger skin rugs. "What's furs?" He asked Will.

"Furs?" Replied Will.

"The sign says furs, what are furs?" Replied Joel inquisitively.

Will laughed. "Hat's, coats, gloves. You know things made of fur."

"Wow!" said Joel shocked. Do people really wear that, real fur? It's like cavemen and Eskimo's?

Will looked at him, surprised. Joel certainly was strange at times. Maybe he was a bit soft in the head, a circus somewhere was short of a clown. He certainly dressed strange and seemed very unfamiliar with normal everyday things.

They had a good wander round, Joel wanted to visit every department and take in the ambience, but Will absolutely refused to go to the ladies' wear department or the lingerie department insisting they would probably be thrown out. Joel tried to convince him that all he wanted to see was a lady's corset (something he'd heard so much about) but Will flatly refused and said indignantly that if he was so keen to see one he should look on his neighbours washing line.

There definitely was something not quite right about Joel. At times he seemed really dim-witted, but as he'd been bombed out and sent to stay with his Grandparents, maybe he was damaged – not physically, but mentally. Will decided to give him the benefit of the doubt, he suggested they take a wander along Bedford Street and Old Town Street. Joel agreed – he was in awe of everything he saw around him; beautiful buildings blackened by years of soot, the facades looking grimy and aged. Trams and buses trundling by. The colourful canopies on the shops - some depicting the name of the store, others striped or coloured. How could the war destroy this beautiful city he wondered? He felt an inner hatred for the German's – a bitter hatred he had never felt before. In his own time, he liked the Germans, but now, at this very moment in time, he felt a part of this city, these people. Innocents going about their daily lives and having no idea how it was to be decimated in the very near future.

Joel suddenly felt an overwhelming urge to take some photographs – who was to know. Who would guess what the small thing in his hand was – he could do it discreetly, no one would know. He slipped his mobile phone from his pocket and randomly clicked away without looking at what he was taking pictures of – they were all from hip height so possibly none would come out too clearly.

St Andrew's Cathedral, although a familiar sight in 2017, it was unrecognisable in 1940 – the surrounding streets were in a different orientation to those that Joel knew and he could in all honesty been in any city in the world. It certainly didn't look like the Plymouth he knew – a city centre built on straight lines, blocks and pedestrianisation. He much preferred this beautiful city; buildings with individual character over many decades – a miss match of lavish skyline; spires, buildings that curved around corners, ornately carved window and door frames. Baroque stonework crafted by hundreds of masons over many years.

Without warning the air-raid siren sounded again; this time, Joel felt exhilarated rather than frightened. The boys made their way towards a sign pointing them in the direction of safety. They, along with what appeared to be a few hundred others entered the busy underground shelter. It was dimly lit and A.R.P wardens in dark blue overalls directed them along the corridors. They took their place on some rather scanty wooden seating, squashed between a baker in his floured apron and a man holding a greasy rag who was still wiping oil from his hands. The air was quite stifling and smelled of everything from engine oil – from the greasy man, body odour, fear and a host of other aromas. It wasn't pleasant, nor unpleasant really. It was rather like being on the school bus with the heating on, on a wet day. There was a lot of excitable chatter, then melancholy talk. Someone suggested a sing song, but just as they started up the A.R.P warden pointed to the sign which stated no signing, as well as other restrictions. When asked why they weren't allowed to sing, the A.R.P warden replied that it would drown out the sound of the all-clear.

After half an hour or so it was becoming very uncomfortable. The benches were hard and bottoms were becoming fidgety. Small children were very restless and a few were crying. It was a Saturday afternoon and the main shopping area of Plymouth had been very busy. Suddenly the mood in the shelter changed; there was a lot of gossip and movement and it seemed that they could now leave the shelter. Joel hadn't heard the 'all clear' but to be honest he wasn't taking much notice, he was too busy making mental notes in his head of the characters in the shelter. He felt a charlatan, an imposter – he didn't belong. He saw the naivety, trust, fear and dread etched on the many faces. They had no idea of what their futures held or that of their loved ones. Would they be killed in a bombing raid? Would they lose their homes, their loved ones? Joel wanted to scream 'I can save you. I can tell you when the dreaded Luftwaffe are going to destroy your beautiful city, I can tell you when to get far away. I can tell you which ships are going to be sunk and when.' But of course, he knew he couldn't.

He watched a little girl of about 5 years old. Her hair tied in to pretty pigtails with dark blue ribbon. She wore a pale blue coat and shoes the same colour as the ribbon in her hair. She was carrying a doll, holding it tightly as though in hope the doll could protect her from the bombs. The whole time she was in the shelter she sat with her head bowed and her legs crossed at the ankle. An adults hand reached out and the little girl took it. The last he saw of her was as she climbed the steps leading out from the shelter, her gas mask slung across her back. Joel hoped she would survive the war.

Will and Joel waited till everyone else had left before making their way out of the shelter. Will said that sometimes things got left behind. He wanted to make sure there was nothing of 'interest.' They had a look about, but other than for a couple of newspapers and a crumpled-up paper bag, there was nothing.

"Come on 'Let's be 'avin you. Come on now, on yer way." A policeman wearing a tin hat, standing at the top of the steps to the shelter waved the boys out. "Coming mister," called Will, and they hurried along, satisfied there was nothing worth picking up. As they got closer Will recognised the policeman – it was Davy Grenfell from number 60 – or Sergeant Grenfell; he being on duty.

"Ow ya doing bey?" Sergeant Grenfell said. "Luckily nothing over our way, but I 'ear Goschen Street and 'amilton Street completely destroyed. Stick bombs I 'eard. Don't know if anyone bought it though. Probably aiming for the Dockyard. "

"Oh," said Will. He sounded a little disappointed. He had secretly anticipating he and Joel venture along and see the bomb damage, but the dockyard was too far to go It would mean taking a bus and the roads would probably be blocked off anyway.

Joel remembered his gran saying her mother had lived near the dockyard – he wondered if it had been her street. He suddenly came to the realisation that his great-gran was actually nearby, right now. A real live little girl. Could the little girl in the shelter have been her? Was he likely to bump into some of his ancestors? That certainly was a strange thought.

 "Best get back and let Gran and Granfer know" said Will. "He'll be fretting as to what's happened."

Joel was disappointed as he'd really wanted to have a look further around the city centre, but under the circumstance it wouldn't really be any fun. Everyone looked shocked and just seemed to want to get home or to find out more information on where the bombs had fallen.

The boys headed back, by way of the Barbican and Sutton harbour area where an uncle of Will's had a small boat. The fish market was bustling by the time they arrived. It was very different to how Joel remembered it only yesterday when he'd walked along the same stretch of ground. Crab pots and fishing nets were neatly stacked. Seagulls circled the skies and there was no sign of any luxury yachts in the Marina – only fishing boats in the harbour. There was a large shed in the same place where Gran had yesterday browsed in a shop called the Edinburgh Woollen Mill. Gran had dragged him round, pointing out things that were 'nice.' There were no fish there yesterday; there had been barometers, ships bells, miniature lighthouses and a multitude of other gifts. The only fish he saw were those that had been deep fried in batter and placed in a glass fronted warming cabinet in fish and chip shops nearby.

There were old wooden sheds where men and women scurried about their business touting their catch, which they displayed on large pull along handcarts with a sloped display shelf on top.

Joel felt adventurous, he slipped his mobile phone from his pocket again and surreptitiously took a few random photographs from hip height. He hoped some would come out. How weird it would be to see the past in colour he thought. Did they even have colour pictures back then he wondered? He'd never seen one. He tried to take a sneaky picture of Will.

 "What's that?" asked Will, grabbing at the object in Joel's hand. "Erm it's nothing. Just a thing my dad gave me."

Will seized it from him "Let's see."

"Wow" He said as he saw the illuminated colour screen saver picture of Gran's dog – Muffin. "That's amazing. What is it?"

Joel wasn't quite sure what to say. "It's secret – it's just something the Military are testing. I shouldn't have it really. I have to give it back to my Dad," he bluffed, grabbed it back and thrust it deep into his pocket. He realised how silly he was to have tried to take pictures. "Don't say anything – it's hush hush." He knew the importance of how in the war if something was 'hush hush' people would keep quiet about it.

"Your dad's not a spy, is he?" queried Will suspiciously.

"Don't be daft" laughed Joel. "He works for intelligence. It's a sort of radar type thing. It's got a tracker on it – bit like a compass. The illuminated painting on the front makes it look like a painting in a frame, so as not to give away it real purpose. They're testing it out ready to give it to airmen when they drop them behind enemy lines. I'm just testing it out here they can be assured of its accuracy before giving it to our fliers?"

Joel remembered a story from one of his Commando comics where a spy was able to gain secrets from the enemy by having a miniature camera hidden in his watch and taking pictures whilst rummaging through secret papers in Berlin. He was then able to feed back the information to the Military on his return to London.

"Crumbs" said Will. "Your dad, a spy for the British?" Joel didn't respond this time, instead he said, "Let's pretend we're spies!" hoping to get Will off the subject of his phone. He'd been stupid to even risk taking pictures. Any good spy would have known that and certainly been more discreet. He was lucky that Will was so trusting – possibly even gullible. If Will did say anything to anyone, he would likely be interrogated and then shot. He certainly wouldn't be taking his phone back into the 1940's again that was for sure. He was even tempted to throw it into the depths of the harbour right there and then. Only the thought of his mum and dad being upset and angry at him losing it stopped him. They'd likely not replace it – and he'd only had a few months. He felt furious at himself for his stupidity.

"American spies!" replied Will excitedly. "Cordy and Jack?" after his speedway heroes' the Milne brothers.

"How about Woody and Buzz?" said Joel, thinking of his childhood heroes – animated but still heroes.

"Woody and Buzz" said Will thoughtfully. "Yes, I like that. I'll be Woody and you can be Buzz. Woody sounds more American, like Woodrow Wilson." Will laughed and thought of the former US president now being a spy.

"You been to see any good films lately?" Asked Will. "I go fairly often, well, at least once a week. I love Western's; Roy Rogers, Gary Cooper, John Wayne." He then trotted off ahead, he began to whistling a tune whilst doing a funny swagger-like walk. "Hey gunslinger, over here." He turned around and pretended to shoot an imaginary gun at Joel, then blew the hot smoking barrel and placed the make-believe gun back in its imaginary holster.

"Not been in ages" said Joel, adjusting the gas mask slung across his back. "Do they still make Laurel and Hardy films?" he asked casually. He remembered watching some old black and white Laurel and Hardy films with his Dad, who had been given a whole box set one Christmas. They were funny, even in 2017.

"Do they still make Laurel and Hardy films?" exclaimed Will. "Where have you been – living in a cave? 'Course they do!" He laughed and shook his head. "You really are funny. Tarzan – you must have seen Tarzan?"

Joel made a Tarzan yell, but it fell far short of the cry made famous by Johnny Weismuller; both boys burst out laughing. They walked on silently for a while, neither sure what to say. Joel scared to say anything that might have him arrested as a spy, and Will, because he was thinking how odd Joel was sometimes. It was as if he lived in a world with very little outside communication.

Joel's mind was racing through a thousand thoughts. He reassured himself that he couldn't be arrested, not really. If the police went to Gran's house in 1940, he wouldn't be there and the family living there would deny all knowledge of him. If they tried to arrest him in the street or wherever, he would then say he would take them to Will's house first where he's say his spying equipment was kept, and then escape via the front door as they left, as long as he wasn't touching anyone - he would just vanish - hopefully. But what if he was wearing handcuffs? A momentary dread was alleviated when he concluded that the person on the other cuff, entering

2017 would be shocked, stunned. They would then start telling everyone it was World War Two and that Joel was a German spy. Within no time at all they would be arrested, sectioned and locked up. Things would be fine.......as long as he was careful.

"I used to have a cowboy outfit." Said Joel wistfully, thinking of their conversation about Westerns' and remembering his Woody from 'Toy Story' costume. "it's too small now thought. I used to wear it all the time......"

Will said he also used to have a cowboy outfit, but again it no longer fitted. His younger cousin Patrick had it now.

They walked and talked; of Texas rangers, Apaches, gunslingers, 'Injuns, bow and arrows, outlaws, saloon bar brawls, cattle drives, and wagon trains crossing the hot and dusty great open plains of America. Will, who had adopted an American accent, suggested that they both take their catapults and do some target practice with bottle tops and stones, aiming at the 'Injun' goods trains that ran along the culvert behind their houses. Joel, not having a catapult and never even having fired one wasn't so sure. He didn't want to get into trouble. He remembered when his cousin Simon got cautioned by the Police for firing a BB gun at the cats that kept creeping into his back garden.

"I haven't got one." Said Joel meekly.

"You haven't got one. Every boy 'as got a catapult!" exclaimed Will, reverting back to his normal accent.

"I...I mean, I didn't bring it with me from Exmouth." Joel meekly replied as an excuse.

"Not a problem, we can make one." Said Will; firing his imaginary catapult at the window of a house as they passed by.

"Oi, put that down or I'll be 'avin you!" Shouted a male voice from the upstairs window. They both looked up. A fair-haired youth, not much older than themselves, who was repairing a broken pane of glass, in a bomb-damaged house stared down at them. Will held up his hands to show his empty palms.

"Go on, be off with you then." Called down the youth. The boys both started running, not to get away; but just because they could. The continued until they reached a small grassy area surrounded by trees and which looked out over the harbour. Out of breath they sat down and leant against a large oak tree. Once their breathing had returned to its normal state, Will stood up and slipped a penknife from his pocket and opened the blade.

"What you gonna do with that!" Shrieked Joel, seeing the offensive weapon.

"Making you a catapult – that's what you wanted isn't it?" Asked Will, puzzled as to Joel's' over excitement.

"Oh right, yea of course," laughed Joel, a little confused. He couldn't quite believe it was the norm for boys to walk around with knives in their pockets. Of course, this was a war situation and possibly the government had advised all young boys and men to carry knives; though he doubted it.

Will started climbing the tree. He examined the lower branches and found one to his liking. With his penknife, he cut a section off and threw it down to Joel. "There you go."

Joel wasn't quite sure what to do or how to turn it into a catapult, so asked the 'expert' Will to show him how. "Is yours a bought one then?" Will asked Joel, surprised at him not wanting the pleasure of making a catapult himself. "Erm yes, from Argos I think."

"Where's Argos, is it in America?" asked Will, as he carefully started removing the bark. "I always remove the bark first as its easier." He said, as he concentrated on the job in hand. "Now it's time to carve the catapult into shape. Take a lot of time here" he said to Joel, looking up. "Especially if you're fussy like me."

Joel watched with interest. "Argos? erm, yea, probably," said Joel. Will didn't seem to hear – but that was fine, he was engrossed in his work, cutting back the bark and smoothing down the prongs of the slingshot. "It needs to be sanded down now and then a piece of leather thong and put on." Joel was impressed. "I'll finish it off when I get time," said Will. Let the wood dry out properly and then I'll oil it to strengthen it.

As Joel sat there, he watched the activity on a hill in the distance He'd seen it when he went out with Gran and it didn't seem to look any different in 2017 as it did in 1941. There were a couple of fortifications with ramparts and lots of trees and things. He could see the glint of vehicle windows, likely Military as they made their way up one of the winding roads towards one of the forts.

"I wish we could walk up that hill," said Joel. "Go and do some spying."

"You'd need a bicycle. We should do it one day if you can get hold of one. We can get a close-up look. Come on, I know the perfect spot," said Will. "There's a road down to the wharves, it comes back on itself; leads right back to our houses. It's great for racing your bike down and the views are amazing. Come on!"

They both scrambled to their feet and Will led the way to a place called Breakwater Hill. Here he explained they were about to walk along a road that had the most amazing views in the whole of England, well, definitely in Devon. As they ambled along, stepping aside for the occasional lorry, Will said that the road was reputed to be haunted by the ghost of a French sailor and many people refused to walk it alone or at night. He had apparently been walking along the road one evening with a group of friends, intent on re-joining their ship which was berthed down on the wharves. In need of relieving himself, he leapt over the wall assuming it to be a field on the other side —not realising it was a fifty-foot drop.

They looked out across the harbour and down onto activity below; a steam train chugging along the Cattewater branch line, serving the industries at the water's edge. A Sunderland flying boat came into view. It gradually came in to land on the water and eventually to a halt. A small boat made its way towards the plane and it's two occupants disembarked and climbed aboard the small rowing boat. They watched transfixed as another plane made its way towards the Cattewater and landed smoothly on the water's surface.

"Have you ever flown?" asked Joel.

Will began laughing, "Course not!" He thought it rather an absurd question. "I've been on the big wheel at the funfair. That was pretty amazing I can tell you." Will remembered the seat he was in climbing higher and higher as the wheel began to turn. The earth being sucked further and further away from him at speed and then plummeting back towards him. It was scary but exhilarating at the same time.

"Why, have you ever flown?" He asked it as more of a joke than anything else.

"Only twice. My dad has to fly quite a lot with his job. He said it's dead boring and often there's nothing to look at – just clouds."

Will laughed and shook his head, repeating "only twice." Joel was a funny sort; his sense of humour could be quite dry at times. He thought it odd that Joel had never mentioned his dad flying planes before but working in intelligence possibly that was all part of the job.

He changed the subject and pointed out Mount Edgecumbe in the distance across the bay in Cornwall, beyond the warships and boats that filled the Sound. To the right he pointed out Plymouth Hoe with the city beyond. They stood a while, observing the activity on the water, in and around the two huge hangars at R.A.A.F. Mount batten, home to the men of 10 Squadron the Royal Australian Air Force, who were part of the Coastal Command. The huge Sunderland flying boats which patrolled the great wastes of the Atlantic and Bay of Biscay in search of enemy aircraft or ships, particularly submarines. At other times searching for surviving seamen from sunken vessels. A patrol could last for up to thirteen hours, explained Will. Down to the Bay of Biscay, across the Atlantic and home again. Their keen eyes, searching every speck of sea.

"Did you know that the first ever trans-Atlantic flight landed there," said Will pointing to Mount Batten. "That was long before the Aussie's came of course."

Joel wondered how much of what he was looking at now still existed. The men working on the jetty would all likely all be no more, and what of the boats and sea planes? Possibly a few still in existence in museums or private collections somewhere. He could see the reflection of the sunlight on the water. Hear the distant sound of heavy engines, voices, chains clanking. The smells from the industries along the wharves mingled with the smells of the sea - they weren't particularly pleasant, but the sea breezes moved them along quickly.

"I did an oil painting at school of this view," said Will. "The one I showed you in the frame at home."

He pointed across the water towards Turnchapel. Joel vaguely recognised the scene. He's never seen the wharves before, only in Will's oil painting.

"At the end of school year awards, I got top prize in art and was presented with a box of oil paints and two canvases."

He pointed to the left of where they were standing, past the Australian air base and at the water's edge to the village of Turnchapel. The pastel coloured houses looked pretty and cars and Military vehicles could be seen winding their way up the roads above the village. Sheep and cattle grazed on the hills in the distance, oblivious to the war. Boats in the harbour carried out their business and along the water's edge pill boxes, sentry boxes and huge coils of barbed wire could be seen. Jerry wasn't getting into Turnchapel, that was for sure.

"Look, there's Fort Stamford," he said, pointing one of a number of fortifications visible on the hill. "See those pylons? They've got red lights on the top and at night they light up. If they go out, you know there's a raid on the way. Uncle Frank told me. He used to work at the Tar works. Got his call up papers last Thursday." He then pointed out the large stone round tower sitting high upon a hill that overlooked R.A.A.F Mount Batten. The turret he said had been used as an artillery defence look out point in ancient times but was back in use with two quick firing guns, protecting the Cattewater surrounding area. "It's named after Captain Batten," he added. "The Parliamentarian naval commander at Plymouth during the Civil War. We learned about it at school."

As they continued on their way, Will pointed down to the rocks and wasteland below. "That's where they found the French sailor body. Some people have said they have felt hands trying to push them over the wall, right here where he fell to his death." Joel told Will that his childish tale didn't scare him. They carried on past the wharves and then followed the stone walled road once more, this time ascending. There was wasteland to the right and industrial units to the left. The view this time was quite unspectacular but turning around he could see the wonderful view again of the hill; the picturesque coloured houses dotting the shoreline opposite and the Military activity in the Cattewater.

"Most beautiful view in the whole of Devon, don't you think?" said Will. Joel had to agree. They carried on and true to Will's word they ended up back at the familiar houses on Cattedown Road, which lead to the tops of Gran's and Will's roads. How had Gran never mentioned this before wondered Joel? He would have to ask her to if they could take Muffin for a walk along there sometime.

As they reached the top of Gran's street, empty stomachs aching to be filled made them decide it was time to head home. Will followed Joel and when they reached his gran's house, Joel realised there was no way of him being able to gain entry without alarming the then occupants. He couldn't just burst in and make himself at home. The house was in the wrong era anyway and none of his things were there – they were somewhere in the blackhole, or whatever it was he had stepped through. He panicked slightly but didn't let it show. "I think I left my pencil at yours." He patted his pockets. "I'm sure I had it when we were in your bedroom. Can I just go and check?" Joel felt sure that if he 'left' via Will's front door, on his own, he should be able to return to the future. The two times he had managed to leave from the door and stay in the past, he had held on to Will's arm. Luckily Will hadn't noticed. It seemed 'holding on' to the past, kept him there and leaving without - 'let him go.'

Joel looked for the imaginary pencil in Will's bedroom and finally decided he must have been mistaken and left it at his Gran's house after all. He bade farewell and left Will to tell his grandparents about the bombs over Devonport. He slipped out of the front door alone and after a momentary 'weird' feeling, was back in 2017.

CHAPTER SIX

"You'll never guess what we're doing tomorrow?" Gran stood there smiling, hands on hips and looking very pleased with herself.

Joel wanted to burst out with "You'll never guess what happened to me today?" and then tell her all about the air raid shelter and Will and the incident with his mobile phone and the walk with the amazing view; but he knew he couldn't.

"Your Grandad has managed to book us two-night break in Cornwall." Said Gran excitedly. "It's a lovely Guest House near St Austell. You'll have your own room and there's some lovely beaches nearby and...."

Joel stopped listening - two nights, Cornwall. That was all he heard. What about the war, what about Will, his granfer, the bombs! What would happen to them while he was away? Would the war carry on without him, or had it already happened and only become 'real' again when, he went back there. It was all very confusing. He needed to let Will know he was going away.

"So, if you bring down any washing you've got, I can put it on now and have it tumble dried and ready for tomorrow......" Continued Gran.

'Two nights' thought Joel. That's three days and two nights. How much time would pass in 1940? Would Will still be there when he got back or would he have been evacuated, or even worse still 'bombed out'! What if when he came back he was unable to travel back to the past?

"Great" said Joel to Gran.

"You could sound more enthusiastic" she replied. "Jim, your Grandad, he said he'll hire a fishing boat and take you out on it. You'll enjoy that."

"Sorry Gran, I was just thinking of something else, Yea, it will be super you're right."

Joel made his way upstairs. He slumped on his bed and felt tears prick his eyes. He knew Gran and Grandad were only being nice and he felt guilty at not being grateful for their generosity. He needed to do something before he went though, to thank Will and his family for their kindness, no

– for just being there. There was a war on and if he could help in some tiny way he would. He lay there thinking of what he could do. Giving away Military secrets that had since become public knowledge and published in newspapers, books etcetera was out of the question.

He decided to send Marley an email. He told him all that had happened, about Will and the false alert. He asked Marley for advice.

"Have you sorted that washing yet?" Gran called up the stairs. "I'm just about to start cooking tea."

'That's it!' thought Joel. 'A food parcel, they're always on about giving out food parcels when there's been a disaster of some kind and having the threat of bombs constantly being dropped overhead certainly counts as a disaster in my book.'

He gathered together bits of clothing lying on the floor and took them downstairs to Gran. He remembered Will asking if his dad could get him some American clothes. He decided his Mercer and Co t-shirt wouldn't be missed too much and decided to give that to Will. It was clean and laundered. "Gran, if you've got anything in the fridge that might go out of date while were away, can I take it along the road to Will's for his mum. Waste not want not and all that."

"That's an old saying 'waste not want not', but you're right. Go on have a look then." Gran now had her back turned to Joel and was peeling vegetables by the sink.

Joel opened the fridge door and began to search the shelves. He found some ham that still had 2 days left on it; that was going. The eggs, he couldn't make out the date stamp on, they were going. There was some cheese wrapped in Clingfilm; that was going. A half-used pack of sausages; they were going. A couple of yoghurts…. No, he'd leave them, how could he pass off Tesco own brand yoghurts as having been purchased in 1940. That was enough, that would do. He knew he'd need to take the sausages from the wrapping as that again was a giveaway. He found a large mixing bowl and carefully placed the items inside, ensuring the ham and sausages were kept apart and the cheese placed on top of the eggs. He then placed a plate on top to keep everything from moving about. He put them in the fridge for safekeeping and remembering a poster he'd seen at school when they studied the war he recalled that tea was also rationed. He remembered how his teacher, an old man called Mr Foster, said all food was in short supply and people had to grow their own vegetables and if they were able to, keep chickens or rabbits, for their meat. All the children pulled faces and said 'Urrgh.' He had said people would join queues outside shops when foodstuffs came in very short supply and often just had to take what they're given.

He went back to the food cupboard and grabbed a handful of teabags from an open pack of 240. He recalled how his Great Aunt Emily had always used loose tea in a teapot, just like, just like how Mrs Roberts made it. He took a cup from the cupboard and shoved the teabags inside. He'd sort that out later. Still looking in the food cupboard, he spotted a packet of Mr Kipling French Fancies that were dated 'best before' a week ago.

"They'll still be safe to eat won't they Gran?" He asked showering her the packet.

"I'm sure they will be, just don't say anything. They'll see the date on the box and make their own decision."

With that Joel un-boxed the cakes and balanced them on the plate. He made a gap in the middle where he placed the cup full of teabags.

"I'm just going to pop down and tell Will I'm going away, I'll be back later on and take these down to his mum after tea if she wants them." As he slipped on his trainers he heard Gran calling - "Tea will be on the table at six, don't be late." As the front door slammed shut, Gran saw Joel had left the bowl of chilled foods on the worktop. She tutted and put them back in the fridge.

Joel had an idea; if it was true that he was time travelling, which it certainly appeared he was - he was going to spend as much time with Will as he could before be going to Cornwall.

On reaching number fifty-two he entered the gate and took a step towards the front door; suddenly, he was thrust into darkness, very deep darkness, no street lighting and fumbling to find the front door he found it locked. He was just about to knock when he realised it was possibly the middle of the night. He stepped back to the gate – it felt as though he had stepped through a warm but invisible 'sponginess'. Not uncomfortable, but slightly heavy. He was in daylight again, 2017 daylight. He stood there for a few seconds and then stepped forward again. This time it was daylight - dull and rainy, but daylight. He called through the half open door. A young woman he hadn't seen before answered. She was dressed in Military uniform and said Will had just left for school but would be home in later on in the afternoon. She queried Joel as to why he wasn't at school, but he said he was being 'home schooled' due to his school in Exmouth having been bombed. Joel asked if she was Vi and when she said she was, she showed some recognition as to who he was. She accepted his answer without hesitation and told him to call back later.

Joel stepped back through the sponginess and waited around for a few minutes before stepping forward again, he did it slowly but with his eyes shut. This time it was still overcast and raining a little harder. Mr Roberts answered his call this time and invited him in. Will apparently was on the 'lav' and wouldn't be long.

Mr Roberts sat down and started talking to Joel about the 'Home Guard.' "Use 'ter be called the L.D.V, the Local Defence Volunteers. They're to offer stout resistance and meet any Military emergency until trained troops can be brought in." He said it proudly, upright, chest out. "Our Ellen's Des, he's to 'elp the R.A.F beys up at the barrage balloon on Astor fields, in the event of an air-raid. He can be there in two minutes – they've timed 'im. Even though he's got a dodgy hip, due to a shrapnel wound in the last war."

Joel had met Uncle Des briefly beforehand. He was quite a character, strong, handsome and intelligent. If he had been given dispensation to have joined the forces he would likely have been a Royal Navy Officer, or a pilot flying alongside the likes of Jason Doyle. He saw in his mind's eye, Uncle Des help heave on the ropes of the giant barrage balloon, tie it up and then jump on a bicycle and pedal furiously to the nearest anti- aircraft gun post. There he would leap into the seat of the Ack-ack gun and begin firing away furiously at the German bombers above, who were being followed by his colleagues manning the search lights.

"… They need the Home Guard to supplement the Regular Army," continued Mr Roberts. Joel could see himself helping Des and his Home Guard colleagues. He would help load the anti-aircraft gun. *Stand Fast'*, *'Stop'*, *'Cease loading.'* Orders would be given out and he would obey, whilst Des, perspiration streaming down his brow would continue to furiously, fire at the enemy overhead.

Mr Roberts then began to talk about his newly appointed position with the A.R.P "…so I'm to carry a book an' take the names of people who appear suspicious. You know the sort; appeared upon the scene in recent times - especially if they 'av a foreign sounding name. What's you last bey?" Mr Roberts queried, always having had some suspicion about Joel.

"Err, Armstrong. "Replied Joel, absent mindedly; his thoughts a million miles away; passing 40-millimetre ack-ack shells to the man standing next to him.

"Herr Armstrong!" Spat out Mr Roberts, nearly dropping his pipe.

"No, I said err Armstrong, as in hesitation," sniggered Joel.

Mr Roberts grunted, slightly disappointed as he wiped ash from his lap. He needn't yet be putting the name Joel Armstrong in his little black book – not just yet anyway. Joel on the other hand was still daydreaming about Uncle Des and his imaginary ack-ack gun; pulling at the lever which would drive the heavy round, miles into the skies. The air around heavy with cordite fumes, the empty shell cases clattering to the ground as the gun violently recoiled. People running to the shelters for cover whilst Des and his other Home Guard cronies as well as the R.A.F, Army and the Navy at sea would chase the unwanted visitors from the skies.

Joel, not having been listening when Mr Roberts said that Des was also part of a rescue and demolition party.

"What's that 'yer wearing?" chuckled Mr Roberts, screwing his eyes up to read the faded writing on Joel's t-shirt.

"It's Superdry," replied Joel.

"It might very well be, but what's it say bey? It's too washed out to see properly." Mr Roberts mumbled and gave up trying to read the faded print, even with his glasses on.

"Re-ignite with Superdry spark plugs," said Joel in a deliberate voice as he pointed to the words individually.

Mr Roberts began to chortle as he pictured the t-shirt having been made from some old advertising hoarding.

The boys sat playing board games, reading comics and chatting generally. Joel liked to listen to Will talk about what he'd been up to. He could make even the most mundane things sound interesting. Will showed off some of his school art work while Mr Roberts, reading a newspaper, chuntered in the background. Joel asked what the weather forecast was, but Will said he had no idea. When Joel queried as to what time the local forecast would be on the news; Will laughed and said it wouldn't be. Weather forecasts weren't issued anymore as they could aid the Germans in planning an attack. Everyone knew that.

After a few hours, the house was beginning to get a little overcrowded; Maggie Roberts had returned from work and Uncle Lennie had come along for some advice on a chicken coop he was building in his courtyard. Cousins Deidre and Pauline, from up the road were also there, they'd been sent along with some chutney their mother had made. Soon after, Des arrived to collect the girls and brought along a garden trowel he had fixed for Mr Roberts. Des walked with a bit of a limp, which Granfer put down to 'a war wound in the last lot.' Des apparently worked in a local wood yard, it was there he had managed to repair the broken handle on the trowel.

"Caught a German last night over on the moors," said Des. His voice full of eagerness to tell the story. "About 10.30 two unidentified aircraft were picked up by the gun operations room in Exeter. They were plotted as approaching the coast from the south east. As they neared land they separated, one turning north and the other continuing overland, westerly. The plane which had turned north was soon identified as a friendly one; and the other presumed hostile." Des took a seat and continue his tale. Everyone seemed keen to hear it. "The raider was again plotted flying somewhere due west of Ashburton at a height of about 5000 feet. He was spotted again just north of Ivybridge. The plotting then stopped and all traces of him were lost. All the gun and searchlight sites were then put on standby as it was presumed he was getting precariously close to Plymouth. At about 11pm a spotter at Plympton, site saw the plane clearly in the moonlight. He immediately identified it as an Me.110. He flashed a warning to the heavy guns here in Plymouth and apparently every searchlight and Lewis gunner's butt cheeks tightened, thinking he might get a burst at the enemy."

Pauline clambered on to her father's knee. He continued. "At 11.07 pm, a neighbouring site again caught a glimpse of the plane – still flying west. As they were watching, it turned and began to circle – the pilot checking his position. Twice it circled and then the pilot switched off his engine. He then took a dive and the people below thought their last moment had come. A couple of people said they were sure they'd seen a parachute silhouetted against the moon. Just as the plane was about to strike it turned off and crashed into the ground, 200 yards from a row of cottages and burst into flames. The searchlight party telephonist called headquarters and a detachment of two search parties were sent out' one to attend to the burning plane and the other to hunt for the parachutist. The plane had crashed not far from a farmhouse, so their first port of call was obviously to the property.

They knocked on the door and it was answered by a ploughman who said "Are you looking for a parachutist?" They said they were.

"Well, he's just arrived not two minutes ago," he said.

They pushed past him into the farmhouse and there sitting in an armchair, dressed in a fleece-lined leather flying suit sat the German parachutist. He threw open his hands to prove he was unarmed and said in broken English "English soldiers – no guns, no bombs." He told them his name was Manfred Horn and where he'd flown from. Apparently, he'd been in the air five hours.

They paid close observation to his clothing. They'd heard and read so much about the previously captured Germans' poor-quality clothing, but this man wore a suit and boots of good quality leather. He wore a gold watch and had a Leica camera strapped around his neck; as well as a map strapped to his knee. The airman then showed them a picture of his wife and son. One of the British soldiers asked if he would like to return to Germany and he quickly responded with 'nein, nein!' One of the lads said this Manfred was a spy – the crash landing, the watch, the good quality clothing. He's now been taken for interrogation."

The conversation about the airman and the war was in full flow and Joel felt a little uncomfortable as it was their war, not his. He made his excuses and said it was time he went back to Gran's for his tea.

Back at his Gran's; Joel said he was back on the pretext of needing the loo. "What's wrong with your friends' loo," asked Gran.

 "His Grandad was in there 20 minutes. Said best leave it half an hour, so I thought it would be better just to nip back here."

After using the bathroom Joel went to his bedroom and picked up a few things that he thought might be of interest to Will; notebooks, a set of pens, and a blue bird print emery board that his Gran had given him the day before when she'd caught him biting his nails. He then went to the kitchen, opened the fridge door, sneaked a mini sausage into his mouth and whilst still chewing asked Gran if there was anything he could take back to his friend's house to eat, as he was hungry.

"I've never seen a boy eat so much. Even your dad didn't eat as much as you, and he was right porker at your age." Joel couldn't imagine his dad being chubby – saying that he couldn't imagine his dad ever being young either.

"I'm a growing lad," replied Joel.

"You'll be growing outwards not upwards if you're not careful," said Gran. It puzzled her how Joel could eat and sleep so much. He'd often catnap during the day and his appetite was that of a heavy manual worker.

"I'll just take a sandwich, if that's ok. I don't like to ask Will's Mum for food."

Gran appreciated the fact he wasn't taking advantage of his friend's hospitality. "Why not invite Will over for tea – I'm making a beef stew and dumplings."

"I'll ask Gran, but he's a bit shy."

Joel absolutely knew without question, that Will would love to come for tea and have a great big plate full of steaming beef stew and dumplings; but he couldn't

He made himself a sandwich and then took two chocolate sponge bars; one for Will and one for himself. Gran was just about to wrap the sandwich in cling-film, but Joel insisted he take it on a plate. She noticed him taking the wrappers from the chocolate bars and throwing them in the bin. She thought it odd and recalled how earlier, when he sorted out the food from the fridge, that might go off whilst they were away, he took the wrappers off the sausages and the eggs from the box and put them all together in the bowl. Joel had always been a bit of a strange one. He'd now become obsessed with World War Two and the 1940's era and talked about it constantly. He often went on as if he were living through it; only the night before whilst watching the late news he had become very animated when watching an item about a Fighter pilot who had taken part in the Battle of Britain and had passed away a year previously at the age of 96. The young airman had received his RAF wings at the age of 19; on the day war broke out. He was later shot down and ended up in the Stalag Luft III POW camp - made famous by film 'The Great Escape.' Joel who had been very tired and quiet all evening, suddenly became very animated and started questioning his Grandad about the film 'The Great Escape.' His grandad who was tired and didn't really know a lot about it said he'd need to watch the film.

The young airman had apparently helped dig the escape tunnel but missed out on escaping, when lots were drawn. He was finally liberated by American troops in 1945. He then almost lost his life during the retreat from Dunkirk when the S.S. Lancastria was bombed from above by the by the Luftwaffe. Thousands lost their live when the ship sank, making it Britain's worst maritime disaster. The newsreader said in recalling his escape from the bowels of the ship, the airman had said: *"It was the longest climb of my life, up one ladder, up another. I saw people bumping into each other as they scrambled on the upturned hull so I literally walked off alongside the propeller into the sea."*

Joel's questions were relentless and to shut him up, his grandad promised he'd take him to the cinema to see the film 'Dunkirk,' which was presently being shown, as he'd be sure to enjoy it and it would answer some of his questions.

Joel took his plated sandwich back along to Will's house. He did get a few strange looks on the way but ignored them. He passed a woman at her gate having a cigarette. It was something she did regularly – he'd noticed the coffee jar full of cigarette ends by the front door.

"Looking after the elderly?" she inquired.

"Na, there's a war on," he replied. "Taking my own dinner; their rations won't stretch to feeding an extra mouth."

The lady looked at him bewildered as though she hadn't understood a word he said. Her gaze followed him along the street until he went out of view.

Back at number fifty-two Joel was able to spend another idyllic few hours with his friend. Well, that was after a little hovering about in the street, trying not to look too conspicuous. His first attempt at gaining entry to the Roberts household, had him walk into pitch darkness and the door locked from inside. He wandered a hundred yards or so, back and forth along the street and then made his next attempt to gain entry. The door was unlocked and Joel entered. He left his backpack at the bottom of the stairs and put the plated sandwich in the kitchen.

Will was just finishing his breakfast and suggested they share the sandwich later on. Joel asked Will to come upstairs, he had something important to show him.

The boys spent what was in 1940 an early-morning, sitting under a blanket thrown over the kitchen table, enjoying the tuna and mayonnaise sandwich Joel's gran had made. They were pretending to be camping out in the wilds, spying on a group of German soldiers who had landed on a desolate beach and were attempting to reach a nearby coastal village. Joel was the 'spotter' and Will was at HQ, deciphering the secret messages he was sent. The plan was to eventually send in snipers to take the enemy out; but as was raining outdoors here seemed better than anywhere else to make camp.

Joel had given Will the blue bird patterned emery board and said it was for discreetly erasing pencil marks from a rubber, so that you could change pencil markings without leaving a smudge, and in emergencies it could be used to sharpen a pencil. When not in use, it should be used as a book mark as to not give away it's true identity. Will was more than impressed with this ingenious tool.

Will had never had mayonnaise before and thought the sandwich they shared delicious. He was more impressed with the chocolate cake bar thing and dreaded the day Joel would have to go back to Exmouth as it would spell the end to all delicious edible treats he regularly brought with him.

Once the rain had cleared they 'broke camp. Will suggested they take a trip to the Empire cinema for a matinee performance in the 'one and three' seats – his treat. His school had been damaged in an earlier bombing raid and he was now having lessons three afternoons a week in a church hall, until other arrangements could be made and today was one of his none school days.

Joel found his cinema experience amazing; much better than any he had witnessed in his own time. The heavy red drape curtains had parted and were drawn back by a pulley. They had sat enthralled watching the feature film; a Western, Will's favourite type of film. This was followed by a public information cartoon about salvage, scraps, paper and bones etcetera, an usherette walked up and down the aisles throughout the film offering drinks and refreshments for sale.

There was a short interlude at one point when the tape broke on the film reel and the lights came up whilst it was replaced. There were hoots and boos from the younger members of the audience, but in no time at all the cinema was darkened once more and the film continued. Joel found it a little off putting that people smoked cigarettes freely, not just in the cinema but everywhere they went.

Will had kindly offered to pay for the tickets, as Joel didn't have any money on him, but promised he would repay him, as soon as his parents forwarded him some pocket money. Will said it was fine, it was his treat; the fact Joel had 'loaned' him a set of four highly secret pens used by Military Intelligence and 'given' him his prized 'American' Mercer and Co,' top. He had sneaked it from his Gran's house and hidden it under the faded old t-shirt he was wearing when he had come around. That one had something on it to do with car parts or something. It was weird because the American's in the films never wore clothes like that, but Joel had insisted that all the people their age wore that sort of thing. He supposed it was to do with rationing and shortages and the American's were simply being inventive. Will thought all in all it was a very good swap for the price of a cinema ticket.

According to Joel, his father had inadvertently left the pens at home when last on leave from his posting with the intelligence services and in a later letter home had asked Joel to look after them in the interim; he didn't want them falling into the wrong hands.

It had been a cold and wet morning, Joel had arrived early around 8 o'clock; Joel had just finished his breakfast and was about to get dressed.

He was smiling and looking rather pleased with himself saying he had something very special to show Will. Will thought it a bit early, but didn't complain, because if it was something important then whatever time it was didn't really matter. Joel had a habit of turning up at random hours. The German bombers didn't care what time of day or night it was when they came calling; at least Joel had waited until a reasonable hour.

They made their way up to Will's bedroom *(it was something so secret that no one else was to know about.)* Joel placed on the unmade bed, two ordinary ring-binder two note books; one with a red cover, the other green. The red notebook already had a number of pages already in use – this was to be Joel's book. He also placed on the bed a set of pens. These pens were no ordinary ink pens, they belonged to the British Intelligence services – each having 'BIC medium' stamped on the side; which apparently stood for 'British Intelligence Cypher - medium level security' - according to Joel. This was whom his father worked for. These pens were NOT for public use. Will was most certainly NOT to tell his sister Vi about the pens or let her see them. She had signed the official secrets act when joining the Wrens and would, by Military law, have to tell her seniors of their existence, Joel insisted. Will understood and promised he would keep them hidden away from prying eyes.

Each pen had a clear case, rather like glass, but not glass, and each had a cap and top in the same colour as the ink inside – blue, black green and red, which was a sort of bakelite material, but rubberier. The ink flowed from each tip perfectly, by way of a tiny metal ball that let the precise amount of ink needed seep out, as the writer moved it across the surface of the paper. They weren't scratchy like a fountain pen and they didn't need refilling either. They could write for weeks and weeks on end without running out, allegedly. Joel said Will could use them as long as no one else was privy to their use.

This was when they decided to camp out in the kitchen with a blanket over the table so that they were unseen pretending to be 'spies.' Joel showed Will how to write in code and encryption. He and Marley had been passing on messages in this way to each other for the past three years, so he was actually quite a good teacher. He explained the hierarchy of the inks colours and when to use them, depending on the type of code they were writing. 'Red ink,' said Joel, was only to be used for words highlighting a danger or urgent. Green ink was to be used when naming a place or person of for their own signature. It was all a lot to take in, but after a few hours they pretty much had their own system weighed off.

"But how can you write me messages If I've got the secret writing implements?" queried Will, when they parted that evening. They had returned from the cinema and Joel made the excuse he needed to pick up his notebook from Will's house before returning home. Joel said not to worry as he was sure his grandad had another set hidden away 'in case of a national emergency.' He couldn't think of anything else to say, he just hoped Will bought it. Who knew what really went on in intelligence anyway.

Back in 2017, Joel took a detour back to Gran's' via the Co-op to replace the set of BIC pens he had given to Will. He also bought a multipack of four chocolate bars, and a bottle of fizzy flavoured water. Arriving back shortly after 4 o'clock, Joel snacked on yet another sandwich and told his gran that he was just nipping out to get a couple of comics, to take with him to Cornwall the following day. He'd not be out long.............

Joel was twice more able to return to 1940 that day; once again going to the Empire cinema courtesy of Will's generosity – in appreciation of the four unwrapped bars of Cadbury's chocolate Joel had kindly presented him with. That visit was cut short when Will's pal Eddie, who had recently returned from Cornwall, turned up for a pre-arranged game of football with some other boys. Joel declined to join them as he felt Eddie begrudged his presence. He hadn't said so directly, but it was quite evident. When Joel had said "Hi guys," Eddie had started to snigger and turning to the other boys had said; "Who does he think he is, James Cagney?" They all laughed at Joel.

Eddie was well built and he could certainly stand up for himself in a fight. He was confident, cocky, and he smoked too. When Joel had casually pointed out that smoking was bad for you, Eddie mocked him and said, "Well why do all the movie stars smoke, huh?"

Joel didn't really want to get into an argument about lung disease and the hardening of the arteries –Will's family already thought him weird, so he just shrugged his shoulders and said. "It's bad for you, that's all I know."

Eddie's replied in an American accent, "You dirty double- crossing rat."

The other boys laughed even more.

Joel had later begged Will to promise not to tell Eddie anything about their code work. If he did, it would be the end of their friendship and he would have to take back the pens. The thought of handing back the pens was something Will couldn't bear. They each spat on their hands and shook on the promise.

On Joel's second to last visit that day, they spent a few hours poring over more complex codes in Will's bedroom. Will showed Joel some more of his art work from school. Mr Reynolds, the art master, was a retired newspaper illustrator. He'd told Will that he wanted to enter some of his work for a national competition. Joel agreed his work was quite impressive. Will said that he hoped to go to Art college one day, but Granfer thought it a bit cissy.

It seemed odd Joel thought; he had only left Will an hour or so earlier and here he was back again and Will was recounting their earlier meeting as though it were days ago; which it had been to him. He told Joel about his glorious morning bicycle ride with his pals Eddie and Andy Gray. They had set off early with a picnic and pedalled across to Turnchapel, on the opposite side of the Cattewater estuary, returning mid-afternoon. They had taken the small ferry boat across the water and rested at the roadside on a couple of occasions just to take in the views which Will described as being miles of hills, hedgerows, forests, fields and sea. They had spent some time watching the Military activity on the short stretch of water, that separated them from home. Seeing the wharves and buildings in Cattedown, as seen from the eyes of those who lived on the opposite side of the water. He described to Joel the mid-morning sun shining through the fleet of billowing clouds that drifted across the sky like silent bombers, navigating their way to a secret target beyond the horizon. The winding country roads, a welcome relief from the boring streets of the city. How Turnchapel, as pretty as it looked from their side of the water was now a rash of barbed wire, pillar boxes, sentries and sentry boxes and looking across towards Plymouth they could see the various barrage balloons floating in the sky above the city.

Joel felt envious, he wished he could have gone with them, but as Will reminded him – he didn't have a bicycle. To be honest though, Joel didn't like spending too much time with other boys. There was always the fear that their inquisitive questions could catch him out. There were other 'displaced' people apparently in the city; and he was aware that many were treat with more than just an element of suspicion.

Will had surprised Joel by presenting him with a 'code board.' He had spent 'the previous couple of evenings' he said, making one for each of them. He had used paper from a scrapbook he had to make the 'code wheels' and a piece of old cardboard from a box he had acquired from Stinson's newsagents. Paper was in short supply and good quality strong cardboard even more so. He had devised each board with ten 6-inch, interchangeable wheels (made by drawing around a saucer.) They were attached to the cardboard backing using a split pin. Each wheel was numbered one to ten and had the letters of the alphabet written around the edges in random sequence. On the cardboard backing, there were also the letters of the alphabet, written in regular sequence. Will explained that the sender and the receiver needed to both have the same code boards. They would choose which wheel from one to ten to use and using the letters on the regular codes on the backing board, write the codes using the inner wheel with its random code, preceded by the number of the wheel. He explained that you could have dozens of wheels, he just didn't have enough paper, and as it was in short supply, it really would be a waste to use any more when 10 codes were ample for their needs. It was at this point Joel decided that the aliases Buzz and Woody weren't really ideal for this sort of code-breaking work and so decided that when they were exchanging secret messages their code names should be 'Enigma' and 'Colossus'. Will was to be Enigma and Joel, Colossus. Their 'street names' as spies though, would still be Woody and Buzz.

CHAPTER SEVEN

Reluctantly Joel returned to his own time, he knew time must be getting late and he still had to pack his bag for Cornwall as well as return to 1940 one final time; to say goodbye and to take the food items he'd put aside for the Roberts family. He remembered to stop off and get a couple of comics for the holiday on the way. Gran noticed how tired Joel was looking on his return and asked if he was alright; he really didn't look too well. He looked exhausted in fact. He'd been perfectly fine when he'd left only an hour or so ago. She offered to send Grandad around to the Roberts house with the bowl from the fridge, but Joel insisted he would take it himself - later on after tea. He lay on the sofa and fell asleep.

Grandad's mobile phone ringing woke him up. He jumped with a start thinking it was the alarm warning him that his plane had gone into a dive and was heading for a crash into the sea. He scrambled about on the sofa trying to find his life jacket, and at the same time, coming to his senses. Within seconds reality hit home and Joel realised it was getting late and he must hurry up and go and see his friend one final time. He headed off reluctantly; he didn't really want to go to Cornwall and miss out on the adventures he could have with Will. There again he had come to see Gran and Grandad and he owed it to them to spend some quality time with them.

He balanced the plate of goodies on top of the bowl and tucked the cardboard box from the cakes under his arm. Outside of the front door, Joel sat down on the step and took the teabags from the cup. He then carefully tore open each one and poured the contents back into the cup. There wasn't much there once all the teabags had been opened, but it was better than nothing. He discarded the wrappings in the bin by the front door and also discarded the empty French Fancies box into the recycling bin. He noticed the packet had already been opened and there were only four were left.

Precariously, balancing the bowl he made his along the street, passing two women standing talking at a gate, one was the lady who regularly stood there smoking and made a habit of watching the goings on in the street, whilst dragging on her cigarette. She whispered something to the other woman and they both giggled as he walked past; he didn't care.

Opening the front gate of number fifty-two, and stepping forward, the sage green painted wooden door that on previous occasions welcomed him wasn't there. Instead he was confronted by a white UPVC door, modern and much like many others in the street. Joel's heart sank. Had his 'door' to the past closed. Had it never been real?

He stepped back out of the gate and into the street, just in case the householder, Mrs Stanfield, had seen him enter the gate. He stood for a moment, wondering what to do, then suddenly a thought – had he left the glass lens at Gran's house? He'd been playing with it earlier holding it up to the light and hoping that was how he could keep it re-energise it; that's if it even needed energising.

He dug deep into his left pocket, his right pocket, then his back pockets. No lens. It was most likely still sitting on the windowsill in his bedroom. He picked up the bowl and its contents, and made his way back along the street, across the bridge, past the two giggling women and back to Gran's house. He placed the bowl on the ground outside the front door and used the spare key Gran had given him to let himself back in. Gran and Grandad were watching TV in the front room. Joel slipped upstairs and much to his delight and relief, the lens was sitting where he had left it. He placed it in the depths of his left-hand pocket and stealthily made his way back downstairs and out the door, ensuring he locked it behind himself. Thankfully his grandparents hadn't heard him; not that that was a good thing really, because if he had been a burglar he could have made off with plenty of valuables. But, as not that many burglars had spare keys, he'd let them off this time.

Joel set off again up the road carrying the mixing bowl and its contents. He approached the two chattering women again. "You look as though you don't know whether you're coming on going." Said the older of the two, who was standing on the pavement outside of the gate.

"Only eight more trips to go." Replied Joel flippantly, as he strode past.

This time when he entered the gate of number fifty-two, it was dark and the familiar sage green wooden door with its brass knocker, stood in front of him. A wave of relief ran over his body. Sylvie answered the door, and a thin sliver of light escaped. She was wearing a silky dressing gown type thing and had on a full face of make-up. Her eyes were immediately drawn towards the cakes Joel was holding. "Come in, get out of the cold." She ushered Joel into the dimly lit passageway, calling out to Will to let him know his friend was here. With a cigarette in hand, she then made her way upstairs from where she had come, and as she did, Will came hurtling down, forcing her to step aside as their paths crossed. Sylvie made some comment about it being bad luck to pass on the stairs but Will ignored her and shepherded Joel along the hallway and into the kitchen. The room was illuminated by a dull but warm orange light. Will, with the most serious face Joel had ever seen, ignored the treats Joel was holding and said; "Have you heard the news? He's dead, Bluey's dead!"

"Bluey?" said Joel puzzled.

"Bluey Wilkinson" responded Will, with a look of disbelief and shock upon his face.

"Bloody hell!" cried Joel. Had his plane been shot down, did his ship sink or was he taken out by a sniper? What had happened, he wondered. Dazed, he nearly dropped the bowl he was carrying. Of course, he didn't know Bluey personally nor had he even seen him race but knew him to be a speedway hero of his great grandfather and of Will's. The 1938 Speedway Champion of the World. He just assumed he'd gotten older, given up racing and gone on to have a comfortable old age. He felt slightly aggrieved that his granddad had omitted to tell him that one very important detail in one his many stories about speedway. A thought flashed through Joel 's mind that maybe Cordy Milne had died in the war too and that's why he hadn't heard of any of his heroics afterwards. 'Please God no' he thought. He knew that the time would come when Will would hear the dreadful news that George Pepper, the quiet, good-natured Canadian Newcastle Diamonds Captain, who had let him sit astride his bike at Knowle stadium and written in his autograph book *To Will, the kid with the nice smile. Maybe see you on the dirt tracks one day,'* was dead. Joel knew the story of George Pepper well, it was one his grandad had often regaled to him, after hearing it so many times himself from his own father.

.... "*You see, George Pepper volunteered for war service with the Royal Air Force Volunteer Reserve in 1940. His speedway career, like most others, put on hold for the duration of the war.*" He remembered how his grandad had told him, that only a few weeks previously George had set a new track record of 74 seconds. A record which according to Grandad stood for many years. *"On 1st September 1939, the Daily Mirror reported that Canadian 'Star rider' George Pepper had been winning all his races with such monotony that his promoter at Newcastle at that time; Johnnie Hoskins, arranged a 'match race' for the following week with Pepper to be partnered by a greyhound, matched against two cheetahs."* Grandad chuckled at the thought of it. *"Thankfully the declaration of war two days later scuppered Johnnie's plans."* Grandad then sighed. *"Instead George Pepper became another short-lived war hero. You see, at the outbreak of war, the team all went their separate ways; some into the Army, some the Navy and some the R.A.F. Johnnie found himself teaching Royal Airforce navigators and pilots, wireless operational skills at Yatesbury camp in Wiltshire. He'd been a been a Wireless operator in the Royal Australian Navy during the Great War.*

George Pepper however was gaining himself a reputation, not only as one of Britain's best ever speedway rider's but also a hero of the skies; a night-fighter pilot. The newspaper loved to report on the exploits of 'Pepper and Salt' as he and his flying partner, Flying Officer Joseph Toone were dubbed. On 31st October 1942, they were part of an RA.F. Beaufighter Squadron. They shot down three, of a group of four Dornier bombers. This was only the second time ever that 'hat trick' had been performed over Britain and George Pepper was awarded the Distinguished Flying Cross.

Not long after, there was a great commotion at the camp where Johnnie was now based. A fighter plane was coming in low and attempting to make a landing on the tiny air strip. 'He'll never make it' the men cried; but somehow, he did and everyone wondered at who the amazing pilot could be. A short time later, Johnnie was taking his class when a young airman walked in to the schoolroom and walked up to his desk. He said "Remember me Johnnie?" Johnnie jumped up and shook hands with the young man – it was George Pepper! They chatted for a while and before George left the base, he came back and said goodbye. Johnnie and his pupils then stood and watched as Captain George Pepper and Pilot Officer Joseph Toone, took to the skies again and headed back to their own base in the south east of England.

The duo were described as the textbook night-fighter flying team. Johnnie told his class about how George had shot down two enemy planes during a dogfight over London and the daring feats that had earned the Distinguished Flying Cross and bar and the Distinguished Flying Order. He often spoke to his class about his speedway days. He told them how George had learned the art of fighting on the speedway tracks; lightening decisions made every race; anticipation of an opponents every move. He told them how he had used these skills in the game of war, to give his gunners the chance for a straight aim. To avoid flack and enemy fire.

One cold November morning some student pilots had come to show Johnnie a newspaper. It said 'Brilliant Air Force Pilot Killed.' On November 17th 1942 George and his navigator had been killed when the plane they'd taken up for a test flight, crashed into a hillside. The engine had cut out and both men failed to evacuate before it hit the ground. George was posthumously awarded a bar to his Distinguished Flying Cross and Toone, posthumously awarded the Distinguished Flying Cross.

Also, in the plane was a boyhood friend of George; Jack Embury. A Corporal serving with the Royal Canadian Airforce. Embury had travelled to England in 1941, as part of the Royal Canadian Air Force and was described as a "Sergeant-Pilot" who was visiting Pepper and went along on the test flight.

Johnnie later recalled going to a funeral service for George in London. Snow covered the ground and the gun carriage, which carried his coffin, was draped in the Union flag. It moved slowly towards the church and Johnnie watched as a gust of wind blew a shower of snow off a low-lying wall onto the coffin. It gave him a small feeling of comfort – like a benediction and a blessing to a brave devoted young man.

After the service George's ashes were flown back to Canada and buried with full Military honours in his home town of Belleville, Ontario. Now this was strange, as this appeared to be in breach of the Allied policy, which stated that casualties should be 'buried where they fell.' Was George Pepper such a hero that even in wartime Military rules could be broken? The same privilege was not extended to Jack Embury, who was buried alongside Joseph Toone, in Maidstone, Kent......"

".....Can you believe it" said Will. "He was killed in a motorcycle crash; in Sydney, Australia. It was back in July, but I only heard about it this morning. Apparently, he was riding his motorbike along the street when it was hit by a lorry that had swerved to avoid crashing into a car. He died instantly; fractured skull apparently. His wife who was pillion survived."

Will hurried back up the stairs from whence he'd came and returned seconds later with the newspaper cutting he had been sent in the post by his uncle Jack, relating to Bluey's death. He also brought with him the catapult he'd made for Joel. He handed them both over solemnly.

Joel read the newspaper story silently and then passed it back to Will, who folded it in half carefully and waited for Joel to say something. Both boys stood silent, dumbfounded- there was nothing to say. They were equally shaken by the awful news. Poor Bluey thought Joel, he was already dead when they had spoken of him so fondly.

He stroking the well-crafted catapult. The elastic was good and strong. He thanked Will for it by limply pretending to fire it; then buried it in his back pocket, not really sure what to say.

"I'll never get that fag card now," sighed Will. He silently ushered his friend into the parlour, both with downcast faces. Will was still lost in his thoughts, mourning for one of his heroes – not killed by the war or a racing incident, but a chance accident that, if he had been a few seconds sooner or later – would never have happened, and he still would be alive today.

Will's sister Vi, who Joel had only met briefly previously, came into the room. She was dressed ready for a night out. She saw the shocked look on both faces and asked what had happened. Will told her about Bluey and showed her the newspaper article. She offered some sympathy, but then said 'Well at least he didn't suffer,' and turned her attention to the dresser unit where she began looking for a needle and thread to sew on a button which had come loose on her coat. Joel wondered if she lacked empathy because she had possibly known of so many local sailors and solider killed by enemy action. Many of whom she would have gone to school with; or was it simply that the war had made people that way – here today, gone tomorrow. Vi was in the Wrens, she perhaps got to hear about people being killed at sea all the time.

The parlour was lit by a tall standard lamp and the heavy curtains were tightly closed, hiding the blackout blinds behind them. A warm fire glowed in the hearth. The grandfather clock in the passageway chimed half past the hour, though what hour he was unsure. It was dark, so it had to be evening.

"You'll catch your death in just that thin shirt" Said Maggie Roberts, who was sat by the fireside with a thick cardigan draped around her shoulders; taking down the hem on a pair of Will's trousers. "Come on in, get yourself warmed up. Ey, what's that you got there then?" she enquired, as she got to her feet.

Granfer Roberts heard the commotion and called out "Where's the fire!" Entering the room, he spied the bowl in Joel's arms "What's this 'yu got bey. We 'avin a Jamboree?"

Joel didn't know what a 'Jamboree' was so ignored the question.

"We've got to go down to Cornwall tomorrow, somewhere near St Austell I think. Gran said I could bring this lot down for you to have as it'll have gone off by the time we get back."

Joel handed the bowl to Maggie. "But doesn't your gran want to take these with her? What with rationing. Or maybe she could swap somethings with a neighbour?" Maggie appeared hesitant to take it.

"No, she insisted," said Joel, taking his hands from the bowl, leaving Maggie no alternative than to accept it. Her eyes widened when she took the plate and cup of tea leaves off.

"Ere, this isn't black-market stuff, is it?" growled Granfer Roberts, taking the pipe from his mouth and peering into the bowl, over Maggie's shoulder. "Your gran, she's not trying to hide her knock off 'ere is she?"

"Course not!" laughed Joel. "She's only trying to be neighbourly." He felt a little hurt, he'd expected them to be a little more grateful at least.

"Hmm" mumbled Granfer Roberts as he deliberated over the kindness of a neighbour whom he had yet to meet. He came to the conclusion that as Joel was an odd sort, so it was likely the rest of his people were too. Therefore, accepting the offerings was probably the right thing to do.

"Go on tuck in," said Joel placing the plate of four French Fancies on the small table in the centre of the room. All eyes were upon them, but everyone seemed hesitant to be the first to pick one up.

Granfer Roberts checked his pocket watch and mumbled something about 'an hour to go'. "You not 'avin one bey?" he said, as he took the decision to be the first one to try the cakes; especially as there wasn't enough for everyone to have one. He slipped the yellow French Fancy from its paper wrapper. "You can't not 'ave one," he said gesturing to Joel.

No honestly," said Joel waving him away. "Gran said I had to give them to you to share."

"Go on," insisted the old man, suspicious of possible poisoning. He broke his cake in two and gave one half to Joel; who ate it without hesitation. Mr Roberts felt slightly more at ease – you couldn't be too careful, not with there being a war on. 'Summat a bit Johnny foreigner 'bout 'im,' he thought to himself.

Confident that the cakes were edible and without any adverse after effects, Will, Vi and Maggie helped themselves to one also. Maggie then took the rest of the contents to the kitchen to show Mrs Roberts. "Eadie" she called as she scurried along the passageway. A few moments later Mrs Roberts came into the room carrying a teapot concealed beneath a red and green tea cosy.

"Sit down sonny." She shepherded him towards the sofa. "So, you're off to Cornwall eh?" she said it in a sombre voice. "I can't blame you really. If we 'ad somewhere to go we'd be off, 'specially after last Thursday. Two attacks in one day! Oh, it was terrible, terrible," she lamented and threw her hands in the air. "The loud whistling of those incendiaries; awful they was." She began to weep and Mr Roberts came over and gave her shoulder a reassuring squeeze.

Joel felt rather uncomfortable and began to blush. He felt rather hot and wiped his sweaty palms on his thighs.

"We only lost a few roof tiles," said Granfer – as he now insisted Joel call him, not Mr Roberts. "A bit of ceiling plaster and a broken plant pot Ede - we got off lightly. Mr Abbott, over on your gran's road," he nodded and directed the comment at Joel "His allotment got a direct hit, high explosive. Lost everything 'e did. Bits of cabbage and parsnips everywhere for 'alf a mile around there was, an' all the 'ouses that back on to the allotment got damaged as well."

The gift of edibles had somehow softened Mr Roberts feelings towards Joel. He had always liked him, just thought of him as a bit strange.

"I know, I know," interrupted Mrs Roberts, wiping away her tears with a handkerchief. "It's just after that fire and all the incendiaries and flying bits of this and that, my nerves are shot."

Joel queried as to 'the fire.'

"Son, you must have heard, well SEEN the flames and the smoke from your Gran's?" Mr Roberts looked puzzled. "If you went down by the wharves you could see the flames clear as day. Even the sea was on fire at one point."

"Err, I went back to Exmouth for a couple of days last week to see Mum and Dad, it must have been then," he fibbed. "You know, before going to Cornwall and not knowing how long I'd be away for."

Will looked at him strangely; how could he not have heard about the attack; the fire at the Turnchapel fuel tanks that had burned for days. Even if he had gone back to Exmouth for a few days, everyone was talking about it.

"Oh, it was terrible, the worst fire that we've ever experienced and hopefully ever will," cried Mrs Roberts. "We 'eard the heat was so fierce that the burning oil melted the metal tankers it was stored in and that the water from the firemen's hoses just evaporated before it got anywhere near the flames. It was terrible, terrible. The newspaper said that when one of the tanks exploded, the burning oil came pouring out over the wall and into the lake beneath it. The water caught fire because of the burning oil on its surface. Two of the fireboats got caught alight, and two firemen died. The others on board swam ashore before the flames completely swamped the water. For five days the horrible black smoke hung in the air. We couldn't even open the windows 'cos of the bitter fumes. They bombed one of the Australian hangars at Mount Batten too. You can see the damage from the wharves."

"Didn't our planes go up and chase them away?" queried Joel. He'd heard so much about the work of the amazing antics of the British planes during the Battle of Britain.

"Not got any night fighters" Interrupted Granfer. "We got night bombers, but not fighters, not yet anyways. Weren't expectin' 'tack's like that on

Plymouth. 'tis all London that the 'guvment have been concerned 'bout so far.

Joel felt dreadful. How could he tell them he was actually going on holiday, to enjoy the beaches, eat fish and chips, have fun, maybe go swimming?

"Gran and Grandad are keeping the house on here. We're just going for a while; like you say Mr Roberts all these bombs. My Gran's nerves aren't too good – she needs the break." He said with positivity. "I'm just not sure when…." He spotted a newspaper on the table. He picked it up and read the headline – and the date, Wednesday 4th December 1940. "we'll be back. Can't see it being before Christmas, things being as they are." Joel wasn't really sure what else to say, he hoped someone else would lead the conversation.

"Well boy, you be lucky to be gettin' away," Mrs Roberts said. "I can only see it getting worse. Every day I worry that it'll be our 'ouse next. Eddie Bullock and his people came back from Redruth after two months away. Should have stayed down there they should 'ave. Their flat got damaged just weeks after they returned an' they've 'ad to move into temporary accommodation while it gets fixed up. Then 'is dad goes and gets injured in a fire on-board his ship and he's in 'ospital somewhere in Kent. Should've stayed in Cornwall I say….."

"Did you 'ear 'bout the Dornier that 'it a barrage balloon?" interrupted Granfer. "Crashed and burned out near Rame 'ead." He shook his fists. "If it had come down this side of the water I'd 'ave been there myself an' dragged the pilot out and given 'im what for; I would you know?" Joel wasn't going to dispute it, he was sure Mr Roberts would have given him 'what for' had he been given the opportunity.

"You'll make new friends down there," mumbled Granfer Roberts as he puffed away, trying to light his pipe. "New school, new pals. You say you'll be back but you'll settle in there bey, likely you will."

"I wish you could come Will?" Joel knew that it wasn't possible, but still he wished he could take his friend with him. Will said he wished he could come too……

Old Mrs Roberts, her mind returning to the purpose of Joel's visit and the eggs Joel he'd brought along. "Where does your Gran get these eggs from. They're brown; I've only ever seen the occasional brown egg before, but these all are. We've always had white eggs. That's peculiar? She sent us down that flan a while back. Is she keeping chickens then?"

"Err no." Joel fidgeted uncomfortably. He didn't know eggs in 1940 weren't brown. How the hell did they change from white to brown? He'd never seen a white egg before. How could evolution change that quickly? It wasn't possible. He'd seen pictures of white eggs and Tabby's plastic play eggs were white; but he'd never thought anything of it.

"I think it must be the breed of them," he said trying to reassure her.

"We should get some chickens or rabbits." Granfer Roberts said, still attempting to re-light his pipe. "It would give us something decent to eat every now and again."

Once assured it was lit, he then went over to an attractively large polished wooden box, which could lay claim to being a piece of furniture in its own right. It was elegantly contoured and veneered. It had an ornate centre part covered in a sort of roughish fabric, a dial, two large knobs and two smaller ones. Joel watched as the old man turned the left-hand knob, which made a 'click' sound. "Let's listen to the wireless." He twiddled another knob and that searched the stations. "See what the 'Home Service' 'ave to say."

Mr Roberts settled himself on the sofa next to Joel, Joel shuffled along to make more room.

"Anyone for more tea?" Piped up Maggie. Everyone said 'please' so off Maggie went to the kitchen carrying the teapot Mrs Roberts had brought along earlier.

They sat and listened to some sketch show called 'Band Waggon' starring someone called Arthur Askey whom it appeared the Roberts family thought 'hilarious.'

The audience on the radio laughed out loud and so did the Roberts. There was music and slap stick and it was humorous in places; especially the character who had the catch phrase 'don't be filthy.' Joel did chuckle, but not as much as everyone else. When the programme ended Granfer got up and went over to switch the wireless set off.

"Might listen to a bit of Radio Hamburg later on," he said.

"Oh, I do wish you wouldn't Charlie." Frowned Mrs Roberts. "It'll only worry you."

"Radio Hamburg, is that the station that Lord Haw Haw's on." Queried Joel. He remembered watching the programme about him on TV only the other night.

"Fascist" grimaced Mr Roberts. "Bleddy blackshirt."

Joel remembered hearing William Joyce's haunting broadcasts. He felt satisfied that Mr Roberts would be pleased that justice was finally served on 'Lord Haw Haw' – though it was years away yet.

Mr Roberts asked about Joel's Dad, but Joel felt it best just to say he was working for the Americans and leave it at that. He told them that his mother and sister were still in Exmouth and they would be staying there. He also stupidly said he would send the Roberts a postcard from Cornwall when he got the chance.

Will brought a pile of comics down from his bedroom, he asked Joel if he would like to take them to Cornwall with him to read, as it likely would be pretty boring down there, especially it being winter. Joel thanked him and leafed through the pile. As well as Commando and Wizard, there were copies of Adventure, Hotspur and The Champion. Certainly, some interesting reading he thought. He'd read some in bed tonight.

Suddenly, Will remembered something and hurried off. He came back holding a large folder and from it pulled some pictures – the art work Mr Reynolds had put forward for the art competition.

"Look, I won first prize!" said Will excitedly. He showed Joel a painting in oils of bombers in the sky, being picked out by searchlights and another, in watercolours of a church standing amid bombed out buildings. "I got a five-shilling gift voucher to buy some art supplies."

Joel felt sad when it was time to go. Maggie brought him the washed and dried bowl, plate and cup and he took this as a sign it was time for him to say farewell; he hoped not forever. In reality, he hoped for just two night and three days. As he was just about to leave he put the bowl down and went to give Will a hug, the sort of hug he would give to Marley when he next saw him, after not seeing each other for some time. Will drew back and looked at him oddly, he held out a hand for Joel to shake.

"Cheerio – keep in touch and don't forget the postcard."

"Take care pal." Joel shook his hand and patted him on the arm. He picked up his gran's crockery and opened the front door.

" 'Ere put the bleedin' light out!" yelled Granfer from the parlour.

As he stepped outside, Joel had the oddest sensation. He felt as though he were being pulled one way and everything around him being pulled the other. He staggered slightly and then adjusted to his surroundings. It was daylight again. He was back in 2017.

His bag was all packed for Cornwall, and so Joel lay down on his bed for a few minutes rest.........

Suddenly he was jarred back to reality by a loud explosion. It was followed by another and another. It sounded like bombs were going off all around him. It was dark; he must have somehow got transported back to 1940. What was happening? He sat up on the bed, he was still at Gran's. He could hear the TV on downstairs. "Gran, Grandad!" he shouted. "What's going on?" He looked at his bedside clock, it said 9.35 pm. Had they all been transported back to the war or had the war somehow come to them? Joel got up and made his way hurriedly down the stairs. Grandad had heard him calling and came out into the hallway. "What's up lad, what's the noise all about?" he asked puzzled and seemingly unperturbed by the sound of the bombings.

"Can't you hear it Grandad? The bombs outside."

Grandad looked and Joel and pulled a puzzled face. He then began to chuckle. "That's not bombs son, it's fireworks. It's the British Fireworks Championships. They hold them here every year. Tell you what, we'll walk along if you want to see them."

Joel was exhausted, "It's okay Grandad, they woke me up that's all." He was still feeling tired and confused and unsure what was real at all. Grandad suggested they all go along to the end of the road to watch from the bridge. Joel wasn't too keen, but as Gran was already putting her shoes on he felt obliged to go. He was still dressed, so slipped on his hoodie and trainers and plodded up the street behind Gran and Grandad. The firework display had just finished when they got there but Grandad said there would be another one on shortly. Gran suggested they probably had time to walk a little further along to where they were and watch them close up, but Joel declined. He wasn't really that interested. He loved fireworks, but tonight he really wasn't in the mood; he was tired and cold. Gran noted his lack of interest when the following display began. She remembered how excited he got as a boy, whenever there were fireworks. How he always loved going to displays. Tonight, he looked tired, washed out. She couldn't understand why. It wasn't like he'd had a terribly long day. She hoped he wasn't coming down with something.

Joel closed his eyes and listened. He was tired, but still captivated by the sounds of the explosions, booms, whizzes, whoomphs, whistles and screeches that filled the air. The ground shaking occasionally. He imagined it was 1940; the Luftwaffe dropping bombs all around him. Will standing next to him, his eyes tight shut and with his hands over his ears to drown out the sound.

Joel lazily opened his eyes and was back in his own time again - he could see Jason Doyle, a few yards further along, leaning on the bridge and grinning as he admired the pyrotechnics dancing in the skies above them. "It's like Sydney at New Year - Ye can't beat a bloody good firework display," he said.

CHAPTER EIGHT

"Double check you haven't forgotten anything." Said Grandad as he secured Muffin's dog cage in the boot of the car. Apparently, the Guest House was 'pet friendly' and so Muffin was getting a holiday too. Joel ran upstairs and checked his bedroom for the second time. Gran had already sent him up only five minutes ago, to check he'd not overlooked anything. Once certain he had everything he got into the back of the car and pulled his ear phones on. He didn't know how long the journey was; he didn't really care. He was going to listen to some music and sleep.

He sat back and tried listening to the music, but other thoughts kept getting in the way. He wondered what Will was doing now in 1940. He wondered what Will was doing now in real life – was he even still alive? That was a scary thought. If Will was the same age as himself – in 1940, then that, let's see… would make him eighty-eight in 2017. Joel began to have niggling doubts about the whole situation. Possibly it was all a lucid dream; something he believed to be real and genuinely experiencing but wasn't.

The lucid dreaming soon became real dreams, sleep dreams, the far away mixed up stuff of normal dreams.

A car door slamming awoke Joel. "Were here!" called Gran, as she knocked on the rear passenger window. Joel gathered his thoughts and belongings and clambered from the car. Grandad was unloading the luggage and Gran was helping Muffin from her cage in the boot of the car. They all made their way into the reception area of the guest house. Joel flicked through a few local attraction leaflets left out on the main desk, whilst Grandad signed them in and got their room keys. Gran and Grandad were in the room next to Joel, it had an adjoining door, but he said he would prefer it if they kept it locked and he would knock on their room door if he needed them.

Once he had sorted out his clothes; by shoving everything in one drawer, Joel got out his phone and entered the 'free Wi-Fi' password. He then perused a map of the local area. He was disheartened to see they weren't just a stone's throw, but rather a drive from the beach. There were a few places of interest nearby though.

The afternoon was spent walking around the quaint little port of Mevagissey. It was typical of the Cornish fishing villages dotted along the whole coastline that he had visited before; he may have been before, he wasn't sure. It was filled with lots of very old houses bordering pavement-less narrow alleys and streets. It still had a working harbour, and fishing and pleasure boats bobbed about on the water. Grandad suggested they go and visit the museum at the far end of the inner harbour. Gran said she would sit outside with Muffin, whilst Joel and his Grandad took a wander round. It was much more interesting than Joel had expected, not only artefacts from the villages fishing heritage, but filled with pictures and personal items from the past. It made Joel think of Will and his family. Especially when he came across mentions of Plymouth and the Blitz. He hadn't realised that Cornwall had been invaded too and that there had been numerous air fields across the county. It seemed odd to think that children had been sent to Cornwall assuming it to be safe, when there were constantly planes flying over-head, too and from France.

The day passed quickly – the museum trip was followed by a fish and chip lunch, sat on a bench overlooking the harbour. Oversized seagulls paraded themselves cockily in front of the wary tourists, vying to grab the next chip or pasty crumb to be dropped. The weather was perfect; sunny, warm and with no breeze at all. They watched children crabbing with bucket and line. Patiently sitting on the harbour side, waiting for a bite. A final stroll around the town led them past an antique shop. It was filled to bursting with paraphernalia from many decades and various livelihoods. There were fishermen's lamps, compasses, 1970's ornaments. A French lamp with European style plug. Large mirrors advertising soap and whisky and boxes filled with random bits and pieces. It was very cramped, cold and damp smelling – but somehow that made it more welcoming. Gran loved second hand and antique shops and spent an age looking at and examining the goods on display, though she left empty handed. This was then followed by a two-hour stroll around the stunning 'Lost gardens of Heligan.' Joel and Grandad took lots of photographs - the vibrant rhododendron bushes, magnolia and camellia trees. The Fern valley, bamboo thickets, ponds. The various fruit and veg in the kitchen and walled gardens as well as the numerous animals on the farm. Muffin's legs got tired and they had to sit down a few times to give her a rest. Grandad had brought his SLR camera so spent a lot of time playing with filters and setting. Gran kept telling him to 'stop it' and tried moving out of shot; she wasn't keen on having her picture taken. "Especially" she said "when it's supposed to look natural and you've got me standing here posing for 5 minutes, while you're faffing about."

Joel clicked away with his mobile phone camera and a couple of pictures that he was particularly impressed with, he forwarded to Mum, Dad and to Marley. He knew he was likely to delete most of the pictures later on, but he still took them anyway.

Dark clouds began to gather as Grandad pulled away from the carpark and by the time they returned to the Guest House the heavens had well and truly opened. Grandad was unimpressed that his car had now got muddy splashes all over it from the dirty rain water that been sprayed upon it by passing cars.

"Every time I wash it this happens. I don't know why I bother, might as well not bother bloody washing it at all." Neither Gran nor Joel acknowledged his outburst. They were used to him having a rant of some kind when it came to his car. They hurried indoors; where the Guest House owner informed them that heavy rain was forecast for the rest of the day. Joel didn't mind, he wanted to do some research anyway. Find out if there was anything he could take back and show Will next time he visited, something that may be of help to him in the near future; well, the distant past.

Joel sat in his grandparent's room using his grandad's laptop. The reception was better in their room anyway. Gran was having a nap on the bed, Muffin curled up next to her. Grandad sat in an armchair reading a book. Joel flicked from web page to web page. He typed in various key words: Plymouth / Blitz / WW2 / rations / bombs. Pages and pages of information flowed forth. He devoured the information; making some notes in the notebook he had brought with him. The more he found out the gloomier he became. He read that Plymouth was as heavily if not more heavily bombed than London, in comparison to its size and population. There were varying accounts of figures, but they were all fairly similar. The city was bombed on 59 occasions. 1,172 civilians were killed, including many children.
Casualties numbered over 4,000. More than 1,000 of them seriously. 7 people were reported missing and never found. 11 Air Raid Precaution Wardens killed, 7 men and 4 women.
3,754 houses completely destroyed and a further 18,398 houses seriously damaged.

49,950 houses were recorded as being slightly damaged. 'Bloody hell!' thought Joel. Fifty thousand houses suffered minor damage. The fact that there were only 42,000 houses in Plymouth before the war, showed that many houses were damaged more than once, some people were in fact bombed out up to three times. Altogether, 30,000 people were deprived of a home as a result of enemy action. The city centre, completely destroyed. Every big store, gone. Schools, libraries, churches – bombed.

"Grandad?" said Joel.

"Yes Joel?" Replied Grandad in the same drawn out tone that Joel had just used, though not diverting his eyes from what he was reading.

Joel shuffled and made himself more comfortable. "Grandad, do you think if you could time travel back to the past you'd be able to change things for the better?"

Grandad looked up from his book and over his glasses. "That's a difficult question." He hesitated and thought for a few seconds. "The past has already been made, it can't be changed. You can change the now and the future, but you can't change what's already been."

"But Grandad," said Joel. "What if, say you really did go back in time. Let's say you went back to the war and you knew what was going to happen and you knew you could help people. Would you warn them, try and change things?"

Grandad put his book down and took off his glasses. Putting both on his lap.

"Have you ever head of the Grandfather Paradox?" Said Grandad.

"Nope." Replied Joel, but eager to hear what it was.

"Well," said Grandad. "Imagine you somehow found a way to travel back in time and you came across me. Of course, I wouldn't recognize you; you not having been born yet. So, there I am, it's 1972 I'm in the Army in Northern Ireland, you take out a gun and shoot me dead. People suspect it's an IRA shooting. No one thinks of looking for a time travelling descendant. But – the reality in your 'time,' is that I went on to meet your Gran and have children, one of whom is your father. If you had killed me back in 1972, how could you be here now? I'm afraid son," Grandad shook his head. "time travellers can't change any past, whatsoever. Fact."

"But Grandad!" Joel said in desperation. "What if when I went back it wasn't to kill anyone, it was to try and do good, you know, help people."

"There's a number of theories Joel, it's not easy to explain. There are contradictions, that's why it's called a paradox." Grandad gave a weak smile and returned to his book.

"But Grandad!" said Joel excitedly. "What if you found yourself back in the war and you could help people escape the bombings and save lives, by giving them little bits of information that might help them later on."

Gran stirred and asked what bombings, had there been a bombing somewhere. Grandad told her to go back to sleep – it was just Joel and his vivid imagination at it again. Joel sighed and threw himself back in his chair frustrated. It was not his imagination and he really had time travelled and been in the war. He began browsing selling sites, he didn't have any 1940's money but he had modern money and he had his dad's log in for eBay which he knew was linked to a PayPal account. His Dad had let him use it before and as long as he let him know that he had made a purchase from it all would be fine. Within minutes he had come across a number of items which he found of great interest and sadly expense. He was sure Will wouldn't be interested in a Sten-gun extractor tool or a British Army Lee Enfield rifle webbing carry case, but it was interesting to browse all the same. He then came across something useful, purely be accident – but brilliant. He came across a listing for 12 one-shilling coins, all from the 1930's. He had no idea what a shilling was worth, so again, ran it through a search engine to check its value. He was surprised to see it was only equivalent to 5p, but in today's money around £2.70. He had a quick count up and 12 x 2.70 would come to £32.40. The bidding on the coins closed in 14 hours and so far, only one bid had been placed. A grand £3.40 was the highest bid and the postage was going to cost £3 on top. He logged in on his dad's account and put an upper bid of £4. If he won it would cost him £7, but with a relative profit £23. He'd pay his Dad back when he got home. Joel set the alarm on his phone for 9.12am in the morning – a 10-minute reminder before bids closed.

He perused a while longer, looking for other coins or notes he could put a watch on. He looked for 'speedway cigarette cards' recalling the ones Will had. There were dozens available. Excitedly he typed in 'Bluey Wilkinson,' not expecting there to be one on offer, but to his surprise there were three! Two singular and one as part of a full set. The single one was on offer to buy now for £3.80 including postage. 'Bargain!' he thought. It would be worth every penny to see the look on Will's face, when he gives it to him. He sent the seller a message purporting to be from his Dad and added a note asking for the card to be sent to his grandparent's address in Plymouth and not his address in Exmouth, explaining it was a gift. He signed it Darren Armstrong, his fathers' name. He then started looking at speedway related pages. He wanted to catch up with news on his hero Jason Doyle; his recent injury and where his Polish club, Falubaz Zielona Góra were in the Ekstraliga.

Reading one article, he saw a link that took him to a page showing footage of old time speedway. He'd seen some before, but now, after having talked to Will about some of the riders and seen his cigarette cards, it felt more exciting. Like watching riders, he now had something in common with. Here were these young men, smiling at the camera, waving to the crowds. Racing just the same as they do today – only these men would soon be involved in a war. A huge war that would see many of them join the armed forces, get killed, possibly taken prisoner of war. Some would come back and race after the war – he knew that, he remembered his grandad telling him stories that his father had told him.

"Look at this Grandad!" said Joel. Speedway from when your dad was young." Joel took the laptop over to where his grandad was sitting. Grandad put down his book once more and they both sat watching the grainy black and white clips. Grandad then began recounting stories his father told him and Joel in return fired questions at him, especially in regards to the riders Will spoke of.

"Grandad, do you remember Bluey Wilkinson?"

"Oh heck, he was before my time, well before my time!" chuckled Grandad. "He was racing in my dad's day. There's probably some footage of him on here somewhere." He reminisced some more of the stories his father had told him as a boy. One about a Dane called Morian Hansen, who rode in the first ever World Final in 1936. He, like most racers, had no fear of danger or speed. He'd earned his pilot's licence in 1935 at a flying club in Essex. Apparently, a number of other riders had taken up flying at the club around the same time.

"There was good money in speedway back then, they were superstars," recalled Grandad. "At the outbreak of war, this Hansen chap joined the R.A.F, the first Dane to do so as far as I'm aware. Anyway, one night, July

1940 it was, ten Wellingtons' of 99 Squadron took part in a raid on Dortmund in Germany. Hansen; then a gunner, shot down a Messerschmitt 1-10. It was the first time a British night bomber had downed a German night fighter and for this he was awarded the Distinguished Flying Cross." Grandad started laughing to himself, paused and sighed. "I don't know how true it is," he said. "but the story goes that on or about the day the war ended, Hansen 'stole' a Messerschmitt 109 fighter plane from right under the Germans' noses, flew it back to Denmark and went on to start a very successful flying training school with it! He was also awarded the George Medal. Do you know what that it?" Joel shook his head. "It's the second highest civilian award. You've to go to Buckingham Palace to receive it. Anyway, so the story goes, he rescued two British soldiers from a burning plane filled with ammunition. The plane exploded just as he pulled them clear."

Joel was awe-struck. "How do you remember all these stories Grandad."

"Well, we didn't have a television when I was a lad and my dad, he was a talker, a storyteller. Television was about, but my mam, she didn't approve of them. She said that they could spy on you from inside the television; watch what you were doing. I was twelve before she finally gave in and got one. Rented it from Reddifusion I remember. Nineteen sixty something it was. You could ask my dad a question on any subject and he would have a tale of some kind to tell you about it. He had some really good stories about the war. He joined the Home Guard you see and did his bit, fire watching and all that, and then in 1943 when he was eighteen, he was called up. He worked as a brickie in the Army – making safe damaged buildings, re-laying bomb blasted runways, putting up Nissen huts, building new structures. Anyway, he got de-mobbed around 1946 and got a job working on the building sites. He hadn't planned on being a builder, but there was plenty of work out there and it was good money. They built a lot of new houses after the war; cities spread out, eating up the green belt. They built houses with gardens back and front. They wanted to break away from the overcrowded back to back houses of the Victorian days and give people greenery and areas for the kids to play. His passion though was speedway. He'd dabbled a bit, got his first motorbike when he was fifteen and I remember him still having one when I was about ten, but then we got a car and Mam made him get rid of the bike. He spannered for a few riders; but his favourite place was always on the terraces, cheering on the action on the track. When speedway restarted after the war, Dad and his pals would go for a drink in the bar with some of the riders. This was probably 1947/48.

He met my mam there you know? She used to go with her friend, Sheila I think her name was. Mam and Sheila were both fans of this Australian rider- oh what was his name?" Grandad paused while he tried to remember. "They called him the 'White Ghost' 'cos he wore all white leathers. Ken Le Breton, they called him. He was a looker, chiselled features, thick dark foppish hair, sparkling grey blue eyes. He was Australian; a lot of the top riders were Australian back then."

That made Joel smile. He was sure if Jason Doyle was racing then he would have been as good if not better than any of them. He wondered what his nickname would have been, but he couldn't think of one at the particular moment in time.

"This Ken chap," continued Grandad. "He'd been in the Australian Army during the war. He served as a gunner in New Guinea. Didn't take up speedway till after the war as far as I know. Anyway, my dad got pally with him and he introduced him to these two girls – my mam and Shelia. Ken had a sweetheart back home, Joanie, her name was. My dad and mam; Winne, they hit it off straight away and so my dad and his pals started meeting up with my mam and Sheila at the speedway every week and standing with them on the terraces.

I remember my Dad saying Ken caught malaria whilst he was stationed in New Guinea. He also suffered from 'Battle Fatigue' – what you'd now call PTSD; Post Traumatic Stress Disorder.

You liked him or you didn't, he could be aloof, but if you understood him you liked him. He knew what he wanted and what he had to do to get there. He'd fought in the jungles of New Guinea and stared death in the face. He was determined to be the best rider he could and if everything felt 'right' he was unbeatable. All the psychology in the sport nowadays – he knew all about it. He had good self-discipline, a direct line of thought and was analytical of everything around him.

He was a good sort and my mam and dad went up to see him ride at Glasgow when he changed teams and rode at Ashfield. They went to Wembley in '49 to watch him in the World Final. Him and Joanie were married by then. He'd brought her over with him from Australia."

"Did he win Grandad, was he World Champion?" Joel imagined a Jason Doyle look alike in white leathers holding the World Championship cup above his head, to the roars and adulation from the crowd.

"No, lad. I can't remember where he came." Grandad then became a little melancholy. Joel waited for him to continue.

"My mam and dad had only been married a few months when they got the news. It wasn't long after Christmas, maybe the New Year. They got a telegram from a friend of Ken's in Australia saying that he'd been involved in a bad crash at the Sydney Showground. He'd suffered severe head injuries and had died the next day in hospital."

There was a short silence between the two of them. Grandad remembering his own fathers' emotion when telling him the story, and Joel thinking of the likes of Bluey Wilkinson and George Pepper.

"You go on about your Dad and his stories, but your just as bad Jim. You'll bore the lad to sleep," snapped Gran.

"No Gran," cried Joel, showing an unusual level of emotion in his voice. "I love Grandad's stories. I want to hear more, especially about the war. "

Gran who was now up and about, rolled her eyes. 'If I hear him mention the war one more time,' she thought to herself as she picked up Muffin's lead and Muffin leapt up expectantly, eager for a walk.

"I'm taking the dog for a walk." Gran slipped her rain coat on and clipped the lead on Muffin's collar. She closed the door gently behind her and they heard her descend the creaking staircase.

"Carry on the story Grandad," encouraged Joel eagerly, as he knelt on the floor and rested his head on the arm of the winged back chair Grandad was sitting on.

"Where was I? Oh aye - my mam was distraught, she was. She said to dad, 'when we have a baby, if it's a boy I want to call him after Ken.' Now's the confusing part."

Joel could tell Grandad was enjoying regaling this story.

"His real name was Francis James – His family called him Frank, his friends called him Jim and for some reason, his pals in the Army had nicknamed Ken, and the name stuck. So, when I was born a few years later they had quite a selection to choose from. I was christened James Francis in memory of their pal."

Joel was touched and saddened by the tale but thought it nice all the same. He'd never realised his grandad was named after a speedway rider. Gran always just called him Jim. He wondered if she knew the story? He wished he'd been called after a famous rider – but he couldn't think of any called Joel.

"Back then, "continued Grandad.

Joel pictured Jason Doyle, in leather flying suit and helmet. The 'Airborne Aussie Ace' would scream newspaper headlines. With war clouds looming, Jason would, like a number of other top riders, acquired his pilot's license in anticipation of being needed by the War Office. He certainly wouldn't want to be a boring old motorcycle messenger or a mechanic working as ground crew.

 Soon after being accepted in to the R.A.F. Doyle would be flying Spitfires... On this particular mission, he finds himself cut off from the others in his squadron. Suddenly he sees a trio of Dornier's chasing him down. He ducks and weaves; avoiding the gunner's bullets that skim past his plane. One of the Dornier's then veers left across his bow, missing him by what looked like inches. The backdraft buffets his plane and sends him into a dive. "Come on come on!" He cries through gritted teeth, pulling as hard as he can on the joystick lever. Steadily he is able to pull the plane back, stabilise it and gain control. Another Dornier's then appears out of nowhere. Jason heads it off in a hail of bullets. It tips its wing, rather like a farewell salute, and plummets to earth; the loud whine of its engine becoming quieter, then silent. Steadying his nerves, he takes a deep breath and wipes the perspiration from his brow. Ahead he can see another Dornier, with obvious damage to its underside – likely caused when he fired on the now downed plane. He looks around, and to his right he sees a fellow Spitfire in close proximity; he radios the pilot to close in. They carry on in formation sitting either side of the limping Dornier, nursing it along but allowing no room for escape. They head it out towards the English Channel and eventually watch as the plane drops lower and lower and eventually crashes into the sea. He and the other pilot give each other the 'thumbs up', turn their aircraft around and make their way back to base.

Soon after returning, Jason would be interviewed by the BBC and the recording played to its millions of listeners. The interviewer, with clipped British accent, would describe Jason as being a hero of the 'cavalry of the clouds' as well as an 'international speedway sensation.' He would ask Jason to describe the dog-fight in which he earned the bar to his Distinguished Flying Cross, but Jason of course would play it down and casually reply in his Australian accent, *"It could have gone either way, it was him or me; and you know, luck was on 'me side; job well done."*

The interviewer would then enquire as to Jason's' plans regarding returning to racing once the war was over and if his sights were still set on the world speedway title.

"Yea, can't wait. I've got a bike here that I get to blast around on some waste ground nearby, when I get the chance. A few of the other blokes here have got bikes too, so we sort of get to race each other when we have some spare time. I'm keeping fit and injury free so far, so yea – the world title is still my aim and as soon as I get de-mobbed I'll be back on 'me bike and looking for a team place and yea for sure, hopefully challenging for the world title."

Joel went back to browsing the internet and Grandad to reading his book. Gran returned from walking Muffin and proceeded potter about the room and chatter to no one in particular.

"Grandad," said Joel, in the same drawn out tone he had used earlier. Grandad, who was quite put out at being disturbed yet again, said "What now?"

"Well, I've just thought of something," replied Joel. Grandad put his book down yet again, he knew this wasn't going to be a quick and easy question.

"Just say," began Joel. "You really were able to time travel."

Grandad rolled his eyes "Here we go."

"No, just listen Grandad," Joel rubbed his hands together. "What say you went to the back to the past and brought something back to the future with you."

"Well" said Grandad. "It would possibly be hard to prove you had brought it back. I mean, it may have been very well preserved, unused, pristine condition. What sort of thing anyway?"

Joel hadn't really thought.

"A newspaper or a comic, freshly printed?" He thought of the comics Will had given him. He had brought a couple of them with him to read – 1940 editions of the Wizard. He'd brought them to read because Will had often spoken about 'The Wolf of Kabul and his sidekick Chung'. There were some crazy inventions suggested in the comics for overcoming the German bombers – rubber roofs over cities, so that the bombs would bounce back and prang their own planes. Monster sized vacuum cleaners to suck the bombers from out of the skies. Machines to squirt chloroform into the upper air to dope and overcome the crews. Of course, all these ideas were ludicrous, but they made people smile and not give up hope.

"No," said Grandad shaking his head. "Things like newspapers are preserved all the time. Unread, stored away in pristine condition. Of course, they could prove that by the ink, print style etcetera that it was from that era, but you couldn't prove you'd only just brought it forward to the future. Even if you brought something back from thousands of years ago, it's possible you might be believed by some people. But ninety-nine percent of folk would just think it a clever hoax I'm afraid."

With that Grandad went back to reading his book. Joel returned to searching the internet for interesting facts about the war. He made snippet notes in his notebook, dates of particular events, casualties, items of news. Things he could bring into conversation to help him fit in – he knew Will thought him a bit simple.

The next morning Joel was awoken by his alarm. He was getting used to having lie-ins, not having to get up early for school. He remembered his bid on the shilling coins and logged in to see how the bidding was going. The bidding still stood at £3.40, but he held of placing a bid until the last minute, knowing if another bidder was keen they would outbid him at the last second and he didn't want to pay more than he needed to. He counted down the seconds and when it reached 32 seconds till close of bids he placed another bid – upping his previous bid to £6. The counter turned over, he was now the top bidder at £3.60. As the final seconds fell away, bids ended at £3.60 and with a fee of £3.00 for first class postage. Joel made the payment and again added a note asking for the coins to be sent to his grandparents' address in Plymouth as it was a gift and again signing it Darren Armstrong. He sent his Dad a quick text to let him know what he'd done and saying he'd pay him back when he got home; ending the message with a smiley face emoji. Hopefully the coins would arrive he before they got back to Plymouth. He wanted to take some back to the war. It then struck him, that he would only have one more full day to spend with Will and a half day the following day. It really wasn't long enough – he didn't really want to have to go back to 'normal' and Exmouth and school and all the boring things like that. He didn't particularly want to live with Gran and Grandad forever, but he just couldn't stop thinking about Will and the war. It played on his mind all of the time; like it was in real time – not 70 odd years ago. Did it stop when he left it? Was it being re-enacted all over again? Had he actually been there 70 odd years ago, not actually around then but somehow teleported from now? Surely that was the only explanation.

At breakfast, he commented to the Guest House owner that he felt the small pats of individually wrapped catering butter, plastic pots of jam and packets of sugar were a waste of food and money as so many were just thrown away. He then went on to describe rationing in the war and how most essential foods were rationed. Mrs Barclay, the Guest House owner empathised with him, but explained that nowadays people were picky and preferred untainted food stuffs, not a jam pot that someone else may have put their knife in or butter that may have been touched by numerous people and with dirty knives. Grandad nudged him and told him to stop being pedantic and apologised profusely to Mrs Barclay. Mrs Barclay said there was no need to; he was a very intelligent young man and patted Joel on the head. She said she remembered rationing after the war and often felt saddened at the amount of surplus food they threw away in the Guest House. "Can't have a four-star rating otherwise" she sighed.

The day was busy and Joel enjoyed a trip to Penzance, where he bought some postcards, wrote them out and posted them – except Will's. He kept that one, he would give it to him when he next saw him. He bought a blue pencil with 'Penzance' stamped on it in gold lettering, he thought it a nice present for Will.

Next stop was an attraction near Helston, an outdoor funfair and indoor museum. Normally, somewhere like this Joel would most likely have hurried around the museum and indoor attractions and spent most of the afternoon on the outdoor rides. Today though he was most keen to see the 'Britain in the Blitz' exhibition; a re-creation of a London street during wartime Britain. He rather enjoyed the Victorian street museum too, imagining Mr and Mrs Roberts as a young couple wandering around there and feeling completely at ease. His favourite bit, the bit that gave him goose bumps, was of course the 1940s experience. The deafening air raid siren made him feel rather queer and as if he really should really run for shelter. It felt weird, but slightly exciting, especially as he knew he was safe – there would be no bombs today. He was particularly taken with the wartime kitchen and couldn't help blurt out to Gran that Mrs Roberts had a kitchen like that. He was rather animated throughout, remarking that the shop looked rather well stocked for goods being on ration as well as other small details, such as the familiar brands: Oxo, Atora suet and Colman's mustard. Gran found his observations rather amusing. Grandad again snapped away with his camera – taking pictures of just about everything. Getting Joel and Gran to pose in the air raid shelter, the bombed-out house and various other places in the mock up street. Joel got to sit in the cockpit of a Shackleton bomber, a post WW2 plane. He imagined it as being very similar to those flown by George Pepper and Morian Hansen.

When the indoor tour was over they moved to the outdoor attractions. Gran and Grandad said they would watch while he went on the rides, but Joel wasn't particularly interested.

"What's up dear, I thought you loved funfair rides?" queried Gran. It wasn't that he wasn't interested, he was just pre-occupied. He did though go on the log flume with Grandad and had a ride on the go-karts. They then went for lunch at the on-site café and Joel scrolled through Grandad's camera, looking at the photographs. He thought it would be a good idea to change the tone to black and white; all second world war pictures seemed to be black and white. He could get Grandad to print them off and he could then take them to show Will. One of him the air raid shelter would be good, or with a bombed street scene behind him. He could say they were taken in Cornwall; which was true.

They arrived back at the Guest house soon after 4pm. Gran made them all drinks and then fed Muffin. Joel took a shower and lay down on his bed, sent a few texts and then he fell asleep.

He was awoken by Grandad knocking on his door. Joel got up and opened it, unsure if he'd been asleep for minutes or hours.

"It's off lad," said Grandad looking put out.

"What's off Grandad?" questioned Joel, looking bemused.

"Speedway. Just had a text off John, says it's off." He waved his phone towards Joel.

With all the excitement of the day Joel had completely forgotten that it was Friday and that Grandad had promised to take him to watch the Plymouth Devils that evening. It was hard to know what day of the week it was when you were flitting from time zone to time zone and day to day. Even more so when you were on a holiday within a holiday.

"Oh," said Joel solemnly. He had been really looking forward to going to the speedway. That was the main reason he had come to stay with his grandparents. That was before he found the time portal and met Will of course.   Before he thought the week would drag.

Grandad put his hands on his hips and said. "it's up to you if you want to come, but I've said to John I'll go over. He lives over near Lostwithiel. I told him were down here at St Austell and he said pop over and see his vintage bikes, so I said okay."

Joel wasn't sure how far away Lostwithiel was, but he remembered driving through it on their way to the Guest House; so, it couldn't be that far away. He'd met John last summer when he'd gone to the speedway with Grandad. He remembered it well. The riders were already on parade at the starting gate when they'd arrived at the track. Traffic had been heavy and Grandad had become impatient thinking they might miss the first race.

Grandad had lead the way to his usual viewing point on the back straight stand and introduced Joel to his 'speedway buddies' Mick and John. The men had conversed about the riders and the state of the track, Grandad said he thought it would be a close match as Stuart Robson was good around the Plymouth circuit. Stuart was a Geordie and Grandad had a soft spot for Geordies, being one himself. Joel cheered for Kyle Newman and Todd Kurtz. Todd was an Aussie, like Jason.

The crowd clapped and cheered loudly when the riders came around on the parade lap. Fourteen 500cc engines all revving together. Joel had told Mick that he didn't get to see live speedway very often, as the drive from Exmouth to Plymouth took just over an hour and his Dad often didn't get home from work till nearer seven o'clock. Mick empathised and said it was a sad day when Exeter had closed its doors for the final time.

Joel remembered the view from the wooden grandstand; he could see in the distance the pits - filled with colour, adrenalin and anticipation.
 The cheery crowds, many wearing the red and yellow home team colours occupied the stand. A few Rye House fans, wearing blue and white stood nearby – they were waving flags and making lots of noise. Joel thought if they carried on being as loud throughout the meeting they would very soon start to get on his nerves.

Mick said he'd first watched speedway at Exeter in 1969 when Ivan Mauger rode for the Falcons. Grandad butted in and said he'd seen Ivan first, at Newcastle in 1965. They then got into a debate of when Ivan was at his best, Joel left them to their argument.

He told John, who seemed to have a much more laid-back view of things, that he'd been to the British Grand Prix at Cardiff for the last five years in a row. That his Gran and Grandad always came up to Exmouth the night before and then on the day itself, Joel, Dad and Grandad would drive up to Cardiff early in the day, leaving Mum, Tabby and Gran to have a day to do girlie things at home. The 'boys' would enjoy the atmosphere of the fan-zone, the crowds milling around the city centre and then sit outside a pub for lunch, before heading to the stadium an hour or so before the racing began. John said he'd only been to Cardiff twice, he preferred to watch it on TV at home. He was on a pension and couldn't afford to go every year. He mentioned having some old bikes in the garage that he was restoring; one a speedway bike, if Joel remembered correctly. John was nice, Joel felt he could talk to him, he wasn't a prick like Grandad could often be; always having to be right. He could hear Mick and Grandad now debating who was better Ole Olsen or Ivan Mauger. He knew Grandad would win the argument – he always did.

The evenings racing had been enjoyable though fairly uneventful other than for four re-runs which dragged the meeting out somewhat – two jump starts and two tape touching offences. Grandad and his friends in buoyant mood, bade each other a farewell till next time.

"Your Gran doesn't mind – she was expecting us to be out for the evening anyway, look." Grandad pointed into their room and Joel came out into the hallway to look. Gran was sat in a comfy chair watching TV. When she saw Joel, she held up an opened bottle of wine and said, "I've been looking forward to this all week. My Friday night treat. I always have a bottle of wine and the TV to myself on a Friday when Jim's at speedway." She grinned at Joel and took a sip from a half full glass. She was obviously starting early.

Joel hurriedly got his hoodie and trainers on, slipped his mobile phone into his pocket and made his way outside to the car. Grandad was already in the driver's seat with the engine running. He could be very impatient at times.

Gran waved them off from the bedroom window.

The drive to John's house only took about 20 minutes. The pulled up outside of a small bungalow with a long driveway and a well-kept garden. Alighting from the car, John was already outside waiting for them. He'd obviously been watching from the window in anticipation of their arrival. Instead of taking them into the house, he closed the open front door and ushered them round to the back of the property to a large wooden garage. He and Grandad chatted while he fumbled with a large bunch of keys in his hand and then unlocked the double doors. The swung open and inside Joel could make out, what he assumed to be motorbikes covered with grimy brown covers. The walls were filled with shelves stacked high with all sorts of paraphernalia; from tools to bottles, and a host of other items he couldn't make out. John flicked on the light and the garage came to life.

"It's not often I get to show my collection," said John, as he patted the grimy cover nearest to him. "Do you want to see something special?"

Neither Joel nor Grandad said anything. They just watched and waited as John slowly and deliberately drew the cover from the motorbike concealed underneath, revealing a sleek and beautiful black and silver machine.

"Ain't she a beauty ay?" He stroked the handlebars and patted the seat.

"She's a T120, won the Isle of Man TT twice. John Hartle in '67 and Malcolm Uphill in '69. He got 'er up to a ton. First time a production motorbike ever passed the three-figure mark from a standing start."

While Joel and his grandad inspected the motorcycle, John went over to another oil stained cover.

"This is my baby," he said, as again he slowly began to reveal the machine underneath. Both Joel and his grandad eager to see, moved closer. John; who was attired in dirty green overalls and work boots, said. "1937 Rudge speedway bike."

Joel said "wow" and Grandad just stared at the labour of love. After a few seconds he said, "bloody hell mate!"

John went on to explain how he's spent the last fifteen years slowly restoring it. The stove enamelled tank and mud guards had been sent off for a re-spray. The wheels had been rebuilt onto re-chromed rims with new spokes. He'd had the seat re-covered and all the cables had been replaced with new ones. The J.A.P engine and the gearbox had been completely overhauled – that had been a difficult job. The exhaust he'd had to replace with a new one. All of the chrome had been re-plated and he'd applied new decals to the petrol tank. The front and rear suspension had also had to be stripped and rebuilt.

Captivated, Joel closed his eyes and placed his hand on the throttle and moved it gently. He allowed his thoughts to stray; he could feel Will standing next to him, excitedly telling him that was the same bike George Pepper rode. He then opened his eyes to take in the beauty of the machine, and gently stroked the low-lying handlebars.

"Careful lad," said Grandad.

"The bey's a'right," said John, appreciating the adulation of his work. "She's a stunner ain't she?"

"Can I sit on her?" asked Joel, feeling strangely odd. As though he was exchanging place with Will, when he had been invited by George to sit upon his motorbike at Bristol speedway.

John nodded. With a feeling of the utmost privilege, Joel held onto the handle bars and swung his right leg over the bike. He then closed his eyes and imagined ...... lost in his thoughts, he pictured in his minds' eye the stands filling up nicely, he could even hear the cheers and the revving of the other bikes in the pits. He'd seen footage online of the crowds of old, the thousands of chanting fans who filled the stadiums decades ago, when riders would slide and leg trail around the cinder tracks. There would be match races and scratch races – whatever they were. Many of the stadiums were now just a long gone forgotten memory; pulled down and made into industrial units or housing estates. The tracks and their memories all ghosts of the past; just like the riders who raced on them. He knew the original Plymouth stadium at Pennycross was now long gone. Will had mentioned Southampton and Bristol; neither had a speedway team now. Joel wondered if it they were large capacity purpose-built stadiums, like those shown on black and white footage he'd seen on the internet. The fans cheering and waving wooden rattles. The high-speed spectacle of the leather clad riders, shoulder to shoulder diving into the first bend. Men and machines locked together in a seeming mass of limbs and wheels, broadsiding around the track. He imagined the ferocious noise of whistles and cheers and claps from the adorning fans when the heroes of the day crossed the finish line. He tried to picture Cordy Milne and George Pepper tackling the small Plymouth track of today. The bikes were different now of course, but it would still be a spectacle to behold.

"Come on lad!" laughed Grandad. "Off you get."

Joel reluctantly climbed from the bike. "John," He said. "Did you ever see Cordy Milne or George Pepper race?"

John laughed and said he was old, but not that old. Joel felt a bit silly, so changed the subject. He told him about his trip to Cardiff to watch the Grand Prix, the previous month and that he'd got to see his hero Jason Doyle, close up. He hadn't managed to get his autograph, but he'd taken some photographs and even managed to get a 'selfie' with Jason in the background. He also said that he'd seen Mattie Bates, the former Plymouth rider, in Primark in Exeter a few months ago, but had been too shy to go up and say hello.

John was now busy, gently oiling the chain of the Rudge. "Should have spoken to him, he's a good lad." He paused as he examined his handiwork. "Got to keep 'er sweet. Treat 'er like a lady."

Joel now wished he had spoken to Mattie. He'd been tempted to at the time, but his friends had wandered off and the moment had gone.

"His grandad used to ride back in the day you know?" said John, as he fumbled with replacing the cover on the Rudge. Joel helped him, it felt nice to let his hands follow the shape of the bike as it disappeared from sight.

"Bronco, they called 'im," said John. "From up Exeter way."

The name rang a bell with Joel. "Bronco Slade?" he said excitedly.

"That's 'im," said John. "Well before my time though sonny."

Joel just smiled. It was nice when he met someone who could relate to riders Will knew of.

John then showed them his 1983 Jawa speedway bike with upright engine. Joel wasn't that interested in it as it didn't look all that much different from the bikes the riders rode today. His grandad and John seemed to find that bike particularly interesting, so Joel made his way back over to the Rudge and pulled the cover back half way, to have another look and to stroke her fine bodywork.

"John," he said. It felt weird calling a much older person by their first name. He always felt he should call them mister or sir or something. "Do you know who this bike belonged to? I mean, it had to be a speedway rider, so was it someone famous like... I don't know. Maybe, Billy Lamont or Ron Johnson?"

"Bey, I've no idea. I bought it from a dealer many a year back now. He said it 'ad an 'istroy, but what it is I've no idea. I've always meant to find out, but never got round to it" John came back over and took another look at his pride and joy. "She was well looked after, that's all I know."

Joel chose to romanticise her past – left abandoned since the outbreak of war, when her owner had gone off to fight on either land, sea or in the air. Locked away and forgotten in some workshop or garage. After the demise of said owner – either occurring during the war; or many years later in old age and the bike having been left abandoned in the intervening years, possibly due to a war wound that halted any hopes the rider had of returning to the shale.

After a pleasant hour or so of talking bikes and speedway, drinking tea and eating biscuits made by Mrs John's own hand, [he didn't introduce her, but Joel did hear her pottering around in the house.] They returned to the Guest house, via a stop off at a fish and chip shop on the outskirts of St Austell. Gran had sent a text asking them to stop off and buy some on the way back as she was peckish and they had nothing to eat in their room.

After supper, Joel retired to his own room and watched YouTube clips on his phone until he fell asleep.

The following morning, Saturday, they packed up and left the guest house shortly after breakfast. Instead of heading east, they headed west. Gran said she had somewhere 'charming' she wanted to take Joel to. They drove for quite some time and eventually arrived at their destination – St Michaels Mount. A Medieval castle reached by crossing a causeway.

They walked across with Muffin trying to paddle in the sea as the gentle waves lapped nearby. Grandad again took lots of pictures whilst they walked the grounds and Gran sat outside with Muffin enjoying the sun whilst Joel and his grandad toured the castle.

Mid-afternoon they set off for home. Joel had phoned his mum and dad, at Gran's insistence when they had stopped for lunch. Whilst he was on the phone she kept butting in – telling him to tell them what a great holiday he was having and how much he had enjoyed himself. He could see Grandad smirking, behind his cup of tea. His was rather surprised when he heard Joel ask if he could stay 'just a while longer,' to which his mum reluctantly agreed, but added that if he was just saying it for his grandparents benefit then to cough. Joel didn't cough. Mum was a little disappointed as she said she missed him and Dad said surely, he must be bored staying with a couple of old fuddy-duddies. Joel was adamant that he was having a good time, and he'd made friends with a boy on the next street.

"Yes, your Gran mentioned him" said Mum. "You should invite him round for tea, I'm sure your Gran would like that." Joel said that Will was very shy, but he'd ask him. When she questioned him further about Will, he said they had a lot in common and Will was telling him all about the war, because he was really into that, and now he was too.

"Well, I'm glad you've got an interest and not all this private eye imaginary stuff" said Mum in reply.

The first thing Joel did when they arrived home, other than accidentally letting Muffin out of the car and having to chase her down the street to get her back; was to check the post. There was one small package addressed to him – the weighty padded envelope of shilling coins. Hopefully the cigarette card would come soon. He picked up the other post and put it on the kitchen table, then hurried upstairs to open his treasure from the past. He ripped own the envelope and watched as the coins scattered across his bed. He then checked each and every one for the date. He couldn't afford to make the mistake of using one that hadn't yet come into circulation. All but one of the coins, a 1942 shilling were usable. He put that one aside, maybe for later and carefully put the eleven usable coins, on his bedside table. He had wanted to go straight round to see Will, but Grandad called him downstairs to help unload the car. Once done, Gran then wanted him to take Muffin for a walk around the block. Joel zipped up his hoodie, and put two of the coins in his pocket 'just in case' – he had an idea......

CHAPTER NINE

"Hullo, anyone in." Joel called through the letterbox, after having knocked three times. The street was in darkness. Joel was unsure as to whether it was very early in the morning or night. There were no street lights or light shining from windows, so it was hard to tell.

Just as he was about to leave, he felt a funny sensation. He looked, his eyes now beginning to adjust to the lack of light. The whole street looked different somehow - emptier. There was a large pile of rubble or something on the road in the direction which he had come from. There were bits of roof tile scattered across the pavements and a good few net curtains fluttered out of broken window panes. He looked in the opposite direction – there was a whole section of roof hanging down from some houses; most of the first-floor walls now lying on the pavement in front of the properties.

Even though he hadn't stepped through the door, he was still a few feet away - he was already in the past – as was Muffin. He took a step backwards towards the gate. The funny feeling came again and he was in his own time. He stepped forward and felt the odd sensation again. He looked around, and could see he was already back in the 1940's. He was mid-step backward again when the door opened.

"What the heck!" Squealed Will. "What just bleddy happened there." He had a shocked, uncertain look on his face, rather than delight at seeing his old friend again.

"Err, I was just about to leave, I though no one was home." Joel felt the funny feeling again; it was like a heavy heady numbness. It was difficult to describe – like trying to walk through deep water.

Will stared at him for what felt like ages but was probably only two or three seconds. "How did you do that?"

"Do what?" Replied Joel, wondering if Will had seen something of what he himself had experienced.

"You just... you just... well, you were sort of there and then you weren't." Will then jumped back in shock. "Where the hell did that come from!" He pointed towards Muffin who was sniffing at the door sill.

"This is my gran's dog, Muffin."

Still looking dazed Will invited Joel into the house, he was in his pyjama's, but with his boots and overcoat on top. "What you doin' here?"

"I've just got back," said Joel rather surprised, having expected a little more enthusiasm from his friend.

"Just got back, what now, from Cornwall?" Will led the way to the dimly candle lit kitchen, where Grandma Roberts sat sipping a cup of tea.

"Err no," replied Joel. He wasn't sure of the time of day, but as Will looked dishevelled, was in pyjamas' boots and overcoat, he assumed it was early morning, and Will had spent the night in the shelter.

"From the Anderson I mean. You know…"

"Your Gran's house been damaged?" queried Will, seeming flustered and continued to busy himself whilst firing a multitude of questions at Joel. He handed Joel a dustpan and brush and carrying a broom and bucket himself, directed them towards the parlour. "Now mind the floor, there's still lot of glass about. I've gotten most of it up, it's mostly plaster and dust now."

Joel left Muffin sitting in front of the kitchen range with Mrs Roberts, whilst he helped with the clear up. He felt somewhat bewildered and realising there had obviously been a heavy overnight raid decided just to go along with Will's instructions and say nothing. After half an hour or so and with most of the dust and glass cleared away, Mrs Roberts called the boys to the kitchen where she had poured them both a strong cup of tea and had cut them both some 'bread and marge.' Muffin looked on expectantly.

"Your dog doesn't look too perturbed after all last night's goings on. I'm surprised," said Mrs Roberts. "Most dogs go daft when there's a raid on, escaping and running wild. A lot 'ave 'ad to be put down. That dog and cats 'ome on Cattedown Road; they been overwhelmed with 'omeless pets since the raids started. They can't take 'em down the shelter neither. Poor dears, 'ave to stay and calm the animals as best they can. You can 'ear 'em all 'owling, when there's a lull between the bombings."

Joel caught sight of the mantel clock, it read 8.10.

" Ee's in shock, let 'im be." reprimanded Mrs Roberts, when Will continued his interrogations as to what damage had there been to Joel's Gran's house and that of her neighbours.

"Your Gran's 'ouse caught it too?" Mrs Roberts enquired gently; she sat down next to him and tried to make him feel at ease. He felt more of a fraud than anything. He'd come to tell Will about his trip to Cornwall and here he was in the aftermath of a dreadful airstrike.

"Err, yea, not too bad, I just came around to check how things were, you know, after last night. I err, I saw the damage down the bottom of the road from the back window and well, Gran said I best come around check if there was anything you needed." Joel felt it best to say something, but nothing too ambiguous.

"Did you see if we had any roof tiles missing at the back?" queried Mrs Roberts.

There was a sudden commotion at the front door, clatters and bumps and eventually the emergence of two men in blue overalls. Neither of whom he'd seen before but Mrs Roberts nor Will showed any alarm. The men entered the kitchen, grunted a greeting and warmed their soot blackened hands at the cooking range as Mrs Roberts took more cups from the dresser and poured them both a cup of tea, from water she had boiled in a heavy black kettle on the range.

'Uncle Des' who at first, he hadn't recognised in his Home Guard uniform, acknowledged Joel with a nod of his head. The younger man, introduced himself as Tom, Des's brother. "Ah won't shake your hand bey, I need to wash 'em first." Joel could see the men were both grimy and tired. Uncle Des motioned to Joel to give up his seat, he needed it more. He sighed loudly as he sat down, taking the weight from his tired legs. "You're goin' to 'ave to get the tin bath out Eadie" he said. "I need to soak me aching bones. Good job you got plenty of coal 'cos there's no 'lectric and no gas. Gas works been badly damaged, likely off for weeks."

Mrs Roberts patted him on the shoulder. "How's our Maid an' the girls?"

"They're doing good. Diedre's got a bit of a cold, but she's nearly over it. They stayed in the shelter all night, like I told 'em to, and the house is fine – just some loose bits 'o plaster. I can get it fixed up." Des eased himself from his overalls and particles of masonry dust fell to the floor. He asked Will to help him off with his boots. "Oh, you are a good 'un," he said. Joel liked Des. Muffin trotted over and began sniffing the at discarded boots on the floor.

"Not sat down or stopped since the siren went off last night" said Des. "Twelve hours non-stop. I'm parched, my hands hurt and my feet ache. I'm totally worn out."

"I 'eard the hospital got it?" said Mrs Roberts looking at the younger man. He nodded. "How many?" She enquired.

"Don't know; too much going on. Siren's, fire hoses, people." Tom suddenly stopped and let out a loud sob and his shoulders began to shake. No one moved nor spoke. He quickly composed himself and carried on. "Thousands of incendiaries apparently, a good few high explosives too. The wharves got hit badly. Reckett's factory – that's gone."

"You need those socks darned Tom," said Mrs Roberts looking at his big toe poking through a hole in his sock. "Get your Beryl to do it before it gets any bigger." There was a short pause and then she asked, "You checked on Beryl and the kiddies?"

Tom took a deep breath and rubbed his weary face with soot blackened hands. "Stayed at her Mother's house last night thank God. I told her yesterday, I said 'take the kiddies to your mothers. There's been bombers circling overhead, likely they'll come back later on.' I said I'd stay and keep watch on the house. I had to stay, I was fire duty anyway. I went and had a check on it earlier; bits of plaster all over the place and few broken plates. I'll telephone her mother's neighbour later on from the phone box, tell her to stay another night. No gas or 'lectric anyway. It's not good for the kiddies to see things like this. There's them lot who go up on to the moors every night to sleep in the open. It's a'right for them, getting away from the bombs, but who do they think is looking after their houses and businesses. Putting out the fires and saving their belongings?"

There was a long pause. No one dared make eye contact. Everyone just stared into the depths of their cup of tea, as if attempting to read their tea leaves through the murky depths and hopeful on seeing a sign of good fortune.

Tom spoke again, "We were lucky, house next door had two incendiaries land on the roof. Luckily the firewatchers nearby saw them. Broke the front door down and got to 'em. One had burned through to the bedroom, but they caught 'em before the whole house caught alight."

Everyone nodded, though again without looking up in fear of catching each other's eye. 'How could that be lucky?' thought Joel. Lucky was going to bed and not having to get up and cower under the stairs or run to the shelter in the middle of the night. Lucky was not having to be worry about bombs destroying your home. Lucky was not having to fear that each time a loved one left the house, it could be the last time you ever saw them. Of course, there was always the risk of that at any time, even in 2017, but not every single day living under such a cloud.

Mrs Roberts looked out of the kitchen window and abruptly got to her feet. "Me yard, look at me yard...." Everyone followed her gaze; there was roof tiles and bits of broken chimney pot shattered across the courtyard. A large chunk of masonry had broken two terracotta plant pots spilling soil and spring bulbs across the ground. "That's me front chimney gone." She sighed, and sat back down heavily, dejected and lost in her thoughts.

"Seen the bottom of our street?" Will directed the remark at Joel. "Here look?" He took something silver from his pocket and showed it to Joel. "Shrapnel, found loads of it. Here, take some."

Joel was strangely impressed. He took a small twisted piece of metal from Will's hand – a melted twisted fragment from a German bomb – still warm, though likely from being in Will's pocket rather than from the impact of it hitting the ground and exploding. He turned it over in his hand and examined the innocent looking shard of metal. Yesterday it had been part of something much bigger, much more dangerous. It had been loaded onto a plane in occupied France, flown by a German pilot across the channel. He pictured the stern featured pilot, probably named Otto or Manfred. He would fly in silence, focussed on the job in hand. His mindset, to cause as much damage and disruption to the lives of the good folk of Plymouth as the Furher and his Generals instructed. Otto or Manfred, like the bomb, were none discriminatory. Loss of life mattered not; as long as he completed his mission and disrupted the lives of those beneath his targets trajectory; then it was a job well done. He had avenged his people for the terror caused by the British air strikes on his homeland. His father possibly having been killed or wounded in the last war. Did he feel he had avenged his people, or was he just following orders? Joel remembered seeing a film about Hitler ordering the burning of all books that were un-German. Did these include children's books, story books, world history books he wondered? Were these pilots all brainwashed young men, still haunted by the gruesome stain left behind by the last war?

"We got it worst in Plymouth 'ere," said Tom. "All the bombs were dropped on our side of the city. They be after the gasometers again. Worst I've seen; houses, schools, hospitals... sick bastards."

Joel expected someone to pick him up on his language, but no one did.

"The gas company, the power station, the wharves, Exeter Street, Tothill Road." The younger man started listing off all the roads he had either seen or been told had been hit. "Greenbank, Mainstone, and railway lines. Cotehele, Laira Bridge, Harvey, Goad, Grenville...." He paused, silent tears ran down Mrs Roberts cheeks. Tom continued, "A bomb just missed my cousin Jean's house, landed four doors down. It was a friend of the family. Mother and three kiddies, all huddled under the stairs. Died where they sat."

"When will it all end eh, when will it all end?" Mrs Roberts sobbed into a knotted handkerchief.

No one replied. Joel wanted to shout out '1945!' but he couldn't.

"Our Sylvie's gone and joined the A.T.S, A wireless telephonist you know," Mrs Roberts tearfully directed the remark towards Joel. "She's gone somewhere up Gloucester way. At least she's away from this bleddy mess."

Will spoke next. Firstly, he beckoned to Joel to come and sit by him on the floor. They sat on a mat with their backs resting against the wooden back door. Muffin joined them; squeezing herself between them for warmth and comfort. She placed her head on Will's leg, he stroked her and spoke quietly.

"Bombers moon last night; big bright moon, weren't it? An 'Air raid night' Granfer said, and sure enough, shortly after the sirens went the raid started. We watched the searchlights for a while from out in the street, but then we heard the planes coming over and Granfer shouted to us to get down the shelter."

He stopped to think for a while, reflecting on the events of the previous night. "Have you noticed how the German planes sound different to ours?"

Joel didn't answer.

"The German planes make a throbbing sound," continued Will. "They have a rhythmic throb, throb, throb, from their twin engines, which apparently are de-synchronised to confuse our sound direction finders, which in turn are directed by the anti-aircraft guns. Granfer was out, riding around on his bicycle and warning people of the raid. Mum was kept busy putting out incendiaries. She saw the bomb that hit the houses at the bottom of our road; really shook her up it did, but she carried on. Word got 'round that Plymstock and Oreston were having a rough time of it too.

There followed another long silence. Will then turned to look at Joel and said. "What happened to the postcard you said you would send?"

Joel felt a pang of conscience. He'd thought of Will a lot while he'd been away, but knew it was impossible to send a postcard through time. He still had it, written out but without a stamp on it.

"I couldn't get a stamp. I'll bring it along with your present next time, I forgot it in the rush, you know with all that's gone on." He nodded his head towards the window.

"And when will next time be?" asked Will.

There was a silence between them. Joel felt a flush of fear, like when he thought he'd been caught out by Will with his mobile phone.

"Soon," he replied quietly. "I have to go back to Exmouth, but I 'll be coming back. It's just awkward – you know, with there being a war on and all that."

"That old excuse," retorted Will. There was a brief silence and he then changed the subject. He was more concerned with now, today and the war that was really happening in 1941. "I'm going to head off soon and see how Auntie Eve is. Bet they got it bad down by the dockyard. Since Uncle Frank got called up, she decided she should do her bit and got a job in the dockyard, all dungarees and turbans now." He seemed to be thinking out loud. "I hope the roads are open."

Joel felt guilty, *'being a war on and all that'* was an excuse constantly being used and he knew it to be a weak justification, but he couldn't honestly say when he would be back, if he would be back. If there was a chance of getting caught in the time warp it just didn't seem worth it. It had even crossed his mind that of the hundreds of people who go missing each year – had any of them slipped through a time warp too and just got stuck there?

The silence was broken by the sound of the front door opening; Mr Roberts then appeared at the kitchen door. He too was wearing blue overalls. Mrs Roberts stood up and ushered him to her seat. Still no one spoke. Mr Roberts silently made his way to the vacant chair. He went to speak then stopped. He pulled out his reading glasses from his pocket, one of the lenses was missing. He poked his finger through the now empty space. "Bleedin' Germans," he said. I can't even read the bloomin' paper now." His shoulders shook and then he took a deep breath. Eadie put her hand on his shoulder, "What is it Charlie?"

 "Brunswick Road got it bad. Numbers five to eleven 'ave gone. I 'eard, yer friend, Maud; 'er 'ouse, took a direct hit – number eleven she lived at didn't she, with her sister? I'm sorry Eadie." His shoulders shook more violently. Eadie let out a gasp and then a whimper.

Joel signalled to Muffin it was time to go and they let themselves out of the house.

He felt sad as he walked along the street, he'd been so looking forward to seeing his friend again and it hadn't just been as he expected. Maybe Will didn't want to be friends with the 'wierdo' anymore. The friend who came and went and was never consistent. The friend who wore strange clothes and said stupid things. The friend who didn't seem to understand the impact of the war, or even know what was going on half the time. He stopped on the bridge that joined his side of the road/railway to Will's side. He stood for a while looking in both directions. The road underneath was busy with its three lanes of traffic. Looking down the road, and along the back of the two rows of houses, he could see in the distance the familiar hills and trees; they looked pretty much the same in both his and Will's time. Nothing looked that much different; the houses had been painted in brighter colours, but other than that and the railway now being a road, it was very much the same view. He looked in the opposite direction – that view that way was completely different. Gone was the

Plymouth and Stonehouse gas and coke company, their sidings and the giant gasometers which stood menacingly, close behind in 1941. In their place was a cinema and restaurant complex; bright lights and a constant hive of activity. Did the war destroy all of what was there in Will's time he wondered; how could it all change so much? He looked back in the opposite direction and felt a wave of comfort as the familiar streets and distant outline of countryside was unchanged.

Back to Gran's house, Joel gave Muffin a dog biscuit and then went to his bedroom to think things over. He now had an extra few days with Gran and Grandad, but if things were so bad in 1941, did he really want to stay in Plymouth any longer? It would be selfish to not go back again, as Will and his family and everyone else was living it in real time, day by day, minute by minute. The reality of the era was very different to reading about it – seeing the emotions for real was what got to him most. He could deal with the rubble and the bomb sites. He'd got used to them now, even though they were still scary.

He would happily pack his bag and ask Grandad for a lift to the station right now if he could - but he knew he couldn't. He couldn't even go back to the war and take Will his present, as it hadn't arrived yet. 'I'm just going to have to tough this one out' he thought to himself. It was likely nearly teatime anyway, and the speedway Grand Prix from Malilla in Sweden would soon be starting on TV.

CHAPTER TEN

It was Sunday – 'nothing much happens on a Sunday,' thought Joel. He didn't feel he could face going around to see Will today. He wanted to wait for the Bluey Wilkinson cigarette card to arrive and take that, along with the pencil from Penzance and the postcard. He wanted to take some sort of peace offering.

Gran suggested he invite Will around for Sunday dinner, but Joel said he was away for the day with his family and so wouldn't be able to come. Grandad said he wanted to get the decorating finished in the dining room and suggested Joel make himself useful. Joel didn't really want to help, but it was better than just sitting around all day doing nothing. He decided to place the glass lens on his bedroom window sill and let it 'charge' for the day, as he wasn't going to be using it.

By mid-afternoon, the dining room was finished and Grandad took some photos to share on social media. Gran was pleased to have her dining room back and said they should celebrate with a bottle of 'fizzy' with the Sunday roast. Joel was only allowed one glass, but it was enough. After he'd helped dry the dishes he lay on the sofa with Grandad's laptop and began doing some more 'research' on the war. He read about how people were asked to give up pots and pans, wire coat hangers, coat hooks, bathroom fittings etcetera, all to help with the war effort. Any household item made wholly or in part aluminium was asked to be given up so that they could be melted down and used to build Spitfire, Wellington, Hurricane and Blenheim bombers. People willingly gave up much needed items, dropping them off at the local W.V.S or to street collectors. Council workmen came around and took away iron railings and gates. It wasn't compulsory, but most people again felt it was their way of contributing to the war effort. A Spitfire apparently cost £5,000 and every town and city in the land had by mid-1941 *apparently* 'bought' a Spitfire.

The grade of metal being contributed though was in no way good enough to make a plane from. The items were often melted down and made in to weapons of war or components needed for the war – but certainly not Spitfires. There were reports of barges dumping tons of London's scrap metal into the Thames estuary because much of the metal was sub-standard. Joel felt frustrated that such a propaganda exercise should be used to deceive the 'blitzed' civilians.

By early evening Joel was bored. He suggested they all go for a walk; he felt he needed to get out and 'do something.' Grandad said he wasn't really keen on going for a walk, but he would take Joel to the cinema if he fancied it. He had promised to take him to see Dunkirk and tonight was an ideal a time as any. There was a low sea mist in the air. It wasn't really walking weather anyway. The donned their showerproof coats - a year-round necessity in the South West and headed off on the short walk to the nearby cinema complex. On the way, Joel observed something he had never noticed before. The garden walls – some had decorative iron railings, others not. But even on those walls with railings, he could see where the previous railings had been chopped off; taken away by the council 'for the war effort.' He mentioned it to Grandad, casually asking if everyone had given up their railings.

"I'm not sure son, you know I think we should look into that – you're a detective sort aren't you? On the way home, we'll walk the long way round – have a look and see if we can spot any really old railings. I know big parks and other places still have their original railings and a lot of grand houses too – they didn't give them up. It was likely voluntary, but you know what with all the pressure from the propaganda machine by way of leaflets, posters, cinema and newspaper adverts that went on – people just went along with it. They felt glad to be helping out in some way and I understand that." Joel liked listening to his grandad tell him stories; especially the ones about when he was a boy and when he was in the Army.

 Joel asked what had happened to the gasometers, as he'd read about the Germans trying to bomb them.

"Oh, they're still there lad, you just can't see 'em." This reply rather shocked Joel – how could they still be there, but unseen. They were bloody huge for goodness sake! The supporting structure with its huge iron columns and trellis girders, where was that? They stood well over a hundred feet high and couldn't just 'not be seen.'

"They just lowered them into the ground. You see, they used to go up and down - telescopic. Up when they were full and down when they were empty. They just let them empty and then left them there. I'll show you."

After they crossed the road to the cinema, instead of going right, Grandad took Joel in the opposite direction. "Just around the corner there's a gate; have a look through."

Joel peered through, and could see a huge gasometer, sunk into its bed in the ground. It was surrounded by a metal skeleton –the trellis brace abruptly snapped off in places, evidence of an attempt to dismantle it.

"There's another further along, and one across the road," Grandad pointed over the road and beyond a high wall. "An even bigger one. Probably just be left there forever. Too big a job to dismantle them fully. Cost too much. There used to be a gasworks here, closed down in the 80's."

Joel looked across the road and through another gateway, he could just make out the white curved top of a ginormous gasometer. He felt happy knowing the gasometers he was so familiar with in Will's time were still there - dormant, but still there. Possibly with a preservation order on them. The German's didn't get to bomb them and now they would likely be left forever in silent perpetuity. He imagined them to be like sleeping giants; if ever Britain were to come under attacked again, they would begin to groan and stretch and the ground around would rumble and shake as they came back to life. The loud screech of metal would be heard for miles around as the rusted iron gasometers rose once again to their full and glorious height. They would stand proud and magnificent against the surrounding area. A warning to the enemy that they were still there, still standing, still undefeated.

"I remember my dad telling me when he was a lad, a bit older than you." Grandad was recounting another one of his stories, as they headed back towards the cinema. "His mam had sent him along to the corner shop with a jug and some money and told him to get milk and two poond o'tatties." He spoke like that – he was a Geordie like me you know." Joel did know, but Grandad always had to remind him of the fact whenever he did the accent. "Anyway, the shopkeeper filled his jug with milk from a huge urn, weighed out the potatoes and said 'pass 'us ya bag' to put the tatties in.' My dad said 'I haven't got a bag'.

"Hev ya got a sack then' asks the shopkeeper. 'No' said my dad. The shopkeeper then said 'Well, I can't give you one pet, there's a war on. I'm not allowed to bag anything that doesn't need to be wrapped.' Then he said 'Howay round here son' and he got my dad to come around the counter and he pulled his pullover out at the bottom and said to my dad, 'Here, just hold it like this,' and then he poured the tatties into the well made by the stretched wool. He pulled it up over the tatties to make a sort of bag. Well, my Dad hurries on home with the jug of milk in one hand and trying to keep the tatties from falling out his pullover with the other. Next thing – the air raid siren goes off!" Grandad started chuckling. "He races as fast as he can along the road, trying not to spill any of the milk. He can hear a plane in the distance coming closer. He makes it home, rushes through the house, empties the contents of his pullover all over the floor, trips on one of the tatties and spills half the contents of the jug all over the kitchen rug. He then belts out of the back door and dives into the Anderson shelter just as the plane flew overhead.... It was a British plane, chasing the Nazi's back across the North Sea. They didn't get to bomb Newcastle that day after all.   His Mam was livid when the all clear sounded and she saw the mess. She gave him a clip round the ear - her rug had to be cleaned and hung out for days to dry and my Dad's over stretched pullover had to be unpicked and completely re-knitted."

Why was a pullover now called a jumper wondered Joel – there was nothing jumpy or jumper-ish about one at all.

"He must have been terrified though Grandad. Imagine hearing a plane coming towards you, running for the shelter and not knowing if you were going to be its intended target." Joel got goose bumps at the memory of hearing the air raid siren for real.

"My Dad had some great stories Joel – you would have loved to meet him."

Joel smiled and thought how wonderful it would have been if Will and his great-grandad could have met. If only they lived closer to one another, he could have introduced them and they could have become pals.

"I remember him telling me about one afternoon. August 1940, I think it was, hundreds of enemy planes appeared above the skies of Newcastle. The sound of the engines was just one tremendous roar. The monstrous racket drew the attention of the North-East fighter squadron, who swung into action and downed 75 enemy craft without any loses to themselves. The intended target had been the shipyards along the length of the Tyne. That's where my grandad worked as a plater."

Joel remembered seeing footage of scenes of Plymouth, Coventry and London burning in the Blitz. He wondered how just many other cities were destroyed in that way. He asked his grandad, but he wasn't sure either. He assumed all the large towns cities were bombed at some time or other, York, Bath, Norwich – all the cathedral cities were bombed within days of each other in 1942 he recalled. "Apparently, Hitler was enraged by the RAF's attacks on Lubeck and some other notable German city, so he picked up a guidebook of English towns and cities and ordered every historic place in England marked with three stars to be bombed in retaliation."

"Do you think that's true Grandad." Joel asked, intrigued.

"Probably. It's a shame my dad isn't still here to tell you; he loved telling a good yarn about the war. Could go on for hours, he could." Grandad paused while he thought of another of his fathers' anecdotes. "He lived near the River Tyne. I remember him telling me about the day he saw a German bomber try to blow up a train which had stopped on the High-Level bridge, which crosses the river. Luckily the bombs missed and splashed into the water below. Probably still there today."

They were now crossing the carpark and heading towards the cinema entrance. Grandad began to pat down his pockets "Thought I'd left my wallet at home." He said with some relief finding it in his inside jacket pocket.

"How old would your Dad be now if he was still alive now? "Asked Joel, trying to picture how old he would have been in 1941. The pair slowed down their pace and Grandad began mumbling to himself as he tried to work it out 'if he was twenty-eight…. That was … mm.. seventy-six…. He'd have been about ninety, ninety-one now."

That made his great-grandad a couple of years older than himself in 1941.

"As I said my dad lived near the river. The whole of the Tyne was a target for the Luftwaffe, 'cos of all the shipyards, marine and engineering works you see. Anyway, it was just after Christmas 1941 and there was a big raid over the city. From the shelter in their garden they could hear bombs exploding in the distance. When they got out someone said that bombs had been dropped in Byker, and some of the houses in Grace Street had been damaged. Now Grace Street backed onto the speedway stadium. My Dad's heart sank thinking the main grandstand had been bombed and the stadium destroyed; luckily it hadn't. Another time he remembered staying at his Aunt's house, somewhere near the city centre. One night, he was sleeping in the attic when the air raid siren went off. Rather than going three floors down to the shelter, he and his cousins watched the sky all lit up by the fires caused by a series of bombs." Grandad demonstrated with his hands the spread of the light created by the fires across the sky. "They heard the first one land a short distance away, then the second one dropped nearer, then they heard the third one coming like the roar of an express train and they knew it was going to be close. They all threw themselves under the bed, thinking it was for them. It landed about ten yards away, just behind the large brick wall which divided his aunts garden from the neighbours. It buried their unoccupied shelter in debris. They ended up going to a neighbouring shelter until it was safe to return home. Thankfully the house was intact; but slightly damaged. When they got up on the morning they found a huge crater in the garden and in it; an armchair from the neighbour's house!"

They entered the cinema and joined the queue for tickets. "Another time, during a day-light raid," continued Grandad – who obviously liked to recount the stories as much as his own father had. "My dad was living at Druridge Drive, Cowgate, it's a suburb of Newcastle. This enemy bomber came sweeping overhead and started firing. He tried to hit the postman who was in the middle of emptying the post box at the end of the street. The postman ducked behind the box and the bullets missed him, leaving scorch marks on the pavement and the walls of the houses behind."

They reached the front of the queue, Grandad bought their tickets and they then made their way up the central stairway and to screen 9. The auditorium was in in semi darkness as the trailer advert and movies were already being shown. Joel, who had the better eyesight of the two found their seats and they settled in. Grandad leant over and began to whisper loudly. "After a recent raid, probably in '41, my Dad found a piece of incendiary bomb in the street. Well, being the sort of inquisitive lad that he was, he thought it would be interesting to see what would happen if he put it on the fire. Encouraged by his pal Bobby Graves; he duly did. After a few seconds, there was a hiss, a bang, a huge flash of white light that lit up the whole room and the scrap of metal casing shot from the fire and flung itself across the room. A white powder, like dust, covered the room. Luckily my Dad was able to clear up most of the mess before his mam got home!" Grandad chuckled at the memory.

"Shhh Grandad – the film's just about to start."

The following morning Joel was awake by 7 a.m. The heavy traffic on the road in the culvert behind his Grandparents house had woken him up. The sound of dull trundle of lorries through the open window kept him from going back to sleep. His mind was in overdrive too. He'd been thinking of what his Grandad had told him last night about his own fathers' memories of World War 2, and then on the walk back from the cinema they had taken a longer route home, by way of the fish and chip shop and Grandad had pointed out the garden walls showing where the railings had been cut off 'to make Spitfires.' There were a few original iron railings still intact and Joel felt a sense of pride at those householders for refusing to give up their railings and gates. Many had been replaced by modern decorative railings, but the crudely cut off iron stumps still protruded slightly from the wall beneath them. Hidden history that went un-noticed to the casual observer. Others had been crudely replaced by breeze blocks painted over, and with 1950's wooden gates that were now showing their age.

Grandad mentioned that his father used to send off for things from 'Exchange and Mart' and when questioned about what it was, he said it was a bit like 'Ebay, but in a magazine.' It advertised items for sale – anything from cars, trombones, holiday lets, second hand furniture to small items that could go in an envelope. His dad had put together a small collection of speedway memorabilia that he had built up over the years. He'd bought a number of items from 'Exchange and Mart' and sold a few on through it too. He'd been an avid 'marter' right up until his sight began to deteriorate when he was in his '70's. Joel had casually mentioned the cigarette cards that he'd seen at Will's, without actually saying he'd seen them. His grandad wasn't sure, but said he'd look through the things he had kept of his father's and see what was there.

Joel made his way downstairs; he could hear his grandad in the kitchen. "You're up early today," he said, hearing Joel descend the stairs. "Got any plans?"

Joel sat and watched his grandad make himself two ham and cheese sandwiches and wrap them in tin foil.

"Just going to see my friend Will, nothing special." Grandad carried on preparing his lunch whilst finishing his breakfast.

"Grandad" said Joel. "Can I look through the things of your Dad's you mentioned? I know where they are, Gran and I found them under the stairs, but we didn't look thorough them. We only looked in a couple of Gran's boxes – photos and things." He omitted to mention the gas mask; he didn't want Grandad to know he still had possession of that.

"I suppose so but be careful. Get your Gran to show you it, I don't want anything getting broken." Joel doubted there was anything he could break in a box of old letters and photo's but said "Thanks Grandad, I will, I promise."

Joel made himself some granola cereal and a drink, switched the radio on and sat patiently waiting for the postman to arrive. Checking the doormat on a number of occasions, in case he had missed him.

At 8.45, whilst in the shower, he heard the familiar 'thud' sound on the doormat. He hurried to get dried, wrapped the towel around his waist and rushed downstairs. There it was; an envelope addressed to him; which he prayed contained the 'Bluey Wilkinson' cigarette card. He carefully slit open the envelope and was not disappointed. In a smaller brown envelope, the pristine eighty-year-old card sat looking as new as on the day it was printed. Bluey sat astride his machine, wearing his West Ham race jacket and yellow helmet colour. Joel smiled to himself, knowing how happy Will would be to receive it, but at the same time sad that the face depicted on the card bared little resemblance to the 'Bluey' he had seen photographs of; the freckled face, the tight curly red hair with a centre parting. The fact he was wearing a helmet and it was a hand-drawn picture rather spoiled it somewhat, but that didn't matter – not to Will it wouldn't. Bluey was dead and Will would never get to see him now; the card would be all he would have to remember him by.

It was a chilly day and rather drizzly, there had been no improvement in the weather since last evening. Joel decided to wear jeans, a t-shirt under his jumper and thin rain jacket. Will was used to him dressing in weird clothes so probably wouldn't notice anyway. He put his shilling coins in one trouser pocket and the glass lens and Bluey card in the other along with the pencil and postcard he had bought in Penzance. Knowing he had a lot of making up to do with Will he wondered what he could do to sweeten him? He remembered people going on about having no bananas' during the war. Apparently, there was a wartime song about it. He tried to think of the words to it;

'Work all night on a drink of rum. Daylight come and me wan' go home. Stack banana till the mornin' come. Daylight come and me wan' go home.' Strange song he thought, especially for wartime, but as he'd never heard any other songs about bananas, that must be it.

He went into the kitchen and took two bananas from the fruit bowl. He called to Gran that he was 'popping down to Wills' and would see her later on. He sneaked the gas mask he had hidden behind the coats in the hallway and closed the front door behind him as he left.

Entering the gate of number fifty-two, he walked straight into the back of another person, a lady who was also entering the house.

" 'Ere watch out you, look where you're goin'. We're not in the black out now you know."

Joel apologised profusely and said he really hadn't seen her and was sorry. They both walked into the passageway. He noticed a bucket of water, a bucket of sand and a small stirrup pump just inside the front door. He wondered what they were for, then realised they were probably for putting out small fires in the event of the house being hit by an incendiary bomb.

"Eadie, it's Doris" called the woman towards the kitchen. "I bought yer beater back." She turned to Joel and said "Mine broke. Can you believe it eh? The Germans come and bomb our 'ouses and mine gets away Scott free. I go to beat 'me rug and find a piece of shrapnel has taken the 'andle clean off." Joel had no idea what a 'beater' was so just gave a look of sympathy.

"Filled a bucket full of shrapnel I 'ave from my backyard. 'Ere, you that boy Will spoke about?" Doris looked at him warily. "An' what's that you got there – bananas'?" Just as she said 'bananas' Mrs Roberts appeared; she'd been filling the coal bucket out in the courtyard.

"Banana's" Said Mrs Roberts "what's this about bananas?" Joel held them out towards her and said "A present."

"Ere, don't go flashing them about or you'll have the whole neighbourhood round. Where did you get them from anyways?" She queried as she grabbed them from his outstretched hand and hurried into the kitchen. Doris still holding on to the carpet beater followed her.

"My Dad, he knows some people. He sent them over – said I should share them so I thought I'd bring you a couple down."

"His American friends no doubt?" Enquired Mrs Roberts, answering her own question.

Doris took them in her hand and examined them like a midwife would, checking over a new born baby. "Need ripening, put them in the oven Eadie," she said, handing them back. "It'll bring them up nicely."

Joel began singing; *"Come, Mister tally man, tally me banana. Daylight come and me wan' go home."*

The two women looked at each other.

"They got bombed out," said Mrs Roberts gently, "Parents sent him 'ere to his grandparents. Don't bother much with the boy as far as I can tell. I think he's you know, a bit affected by it all."

Doris gave her a knowing look. Mrs Roberts was tempted to try one of the bananas there and then but decided to wait till everyone was home.

Doris placed the carpet beater against the back door and then left.

Will heard his pal's familiar voice, as he entered the house. He was wearing his school uniform. "Hallo stranger" he said. There was still an unusual distant tone in his voice. He looked at the bananas, raised his eyebrows but said nothing.

"I've brought your postcard and present round, the one I said I got you when I was in Cornwall. I must have forgot to post the card – sorry." Joel said, trying to sound upbeat and excited. He desperately wanted Will not to fall out with him, because if he did – well, it would mean an end to his time travelling trips back into the past. He would have no reason to return if Will shunned him. "Here." He handed Will the postcard, blue pencil with 'Penzance' stamped on it in gold lettering and the small brown envelope. Will appeared to appreciate the pencil. He studied the sepia coloured postcard and then took out the small card cautiously from the envelope. A huge grin spread across his face as he realised what it was. He walked over to Joel and giving him a manly chuck on the shoulder said. "Cheers pal, it means a lot, it really does," which rather took Joel by surprise.

"Where did you manage to get it anyway?" enquired Will, as he examined the detail on the card.

"Saw it advertised in Exchange and Mart, so I sent off for it," lied Joel.

"Hold on." Said Will, and he dashed upstairs, returning moments later with his Players cigarette album. He placed it on the table and began rummaging around in one of the drawers on the large dresser. "Found it." He said and came back to the table with a small tin of what appeared to be glue. He opened the back page of the album and stuck Bluey's picture in to its allocated space, between Colin Watson of Wembley and George Wilks of Hackney Wick.

He admired the picture for a few moments, flicked through the album then putting it back on to the table said "So, what you been up to these past few weeks Joel?"

Joel felt uncomfortable, but he briefly mentioned a few of the things he'd done on holiday, without making it sound like he was on holiday. Will reminded him it was weeks ago that he'd been to Cornwall. He wanted to know what he'd been up to since. He said it rather coldly and it made him Joel want to leave, but at the same time he didn't want to leave. He really cared about his friend and his family and knew that soon their lives were to be changed forever.

Joel wanted to tell him about going to see the film 'Dunkirk' with his Grandad. How he had imagined Jason Doyle as Tom Hardy. He himself as Peter, the boy in boat; even though he looked more like Will. Will he had imagined, to be the young Scottish pilot who they managed to save from his sinking Spitfire. Granfer had to be the old man who steered the boat.

He'd quite enjoyed the film, but Grandad had said they'd used rather a lot of poetic licence and it was aimed at the American market. Joel didn't mind, he'd enjoyed watching the Spitfires.

"I've got something to show you." said Will. "You're going to like this." He motioned to Joel to follow him upstairs.

From inside the top left-hand drawer of his chest of drawers, where Will kept his sketch book, pencils, paint and other art paraphernalia; he pulled out a picture.

"Here, I did this for you when you were away. I thought of you and Muffin in Cornwall. You throwing sticks across the beach for her to go and catch."

Joel was touched, it was a beautiful picture.

"Keep it," said Will.

He then changed the subject and pulled out a box from under his bed. It was plain brown with a large pink paper sticker on top. "Look what I got for my birthday," beamed Will proudly. Joel read the sticker 'ELECTRIC SPEEDWAY – the greatest game of chance of all time.' He raised his eyebrows and grinned. "Let's have a look see then."

Will carefully unveiled what was inside the box. There was a green wooden circular board with six different coloured speedway bikes on it. He explained to Joel that players were invited to put their bets on to a Roulette-like board – pennies, counters buttons, it didn't really matter. Once the bets were placed, a switch was flicked and the wheel would begin to spin. He switched it on and demonstrated how it worked. As each bike went past a connection, their colour light would flash on, and with a fast spinning wheel, all the lights would be flashing, adding to the excitement. When the wheel slowed down so would the lights and then when the wheel stopped, one light would stay on and that rider would be the race winner. The winning bidder then collected their bets and another race could start. The winner must be the one who has the most money when the game ends.

Joel picked up the lid of the box and read the description label. 'An exciting game that has taken the world by storm. As the six riders speed around the course, coloured electric lights flash dizzily before you. What thrills! What excitement as the end is nearing! Whirling riders, flashing lights. All the thrills of speedway in your own home. The game that has set the country talking – the game that makes every party a success.'

"Mum bought it from one of the blokes on the buses. His house was hit and they had to get re-housed. They did a clear out and sold stuff they no longer needed, his lads being in the Army now."

Joel thought the game quirky, and certainly different. They played a number of games, using coloured counters to bet on the result, choosing 2 riders each time to be 'their team.' Joel bored of playing long before Will did. He thought it a bit silly to have six riders when speedway only had four.

"Did you know lots of speedway riders trained as pilots before the war?" Said Joel, remembering his Grandad's story about Morian Hansen.

"I read something about aviation being popular, over London way. That's where they've got a big airfield apparently. Vic Huxley and Jack Ormston I think it was I read about. Ormston's from up your grandad's way, isn't he?" questioned Will, looking up. Joel didn't know, so didn't reply. Will then began to laugh, remembering a story his dad had told him.

"My dad heard this story off a fella at the speedway. A few years ago, Roger Frogley was piloting his own plane, when the wind forced the door open, and he ended up flying upside down." Will seemed to find it very funny and not at all dangerous. "He crash-landed the plane and the next day beat Jack Parker at Wimbledon! My dad says all riders are just like schoolboys at heart, always ready for a dare."

Joel had no idea who Roger Frogley nor Jack Parker were.

"You know Morian Hansen?" said Will. Joel looked up and acknowledged that he did know of Morian; his Grandad had told him of his wartime exploits while they were on holiday in Cornwall. He was expecting to hear a story of great heroics and aerobatic exploits, but instead Will simply said - "He used to fly a lot too. Joined the RAF apparently."

Joel felt the urge to tell him about Morian Hansen's exploits after the war with the stolen German plane; but he couldn't, because it hadn't happened yet.

Eventually Will suggested they go for a walk down by the wharves, to see if there was anything interesting on the shoreline. He said it was surprising what you often found washed up by the shore. He'd once found a small leather purse containing a whale's tooth and an old shilling cut in half. "Probably a lucky charm I expect."

Joel ensured he held on to the back of Will's coat as they left the house and headed off up the road. Wanting to show his friend he now finally had some 'real money' he reached into his pocket and pulled out three shilling coins. "Here you go," he said handing them to Will. "What I owe you back for the cinema." He knew the seats had been one and threes, but one and three of what he wasn't sure.

"Crikey" cried Will. "Three bob, you made of money? We could go to the cinema - twice, get fish, chips, lemonade and still have change out of that!"

Joel shoved the rest of the coins back in his pocket. He had no idea of what 1940's money was worth in purchasing power.

"That's an idea; come on, let's get some fish and chips instead," suggested Will. "Best go tell Gran first, so she doesn't save me any tea."

Joel realised that it wasn't just a dull morning like in 2017, but early evening closing in; a very chilly evening too. The boys made their way along the now familiar streets and back lanes, past two new bombsites. Will pointed out the shrapnel scars on the walls and all across the pavement; showing the direction of the blast from a high explosive. He said there'd been a scramble for shrapnel by the local children the morning following the raid. Collecting shrapnel had now become quite a hobby. Mainly the silver star shaped pieces, from the anti-aircraft guns; it was everywhere. It wasn't how much you had that mattered though, but how big it was – that's what people were after now; the biggest pieces. He showed Joel the strange scars on the pavement caused by the incendiaries burning into the tarmac or melding with the slate paving stones; only the tail fins would survive as recognisable souvenirs. He talked about how the younger boys especially, were getting more and more daring, going further and further into the bombsites, before they had been declared safe. He asked Joel if he'd heard about Mrs Finnegan. Joel said he hadn't. Will said that only a week or so ago, whilst Joel was still in Cornwall, a nine-year-old boy called Maurice Johns, had dared to clamber over the bomb site to reach what looked like a huge piece silver metal. As he got nearer he heard a whimpering sound and realised there was a person still trapped in the rubble. He called for help and quickly the area was awash with Home Guard and Military personnel, all clawing away at the bricks and timber. After twenty minutes, they were able to pull clear a woman; still clinging to her silver tea service. Joel asked why she was holding a silver tea-service during a raid. Was she planning on taking it down the shelter?

"Probably afraid of looters," replied Will. "Goes on you know."

They stopped and had a good gawp at some ruined buildings. There was something mesmerising about them. Was it the way something so solid could suddenly become so fragile? People tried not to stare, but they just couldn't help it. Maybe it was just getting to see inside other people's houses?

"Cor look," said Will in excitement. "They've got a bath!"

Joel looked in the direction Will was pointing. Sure, enough there was a porcelain bath sitting vertical rather than horizontal against an outside first floor wall. A toilet next to it was still attached to the wall and much of the tiling around it, intact. Joel imagined someone in the bath at the time of the raid and when the bomb fell they were tipped out, just like water running down a plughole, and were buried somewhere beneath all the rubble.

They picked up a few small fragments of shrapnel from the ground. Joel noticed some pieces had embedded themselves deep into the fabric of slate paving stones and would likely be there forever. The hot molten metal now at one with the cold stone around it. He wondered if he took Muffin for a walk in the area in his own time, would the scars still be there?

They passed the former playing field; now equipped with a large silver barrage balloon, which was moored to the ground by stern rigging, concrete ballast and sandbags. It was manned 24 hours a day by the R.A.F. Ten men working in teams of five. The balloon had apparently been nicknamed 'Hector,' and the locals would often hear a shout of "Hector's going up!" suggesting that the air raid siren would shortly be sounding, and a daylight air raid being imminent. The field also housed living accommodation for the servicemen who manned the balloon.

"I met the Duke of Kent on Friday" said Will proudly. "He came to inspect the representatives of the City's Civil Defence Corps - I've joined up."

Joel burst out laughing "But you're too young."

"I'm not, I'm nearly fifteen," replied Will indignant. "I'll be doing my exam's soon, leaving school. We all have to do our bit and in the event of an air raid. I, along with the other messengers, provide a line of communication between the A.R.P Command Posts."

Joel felt rather proud of his friend. He'd never imagined young teenage boys playing their part in the war; running through the streets, taking messages from one command post to another, whilst bombs rained overhead. He imagined Will would be very good at that sort of thing, he was tall and thin and could run and manoeuvre quickly.

"If there's an air raid warning I have ride around on my bike blowing a whistle - long blasts for the 'Warning', and short blasts for 'All Clear'. Got a helmet with a big white 'M' on it for messenger, and overalls, just like my Mum and Granfer have."

"I wish I could do something like that." Joel thought out loud.

"You're not here enough, though are you? To be honest you are not here, more than you are here." It did hurt Joel's feelings, but he didn't let it show, after all there was a huge element of truth in it. He changed the subject and told Will the story about his great grandad and the incendiary bomb, though said it was his cousin, as it seemed unlikely an old man would be silly enough to play with bits of bombs. He thought Will would be impressed, but instead he voiced his dissatisfaction at his cousins' stupidity and told Joel how one if his school pals had found an unexploded incendiary bomb which had made a soft landing on an allotment at the bottom of his road. It was obvious it was a bomb, as it was a thick metal tube with 4 tail fins at the bottom and had a rounded nose cone. He had taken it back to his house and with a devil-may-care attitude, unscrewed the nose cone and tipped out the thermite powder from inside - the chemical which on impact was supposed to be ignited by the fuse. This, when lit, would burn with a fierce white heat which in turn would then set the casing on fire and was difficult to put out. His pal thought he would light the powder to see what would happen. It caught fire; swiftly setting the whole room ablaze. The entire house then caught fire and was lost. His friend received second degree burns and was still in hospital. His family had been re-housed but had lost everything.

'Don't let anything get in the way of a good story', thought Joel to himself. Will was growing up before his eyes. He was literally; certainly, going by his trousers leg length, which hung just above the ankle. He had aged in real terms five months at least, but in Joel's time only a week. He appeared much more serious too. Maybe it was the war taking its toll on him.

The delicious aroma of frying fish in the cold night air wafted towards them. A queue that led out of a doorway and along the pavement indicated the precise source of the smell; 'Hodge's Fish & Chips.' The queue reduced quickly and the boys were soon inside the small warm shop. Greasy steam filled the air and condensation ran down the window.

"Cod and chips twice please." Said Will confidently, as they reached the front of the queue, "and some batter scraps if you've any left."

"Only got pollock, will that do? and there's no scraps. Everyone's asking for scraps there days," said the young girl behind the counter. "You heard about Jimmy Chapple?"

Will nodded.

"He used to go to school with our Vera," continued the girl as she took a scoop of chips from the fryer. "Only nineteen, awful isn't it. She looked up. "Salt and vinegar?" Joel caught her eye. "Who's your friend Will? Haven't seen him round here before."

"Hi." Said Joel and smiled. The girl grinned back.

"This is Joel, he's American. Joel this is Ellen Hodge, we used to go to junior school together"

"American?" Replied Ellen. She smiled and looked him up and down. "You do look different – it's the hair." She furrowed her brow but didn't seem satisfied that was what it was. "No hang on, it's the clothes. You can always tell a foreigner by their clothes." She placed the fish and chips on some sheets of newspaper and began wrapping them up. "What part of America are you from?"

"Argos." Replied Will, before Joel got a chance to reply. His response made Joel smile. "It's in Indiana." Will glanced at Joel knowingly. "I looked it up on a map at school."

"Well, welcome to England, said Ellen as she wrapped the fish and chips and handed then to Will.

"Hey" said Joel in his best American accent, eyeing some bottles on the counter behind the girl. "Two bottles of your finest English lemonade if you please young lady." It was now Will's turn to giggle.

"Certainly, young man," she reached behind for the bottles. "Want 'em open?" She enquired.

"Err, sure. What other way is there to drink lemonade eh?" He responded, noticing they had caps on like beer bottles. She swiped the caps off with a bottle opener and handed the bottles to Joel. "Thank-you ma'am," he replied as he took them from her grasp. He handed over the money and waited whilst she counted out his change. As he stood there he heard an older youth behind him comment on his strange trousers. Joel was wearing a pair of pale blue jeans; very different to the plain dull flannel trousers, with or without turn-ups that every other man and boy wore. Denim jeans obviously, weren't popular, or possibly hadn't yet been introduced to Britain at this point in time he realised.

"Good ol' American denim." He said pointing to his trousers. "All the ranchers and gunslingers wear 'em. You watch those westerns' - John Wayne, Roy Roger's? They all wear 'merican denim. Toughest material in the world. Why, I doubt there's a man alive who could tear it apart with his bare-hands." He proceeded to pretended to tip his imaginary Stetson and fire an imaginary gun at them as he and Will exited the shop to wide eyed stares – and then excited chatter. The youths behind were rather taken aback at having an American boy in their neighbourhood and started gossiping with the girl behind the counter and asking if they thought he may be related to American born Lord and Lady Astor - he being the present Mayor of Plymouth and she the MP for their constituency of Plymouth. Maybe he was a nephew over on holiday or 'vay-cation' as they called it in the movies.

Will and Joel made their way towards a quiet railway siding to eat their food. Will said there was a 'den' there and it was away from the wind. They walked in silence, Will seemed to have something on his mind; it made Joel feel uncomfortable, he didn't know why it just did.

They clambered over some rubble and bits of wood and other bits of what could have been bombed or discarded household items. They found the den, which was as Will had described – cosy and sheltered. Will opened the newspaper to reveal the steaming hot food; they both proceeded to demolish what they agreed was probably the best fish and chips they had ever tasted. The lemonade was rather good too. Once finished, they lay back on what had once been someone's sofa, or part of – one of the arms was missing. Joel picked up the now greasy newspaper, in which their supper had been wrapped; 'The Western Morning News' dated Friday 11th March 1941.

"What's the date today?" he asked.

Will thought for while "The 14th Why?"

Joel felt an inner fear, his tummy squeezed. He knew the terrible blitz the shook Plymouth and destroyed the beautiful city that he had only recently got to know, was only less than a week away. Will, all his family and everyone else who was here now; living breathing people, were in in great danger; but what could he do? His tummy knotted tighter.

"I heard Portsmouth got it bad on the 10th and 11th, they got battered by hundreds of incendiaries and high explosives. Probably after the dockyard. Could be us next."

Will sat up and looked at Joel. "Could be us next? Come on then mystery boy, what do you know? We both know you aren't who you say you are. How do you know about the bombings on Portsmouth; and what is it with all this American stuff anyway?" he said angrily.

Joel felt scared. "Just a feeling, err…. I read about it in the papers, that's all."

Will gave him a hard stare, he knew the papers wouldn't have gone into any such detail. They may have said a town on the south coast or a Military town, but not named it outright.

 "Look, I know you're not a double agent, you're too daft for that, even Granfer says you're not a full chiming bell. You wear the weirdest clothes." He pointed at Joel's jeans and trainers. "You're a strange one and no mistake. I went along to your 'supposed' Gran's house the other day. I spoke to the lady who answered the door and she said she'd never heard of you. She wasn't old enough to be a gran either. She asked around her neighbours to see if they knew you – none of them did." He paused and then looked Joel in the eye.   "Nobody knows who you are."

Joel felt his cheeks flush.

"Show me your Identity Card," demanded Will.

"No." said Joel, now really afraid. He didn't have an identity card. He knew everyone had one during the war, but he had no way of getting hold of a blank one in 2017 or in 1941 for that matter, unless you knew someone who could get one through the black market. "I've not got it with me."

Will stood up and put his hands on his hips. "As an A.R.P member, I have the permission to demand to see your identity card and if you are unable to produce it, I have the authority to have report you to the Police and you are obligated to produce it at your local station within 48 hours."

He was lying; well, bending the truth somewhat. He didn't have the authority to demand to see Joel's identity card. His parents or grandparents would have been looking after it anyway; Joel being under sixteen. He could though report him to the Police if he really didn't have an identity card.

"I'm not a spy." Was all Joel could say. He didn't look at Will, he couldn't.

"There's something naïve, possibly even stupid about you. I believe you're not a 'spy' as such. Your dad, you know this job he does with the Americans. I remember you said you were testing that radar thing out for them and well, it all fits in doesn't it. Who other than an infiltrator is going to have a gadget like that? No one's going to suspect a 'boy' of being a mole. They just think you're an evacuee and put your strange ways down to not being local.... The American's are gonna come and help us, aren't they?" He said the last sentence questioningly.

"'Course they are," replied Joel confidently. "Just not sure when, that's all." He'd read up on it and he knew it wasn't going to be as soon as people hoped.

"I've got you worked out you know?" said Will, lying back on the sofa, putting his hands behind his head. "Every country has their own organisations that gather information, troop movements, supplies, etcetera. Your dad has likely trained you in the skills of intelligence gathering; possibly without you even being aware of it. Your movements are being monitored by that radar thingy-bob and when you write to your dad or speak to him or whatever, you tell him what you've been doing, what you've seen, general stuff like that. Overheard snippets of conversations – you're passing all that back to him and he is passing it to the intelligence services."

Will turned onto his side and looked directly at Joel. "These bananas, cakes, eggs, the Bluey Wilkinson cigarette card; they're all rewards, aren't they?"

"I don't know, are they?" Joel replied, amused.

Will was now sitting upright. "I can't believe I hadn't linked it all together beforehand. I'm your lackey, your patsy aren't I?"

"Patsy?" Joel screwed up his brow, with a look of confusion.

"You know, your mole. They thought you could take advantage of me, befriend me and then pass on information either to me or to you – I'm not quite sure which yet. Too or from, it's puzzling." Will now looked confused.

"So, I'm working for the American's, passing on information to the Germans, am I?

Both boys looked at each other and began laughing. Joel pushed Will off the sofa and they began play fighting. Will, the taller and stronger of the two, got the upper hand and was able to pin Joel down. He sat astride him holding his arms at his sides so that he was unable to move he said, "You're not getting up till you tell the truth."

"I'm not lying," cried Joel.

"TRUTH!" shouted Will.

"Get off, you're hurting me." Joel tried to wriggle his way out of the hold Will had on him.

"If you don't tell the truth I'll have to hand you in. I bet you know when the next raid is going to be don't you." He slapped Joel across the face, not hard, but hard enough to shock him.

"I'm not a bloody German spy, an American spy or a British Spy." Will slapped him again, harder. Joel began to fight back. He reared up and was able to throw Will off, but Will grabbed him by his jacket and landed him a hefty blow to the side of his face which caused a nosebleed. Joel had never been in a proper fight before and began to cry. Will, who had been in a number of scrapes over the years felt a pang of guilt, seeing his friend in tears. He reached into his pocket and pulled out a slightly used handkerchief. "Here," he said, as he thrust it towards Joel. "Clean yourself up." Joel took it from him and held it against his bloody nose. His top lip hurt too and he could feel it swelling up as he ran his tongue along it.

"I'M NOT A FUCKING SPY!" he screamed at Will.

Will looked shocked, Joel had just used probably the worst swear word in the world. He himself had only ever whispered it and even then, felt guilty he might get found out. His mother no doubt would wash his mouth out with carbolic soap. He was stunned Joel could even utter it, never mind scream it at him. He lunged for him again and in his rage, shouted at Joel; "So where do you go when you disappear off for days or weeks on end then. Just WHO ARE YOU?"

"I've told you before, I'm not a fucking spy!" Screeched Joel, wildly trying to fight Will off. "If you must know, you and all this around us," Joel blurted out, tears streaming down his face and with his arms flapping wildly around, pointing to the houses, trees, traffic and railway sidings surrounding them, "are all in the past. I'm from the future. This isn't my time, this is your time. You probably don't even exist in my time."

Joel sat on a wooden chair by the side of the kitchen range, with a clothes brush, doing his best to remove the dried-on mud from his jeans. Will was sponging down his jacket by the sink.

"What 'appened to you beys. Get in a scrape with some louts? Too many ruffians today – didn't have 'em when I was a young 'un. It was safe to go out then." Granfer Roberts, looked at Joel then at Will. "I see you came off worst bey – need to have some boxing lessons. Won't touch you again after you give 'em a good ol' right hook." He took a swing at an imaginary 'ruffian.'

"It's fine Granfer, no harm done." Joel said but didn't look up, he carried on brushing the dirt from his jeans. Hopefully he wouldn't need to explain anything to Gran; with any luck, the swelling on his lip would go down before he returned home.

Mrs Roberts came in; saying the teapot needed filling up. "Oh, look at you two. If it's not bad enough with a war on you two getting into fights." She tutted and then reminded the boys she'd kept then back a 'bit of banana.' She had as her neighbour suggested, heated them up in the oven. The bananas were now of a brown mushy consistency, just like Joel remembered having as a very small child. He had a taste, but said he preferred raw banana.

Once the boys had got off as much dirt as they were going to, Will made them both a cup of cocoa and they went upstairs to his room. He closed the door behind them and began talking in a low whisper.

"So, tell me it again; you go through a 'time portal' at the front door?" Will thought for a moment. "So that time you sort of went blurry and then normal again, that was you going through the portal?"

Joel nodded.

"Jesus!" said Will out loud. Making the sign of the cross on his chest, even though he wasn't Catholic.

Joel explained the whole story about the time difference and the glass lens and how he was able come and go. He emptied out his pockets to show Will. There was the handkerchief, a key, pencil, small notebook, a shilling coin, a few smaller coins; the change from the fish and chips, and a couple of sandy pebbles he'd picked up on the beach at Pentewan, in Cornwall. He searched again and even looked in his gas mask bag, even though he knew he would never have put it in there. Panic set in as the realisation set in that he had lost the lens, likely when they had fought. If he didn't find it then he would never be able to get back to 2017; he would become a missing person. His Gran and Grandad would feel responsible for his disappearance and worst of all, he would never see his parents or little sister again. He burst into tears for the second time that evening. Joel wasn't one for showing his feelings, especially in front of other boys – but tonight he really didn't care.

Will then remembered when his grandad had come back from the bad raid in January and said he had lost one of the lenses from his reading glasses, when his glasses had somehow been knocked off as he was hurriedly ushering people towards the shelters under Astor fields. Was it the very same lens that Joel had found and had somehow made its way into the future, becoming his gateway to the past? He read the panic on Joel's face as he recounted the occasion, and knew this wasn't just an elaborate story to get him off the hook. Joel was really terrified. He started to shake and said he felt faint. Will got him to lie down on the bed and immediately began to put a plan into action. It was too late to go out searching now, it was getting dark and they couldn't take torches because the A.R.P or the Police would likely see them, or someone from a house overlooking the sidings would see them and report their suspicious behaviour. Joel had to stay at Will's house overnight and they would go out looking in the morning; early, before he went to school – his school now having had the bomb damage of a few months previously repaired, and extra temporary classrooms set up in the playground. He would tell his gran that Joel's grandparents had to go and visit a sick relative and Joel didn't want to stay in their house on his own, in case there was another raid.

Will explained the situation to his gran and she agreed it was best that Joel stay with them until the morning, especially as there was a chance there could be another air raid. Maggie said he could borrow a pair of Will's pyjamas and sleep on the camp bed, which was already in Will's room and just needed to be made up. She made them both another cup of cocoa and gave them each a slice of plain sponge cake. She could see Joel looked upset and said she hoped his relative would be fine. She felt sorry for him, as it must have been bad for his grandparents to have to go away at such short notice and leave him behind.

The boys went back upstairs and Will quizzed Joel more about 'the future.' Joel was cautious and said his grandad had told him that it was dangerous to interfere with the past as it had already happened and altering it could have catastrophic consequences in the future. "You can't change what has already happened, only what is yet to happen," he'd said. Joel refused to tell Will what year he had come from, but if he did get back to the future, he promised he would bring him something back as proof.

As much as Will at times thought it an elaborate hoax, he did have to admit that Joel looked terrified [as maybe a spy caught out would be] but there was something so innocent about Joel that he had to give him the benefit of the doubt.

 "You said I probably didn't exist in your time," said Will. "Are you from far into the future; like hundreds of years?"

"Not quite that far," replied Joel. "But far enough."

"Is the war still going on in your time?" asked Will.

"No," replied Joel confidently. "This war ended a long time ago, but there's been other wars, in other places. There's always been wars and always will be sadly."

Will thought about it and had to agree, in school when they studied history it was always about wars.

"Will I have to go to war?" He queried, wondering how long this war would continue for. It wasn't something he really wanted to do, but he knew it was a possibility, if this war dragged on like the last war. That one lasted four years.

"I don't know," replied Joel. He genuinely didn't know. He knew that there were wars, in the jungle or somewhere he thought, after the Second World War, and there possibly was still conscription, but he honestly didn't know if Will would have to participate.

"I've noticed how you look at things funny," said Will. "Is it really that different in the future?" He wasn't going to give up. He had to gain some knowledge of the future for goodness sake, he had a real time-traveller in his bedroom. If he had to beat him up again he would, he saw how easily Joel crumbled last time he thumped him. He liked Joel though and didn't really want to have to lamp him one again unless he really had to.

"Not that different really, well, sort of not," said Joel, enjoying the attention." There's lots of inventions and thing. We still have cars and motorbikes and radio's... I mean wirelesses. Television is really popular and we still eat fish and chips and stuff like that. Food is a lot more interesting than now." Joel thought about McDonald's burgers, pizza's and Chinese and Indian takeaways. He'd not seen any such places in Will's era. "I suppose with there being rations and all that you might have had the same stuff as us before the war. Have you ever had Chinese?"

"Chinese what?" asked Will, puzzled.

"Chinese food," replied Joel. "You know, noodles, chop suey, chow mein. We have Indian food too," said Joel, and then putting on an Indian accent said; "Tikka masala, vindaloo, bhuna, balti, pilau rice and naan bread." He dragged out the word naan, which made Will hoot with laughter and this encouraged Joel to repeat himself again. "Tikka masala, vindaloo, bhuna, Balti, pilau rice and naan bread."

Once they had both quietened down and the tears had stopped streaming down Will's face from laughing and his stomach muscles had relaxed, he asked in all seriousness, if things had got so bad after the war that Britain had had to rely on other countries to help feed the population. Joel assured him that things hadn't and that 'foreign food' would be all the rage in the future and he'd get to try some for himself.

Will remembered in French lessons how French people enjoyed l'escargot and Cuisses de grenouille – snails and frogs' legs. He wasn't too sure about trying foreign food.

Joel then told Will about a few other advances that were prevalent in his time but seemed none existent in Will's. "There's robot type things that do a lot of the work that humans do; built things like cars and stuff. Robots do a lot of precision work, stuff that humans find hard to do. Some are just machines, programmed to do certain tasks. Others are a bit like humans and ......" Joel trailed off the sentence and quickly changed tack. He knew he shouldn't really talk about the future; but what harm could little snippets of information do? It's not as if in years to come Will would remember everything he had been told and even if he did, what difference would it make.

"People's houses are pretty much the same." He said. "It's not all that different really, just some stuff's different. Clothes are a bit different. Fashion apparently changes all the time. In my time people wear clothes with rips and tears and holes in." As an afterthought, he added. "Not everyone of course." He couldn't see his gran walking round in ripped jeans.

"Don't they sew them up when they get holes in?" Will said incredulous to such a thing.

"Oh they do, but these clothes they buy ripped," said Joel. "Holes and frays up the legs. I've got a pair of jeans with holes in the knees."

Will thought of the top that Joel gave him with the faded writing on that reminded Granfer of an old flour sack. Even the date was from decades ago. What sort of future was it where people had to buy clothes that were the sort of thing you'd give to the rag-man?

"There's still footy and speedway of course," Joel continued "but for some reason football's is more popular."

Will was still thinking about people walking around wearing ripped clothes; rather like street urchins. People's priorities seemed very different in the future. His mother would never let him go out in clothes with holes in, never mind buy them like that. He wasn't that bothered about football. It was something you played with your mates in the park. If you had clothes with holes in you'd wear them maybe for playing football, climbing trees or gardening, but not every-day wear. You could get famous playing football, but not nearly as famous as being a top speedway rider. He thought maybe football was more popular because it was an inexpensive sport to participate in? All you needed was a ball, some waste ground and as many lads as you wanted to knock it about, whereas in speedway you needed a motorbike, equipment, a track to race on and riders to race against. Likely after the war, with fuel rationing along with all the other forms of restrictions and cutbacks, people wouldn't be able to afford to rides speedway. Maybe that had something to do with the clothes with holes in and football being more popular.

"Does Jason Doyle wear clothes with holes in?" Asked Will. Surely superstars could afford to buy proper clothes he thought.

Joel thought for a while and then said, "I doubt it. He's too old for that. It's mainly young people who wear ripped clothes."

 Will wondered how old Jason Doyle was, he must be at least twenty-five if he wasn't young. He'd always imagined him to be about nineteen or twenty, with slicked back hair and a cigarette perpetually hanging from the corner of his mouth. He'd never imagined him as old as Cordy Milne. He was twenty-seven now. Saying that, Lionel Van Praag had been twenty-eight when he won the first speedway World Final in 1936.

"Codes are really important too," continued Joel, changing the subject. "People have codes too you know. It hasn't been discovered yet in your time, but it will be."

Will was rather sceptical at the idea of people being coded without them even knowing. It was things like this that made Will wonder if Joel was making the whole-time travel thing up. If he was though he was very good actor.

 "So, what does it look like this code thing. I mean, how can people have codes?"

Trying to think how to describe it, Joel said, "It's inside of you. You get half of it from your mother and half of it from your father. They get their halves from each of their parents – so you have a quarter of each of your grandparents' code, but half of your parents. It's complicated; each generation back you get a bit from each of your great grandparents."

Will couldn't understand that at all. "So where is this code stored then?" he asked. He pictured a person being cut open and having miniscule lettering throughout their body, rather like a stick of seaside rock.

"You can't see it," said Joel laughing. "It's inside all of your cells." He shook his head. "It's too complicated to explain; but it is there. I promise you. It's to do with how you get your eye and hair colour, your height and all that. It's all determined by your DNA."

"What's that?" questioned Will.

Joel thought for a while. "I don't know really. That's just what they call it."

They both lay there thinking about their own codes. Joel pictured the double helix diagrams he'd seen in a text book at school. It looked a bit like a winding staircase or one of those stunt kites he'd seen at the beach. Will pictured a blob filled with lots of tiny letters and numbers in miniature, that could only be seen under a microscope.

"This Jason Doyle you mentioned," said Will, changing the subject. "Is he World Champion in your time?"

"That's for you to find out," laughed Joel. Hoping and praying that in the next few weeks he would know for sure that he was. He pictured Jason standing on the podium at Melbourne holding aloft the 2017 World Speedway Champion trophy and the crowds cheering wildly as the riders sprayed each other in champagne to the sound of fireworks crack and pop all around them. In the post meeting interview Jason would thank his wife, his clubs, all his pit crew and sponsors for their support over the season, and then giving a special mention to Joel would say; "Yea, and I want to give a special mention to me young mate Joel. He keeps me focused. Cheers pal." He'd wink and give a thumb up sign to the camera.

"If Jason was around now he would be a real hero and he'd beat any rider you've ever seen, hands down. He'd win all the World Championship, Victoria Cross, Distinguished Flying Order and loads of other medals. Do you know; he's broken his neck twice, both times in track crashes. If it had been a millimetre either way it could have left him paralysed, but like he said, you can't live your life never taking risks. He refuses to change his lifestyle saying 'you never know when your time us up.' He's punctured his lung, broken his elbow, his shoulder; all sorts of injuries, but he never gives up. He's riding with a broken foot right now. It's got pins and things in it to hold it together."

This Jason Doyle did sound a pretty remarkable tough character thought Will. Maybe in the future people would be tougher. Maybe the war would make them that way; more resilient. He then looked at Joel who had already blubbed twice that evening and decided that couldn't be the case. Joel had mentioned about robots in the future; could Jason maybe be one of these robots?

"He rides all over," continued Joel. "Sweden, Poland, England, Denmark; everywhere. He can ride in a few different countries in one week. He's either on the road, in a plane or on his bike."

"He flies as well?" Will was impressed. Flying himself from meeting to meeting, likely in some small fixed winged biplane. Though how he got his bikes on-board he was unsure.

"He doesn't fly the planes himself," replied Joel, mockingly. "He's sits with all the other passengers, you know; businessmen, holiday makers?"

Will didn't know. Who went on holiday by aeroplane anyway? Certainly, nobody he knew. He then changed the subject. He wanted to know more about his hero. "Do you know if after the war, Cordy Milne becomes World Champion?" Surely Joel would know that?

"I'm not sure." Joel replied dismissively, he didn't really want to talk about 'after the war,' it made him feel uncomfortable. He was thinking of the coming weeks; he was in 1941, there was yet another four years until 'after the war.' The utter devastation that was soon to befall all the people around him now was his main concern. He doubted that this time next week, Will would give two hoots as to what Cordy Milne did after the war. These people here and now were the ones who mattered; Mr Roberts and Maggie doing their A.R.P work. Old Mrs Roberts and her nerves. Will and his school pals. Who of them he wondered, would be caught up in the utter carnage of the Plymouth Blitz?

"It was a long time ago in my time. "Joel hoped his answer would satisfy Will. "And it's not like I've got a magic box of answers." That was the biggest lie - he did; he had the access to the internet; a network of networks that all connected together and thus becoming the world-wide web, a highway of information. Joel could find the answer to many of Will's questions, but it would be wrong to do so. Like his Grandad had said; interfering with the past and its natural pattern of events would change the future.

Joel had read that Cordy Milne carried on racing through the early war years; in Australia and America. He'd married his second wife in 1940 in Australia, whilst racing there and as far as he could tell and appeared not to have participated in the war. The American's didn't officially join until 1943. Maybe Cordy had been given dispensation due to his mechanical skills being needed in his native Passadena? He read that Cordy had set up a business with his brother Jack, in their home town using the winnings from their racing careers; selling bicycles, then motorcycles and later cars. That made him feel rather sad for Will, as Will imagined Cordy to become the ultimate hero; winning the congressional medal of honour and then after the war, returning to win World Championship after World Championship. Life wasn't like that though, as he would soon find out.

The boys continued to talk late into the night. Will asking question after question about the future and Joel trying to answer as best he could, but at the same time being evasive. Some things he didn't think it mattered telling Will the truth about, as he wouldn't understand anyway. He did though give him a clue that really, he shouldn't have.

"There's a book. It was written a long time go in my time, maybe it's already been written or maybe it will be in the near future. It's called 1984, by George Orwell."

Will said wasn't sure if he'd heard of George Orwell or not.

Joel continued. "Mr Saunders, my English teacher, he says it's a scarily accurate view of our time."

"Are you from 1984," asked Will. Saying the words sounded strange to him – talking about a time, very far into the future.

"No," replied Joel. "I wasn't even born then. How do you see the future?" he asked Will, changing the subject slightly but genuinely interested to know. Will had to think, he'd never really thought about the future; one day just followed another.

"I suppose there'll be more machines and inventions like you said. Advances in medicine, like after the Great War. Bigger, faster cars, trains and ships. Big tall buildings like those in America, stuff like that....I don't know really."

Will then asked how many other time travellers there were, Joel answered honestly in that he didn't know. He didn't actually know if there were any others; but if he was capable of time travel, then he assumed lots of other people were too. It was just about finding a door to the past.

"Have you read 'The Time Machine' by H.G. Wells?" asked Will. Joel said that he hadn't and so Will proceeded to tell him the tale of an inventor, living in Victorian England, known throughout the book simply as the 'time traveller.' The story said Will, was about an inventor. During a discussion over dinner, he tells his guests that he had built a time machine. He shows the men gathered, a miniature time machine, the size of a clock, made of ivory and crystal. The inventor explains how one lever on the clock sends the machine into the future, and the other one sends it into the past. He encourages one of the guests to push the forward lever; the machine disappears. He then claims that the machine is now gliding forward into the future. The guests question why they can't see it, since they too are moving into the future, and the time traveller explains that it is moving forward too quickly to be seen, like the spokes of a wheel or a speeding bullet.

Joel interrupted and said "Crystal glass - like my lens."

Will paused and gave a look as though to say, 'this is my story. Please be quiet,' and then he continued.

"The time traveller then shows them a much larger machine, with which he plans to use to explore more areas of time. This machine he says, is capable of carrying a person through time. The guests of course think it's all a story, a clever, inventive and colourful story.

The following week the guests arrive for dinner and are instructed by the housekeeper to begin dinner without their host. When he does enter the room he's incredibly grubby and dishevelled. Some of the guests joke that he's been travelling in time, others are dubious and make sarcastic remarks. The time traveller goes off to clean himself up and when he returns, tells them an incredible story. He tells them of the dizzying sensation of moving forward in time. Pushing the lever on his machine forward and then forward a bit more – travelling further and further into the future. Night and day beginning to fly by in rapid succession. Soon his laboratory and house disappear. He can see the hazy outline of buildings. The suns path moving up and down in the sky with the passing seasons. He deicides it's time to stop and slowly pulls the lever to slow the machine down. The first thing he sees is a giant statue of a white sphinx on a bronze pedestal. He begins to wonder what man may have evolved into. He sees large buildings, and people wearing rich robes. They speak in a strange tongue, not really words, but more like sounds. They seem free of fear, lazy and lacking intelligence. He puts the control knob from the lever on his time machine into his pocket, so that no one else can use it."

Will, realising the story could go on for a very long time, decided to cut it short.

"The time traveller tells his dinner guests of him of him saving Weena, one of the people he befriends, from drowning. She was from a race called the Eloi. He then comes across some ape like creatures who steal his time machine. They were called Morlocks and lived underground. He realises the only way to recover his time machine is to enter into the world of the Morlocks. He discovers they are frightened of fire and he sets alight a number of fires in their underground caves. After some time, the Morlocks unlock the secret door on the sphinx where they had hidden his machine. He guesses they plan to trap him by closing the door once he is inside. As he enters the door shuts behind him, just as he had suspected. The Morlocks pounce, and he jumps into the seat of the machine, screwing on the forward lever that he had kept in his pocket so that no-one lese could fly the machine. He pushes it forward. He travels further on into the future, eventually stopping 30 million years ahead of where he began. He then puts the machine into reverse and arrives back in his own time, telling his guests he had returned, just three hours after he had originally left. To prove he was telling the truth he produced as evidence, two strange white flowers Weena had put in his pocket.

His friends discussed the flowers, not being ones, they were familiar with. The following day one of his friends returns to his house and finds the time traveller preparing to go on another journey into the future. He promises he won't be gone long, no more than half an hour His friend waits. His housekeeper looks after the house – but after three years he still hadn't returned."

"Not a bad story," said Joel. "But it is only a story. You'd combust long before you reached speeds that fast." He then started talking about something called 'Time and relative dimension in space' – TARDIS for short. He told Will how scientist had been researching for years, black holes, worm holes, traversing time and the like. There were secret Military installations where they experimented on things and people, de-materialising in one place and re-materialising in another. There was the quantum theory, which was just that – a theory; the idea that alternate histories and futures were real and possible, though in a parallel world.

Will thought it all amazing, but how if Joel was from a long time into the future, were things still so similar? Could they be actually living side by side, right now – but in a parallel world. Joel said he didn't think so as the things that were happening in Will's time were recorded in history and so couldn't be parallel, they had to be in the past.

Will was relentless with his questioning. He queried as to whether Joel could possibly be being used as a guinea pig by the intelligence service his dad worked for? Had he been sent into the past to change things so that the history people read about and remember happening in the past did happen, but only because of Joel's intervention? It sounded a pretty plausible explanation to him. Joel, in all his innocence had conveniently been sent to Plymouth to stay, and his dad giving him the radar tracking thing on the pretence they were using it to test its accuracy, when in fact it was for something very different. That had to be the answer!

Only it couldn't be true, as Joel's dad didn't really work for the intelligence services or the Military and he'd never brought his mobile phone 'radar thing' with him again since Will had caught him trying to take photographs with it. Joel explained the 'radar thing' was something everyone would have and it wasn't tracking him... well, not in the past anyway. The technology hadn't been invented to do that. Will was rather disappointed, but as Joel explained, a lot of things wouldn't make sense and that's why he didn't talk about them.

Will noticed Joel used the words 'like' and 'so' a lot when he talked, he seemed to add it into sentences randomly.

Joel talked about his own time in the future. Saying how people took photographs all the time, it was a huge hobby. People took cameras with them everywhere and took snaps of just about anything they found interesting or amusing. There was a popular thing called a 'selfie' because it was a picture of one's self. Will thought that really silly to waste so much film.

"Have you got a camera," asked Joel. Will said his dad had one, but it rarely got used. Joel had an idea. He asked Will to find it and suggested that the next time he visit, he would bring the money to buy a film and would give Will the money to have the film developed later on. Will thankfully didn't question why 'later on.' Joel remembered his dad saying that cameras used to use 'film' whatever that was and that it had to be sent off to be developed.

"People still eat fish and chips" said Joel, feeling a little more confident. "To be honest they have chips with everything. There's crinkle cut chips, triple fried chips, frozen chips, chunky chips, sweet potato chips, skinny chips, beer battered chips, oven chips, micro chips, nano chips, LED chips. The world in my time relies on chips." They both began laughing. Joel was telling the truth, but not in a way his friend would understand. Will thought it odd that future generations would rely on something as simple as chips – and so many variations.

"Can you bring me a cigarette card of Jason Doyle," asked Will, changing the subject.

"They don't make cigarette cards in the future," laughed Joel. "Smoking's bad for you. Instead they put pictures of diseased hearts and lungs on the packets."

Will thought that grotesque, but still implored Joel bring him back a picture of Jason Doyle. Joel had to think about it but didn't really see the harm in it. No one would know who Jason Doyle was anyway. He wouldn't be born for a very long time yet, so one photograph wouldn't affect the course of history in any way. He had after all, seen pictures of Will's speedway hero's.

"Something I can tell you about the future though," said Joel sounding most adamant. "Don't let the Corporation take your flippin' railings. They don't use them to make Spitfires. They'll bury them in a dump down by the wharves, or out at sea. I swear it, I read about it."

Will found that a little unbelievable, as the Government had already removed thousands of tons of decorative ironwork and railings from British streets, supposedly for re-cycling into munitions and the war effort. They were also encouraging people to give up aluminium pots, pans.

"It's all propaganda. It's to make people believe they're helping the war effort. They'll recycle the aluminium and copper and bits of shrapnel, but not your railings, they'll just dump them," insisted Joel.

The boys lay down, and eventually fell asleep, not long after midnight. Thankfully there were no air raids or alerts and they slept until seven a.m. when the alarm clocks' loud 'bringggg' jolting them awake. The bedroom was cold, unlike the centrally heated rooms Joel was used to. Will let him borrow a pullover and they made their way downstairs. He didn't like having to use the outside 'lav' either, but as no one else complained he wasn't going to make a fuss. The boys had to wash in a bowl, filled with water, heated up in the kettle with Maggie Roberts brought up for them. He noticed the soap was the same as him mum used, a sort of clear brownly coloured bar with 'Pears' imprinted in the…. well, whatever it was made of – it gave him a comfortable feeling of home. When he asked if Will had any toothpaste, he received the reply, "Got tooth powder?"

Will offered Joel a small round metal pot of pink coloured powder that smelled of antiseptic. Joel was unsure of what to do with it – put it in water and drink it, dab it on his teeth? He watched as Will dabbed the bristles of his wooden handled toothbrush in it and began rubbing it on his teeth. Joel hadn't a toothbrush with him, so licked his finger, dabbed it in the powder and rubbed it on his teeth. It didn't taste too bad; it had a sort of mild liquorice taste to it – but he definitely preferred toothpaste. He felt his adventure was rather like camping; but indoors. He'd been camping a few times in the past, but there'd always been a nice warm shower block and toilets with soft toilet paper.

They brought their clothes downstairs and held them in front of the kitchen range to warm up before putting them on. At 7.25, after a bite of jam on toast and a cup of tea, the boys made their way back to the railway sidings. The found the old sofa easily enough, also their discarded newspaper chip wrappers shoved down the side of one of the arms. Joel feel rather guilty at having left them there but didn't attempt to take them out and discard them properly – he had more important things on his mind.

They both got down on their hands and knees and checked the over the sofa, then under it, and then slowly working their way around it, widening their circle as they crawled anti-clockwise. After having covered ten feet of ground away from the sofa and with very wet knees they'd found nothing. Will suggested they try to work out where they were when they had the fight. They both carried on crawling stealthily across the cold wet grass and down the slope towards the railway track. Will thought he had found the lens, but it was a fragment of broken glass, probably from a bottle thrown from a passing train.

Finally, after a cold twenty, wet and fraught minutes Will held the lens aloft, catching the early morning rays of sunshine. They both cheered and embraced each other. Joel carefully took the lens from him and squeezed its cold exterior tightly in the palm of his hand. Checked there was no damage to it and then thrust it deep into the safety of his pocket.

"So what happens now then?" Asked Will.

"I'll go back to my time and come back again soon I suppose." Joel knew that he had to come back soon, the Blitz was imminent and he couldn't afford to miss it. Neither for himself or for Will. It was an experience he would (hopefully) never have again and also, he felt it imperative he kept his friend away from the devastation that was about to claim so many lives.

Will suddenly said "If that lens is your portal into the past, my time. How was it last night when you didn't have it with you, you were able to stay in the now time and come back into the now time this morning, without going back into your time."

Joel had to think about that for a while How was he able to go through the portal, but stay in the past without the lens? The conclusion he came to, was that because the lens was still in the past then he was also stuck in the past. If he had gone back to Will's and someone had thrown the lens through the portal, then he would have been stuck forever, in the past. If on the other hand, he had thrown it through the portal from the future, he would have been stuck in his own time forever and unable to return to the past. Both boys agreed this hypothesis was probably right. They returned to Will's house, as this was the only entry and exit point Joel knew to the past. Will asked if he could come back with Joel 'even just for a minute?' Joel felt this really would be playing dangerously; but if it was only for a minute, he couldn't see there being too much harm caused. Who would believe Will anyway?

They both entered the house, Will went to his room to change for school. Joel waited by the door anxious and excited at what they were about to do. Even when they were about the leave, Will still felt it was likely to be some kind of a joke. He took hold of Joel's arm, as Joel had done to him on previous occasions. They stepped forward; Joel felt the weird heady sensation as did Will.

CHAPTER ELEVEN

Will looked all around him in wonder. He blinked a few times and his mouth dropped open like a guppy fish. "Wow," he said in astonishment. "It's still nineteen bleddy forty-one!" He turned around to challenge Joel, but there was no one there to hear him.

Joel found himself back in 2017 and on his own. He looked around but couldn't see Will. He was disappointed but assumed Will must have seen him vanish. What more proof did he need than that? He was tempted to step back in to the doorway but decided not to. Will would now surely believe, and anyway and he had no idea how long he had been away; Gran might be frantic. He dashed along the street, crossed the bridge and back down Gran's road. He entered the gate and rang the doorbell. Gran answered and appeared rather unconcerned at his lateness but queried is dirty clothing. "We had a game of football, I fell over, that's all."

Joel was getting good at the white lies now. He wasn't particularly keen that he was telling them, but because they were a necessity, they didn't really feel they were dishonesties – more requirements.

Gran said he had just missed lunch, but she could make him a toasted sandwich if he wanted. Whilst she was busy in the kitchen, Joel began to draw up his strategy for the coming days. He had to ensure he could stay in 1941 for at least 48 hours. He couldn't risk coming back and then returning in the middle of an air raid.

He began checking the dates and times of the raids over Plymouth. He then set up Grandads' printer and using some photo paper, printed off a few pictures from his mobile phone. One of Mum, Dad and Tabby; taken by himself at Dawlish last summer, also a picture of Gran and Grandad taken only days ago. A colour picture of Jason Doyle he'd found online for Will, and finally one of him and Marley – a selfie, taken on a school trip the previous year.

Gran said she wanted to pop into town and made it quite obvious she wanted Joel's company. He felt he couldn't really say no, he had asked his parents if he could stay longer to actually spend time with her and Grandad. It wouldn't be fair if he said he had other things to do.

As they walked to the bus stop Joel pointed out the shrapnel damage on the side of some houses. When Gran asked how he knew it was caused by shrapnel, he said that Will had told him. She smiled to herself; this Will boy sounded just like Joel she thought, full of imagination. She just couldn't understand why he hadn't brought him round to meet her.

Joel had brought his backpack, just in case he saw anything he may feel necessary to take back to 1941 with him. He did in fact buy a woolly hat which he saw in a sale bin for £3. Gran asked why on earth he wanted a woolly hat in the middle of August, but he said as she didn't know much about fashion it wasn't worth trying to explain. They then stopped off in a department store cafeteria. Gran had coffee and Joe had coke and a cake.

"Gran," said Joel.

Gran fully aware of what his tone of voice indicated, looked at him over her glasses and waited for him to continue.

"Will's family have asked if I can go on a day trip with them tomorrow. I said I'd ask. They're going to Padstow in Cornwall and I really want to go. Please Gran," he pleaded.

Gran sighed and said he would have to phone and ask his mum and if she said yes, then she would agree to it. She took her mobile phone from her handbag and called Joel's mum.

"Hello, Jenny, it's Anna……."

The chatted and chatted and Joel got bored waiting for Gran to ask the important question. He'd long finished his drink and cake and Gran still hadn't asked about the day trip to Padstow. Eventually the subject was brought up. His Mum was obviously asking all sorts of questions about Will, as Gran mention something about not having met him yet. Joel gestured to her to pass the phone over. He then proceeded to tell his mum what a wonderful time he was having and how 'ace' his new friend was. Eventually, after what seemed one hundred questions, Mum agreed to his day trip, as long as he phoned her as soon as he got home.

The rest of the trip round town with Gran was uneventful but interesting. He took note of what he may need to take back to 1941 with him, spending a good twenty minutes looking around a camping shop, while

Gran went clothes shopping. He picked up a neck scarf that matched the colour the woolly hat he had purchased earlier. Neither would save him from bombs and burning buildings, but somehow that added bit of protection made him feel a little safer – and they would keep him warm. He was tempted to buy some Kendall mint cake he saw stacked up by the till. He'd seen it advertised as being popular with explorers and mountaineers – due to its high sugary energy value. He decided that taking a few chocolate bars back with him would tastier, cheaper and more enjoyable. He purchased those at a newsagent's shop, along with a bottle of water. Everything else he needed he felt he had already, or at least Will likely would.

Once home, Joel offered to water the plants in the courtyard for Gran, whilst she put her shopping away. He enjoyed being in the pretty courtyard filled with flowers. He smelled the relatively clean air – there were traffic fumes and the light aroma of the sea, but nothing bad. So very different to Will's world where the industrial smells overwhelmed at times. Seagulls squawked overhead; that hadn't changed. More than likely descended from the birds that stole from the Barbican fish market and boats in 1941 were flying overhead now - never having to move further afield in search of food.

He listened to the traffic trundling along the busy road that ran along the culvert behind the house. From Will's courtyard, he had watched goods trains puffing smoke, and making their way along the same culvert; not a car in sight.

"Gran," called Joel through the open kitchen window. By the tone of his voice, she knew there would likely follow a multitude of questions.

"Yes Joel," she sighed.

"Did you know the road behind your house used to be a railway line?" He called through the window. Gran continued to put away her groceries. "Yes, I did, but that was before we moved here. We moved here when your dad and your aunties were small. We lived upstairs, the house was two flats back then. We used the same communal hallway and the courtyard with the old couple who lived downstairs – Mr and Mrs Morris, they'd lived here for years, all through the war I think – with four kiddies, all cramped into the downstairs flat. They moved away; bought a bungalow somewhere, with views over the moors."

Gran having finished putting away her shopping, came out into the courtyard and joined Joel. She sat on the wrought iron bench Grandad had renovated after having bought it from a scrapyard – frame minus wooden slates. She put up her hand up to protect her eyes from the sun, having left her sunglasses indoors.

"The downstairs flat was empty for months – needed lots of work doing on it and the Landlord didn't want to spend the money. After six months of it sitting empty, your grandad put in an offer, a good price considering how much work it needed doing on it. The landlord accepted and Jim was in his element, he spent the next goodness knows how many years hammering, chiselling, sanding, painting, pulling down and putting up."

Joel now having watered the plants, came and sat next to Gran.

"Did you have two bathrooms?" queried Joel, wondering where the downstairs bathroom had once been, or had it been like Will's house with only an outside loo.

"Oh no," said Gran, still shading her eyes with her hand from the sun. "It was pretty primitive. We had a bathroom, it had been put in before we moved here. Mr and Mrs Morris, they just had the outside loo, well, two as there was one for each flat. I remember we used to let them borrow our bathroom every Tuesday night, so they could have a bath. They thought it a real luxury they did!" Gran laughed. "Your Grandads' done a lot of work on the house since then of course. The kitchen," she nodded towards the kitchen. "That's where the outhouse was. For months, we still used the kitchen upstairs. We then had the upstairs one ripped out and made it into a bedroom for Darren, your dad, and had a new bathroom put in. The kiddies all slept in the same bedroom for months while the work went on.

Joel wondered about Mr and Mrs Morris, he wondered if he had over come across them in during his time travels. He knew Will had met Mrs Morris, when he had gone calling for Joel and she said she'd never heard of him.

"Did either of them ever mention the war, you know, whether the house got bombed or anything?"

Gran thought for a while. "I remember Mrs Morris saying the whole area was badly bombed. Quite a few houses had to be pulled down because the damage was beyond repair. I'm sure she said every house suffered some sort of damage.

"So what happened to the Gas company and the railway lines, were they bombed?" Joel need to know answers. His question took Gran by surprise. How did he know about the Gas company? But of course, his friend Will lived with his grandparents and they probably told him what the area used to be like.

"You're probably better off asking your friends grandparents if they've lived here longer than us," Said Gran. "I remember in the early 1980's the council decided to demolish a lot of houses and build a new road. They put a compulsory purchase order on a lot of houses at the top of our street, Will's street and a number of houses on the other side of the new dual carriageway. A lot of the houses that had been left standing after the war, over the way." She pointed towards the area that now looked so different from Will's time. They wanted to pull then down and build industrial units. They then put the road in; behind our house, the old railway line. They built a footbridge over the new road. I remember your Grandad being livid at one point, because he thought our house might have become part of the programme and be pulled down too".

"The war didn't destroy it all then?" asked Joel, needing reassurance.

"No," said Gran. "It's progress, things have to change and move on. Look at that wonderful cinema and leisure complex we have now. Used to a smelly horrible gas and coal yard."

As much as Joel had to agree it was nice to have a cinema and leisure complex nearby, he did prefer the 1940's era. He didn't know why, he just did.

They went indoors and Gran poured them both a glass of lemonade and offered Joel a packet of crisps. They went back outside and returned to the wrought iron bench. This time Gran had remembered her sunglasses.

"I remember a lovely lady called Edna, I used to often bump into her when I was out with the children in their pushchairs. She lived on Brunswick Road. The council told her they wanted her out and offered her some measly amount to buy her out. In a right state about it, she was. Her family had lived in that house since before the war. It had withstood the German bombs, when many of the houses around were destroyed and here was the council wanting to pull it down in the name of progress! Her husband had a stroke and died not long after. They put it down to the stress they were living under. Poor fella. Edna carried on the fight, but she was forced to accept their offer in the end. She could have taken them to court but it would have been at her expense and she would have lost out anyway." Gran sighed. "Lovely lady she was. I don't know what happened to her after that. Moved away; to be near her daughter I think."

Joel knew Brunswick Road, he'd walked along it a number of times with Will.

"Is that the road with the newsagents on the corner?" he asked. Gran said she couldn't remember. Joel tried to think, he remembered a lady with the two little boys. Will said it was Aunt Ellen's friend. "Edna, did she live at number four?"

"I think she did you know," replied Gran, sounding rather shocked. They both sat silently drinking their lemonade and listening to next doors radio, which filtered out of the open back door. Gran wondering how on earth Joel could have known which house Edna lived at, and Joel, thinking it such a shame that all those lovely houses were pulled down, all in the name of progress.

After tea Joel had a long soak in the bath, he still ached a little from the tussle he'd had with Will. Thankfully his fat lip had gone down quickly. He'd rung his Mum and Dad, and then shad a few words with Tabby.

It was close to midnight when he finally fell into bed. He had checked, packed, unpacked, re-checked and again packed his back pack for the following day – his Blitz survival pack. There were chocolate bars, some toffees, a bottle of water, the catapult Will had made him, notebook, pencil. A hand drawn map of the local area and a small torch, as well as the woolly hat, scarf and an extra jumper in navy blue.

The following morning Joel awoke at 8.20 a.m. He'd gotten used to the long lie-ins, but he wanted to make the most of today. With Military planning, he double checked his backpack. He also wrote a letter for his family telling them how much he loved them and that if he didn't come home, then not to worry too much. He told the truth about his time travelling experience and that he very well was likely stuck in 1941 due to the bombings but would hopefully find a way back soon. If he didn't return after a few days then he had possibly been killed in 1941 and they should look on the Commonwealth War Graves site for civilian casualties, to see if his name was listed there. He'd previously checked the site himself and his name wasn't on it; which was a good sign – but as he was now meddling with the past and changing it; that possibly meant nothing. He put the letter in his bedside drawer and just prayed Gran didn't go poking about before his return. He also deliberately left his mobile phone on the bed, on silent – making it look as though he'd just forgotten to pick it up.

At 9.15 he was ready to go. He told Gran not to expect him back for tea, it would be early evening at least before they got back. He said he would see her later on and gave her a tighter hug than usual. Gran gave him two £10 notes for spending money, as he'd need to buy lunch and probably want an ice-cream. Joel knew the money wasn't going to be of any use to him where he was going, but a trip to the Co-Op on the way did mean he could buy some supplies to take with him. He gave Muffin a last pat on the head and set off. He walked up the road as usual, crossed the bridge and carried on, through the park and to the local Co-Op. There he bought another bottle of water, two packs of sandwiches, and a family sized bag of crisps. He squeezed them all into his back pack and headed off to Will's house.

Before entering the gate, he inspected the iron railings on the garden wall. They were fairly modern, as were all the others in the street. He felt a sense of disappointment, that Will had not talked his granfer into heeding his advice about not allowing the Corporation to take their railings away. Then again, they could have been changed any time after the war. It had been over seventy years after all. He then stepped through the gate and the into the sponginess of the time portal.

The front door was locked. He assumed they'd gone out, but just as he was about to turn around and leave, a stranger came in the gate behind him. "Hallo Sonny, didn't see ya there. Nice morning." He bent over and placed a bottle of milk by the front door, and at the same time, picked up two empties. Joel heard a snorting sound, which made him jump. He turned to see a horse, which neighed and clomped his feet on the cobbled road, eager to get on with his route. Joel watched as the milkman, dressed in white coat and wearing a cap, rather like a modern-day policeman's, make his way along the road. The horse and cart stopping at each house where he was to make a delivery.

Joel pondered on how it was he was able to travel back to the past without any interference from it. His portal was the lens combined with Will's front path; he'd worked that out. But why was he only able to stay in the past when he left the house by holding on to another person? Was that origin of the saying 'holding on to the past' – surely not? Why was 'this' particular spot a portal to the past? What was the connection between the glass lens and that exact spot? Were there other portals that he could inadvertently walk through and find himself transported to another time in history? He had previously checked out the longitude and latitude of the exact spot by typing them into an internet search engine, in hope of finding some anomaly such as an ancient ley-line but came up with nothing.

His thoughts wandered from what Marley was up to in Scotland and if he was now in the car and on his way to Edinburgh. Marley had texted the previous night to say he was off to Edinburgh in the morning and was hoping to visit both the castle and the zoo. Joel had texted Marley and Ben just before he left Gran's to wish them and entertaining day in whatever they were doing and to say he wouldn't be contactable as he was off to the Blitz. He said he was scared but excited and would tell them about it on his return. He knew Marley didn't believe him and responded all his messages about the war with either a joke or ignored them all together. Today's response reflected his scepticism. Marley simply said 'Hope you have a blast!' followed by some 'bomb' emoji's. Ben hadn't replied by the time Joel left his phone on the bed. He was likely still asleep.

He wondered what Jason Doyle was up to; possibly he'd woken up early, around 5 a.m. in preparation of catching an early morning flight to a meeting somewhere in Europe.

What was his great grandma, a girl younger than himself, was doing right now? She really was in this very city right now, living through the war. He wished he could go and visit his great-great grandparents. Just to see them, he didn't want to interfere in the past and speak to them. He remembered what his grandad had said about the grandfather theory.

He watched as people and the occasional workman's lorry drove past, all just getting on with their business. A double decker bus painted battleship grey with wire mesh covering the windows drove by. It stopped further up the road and a number of people got on. He wondered why it had the metal covering over the windows and assumed they must be in case of a bomb blast. A man pushing a barrow with a long wooden ladder tied to it strode by; he was whistling away. Joel pondered over his occupation and assumed a builder or possibly a window cleaner. He'd noticed a lot of people whistled during the war. It wasn't something he heard much in his own time.

A boy, probably aged about ten, stopped at the gate, he was just about to open it when he saw Joel. He handed a newspaper towards him. Joel stepped forward to take it but knew he couldn't venture further than the sponginess without stepping back into his own time.

"Just chuck it," he said to the boy.

"A'right," replied the paper boy, and threw it swiftly towards Joel. He then carried on to the next house on his round. Joel looked at the newspaper. It was the Western Morning News, dated 20th[th] March 1941. He had timed it well; today was the day he had been eager to return to – the first day of the Blitz of Plymouth. He sat on the doorstep and flicked through the paper. It was quite vague about the war and bombings, but then he supposed maybe it had to be due to spies passing on information. After a while he got a little bored, he didn't want to have Mrs Roberts or Maggie finding him sitting on their door step, so he posted the paper through the letter box and stepped towards the gate and back into 2017. The street was very different, packed with cars and different smells. He rather preferred 1941, it somehow had an innocent mystery about it. People appeared much friendlier, chattier and lived at a slower pace. They didn't walk around with their faces glued to a smartphone or walk around talking to an unseen friend many miles away through an ear piece attached to their mobile phone.

The street was crammed with parked cars on either side. He watched as five people walked past and not one acknowledged him. He felt invisible, but that was good because he was only passing time. He turned around and was just about to go back to 1941 when the driver from a delivery lorry that had pulled up outside entered the gate and knocked on the door.

"Hello sonny. Is your mum in?"

"Er, I don't live here." Said Joel, as he stepped back on to the footpath. A tall dark-haired lady opened the front door. She looked friendly enough and smiled when she made eye contact with the driver. Joel watched as his mate began to unload something from the back of the lorry. The driver then went to help him and Joel stood at the gate, holding it open for them to carry in whatever it was they had to deliver.

"Are you Mrs Stanfield," asked Joel, noticing the lady watching him with amusement. He assumed her to be his gran's friend, the lady he was supposed to have delivered the quiche to.

"I am," she replied laughing. "Who's asking?"

"I'm Joel Armstrong. You know my gran." He looked past Mrs Stanfield and into the hallway of the house. The vestibule had pretty blue wallpaper. Further up the hall the staircase was painted white. Will's house had different tiling and wallpaper and the staircase was painted a light green colour. He thought Will would be rather impressed how an owner in the future had obviously looked after the house. He paused to let the delivery men carry in a dark wood wardrobe. The lady stepped outside on crutches and let them through.

He couldn't help himself. "There used to be wooden panelling and tiles in your porch. Yellow and green flowery ones; sunflowers."

Mrs Stanfield smiled and said there hadn't been any tiles on the wall when she moved in. Joel started chatting to her about how the houses looked in the 1940's; the green or brown painted woodwork and real fires instead of central heating. He asked if she still had an outside loo, and she laughed out loud. One of the delivery men then called her away. She made her excuses and said she had to go, but it had been nice talking to him. Joel wondered if he could maybe get Gran to take him round to visit her house? Without the lens in his pocket he would easily be able to visit Will's house in 2017.

Mrs Stanfield retreated into the house on her crutches but left the door open. Joel wondered what would happen if he stepped inside – would it be 2017 or 1941? He bravely entered the gate and walked towards the front door. The delivery men, having offloaded their goods were now making their way towards him along the hallway…. and then he saw Mrs Roberts. The kitchen door was open and she was busy with a large pan on the stove, a box of 'Sylvan Flakes' sat open nearby. "Hello Mrs Roberts, something smells good," he called out. Announcing his presence.

Mrs Roberts began chuckling and replied, "If you like long johns then you're welcome to try some." She picked up a pair of wooden tongs and lifted a steaming pair of long-johns from the pan. "Boiling Charlie's underwear." Mrs Roberts didn't know if Joel had a wicked sense of humour or was just a bit daft, but he certainly made her smile with some of the things he came out with.

Joel had no idea why she would do such a thing as boil underwear, but had learned not to ask questions about the peculiarities of what people did in the past. Maybe Mr Roberts had lice, like the soldiers got in the First World War. Why she was adding Sylvan Flakes he had no idea, or maybe she'd just had them for breakfast and hadn't yet put them away?

Maggie came out from the parlour room with Aunt Ellen, they were dressed in outdoor clothing and chattering enthusiastically. Maggie said she's received a letter from her husband that morning saying his ship, the newly commissioned HMS HECLA was at present patrolling the Scottish coastline hunting down enemy submarines. Well, he hadn't exactly said that; but they had worked out his coded message, so that she would know where he was when he wrote home. It had been Will's idea to use cryptic words that only they would understand. Apparently, a lot of Military personnel did it.

They were laden with items they had collected from friends, family and neighbours, and were about to take to the Red Cross collection centre. As Will was still at school and Joel wasn't, they asked if he'd like to help them, as it would be a struggle for them to carry it all themselves. He felt he couldn't really refuse, as it's not like he had school as he'd previously told them he was being 'home schooled.'

The three of them set off on foot, loaded with no longer needed clothing and household items; much of it reluctantly given up, but forfeited knowing the money raised from the sale would be of great use towards gifts for prisoners of war and soldiers, sailors and airmen abroad. Joel held onto Ellen's coat as they left the house. She gave him a funny look but said nothing. He found his load cumbersome but refused to leave his backpack at Will's house in case Mrs Roberts decided to take a nosey inside.

As they walked they chatted, Maggie mentioned about having two days off and not looking forward to returning for an early turn on the buses Saturday – she was tired and just felt like having a whole day in bed, but there was too much to do.

"What time is it Mrs Roberts?" he asked.

"Must be about nine forty-five I think, why?" she said.

"Do you think we can get word to Will – it's really important." Joel knew it was more than that, it was imperative. Maggie Roberts said Will would be home from school at lunchtime, if it could wait till then.

During his research, Joel had found out that on that day, 20th March 1941, the Blitz of Plymouth had begun. The King and Queen had visited Plymouth and even more importantly they had taken a car to Cattedown and stopped at the bottom of Will's street, where they had dismounted and gone on a short walk, viewing damaged properties and chatting locals who had suffered in the previous bombings. That meant they, including himself, had a good chance of actually meeting the King and Queen!

Joel wasn't sure how to address Ellen. Whether to call her Ellen, Auntie Ellen, Mrs – he didn't know her surname. He looked at her and said "Can you tell your people to come over by 2 o'clock? I promise it's not a wind up, I'm deadly serious; and tell them to wear their best clothes."

Joel had noticed how when he was in the 1940's Will's family rather than referring to their family as 'family' – would call them their 'people.' The women both looked at each other. "Not until you tell us what's going on," said Ellen, a little concerned.

"I can't say much, but I've heard there's some dignitaries are coming to look at the damaged houses in your street. The Western Morning News are coming along too, to take photographs."

The women both looked at each other again questioningly, unsure if to believe Joel or not. He was an odd sort, that was for definite, but he seemed sincere in what he said.

"Who told you this then?" Maggie said laughing. "Why would dignitaries want to come to our street?"

"My grandad, he knows a reporter from the paper – got told last night," he fibbed excitedly. "Honest, you might get your picture in the paper!"

Joel was getting good at sounding truthful – probably because it was the truth, only not 100% but still the truth; in an indirect way.

The three of them quickened their pace, they dropped off their collections and Ellen then headed off to catch a bus to where her husband Des worked, to tell him about the newspaper photographer. Maggie and Joel headed home, it was now Joel felt he should tell her the truth.

"I don't want you to get excited Mrs Roberts, but I've heard on the 'hush hush' that the King and Queen are arriving by Royal train at Millbay station at 10.30. They're going to be met by the Lord and Lady Mayoress and then going on a visit of the Naval establishments, inspect the troops and meeting lots of other dignitaries. After lunch, they're going to the Guildhall to meet people from the W.V.S, St John's Ambulance, the Red Cross and a few other organisations."

As soon as Joel said the Red Cross, Maggie remembered the excited flurry at the depot. People seemed pre-occupied and there was lots of chatter. One lady in particular; in uniform, was busy hurrying people along and making sure everything was 'spick and span.'

"Like I said," he continued smugly. "I can't say too much."

Joel hung around the Roberts front door, popping in and out of 1941 and 2017 every few seconds, until he heard Will voice coming from the hallway and knew it must be lunchtime. He knocked on the door and popped his head in, as though he'd just strolled by on the off chance. Will invited him in and Joel explained the impending Royal visit that afternoon and implored they get a film for his dad's camera. Joel offered Will three shillings – he had no idea how much a film and processing would cost but assumed that would cover it. He had asked his grandad how people got their pictures printed in the old days, because he couldn't understand how you could print a film. His grandad had said something about taking the roll of film to a photographers or chemist shop and they would either develop it there in a dark room or send it off. You could send them in the post to and get your pictures back in the post a couple of weeks later. He'd briefly told Joel about the developing process, but it didn't make much sense.

The boys hurriedly set off to buy a film from a photography shop and with some help from Mr Roberts, Will put it into his Dad's camera. Joel, never having used a proper camera before, eagerly took the camera from Will and took a picture of him. He then discovered the camera wouldn't work when he tried to take a second picture.

 "You haven't wound it on," said Will. He showed Joel how the camera worked. It seemed a bit strange to Joel that you had to 'wind it on' after every picture and you couldn't see what picture you'd taken either. Will looked at Joel like he was stupid and explained you couldn't see the pictures until the film was developed. Joel was disappointed as he'd hoped to take lots of pictures, but the film apparently only allowed for twelve images to be taken.

It was a lovely sunny afternoon, spring was definitely in the air. Word of the Royal visit had somehow got around and small clusters of people had begun to gather on Elliot Road, where the King's car was due to travel along. Some people were there because they were 'in the know' or whose presence had been requested; those whose houses had been badly damaged. Others out of curiosity. A few women were still wearing their indoor wrap-around aprons, having only to come out to see what all the commotion was.

In the distance, they saw two cars approach, the leading one with the Royal Insignia on its bonnet. The street was now lined with curious faces. As the car neared, the crowds began to cheer and Union flags were waved in the air.

"Where's your gran, I thought she'd be here?" asked Mrs Roberts, looking around for an unfamiliar face.

"She's had to go, my grandad too. Aunt Jane's taken bad again."

The cars stopped and first to alight were Lord and Lady Astor, followed by the King and Queen. They nodded and smiled and began walking towards the gathered throng. The King was in his Naval uniform and looked incredibly smart. The Queen, who was smaller than Joel had imagined, wore a royal-blue coat and matching hat, which sort of sat upright and sideways on her head. She wore fur cuffs that came up to her elbows and delicate grey coloured leather gloves. As she came nearer to where he and the Roberts family were standing, he noticed the multiple string of pearls she wore around her neck and the pretty silver brooch, with real white and pink flowers sticking out from the top. They were the sort of thing his Queen in his time would wear. It then registered with him that the lady he was looking at was the mother of his Queen - Queen Elizabeth. He looked around to see if the then young Princess Elizabeth was with them; sadly, she wasn't.

Will Nudged Joel and asked him to take a photograph of him with the King in the background. They then swapped places and Will took a picture of Joel smiling at the camera with both the King and Queen behind him. They were chatting to a lady holding a small child. Joel took the camera back off Will and took another two more discreet photographs; Mr and Mrs Roberts, Maggie, Des and Ellen, all in shot; ensuring he got either the King or Queen in the background.

As the King came nearer, Joel was just about to take another photograph when a policeman stopped him. "No photographs sonny. Only official photographers." Joel felt disappointed, but luckily, he had been able to take a few pictures without being noticed.

There was a small group of individuals assembled, who had obviously been invited to be presented to the King and Queen. An official looking young Naval officer was having words with them and telling them where to stand.

"Word 'as it, they've all been bombed out or at least suffered considerable damage," said Mr Roberts. He had been reliably informed by Wally Thomas, who was also an A.R.P warden and knew one of the women in the small gathering.

As they Royal couple neared, the King caught sight of Mr Roberts, who had insisted in going along in his blue dungarees and tin hat.

"Ah, you must be the air-raid warden," enquired the King. He stood with his hands behind his back and looked Mr Roberts up and down. "Were you on duty and did you have a bad time during the raids?"

Granfer answered to the affirmative and said "We're British and we'll stick it out, keep our chins up too." He then nodded towards Eadie. "This is my 'ere wife. She's 'ad no gas, no 'lectric, but still manages to keep the 'ouse runnin' an' the family fed."

The King nodded his approval. "This gentleman," he said, turning towards the Queen, who had now joined him. "Said his wife has had no means of cooking or washing, but still managed to keep the family fed."

The Queen proffered her hand to Eadie, who took it and curtseyed at the same time. Joel really wanted to take a picture but knew he'd likely have the camera confiscated.

"Your Majesty," said Mrs Roberts, who was holding a small paper Union flag in her right hand. "I'm honoured to meet you."

The Queen smiled, and said "Nice to meet you," and moved on. Still smiling and nodding. Will was still in his school uniform and Joel in his modern-day outfit. The Queen smiled at both Will and Joel and her gaze seemed to hold just that little while longer on Joel. He wondered if she knew his secret.

He then watched as the King, Queen and other dignitaries made their way along Elliott Road, looking at damaged properties and chatting to the small groups of mainly women and children who were there by invitation. When they eventually made their way back to the car, they had to pass the Roberts family again. The policemen standing guard saluted and everyone began cheering and flag waving. As the Royal couple reached the car, Mr Roberts shouted out "God save the King!" A huge frenzied cheer went up and the crowd broke out in song; *"God save our gracious king. Long live our noble king. God save the king. Send him victorious, Happy and glorious. Long to reign over us, God save the king.........."*

As the car drove away, the crowd continue singing, until the final line was sung and the Royal car out of sight.

As they strolled back up the pavement towards to number fifty-two, Mrs Roberts said it was a day she would never forget; Joel knew that to be true.

"I took the hand of the Queen of England, and she spoke to me," said Mrs, Roberts. "Until the day I die, I'll never forget that moment. Just think, the Queen visited our street."

Mr Roberts, strode on ahead – feeling proud and patriotic. He had spoken to the King; he had roused the gathered crowd into singing 'God save the

King,' to the King! He would never forget that moment; he felt incredibly proud. He felt as though he had single handedly bolstered the spirits of the British people.

Joel and Will ambled along behind, both lost on thought. Will thinking of the letter he would write to his father saying how he had met the King and Queen and that they had spoken to Granfer. Joel feeling satisfied he had now proven time travel. Once the film was developed he could show it to his grandad and prove he had travelled back in time to 1941.

"This camera," he said to Will. "You must keep it somewhere very safe. You can't have the film developed for a week or two. Just promise me you will keep it somewhere safe, like in the Anderson shelter or somewhere it can't get broken."

As they walked back, Mrs Roberts said, "Cod's roe fritters, boiled potatoes and winter salad for tea tonight. You're welcome to join us." She felt rather indebted to Joel and would do forever more. If it hadn't been for him she would never have met the King and Queen. She was walking on air – Royal tinged air.

Joel accepted the invite – he wasn't planning on going back to Gran's anytime soon. He was excited, nervous and scared. A mixed bag of emotions. He couldn't wait to see the search lights and bombers, experience the war for real. At the same time, he was dreading the cost; the lives he could not save, the buildings that would perish. The destruction that was to come and of which he had no control over at all.

Back at number 52 the boys headed up to Will's bedroom. He changed out of his school uniform, into an outfit very similar to the uniform he had just taken off. He topped it off with a sleeveless striped pullover that added some colour to his drab clothing.

"I've a treat for you here Will," said Joel "Tuna sandwiches." He took a pack of sandwiches from his backpack, opened them and handed one to Will.

"Brown bread," exclaimed Will, disappointedly.

"It's wholemeal, it's healthy," replied Joel.

Will took the floppy half sandwich Joel offered him, twisting his face as he examined it. He took a bite, and then another.

"It's alright, but I prefer white, don't they do white bread in the future?" Joel just laughed and shook his head. Will was incredulous that with all these 'inventions' Joel spoke of, they couldn't make decent bread in the future, it was all thin and soft.

Joel then opened the second packet of sandwiches he had brought and the pair happily shared a bacon, lettuce and tomato sandwich. Will said it seemed weird eating tomatoes and lettuce in March. He'd only ever had them in the summer before. When Joel asked why, he was surprised at Will's reply, that they were 'seasonal' – you can't have tomatoes in winter when they only grow in the summer. "Unless you have a greenhouse of course."

"So what's a winter salad, then? Your Gran mentioned winter salad with the cod things," asked Joel inquisitively. He'd never heard of a 'winter salad' before.

"Well, it's white cabbage, red cabbage, carrots, stuff like that." Joel assumed he meant coleslaw, it sounded rather nice. He was looking forward to tea.

Joel began to get nervous – he couldn't stop thinking about the impending terror campaign. Every second brought it closer. An air raid alert had sounded earlier and word was passed around that German aircraft were in the vicinity, though none were visible and the assumption was that they were on reconnaissance.

Eddie Bullock called around and sat chatting about the King's visit, which he's missed; and the boxing club which he'd recently joined. Eddie had his boxing gloves strung across his shoulders and asked Will and Joel if they wanted to come along and have a spar. He showed them some of the moves his trainer had taught him and said he was planning on taking on Joe Attfield; a local pugilist, in a few months' time. The boys turned down the offer of a spar and said maybe another time. Joel had never boxed in his life and didn't fancy getting a pasting from Eddie, who was far taller and thicker set.

"who d'ya prefer eh, Mae West or Greta Garbo?" said Eddie as he pulled from his pocket a battered edged photograph of a semi naked woman. "Stunner in't she?" he said.

Will grabbed the picture and studied it. "I'd take either of them," he laughed. Joel didn't know who either Mae or Greta were, so he just looked at the photograph in Will's hand and said nothing.

"Who is she anyway?" asked Will, handing back the picture.

"Cousin of our Jimmy. I can get more like that if you want, but it'll cost you." Will looked a little flushed. Eddie gave Joel a cursory nod, but Joel just gave a short chuckle and shook his head.

Eddie got up to leave, his gloves still dangling over his shoulder. "Catch ya later, if Jerry doesn't first."

Will felt guilty as Eddie left and called after him. "Come around Saturday and we'll go to the pictures."

Eddie, who was lighting a cigarette, waved his hand in the air in acknowledgement.

There was a mutual distrust between Joel and Eddie; neither liked nor particularly disliked each other. They just weren't quite sure of each other. They'd never be proper friends that was for sure and even Will realised that. Joel had always felt intimidated by Eddie. For starters, he was a lot taller and bulkier than Joel, and he asked a lot of questions – too many questions. When Joel asked Will why they were best friends, as they didn't particularly have any shared interests, Will had to think about it and then said it was because they had sat next to each other at infant school. Joel had laughed and said something which sounded quite sarcastic about hopes and aspirations.

Will then suggested they played with the 'Electric Speedway' game. It made Joel a little sad to see the delight on Will's face as he pictured in his mind the painted lead figures, to really be his favourite riders; Cordy, Jack, Bluey, George, Lionel, Tiger and all the others he had mentioned. It was like with Will's paintings and drawings – they all seemed so real to him. It was like he had a real emotional attachment to these inanimate things.

The cuttings and cigarette cards in his treasure box. His paints and colouring pencils. It was then Joel realised that they were real – just as his pictures and video clips on his phone. His music through his headphones, his computer games. They weren't really there, they were recordings which stimulated memories and feelings. Will's attachments were to inanimate but actual physical things. Joel's were to things that just held a recording. It made him feel the much shallower of the two.

"What's up? You're really quiet today," said Will. "I thought you'd be all excited, meeting the King and Queen and all that. I mean it's not everyday something like that happens." He flicked the switch and watched as the riders spun around the circular track and the lights flashed brightly. As they slowed and drew to a stop, Joel decided it was time to tell Will the truth, well, something of the truth – not the whole truth, but enough to prepare him for what was in store. He looked at Will and said; "I've got something to tell you, and I want you to be very brave." This is how he remembered his mum approaching the subject, when his pet rabbit died. He was only ten, but he knew by the tone of her voice it was not going to be good news and that he was likely to cry.

Will just looked at him as though he was stupid, furrowed his brow and said, "What you goin' on about?" He flicked the switch on the board once more and watched as the riders once more spun around the track.

Joel realised his soft soap attitude was all wrong and he wasn't breaking the news to Will that his pet rabbit died. To be honest, he was well aware that during the war people ate rabbits and if it were really true that Will had a rabbit, and it had died – he may be a little sad, but also glad that there would be some decent meat for tea.

"There's going to be a raid tonight," replied Joel solemnly. There was no point in beating about the bush.

"Pretty much thought so to be honest," said Will nonchalantly, without looking up. "With the alert earlier. I noticed Hector is flying high too. I'll have to go to the A.R.P post as soon as the alert sounds. You'll need to get home. Best be heading-off straight after tea, just to be sure."

"I'm not going anywhere," said Joel defensively. "I'm staying here with you – look." He showed Will the contents of his backpack. Will took a deep breath and asked what was going on, or words to that effect.

"At 8.39p.m. tonight there will be an air raid warning. The first wave of bombers will be pathfinders- dropping flares and incendiaries. This will light the way for the main bombing force, who will be following not far behind. There's going to be over one hundred planes and they're going to pound the city. They're going to drop over one thousand bombs and over thirty thousand incendiaries.

"Sod off!" Said Will, pushing Joel away, the colour slowly draining from his face. It couldn't be true - surely not? But Joel looked serious and as much as he might be strange and allegedly from the future; he wouldn't lie about something like that. Will had to think and think fast.

"What planes are coming?" asked Will.

"Heinkel's and Junker's" said Joel, "The Heinkel's engines make a distinctive grinding sound as though they're stuck in first gear. It's due to the heavy load of their bombs. The noise will change as they pick up speed and then you'll hear a loud whistle as the bombs fall to earth. They're aiming for the city centre, the dockyard and the gasometers."

They both sat in silence; Will, trying to take in the scene and Joel, because he knew he'd said something he couldn't now take back. He had already changed history by pre-empting Will of what was going to happen.

Will spoke first. "Right come on, let's get our stuff – down into the Anderson. There's room under the bottom bunk to store things safely."

Joel picked up his all-important backpack and contents to put in there too. His plan was, once the bombs began falling, to go outside and see the battle overhead for himself.

The boys slipped out the back door and discreetly hid away their valuables. Joel took the torch from his backpack and gave it to Will. Will was just about to turn it on when Joel told him not to, as the beam was very powerful. He told him to keep it on him, and when the warning sounded, he should take it with him to the air-raid precaution station. If he got into difficulty he could use it as a warning or call for help. Joel told him how to twist the end of it and that the beam of light would be similar to those of the searchlights, only with a much shorter range, but still very effective.

They went back indoors and Maggie was dishing out tea, there wasn't a great deal on the plates but the fish cake thing looked okay. He cut into it and took a bite and it tasted ok, but different. Looking down Joel noticed it was grainy and crumbly, not potatoey or with fishy chunks like a fishcake.

"I've never had this before, what is it exactly?" he asked, looking around the table. Granfer, sitting opposite replied.

"It's the roe of the cod, you know – the eggs the female fish lays when she spawns."

Joel laughed, he was sure Granfer must be joking, but no one else laughed. He felt a little bit sick come up into his throat. It actually now did look like fish eggs. He couldn't eat any more, he knew he would be sick. He chopped up and ate the 'winter salad' and the batter around the fritter. The roe he offered to Granfer as he 'wasn't feeling too hungry.' Vi, who had a rare evening at home said she would have it, she loved cod's roe.

Everyone at the table seemed much jollier and chattier than usual. The talk was of the King and Queen and even Vi had got to meet them when they had visited the dockyard, earlier in the day. She had recently begun 'walking out' as she called it, with a chap called Fred. He was in the Navy and was shore based for the next three months while his ship was in for repairs. She asked Maggie if he could come on the Sunday afternoon for tea. The women folk then began gossiping about Fred. The mood was buoyant and no-one seemed to notice how Joel and Will were somehow quieter than everyone else. Well, Mr Roberts noticed it, but put it down to Joel having been abandoned by his family and if he saw his gran, he was going to have words with her.

"Tell you what son; you stay here tonight. You'll be safe 'ere with us. Can't 'ave you goin' 'ome to an empty 'ouse." Granfer patted him on the shoulder then got up and went into the hallway to smoke his pipe, closing the kitchen door behind him. He couldn't understand how Joel's family could just abandon him; though there were others who just let their youngsters roam the streets. Joel was clean, and spoke well – he spoke articulately, but say some odd things. There was a slight niggling sensation in the back of his mind that all wasn't right. Joel used words in the wrong context; randomly using strange words. It was like the time Will had shown him the crystal radio set he and his uncle Des had been trying to tune in. Joel had looked really keen and said it was 'cool.' When asked what he meant, he looked at them as if they were stupid and said "Cool, you know, like it's good?" No one knew what he meant. Mr Roberts had slipped off quietly to have a look in the German/English dictionary he had been entrusted with – should he capture a German airman and need to translate. It appeared the word 'cool' in German meant the same as in English; not warm, cold. Joel had used the same word a number of times since and Mr Roberts conceded that it must be a throw-back in his once local accent – the vowels 'oo' being predominant.

After fifteen minutes or so of meditative thoughts, Granfer stubbed out his pipe and returned to the kitchen. In anticipation of an air raid, Mrs Roberts had gotten his boots, coat and canvas haversack ready for the impending call to his post at the end of the road. Maggie had the kettle boiling on the range, where she had previously cooked tea. It was good that coal was in plentiful supply because the range appeared to be constantly in use. Curtains were closed and candles were lit and strategically placed to give out the best light possible. It was getting dark and everyone was now huddled in the kitchen. There weren't enough candles to illuminate all the rooms.

The light wasn't strong enough to read by, so Granfer decided to reminisce, about when he was young. He put on his best Devonshire burr, which was pleasurable to listen too, but also made Joel laugh.

"When 'ah wur a young 'un we 'ad 'orses, two of 'em. Daisy 'an Titch." Recalled Granfer. "Daisy wur a bit of an 'an full, but Tich, Tich wur moy favourite 'orse."

Joe began chuckling and Will threw him a quizzical look; he was trying to listen. He loved Gran and Granfer's stories of the olden days. Joel tried to stifle his laughter. Granfer carried on talking of life in the village where he grew up and of the animals, of whom all had a name.

"Oi recall moy muthur saying we be 'avin Henrietta for dinner on Sunday," He said, in reference to one of the chickens. "Oi would grab the chicken from the coop an' teke it to fatha. 'e would then say, 'Oo's turn be it this toyme 'an I would say Henritetta or Martha, or whoever's turn it may be that day……"

CHAPTER TWELVE

Joel heard the clock begin to strike eight o'clock, he knew that soon the bombers would be coming overhead. They were already more than half way across the channel. One hundred and twenty-five aircraft from Luftflotte 3. The heavy engines of the Heinkel 1-11's rumbling through the night sky. His tummy knotted.

"They're going to drop land mines," he whispered to Will. "Great big buggers, the size of cars."

"What you on about?" Will whispered back, without taking his eyes off Granfer. He was still slightly disbelieving the size or scale of the attack that Joel was indicating.

Gran and Maggie had been pre-empted to take supplies down the shelter earlier, as a warning had been made that there was likely to be an attack that night. Joel had also earlier 'mentioned' that his Gran and Grandad had gone away. He said the same relative, his Aunt Jane, was very ill and she needed help with the children as her husband was away at sea. Mrs Roberts fussed around him, 'poor boy' she thought. He was being shoved from pillar to post and his parents weren't even prepared to take him in whilst his grandparents were away. It was child abandonment and they should be charged for it. The poor lad had been walking round all day with a haversack thing on his back – likely all his worldly possessions. The bombed-out boy, with only a bag full of belongings, and clothes that – well, goodness knows where they came from.

Joel hoped he could be forgiven for his lie. In truth, Aunt Jane was healthy and happy and lived near Dorchester, she had no children and her husband was a dairy farmer.

Soon after the alert sounded.

"Come on, let's get to the shelter, hurry up." Joel jumped to his feet and Will followed swiftly behind. He knew it wasn't a joke, Joel was telling the truth. His stomach squeezed, anticipating what lay ahead.

Joel, Mrs Roberts and Vi, clambered into musty smelling shelter. Vi lit two candles which she placed inside glass jars, so that if they fell over, they wouldn't set anything alight. Everyone made themselves as comfortable as possible and sat in anticipation of what was to come. Granfer, Maggie and Will didn't join them, they went off to their A.R.P posts. Granfer said he'd pop back and forth and let them know how things were going.

After five minutes or so Joel got fidgety, he wanted to know what was going on. He could hear the booms and crumps of falling bombs. The inferno that was about to change the city forever had begun. He crept out of the shelter, to many protestations from Mrs Roberts that he'd likely be shot at. He didn't care, he wanted to see the war for himself, first hand. Standing in the backyard, he observed the anti-aircraft searchlights criss-crossing the sky. They were following two pathfinder airplanes which were circling overhead. He watched in amazement as he saw a multitude of flares and incendiaries being dropped from the planes – lighting a colourful trail of blue, green and crimson pyrotechnics, that were not for the entertainment of the watching folk below, but to light the skies for the wave of heavily laden thundering planes that were heading towards the city. Bright lights dotted the skies, and below, fires were starting to break out all over the city. Vi popped her head out to plead with Joel to return to the relative safety of the shelter, but he was mesmerised by the events overhead. He could hear the dull heavy throb-throb of the Heinkel's engines. He couldn't see them though – a thick blanket of smoke now covered the city. He could hear the distinctive grinding sound of their engines change as the planes homed in on their intended target; this was followed by a loud whistling sound as the bomb began to fall.

That was when it started; the thunderous roar; as dozens upon dozens of bombers began dropping their load across the city. Joel crept back into the shelter and sat huddled with the girls. Mrs Roberts and Vi began singing.

After what seemed an eternity of bombs falling, there followed a period of silent anticipation which then came to life again as the staccato bark of ack-ack guns interspersed even more unearthly sound of bombs, part wail, part screech, falling through the air. Suddenly, there was a rush of air through the shelter door; everyone shrieked. This was followed by the bitter smell of burning and a dark heavy object landing in the middle of the shelter. The whole world appeared to be screaming – or so it seemed to Joel; he certainly was.

The thing then slowly began moving and a small ray of bright white light began to emanate from it. The silence was now as deafening as the screaming. All eyes were on the mass on the shelter floor; it's movements casting ominous shadows across the corrugated roof of the shelter.

"Granfer, said it's too dangerous for me to be out there. He told me to get down the shelter, nothing more I can do." It was Will. His face smudged in soot and his clothes emanating the unpleasant smell of burning buildings. Maggie then clambered through the shelter door; much less dramatically. She sat down on the bunk next to where Will was now sitting. She pulled him close and began crying, "My boy, my boy."

"What's 'appening?" cried Mrs Roberts.

"The whole city's on fire Gran!" exclaimed Will, shaking. "All of Cattedown, Lipson, the city centre, Keyham, dockyard. There's over a hundred bombers up there. The fire engines aren't coping and the ambulances can't get through."

"Oh my!" cried Gran.

Maggie had now turned her attention to Vi, and was clinging on to her, singing a hushed mantra and shaking like a leaf. After a minute or so, she then gathered her wits and said she needed to go back out, it wasn't fair on those who were still out there – they needed her.

Will offered Joel back his mini torch, but Joel put out his hand to stop him. "You need it more than me, keep it."

"You were right Joel," whispered Will, appearing somewhat dazed. "Huge great bombs, size of cars. Thousands of incendiaries. It's crazy!"

Granfer had now retreated to the backyard. Every so often a triangle of orangey sky would appear as Granfer moved aside the heavy wooden door and silhouetted against the brightness of the search lights and fires, he would call out "Everyone a'right in there?

On his fourth visit he said, "It's getting hot out 'ere. I've put out over forty 'cendries already an' there's four of us working this street. You lot best stay put. I'll pop back in a bit," and off he went again.

Will lit the torch, which sent a warm glow throughout the shelter. Mrs Roberts began yelling for him to put it out as it might attract the attention of a bomber.

"They can't see us in the shelter Gran," yelled Vi. "And I think they've got more important targets in mind than us, don't you?"

Un-noticed Joel was putting his back pack on and was ready to head out of the shelter door. It was only as he pushed past Will, that Will realised what he was doing. He tried to pull him back by grabbing a hold of his gas mask.

"I'm not missing this for anything," said Joel as he slipped from Will's grasp, leaving his gas mask swinging in Will's hand. Joel headed off up the courtyard and through the house.

The sky was aglow; a mixture of searchlights and fires caused by the incendiaries, which lit up the whole sky. He looked around in amazement. He watched as a few doors further along, firemen on a truck with extendable ladder, were putting out an incendiary fire on a roof. Shrapnel, broken glass and bits of masonry lay scattered in the road. Then all of a sudden it hit Joel – he was still in 1941. He had left the front door, on his own, and was still in the past. He spun around; right behind him stood Will.

"I followed you, I tried to stop you as you left the house."

They both then realised what had happened. Will had inadvertently and thankfully, stopped Joel from returning to the future.

"Come on, what are you waiting for?" said Joel excitedly. He opened his back pack and took from it the woolly hat and neck scarf he had bought for this very moment. Together they headed off up the road, past the firemen, Home Guard and A.R.P volunteers, all doing their bit. No one noticed the two boys running past. It was actually surprising how many people were out and about; groups of people watching the spectacle overhead, other making their way home from wherever they had been, despite there being a raid on. Assuming their own shelter to be safer than a public one.

The boys carried on past the top of Joel's Grans' street and along the road which lead down to the wharves. When Will asked where they were going. Joel replied that he wanted to see the fires for himself and from what he knew, they should be safe from the bombs where they were going, as the planes were aiming for the gasometers and the city centre. He couldn't guarantee they wouldn't be hit by an incendiary, but it was a risk he was prepared to take. Will had an advantage over Joel in that he was wearing his A.R.P helmet.

During a lull, between bombing raids, they hurried past the gasometers and then, with a good viewing position across the city they stopped, both out of breath. They sank down onto the ground and sat with their backs to the wall that banked the side of the road. Joel took from his back pack two bottles of water. Handing one to Will; he shrieked and dropped it to the ground.

"What's up, what's wrong!" yelped Joel; assuming an incendiary or similar had landed nearby.

"The glass, it moved. Honest to God, it just sort of melted in my hand!" He sat staring at the bottle on the ground. Joel picked it up, it looked fine. He opened it and handed it back to Will; again, he shrieked and dropped it, spilling some of the contents. "It did it again, it melted in my hand!" he cried out.

Joel thought he might be suffering from shock, and that was quite understandable to be honest. He picked up the half full bottle and held it to Will's lips so he could take a drink. As he gently took the bottle away, Will removed it from his grip and squeezed it slightly once, and then again. A look of incredulity spread across his face. "Bendy glass?" he said looking at Joel.

"It's not bendy glass, it's made of…." He wasn't sure if plastic as such was around in the war, so instead he said "stuff like glass, but not glass I brought it from the future."

Will again began squeezing it, only slightly harder. He began laughing; it seemed hard to believe there was a reign of terror going on overhead, the likes he had never experienced before and here he was, sat on a road – with a time traveller, laughing at 'bendy glass.'

"Come on," said Joel. Let's watch, there fires."

They found a good vantage point and Joel got out his binoculars through which they watched the fires across the city slowly spread. They could also see out into the harbour and the Sound. The guns from the ships fired tracer bullets of various colours, and searchlights darted across the sky, occasionally revealing an enemy plane fly overhead; in search of their target.

Suddenly they heard a loud 'whoomph' followed by the sound of falling rocks. It was reasonably close by.

"You said we would be safe here!" yelled Will.

 "I thought we were, I mean I'm sure we are." Joel was cross with himself. He'd been sure that no bombs were going to fall in that area that night. There wasn't any recording of a bomb landing there; on the bomb map he had looked at. Had it not been recorded or had he made the mistake?

 They could hear a strange cacophony of sounds – sirens, airplane engines, crackling fires, the scream of bombs being dropped, explosions, shouts; a mixture of terror and fear. The acrid burning smell was becoming stronger and the sky began to glow brighter; especially towards the city centre. Joel imagined it being like watching a film in 4D, not that he believed they could make it this realistic; there was just so much going on. He started to feel a bit funny; overwhelmed by it all. The whole area was illuminated like it was daytime. They then saw the distinct markings of a German Bomber, illuminated by the fires. It seemed so low that it looked as though it had been hit and was coming down. Whether it did or not, they didn't wait to find out as they both agreed it was time to be heading back to the shelter. Their ears had begun to hurt with the discord of noise; rumbles, whistles, thuds, cracks barks and the ringing of fire engine bells. Their eyes also stung from the smoke and fumes in the air. They made their way stealthily back through the debris littered streets; roof tiles, anti-aircraft shrapnel, bricks and burned out incendiary bombs.

At the open door of number 52, Granfer was standing in the vestibule drinking a cup of tea, poured from a thermos flask – he'd done all he could. He said he'd sent Maggie back down the shelter as it wasn't safe for a woman to be out on a night like this. She'd argued that ambulance drivers and other A.R.P's were out, but he'd told her she was better off looking after her family in the shelter than risking getting hurt in the street. There were plenty of fire-watchers out, they'd be alright. 'There's only so many stirrup pumps and buckets of sand,' he said.

When he asked the boys where they'd been, Will said they had only just slipped out for a minute to see the glow from the city centre, but were heading back to the shelter. Mr Roberts said he would clip them round the ear if they did it again.

Back inside the Anderson shelter, the women didn't appear to notice how long they had been gone. Maggie, Mrs Roberts and Vi, were all holding hands. Every time there was a sound nearby they would duck down and pray out loud that they would be spared.

Eventually, after several hours the all clear sounded. Granfer came and called them from the shelter. Cautiously they all trooped indoors, took a cursory torchlight look around and decided that as there was nothing they could do at such an unearthly hour, and they should all go to bed and get some sleep, and in the morning, face the clean-up operation.

A few short hours later, the whole city seemed to be awake and in action; though the likelihood was it had never slept at all. Many hadn't gone to bed; they no longer had a home, never mind a bed. Emergency evacuation centres were being set up in church halls. Families trudged across town in the dark, hoping a relative would put them up. Hospitals in Plymouth and further afield were working overtime. News of casualties and deaths was being passing from house to house, neighbour to neighbour. Everyone on Will's street seemed to be outdoors, clearing up bits of rubble and shrapnel from the pavements and roadway or patching up theirs or a neighbour's property. There wasn't the jolly chatter of a normal day – just quiet subdued conversation. The Milkman still came, though a few hours late.

Mrs Roberts asked Joel if he wanted to send a telegram to his parents to let them know how he was. He didn't really see any point, but felt he should to keep her happy, as earlier he'd heard her talking to Maggie about 'that poor boy.' and how his parents should be ashamed of themselves.

Maggie said she would go with him to the Post Office, as she was going to have to walk into work, although she doubted any buses were going to be running, especially on her route. Vi said she would have to walk the four miles to work at the dockyard, though hopefully buses would be running part of the route or if she was lucky she might be able to catch a lift off a passing lorry.

 Luckily Joel had some money in his backpack so would be able to pay for the telegrams. He didn't know if the people at the Post Office would check the addresses, but he supposed it was best just to send one to Aunt Jane's farm, which was at least 200 years old. His parents' house – that was a different kettle of fish altogether. Their house was built in the 1990's on former farmland. He'd need to give a real address, a house that was standing in 1941.

They hastened along and could see that St Johns Road and Brunswick Road had taken a pasting. The glowing sky to the left indicated to Will that one of the schools or maybe all; infant, junior and senior, were ablaze. He and Joel ran on ahead to check. The junior school had been totally burnt down, although the adjacent Infants' School was undamaged. As they neared Holborn Place, it was already obvious that no telegrams or letters were going to be sent today. The whole area was cordoned off and where the Post Office had once stood was simply a collapsed and burning mass of masonry and timber. Maggie stood dumbfounded. She stood behind the cordon staring at the sight in front of her.

"Nothing to see here missus," said a Policeman. "Now move along please."

"Was anyone hurt?" asked Maggie, quietly. Her voice little more than a whisper.

"I'm sorry missus, they all bought it."

"All of them?" Maggie's lip began to quiver.

"Yes Missus, all nine of them. Even the little kiddies. I'm sorry." He put a comforting hand on her shoulder, but Maggie's face folded and she turned and fled in the direction of home. Joel raced along behind her. A neighbour seeing her running down the street in tears, alerted Mrs Roberts. Eadie rushed out on to the street to meet her.

"They've all gone Eadie!" She cried, "even the kiddies." Maggie ran in doors in tears, rushed upstairs and slammed shut the bedroom door. Mrs

Roberts asked Will and Joel if they would go along to the bus station and tell the Inspector Maggie wouldn't be in today. She'd suffered a loss.

As they walked away they could hear Maggie's howls through the closed bedroom window.

The walk to the bus station allowed them to see some of the damage caused by the previous night's raid. Vehicles were diverted by policemen as roads were blocked or un-passable due to bomb damage. They saw ambulances carrying the injured to hospital, likely dug out of the rubble of what was once their house. Yesterday a home - today a bomb site. There was more shrapnel lying around than any school boy would really ever need or want. Army lorries were parked up and soldiers were shovelling debris into wheelbarrows, which in turn were being emptied into the lorries by way of a wooden ramp. There were more people than usual outdoors; people moving furniture from damaged properties, others checking up on friends and relations, or queuing up outside of shops in fear of running out of food to feed their families.

They bumped into Andy Gray. He had a rather colorless look about him. His eyes were glazed and he seemed 'not with it.' He approached the boys, still staring blankly ahead, but obviously aware they were there.

"He died last night, he was only a babe," he said. "My aunt was badly injured too. I've just been up the 'ospital with my Nan."

"Who died?" asked Will.

"My little cousin, he was only a babe., two he was.... just two." Andy's bottom lip began to tremble. Although Joel didn't know Andy all that well, (he had played a 'kick about' in the park with him, Will and a few other boys,) he was tempted to give him a matey hug, but it didn't really seem the done things between boys in that era he'd noticed; so, he said and did nothing.

"They were in the public shelter on Stillman Street. Took a direct hit it did. Their house was fine...." Tears began to run down Andy Gray's face. Without saying another word or wiping away his tears he walked on.

Will didn't speak, he just looked on helplessly as he watched Andy walk away. Joel wanted desperately to tell Will what the coming night had in store, but he couldn't. He couldn't even hint at it. Everyone they passed seemed to have the same glazed look as Andy. Joel asked why Will's Mum was so upset.

"My auntie Doris," replied Will. "Mum's sister. She lived above the Post Office."

The day passed in a haze of busyness and confusion. Will, Joel and Granfer, walked to Mount Gould to check on Aunt Bertha, Uncle Herbie who was in the Home Guard; and the family. Every so often they were stopped by strangers asking them were they lived and what the damage was in their street.

No one was home when they arrived, but a neighbour, outside fixing a wooden fence that had been shattered by bomb splinters, said Bertha had "Gone up the infirmary to check on Herbie." As they were chatting an older boy, probably aged about sixteen, came along on a bicycle. He stopped next to them with a squeal of brakes.

"Granfer," he called out. "Dad's up the infirmary. Got dressings on his arms and chest. Got burned helping Joe at number twelve. He was putting a fire out. An incendiary came through the window and landed on his rug. He's gonna be a'right though. He sent us down the shelter an' said he'd be along straight after, only he didn't come, he got taken to hospital."

Mr Roberts asked where the other gran-kiddies were and the boy said they were at Bandy Lena's house. Alfie, as his name turned out to be, was Will's cousin. He got off his bike and pushed it along the road, as the ensemble trotted alongside, spread out and in single file as to avoid the working parties clearing up.

"I've just been up in town on my bike," said Alfie. "You want to see it there. They're saying thousands of incendiaries were dropped. Can you believe it? There's fire engines everywhere. Apparently, they ran out of water." He seemed to find it terribly exciting, rather than horrifying. "Old Mr Jones sent me home from work, said I best see to my own people as there was nothing I could do there 'cos of the gas and electric all being off. Is yours off too Granfer?"

"Whole city is I 'spect," said Mr Roberts. "Bleeding Jerries."

"You won't believe the city centre," said Alfie, aiming his remark at Will and Joel. "All the big shops - gone. Spooner's gone. Police wouldn't let anyone through. Massive craters in the roads as well; from 1000lb bombs apparently. One chap said that the fire brigade called in help from other counties, but by the time they got here the water supply had been cut or their hoses didn't fit. Had to pump water from Sutton Harbour so that they could keep fighting the fires when the water mains got cut. Isn't that right Granfer?"

Mr Roberts agreed and said he'd heard that the Navy had brought out their own pumps from the establishments roundabout and had their dispatch riders taking messages to aid the Police as there was little in the way of communication, due to the speed and intensity of the spread of the fire.

It was going to be a long day for everyone, especially as many had not slept since the night before last.

"The emergency services are still digging people trapped in buildings," said Alfie. "I could see them at it on my way home. I had to carry 'me bike over a road filled with debris – a gable-end it was. Unexploded bombs apparently too."

They walked on, paying attention to where they stepped. The air was thick with smoke and poured from buildings that were still burning. The firefighters who had begun tackling them fires over fifteen hours previously, still working.

At Bandy Lena's house, the young cousins all seemed happy enough. Lena was a short statured woman with incredibly bowed legs. She rocked from side to side as she walked. Joel couldn't help but stare. He knew it was rude, but he'd never seen anyone with such a strange gait before. As well as moving forwards her trajectory, took her twenty degrees to the left and then to the right with each step.

The cousins were more interested in listening to a story from Lena's son George about his fascinating find in a bombed-out house. There were lots of titters and gasps as he amused them with the tale of his apparent 'secret' find.

Granfer thanked Lena for taking in the youngsters and signalled to them that it was time to leave. He said he'd take them to a nearby emergency kitchen for their dinner, as there'd be 'naught but marge and bread at 'ome. '

At the Emergency kitchen, they were all given corned beef sandwiches and cups of tea by the Women's Voluntary Services. Granfer asked a number of people there what damage they had suffered, and everyone had similar sad stories to tell.

They then delivered the young siblings, along with Alfie and his bike, back to their home address and into the care of their parents, who were now home from the infirmary. Uncle Herbie was lounging in an armchair, naked from the waist up, covered in numerous dressings and looking quite sorry for himself, and Aunt Bertha was clearing up some of the fallen ceiling plaster – their only damage.

On arrival, back at the Roberts residence, Mrs Roberts said that Lennie and Elsie had called around. Apparently, Elsie had been caught on the arm by a shard of broken glass that had been blasted through the door of their under-stairs cupboard. She hadn't wanted to go to the public shelter as she couldn't cope with all the other people there, and they didn't have an Anderson or Morrison shelter. She'd had her arm patched up at a First Aid post and then sent on her way. It had only been a small cut, more of a scratch really. There were far more badly injured people to see to. Eadie couldn't offer them anything more than a cup of tea with evaporated milk

Whilst Elsie and Lennie were there, they mentioned they'd seen a commotion nearby, an ambulance near and a huddle of women near to a previously bombed-out property. It wasn't until Doris, the neighbour who had her carpet beater sliced in half by shrapnel, came around and told them that she'd heard a little boy had died just after arriving at Greenbank Hospital. He'd apparently been playing on the flattened bombsite with his pals. It was the properties that he been hit in the first raid last July, which had included a Post Office. Unbeknown to him or anyone else, an unexploded bomb had landed in exactly the same place during the previous nights' raid and he had either stood on it and detonated it, or it had been a time bomb and he was just unfortunate to be at that spot the very second it went off. His mother had seen the explosion from her window, opposite.

Vi had been told at work that another night of heavy bombing was expected and she had been sent home early, catching a bus that took her to their side of the city centre, via a roundabout route. She had then made the rest of the journey on foot, trying not to look at the horrible burned out shell, of once beautiful buildings.

As twilight crept its way slowly across the sky, the Roberts and Joel prepared themselves for another night in the shelter. A warning had been sent that another attack was most probable. Hollow-eyed for want of sleep, Maggie said she hoped it was a false call as she really wasn't feeling up to it.

Joel thought it was time he brought out the family sized bag of crisps he'd brought with him; he thought it might cheer them up a bit, their diet being so bland and meagre. Tea had been Jam sandwiches and water, due to their being no gas or electricity. He poured the contents of the packet into a bowl Mrs Roberts had left out on the kitchen side and discreetly hid the packet away in his pocket. Mr Roberts took a handful and then nearly spat them out. "What's goin' on with these 'ere things? They taste funny."

"They're cheese and onion," replied Joel.

"Cheese and onion. What's them when they're at 'ome? Where's the little bag of salt?" Mr Roberts was not impressed.

Joel didn't know what he was on about but tried to explain they were pre-flavoured. Mr Roberts didn't get it and so tried a few more. He admitted he could sort of taste cheese and onion, but it wasn't what crisps were about. Everyone else had a few, but they weren't particularly impressed with the flavour. Maggie sprinkled a good dose of salt over them to enhance the flavour.

Joel slipped the empty packet from his pocket and hid it in his backpack so as to avoid further questions.

Vi complained the crisps kept 'repeating on her' and wished she hadn't had any.

Mrs Roberts probed Joel on his grandmother's strange ideas of cooking, and to Maggie she questioned his whole upbringing. "He's an odd boy and that's no lie. They go off an' leave him and not even a word from his parents, poor thing. When this is sorted I'm going to get in touch with the authorities 'bout him. It's not right it isn't."

Joel overheard her remark but declined to say anything in his own defence. He knew what was in store for them over the coming weeks and knew it was unlikely she would even remember her concerns for him in the coming days and weeks.

Maggie had been very quiet all day, interspersed with frantic activity and periods of lots of crying. Joel had decided earlier on in the day to just go with the flow of events. Never in his wildest dreams had he thought of the war being like this. Of course, he'd read about it and knew people died and how the city was destroyed, but somehow the human face of it had passed him by. Maybe he thought it was because he'd never had to face anything so horrifying in his own time...... but nor had they he supposed.

Tonight, the shelter was prepared in readiness and so were Granfer, Maggie and Will. They had their regulation uniforms ready to put on and had taken anything of great value into the Anderson shelter, including insurance documents and family photographs. Whilst looking out of Will's bedroom window, towards his grandparents 'future' house, he noticed something that made his heart miss a beat. The railway sidings that sat in the culvert between Will's street and his, housed a train carrying boxes of what to his mind could only be ammunition. The boxes on each carriage had on them the Military broad arrow symbol.

He knew that this night's bombing raid was going to be heavier than the night before. Had he somehow inadvertently changed history and the whole area going to be blown to bits, he, Will and everyone else. He decided not to say anything, because if they were all going to die it would be his fault. His Grandad had warned him about meddling with the past.

At approximately the same time as the previous night the siren sounded. The train loaded with ammunition still hadn't moved. They sat in the shelter once again and like the night before heard the bombardment start.

"Dear Lord," sobbed Mrs Roberts as she clung on to Vi. "Will there be anything left in the morning?"

Joel sat on his own as Will; just like on the previous night, had been sent out to act as Messenger for the A.R.P.

The bombs whistled overhead but sounded slightly further away – likely finishing off what parts of the city centre they hadn't managed to destroy the night before. There was no way Joel was venturing out tonight. He had read that the attack was carried out on areas adjacent to that of the previous night and more aircraft were involved. As well as bombs, the aircraft were loaded with over thirty-five thousand incendiaries

Maggie, seemed to come to life when the siren sounded – she now had something to focus on, a distraction from her most awful day. She was already in her overalls, wellington boots and grabbing her steel helmet headed out into the street. She strode with such purpose that you would have believed she was single-handedly, with her stirrup pump and bucket of sand, going to take on the whole Luftwaffe – and win.

Mr Roberts headed out with his notebook. He had earlier in the evening gone out checking which houses on his 'patch' were unoccupied or damaged. He'd checked on neighbours, seeing if anyone had infirmities and needed help getting to the public shelter and those with small children. He gave firm advice to those who decided to sit it out and could only but point out the terror of the previous night was unlikely to have been a one off.

Will stood in the back doorway of the house, watching the Nazi 'circus' which had come to town once more and was determined to put on a show that the people of Plymouth would never forget. The small groups of aircraft in the pathfinder force circled overhead, accurately positioning themselves before dropping their loads.

It started with flares and incendiaries - a precursor to what was soon to follow. Will called Joel to come and watch, but Joel didn't want to. He poked his head out the shelter door and demanded Will come back in and sit with them, out of harm's way. Will laughed and pointed to the sky, "It's like Guy Fawkes, come on, come and look."

Swaying search lights illuminated the skies above. Will was happy to watch from what he felt was the safety of the courtyard. He had his tin hat on, he was fine. He could hear bombs exploding in the distance and the anti-aircraft guns firing at the planes overhead. The echo from the guns bounced off the rooftops and reminded him of the sound of teeth chattering.

The sight of the numerous enemy aircraft directly above him was thrilling and terrifying at the same time. He could just make out the markings on the underbellies of the planes. He wondered how the German pilots felt, inside their fighting machines? Did they feel vulnerable to the guns on the ground or did they feel superior and all powerful up there in the sky?

"Bugger off home!" shouted Will. "Go on, bugger off and leave us alone."

He wanted to see one of the aircraft get hit and spiral into a dive towards the ground. He wanted the pilot to feel fear, the same adrenaline filled fear that he felt at that very moment. He hoped that at least one of them had gone to the toilet in his flying suit and would have to sit in it until being shot down and captured or having the humiliation of having to sit in it all the way back to base.

Joel on the other hand was more concerned about things at ground level. He prayed that there were soldiers guarding the train behind them in the culvert and it hadn't just been left there overnight, assumed to be in a safe place, out of the way. He prayed out loud to God, Jason Doyle, his parents and to any other time travellers out there that very moment. He prayed that he hadn't inadvertently changed events, but if he had, please let it mean that more lives would be saved rather than lost.

Vi and Mrs Roberts didn't hear his garbled ramblings over the distant 'booms.' They had begun singing 'It's a long way to Tipperary.' It didn't stop the bombs but it gave them strength and brought a moment of normality to the madness around them.

Maggie and Will came into the shelter after what seemed like at least an hour. By this time Joel was lying down with a blanket pulled up over himself and covering his ears; trying to ignore the ferocious barrage outside. He had calmed himself down by breathing slowly and deeply and imagining his hero, taking to the skies in a Bristol Beaufighter night-fighter; the sort George Pepper flew in 1942. Sadly, in the here and now of 1941, the British hadn't yet perfected the night-fighter. It would be at least another year until they came into usage.

..... 'Seeing the flames yet again light up the night sky over Plymouth, Jason couldn't bear to see the city and countryside around it that he had grown to love, destroyed. He stood outside of his accommodation block at R.A.A.F. Mount Batten and watched as the ships in the Sound fired upon the incoming enemy craft. He had an idea. He grabbed his leather flying jacket, goggles and cap and made his way swiftly down the slipway. He wasn't going to ask permission; it would only be denied. Jumping into a small boat he rowed himself across to where the flying boat was secured. He disengaged it from its mooring and started up the engines and began taxiing out towards the Sound. Building up speed the plane was soon in the air, flying at low level to avoid the strafe from the ships in the harbour. Once clear of the city he began to gain height. The sky was clear but dark and with no lighting below, he had to rely on his instrument panel and compass to tell him where he was. His radio began to buzz and Wing Commander Holder demanded to know his whereabouts and destination. Jason replied that they would find out when he returned and switched the radio off.

He continued to fly through the night, the gentle buzz of his engine his only companion. He kept a close eye on his compass – he knew exactly where he was heading. As he approached Swindon he made out the airfield he was heading for, it was going to be a messy landing though as there wasn't any water nearby to land on. He came in as slowly and carefully as he could he nursed the plane in and slid it along the grass at the side of the runway, eventually it came to a halt. He jumped out of the plane and made his way across to the hanger in which he knew there were Bristol Beaufighters; he'd been practicing in one only recently.' Joel liked his dreams, he could make any outcome he wanted in them.

"Hey, what ya doing pal?" Called out an air mechanic, seeing Jason pulling open the doors of the hangar he was working in and letting the light flood out onto the runway.

"We got an emergency on in Plymouth Bud. The day fighters saved Britain from invasion, and as sure as hell these night fighters are going to save her cities from destruction. You guys have had long enough to get the radar sorted on these things. Now I need a navigator – who's up for it?"

A crowd had now gathered and one man, a swarthy looking chap with slicked back hair and a pearly white grin stepped forward. He saluted

Jason and said, "I'd be proud to be your navigator Sir!" Recognising Jason from newspaper reports as the 'Flying Aussie Ace.'

"Jump in bud, we've no time to lose," yelled Jason as he clambered aboard and started the engine. "What's your name pal?"

"Cal McCready," replied the Navigator.

Navigator on-board, Jason told him of the plight of Plymouth and that if they could even down just one enemy aircraft he would be happy.

Within fifteen minutes of being airborne, the bright light that was Plymouth lit up the sky. As they neared they could see an incoming wave of German bombers, the preceding wave having left after emptying their load on the city.

"C'mon then 'Cats -eye's' McCready, let's see 'em off."

Jason pulled the plane up high, much higher than the incoming enemy aircraft, the engines screeched as he pulled hard on the gear stick. Then they began firing. Almost immediately they saw an enemy plane veer off to the left, a gaping smoking hole in its wing.'

At this point, Joel had to leave Jason and Cats eye's McCready to continue the battle over the city alone. Will had interrupted his dream, by clambering back in the shelter and shoving him along the bench, saying he needed a drink as he had a dry throat and his eyes were stinging all the smoke in the air.

"It's much worse up town tonight, "said Will as he poured some water from a jug into a tin mug, He wiped encrusted dusty grime from around the corners of his mouth. "Granfer said I should stay with you lot now. Not so bad here thankfully," he nodded outside. "Mostly incendiaries. Mum and Granfer have it quieter, but I know some folk have had to go and help in other parts. There's going to be a lot of people with no homes to go to in the morning." He said it dejectedly whilst staring into the depths of his tin mug, in the dull candle light.

There was a loud crump and the ground shook. Mrs Roberts swore and cursed. Vi wrapped her arms around her and sobbed. Joel waited for what seemed like an age for the train behind them to explode and blow them to Kingdom come – but it didn't happen.

A few minutes later Granfer entered the shelter. He seemed flustered. "They're sayin' all of town is gone. Bedford Street, Cornwall Street. Just burning piles of rubble. The Guildhall and St Andrews Church, burnt out. Further on towards Devonport, again it's all alight; the Octagon, the Westminster Hotel, all down towards the Hoe, lost. Schools, churches, businesses; all gone. They've even bombed the bloody Pier!"

He sat down and simply stared ahead. He was thinking, assimilating what had just happened. This terrible 'thing' that they had all been a part of.

Mrs Roberts looked aghast at hearing the pier had been bombed. "Oh Charlie," she said, her voice trembling. "Remember all those dances we used to go too when we were young?"

Mr Roberts wiped some dirt from the breast pocket of his soot and grime covered overalls and without making eye contact with his wife, simply said. "All gone my luvver, all gone."

Vi asked him about their house and he said he thought a few windows had 'blown.' There was another long silence and then Mr Roberts began telling them the snippets of news that had been relayed to him. Every sentence ended with 'all gone.'

No one spoke. Even when Mr Roberts had finished telling them of the damage to the city, no one questioned him nor gave an opinion.

There appeared to be a lull in bombings; likely one wave having left and another on its way. Maggie then stood up and patting Granfer on the shoulder said they should both go back to their posts. Even though the activity in the skies above appeared to be lessening.

When the all clear sounded, in the early hours, Granfer roused the sleep deprived inhabitants of the shelter and bleary eyed, they clambered out. Joel took a look behind to see what damage if any had been inflicted on his grandparents' house. Well, the then occupier of his Gran's house, whoever that may be. It took a few seconds for his eyes to adjust to what he saw – because it didn't look quite right.

The flames from the fires burning only a mile away in the city centre lit up the sky, so it wasn't due to the lack of light that it didn't look right. The skyline somehow looked different. There were tall things sticking up, like giant chimneys. The whole picture just looked wrong. Mr Roberts saw him staring in dismay. "Sorry bey," he said, placing a hand on Joel's shoulder.

"Like a pack 'o cards, them there roofs went. Only the chimney breasts left standing. Don't know what the damage is indoors. We'll have to go see Bill Pengelly, he's the warden for your Gran's street."

Mr Roberts then told the boys to gather their 'bits and bobs' from the shelter and to go into the kitchen and wait for him there. They returned to the dank shelter and felt around in the murky darkness, beneath the benches. Joel pulled out his backpack, he could smell the cold damp earth on it. Will struggled with his arms full; the speedway game, his tin box, the camera and other items such as the code wheel and pens, that he had felt important enough to hide from the German bombers. Joel exited the shelter first and Will passed a handful of his prised belongings out to him.

Once everyone was indoors Mr Roberts lit his torch. He said he'd been through the house and there had been a 'bit 'o damage to the front.' He then said they'd need to gather some basic belongings because it wasn't safe to stay; the front of the house was a little precarious.

"Eadie, fetch our papers and get a few bits together." Mrs Roberts headed to the cupboard under the stairs. She kept an emergency supply of items there just on case of such an event. She'd watched a public information film at the cinema which had advised 'good' housewives to have a ready supply of basic items to hand if they needed to vacate their property at short notice.

Mr Roberts made his way upstairs saying he would get some blankets.

It was still dark, but using the torch that Joel had lent Will, Mrs Roberts was easily able to look in the pantry and take out what perishable food there was and put it in a basket. She also added some extra candles and matches. There certainly wouldn't be any power supply today.

"I've got our papers and my purse Charlie," she called up the stairs. "You take that son," she said to Joel, handing him the basket. "We'll have to go to our Ellen's for now, and when it's light, we'll get something sorted. Message your parents too. They'll be ever so worried."

She didn't mention his grandparents; she was very unimpressed with them and even after the raid and all that had happened she was still adamant she was going to report their neglect to the authorities. Why should she take on the responsibility of the boy? His Gran didn't even have the decency to leave him with his ration book!

Vi opened the vestibule door, its two glass panes already shattered, fell to the floor. The wooden front door beyond was opened flat against the interior wall and on the ground outside lay a large pile of rubble. Looking up at the ceiling, there was a large crack; it was obvious the front of the property had received quite a lot of damage, rather than the 'bit' Mr Roberts had described. likely from a bomb that had exploded at roof top height, designed to create damage over a wider area.

Mr Roberts pushed past everyone and he and another gentleman, also in warden's uniform; a tall thin man whom Joel recognised as a neighbour, began helping them all clamber across the rubble.

"Now be careful, because there's loose masonry up there and tiles of brickwork could fall at any time." Granfer, and the tall thin man helped a tearful and shocked Mrs Roberts, who was wearing Will's tin helmet, climb over the rubble.

"Now now Eadie," said the thin man. "Don't fret dearie. It's not as bad as it looks; I've seen worse. They'll be able to repair it."

Once Mrs Roberts was over the rubble, the helmet was passed back to Vi, who had put on her *very expensive* sable fur coat "ust in case someone comes in and takes it." She then was helped to carefully make her way across the pile of debris, holding onto both men for support.

"Mr Roberts," called Joel "Let me pass you Will's stuff."

Will had put the camera around his neck, but he wasn't going to be able to clamber over the rubble whilst also holding the speedway game and his tin. Donning the helmet, as it was passed back to him and taking the cardboard box first, Joel clambered half way out the door way with the help of the other warden and passed it over. Granfer moaned about it not being essential – but to Will it was; It was his hold onto normality. Looking along the road Joel could see the Roberts and the next two houses along had both suffered similar damage. He climbed back down and taking Will's precious tin, passed that over too. At this point, there was a shout from a neighbour further up the road, having returned to their property from the communal shelter, they had found a small incendiary fire burning in their house. Maggie was just in the process of clambering over and once on the other side, the tall thin warden said he had to go and ran off to get a bucket of sand to put out the incendiary fire. Will clambered over next. He then passed the helmet back to Joel. Joel adjusted his backpack and began to precariously clamber over the mound of broken glass and rubble. He held his arms out to balance himself on the uneven footing. A brick gave way and he stumbled and fell, the helmet slipping from his head.

CHAPTER THIRTEEN

It was daylight. Joel was lying on his side in the middle of the pavement - his elbow hurt; he sat up and gave it a rub. It had grazed slightly but wasn't bleeding. He reached out and picked up the helmet and then turned to call to Will…. and then it dawned on him; he was back in 2017. There was no rubble or bomb damage. There was a boy coming towards him on a skateboard though. He got to his feet and stood there for a few moments gathering his thoughts. The skateboarder whizzed past. He was plugged into his iPhone and oblivious to much of what was going on around him.

Joel picked up the helmet that had rolled onto the roadway nearby, half under a car. He had gone from being in the middle of the Blitz to, well this; this 'normalness' and it just didn't feel right. He didn't want to be in 2017, he wanted to be back in 1941 with Will, Maggie, Vi and Mr and Mrs Roberts. He wanted to know what damage had been caused to the other houses in the street, to his Gran's house. Were the occupants of that property safe? What about Will's other family members. How was Andy Gray, Eddie and the others?

He slowly opened the gate of number 52 and stepped towards the modern white UPVC door. A searing pain on his shin came from a piece of masonry he had just walked into. He climbed the mound of rubble and stood in the doorway calling out to Will. No one answered. He rubbed his leg and felt the lump forming on his shin. Pulling up his trouser leg he could see a small graze but no blood. He then checked his elbow, it was the same.

He entered the house by forcing open the front door. It had been pulled too, but not locked. The wood had splintered and it no longer fitted in the frame properly. He walked around the ground floor rooms. He noticed a few things missing and assumed Mr Roberts had been back and taken them. The house certainly wasn't liveable in at present. The front room window had been boarded up and glass was strewn across the floor. He wondered where Will was and if he would be back soon. He needed to see him; they hadn't even had a chance to say goodbye. He decided to leave the tin helmet on the parlour table. That way Will would know he had been back looking for him. Returning to the front door he saw a group of workmen standing outside.

"This your 'ouse son. Come to get your things?" asked a bushy moustachioed man. Joel said it was his best friend's house and he'd come looking for him. The workman nodded understandingly and asked if anyone had been injured. Joel said just him and showed the workmen his elbow and leg. They all chuckled and told Joel to be on his way. They then turned to their truck to off load their tools and wooden barrow. Joel climbed over the rubble once more and slipped back into 2017.

Where the bleddy 'ell 'as he gone?" said Mr Roberts in a confused tone. He'd only turned to speak to Eadie, who was adamant they needed to go back into the house and collect a few more things.

"He must have run off back to his Gran's," said Will, knowing full well that Joel had leapt forward and into the future. He wished he could have gone with him too; away from the nightmare he was living in 1941.

Mr Roberts tutted, as they all plodded up the road to Ellen and Des's house. He was puzzled as to why Joel had suddenly decided to run off like that.

"He'll come around our Ellen's soon," said Vi. "He just wants to check his Gran's house and probably tell Bill Pengelly where he can contact them. You told the boy he needed to see Bill."

Ellen and the girls, Diedre and Pauline had been in the shelter and were now back in their own beds. Des was out with a rescue party on Brunswick Road, he'd not slept at all in over 24 hours. The Roberts made themselves as comfortable as possible, in armchairs, the sofa and on the floor. Mr Roberts advised they all get some sleep until it was daylight. "Naught can be done till then," he said.

Will took the camera from around his neck and placed it on the mantelpiece. He then lay on the floor and using his pullover as a pillow and his coat as a blanket, he held onto his speedway game and tin box. His mind was spinning with the events of the last two nights. It was spinning so fast it dragged him off into a deep slumber.

Joel made his way back to Gran's house. It was definitely 2017, there were no armed guards on the bridge and the cobbles of yesteryear were long buried under layers of concrete and tarmac. He felt as though he'd been away for weeks. He wasn't quite sure how long he'd been away, but he was hungry, tired, disorientated and just wanted to get some sleep.

Gran answered his knock at the door; she looked a little surprised to see him. "You're early. I thought you'd be another few hours yet."

"What time is it?" he asked, having no idea, but glad in a way that she wasn't concerned about his lateness. He had visions on the way back of her being frantic and having called his mother and the Police, having reported him as a missing person.

"It's only just gone three thirty. Come on in and tell us about your trip; Mrs Stanfield's here."

Joel walked in to the lounge and put down his backpack and sat on the sofa.

"Want a drink?" called Gran, who had gone to the kitchen to make her and Mrs Stanfield a coffee.

"Please!" he called back. "And something to eat, I'm starving."

Mrs Stanfield smiled at him and asked if he'd enjoyed his trip. He lay back on the sofa and said it been 'different', but he wouldn't have missed it for the world. He wondered if she knew about the time portal? He was too tired to care to be honest. He lay down on the sofa, kicked off his trainers and made himself comfortable.

When Gran came back into the room she commented on the funny smell. It was like a wood burning smell, earthy and woody. Mrs Stanfield said she could smell it too, maybe Joel and Will had had a barbecue, she

246

suggested. Gran picked up his backpack and began to empty its contents, taking out the empty crisp packet, the flattened plastic water bottles, binoculars, catapult and paraphernalia Joel had taken with him on his adventure. "What's this," she said, taking out some bits of shiny silver bits of metal.

"Just bits of shrapnel from the war," mumbled Joel. Both women looked at each other puzzled. Mrs Stanfield raised her eyebrows and Gran pulled a face and said Joel and his friend Will were 'into the 'war' and had probably picked them up in a bric-a-brac shop somewhere.'

"So, what did you get up to," asked Gran, still examining the small pieces of metal. "Tell us all about it."

But it was too late; Joel was fast asleep.

Will wearily came too at around ten o'clock in the morning. Gran and Granfer were both discussing with Uncle Des, their options. Their house was uninhabitable for the foreseeable future. There were hundreds of damaged properties across the city in need of repair and it would take time to get around to their house; there was a list of previously damaged houses still awaiting work to be done of them. It was going to take weeks, possibly months. They needed to look at temporary accommodation in the meantime; possibly moving in with relatives or to a house left vacant by occupants previously having left the city. They would need to ask the Corporation for advice or check the paper for houses to let. In the interim, Ellen said they could stay with her and Des in their three-roomed flat. It would be cramped, but manageable. Will wanted to go to Joel's Gran's house – but he knew Joel wouldn't be there; not yet anyway. He opened his treasure box; it was his memory box too, the newspaper clippings inside made him happy; Cordy Milne, Bronco Slade, George Pepper – all happier times. He was surprised though to see an envelope he hadn't seen before. He knew he certainly hadn't put it there. Cautiously he opened it. Inside was a folded letter, a coloured picture and a small piece of card.

Dear Will,

I am writing this letter in the future, to leave for you in the past. Now that you are reading this, I will either be back in my own time or dead. You are only reading this because I'm no longer with you. If I was still with you I would have taken this letter back and given you these items myself. I already knew the raid was going to be bad and I worried we might get separated. I also knew I had to get back to my own time after the all clear sounded.

Hopefully I will be back with you soon, but time seems to work differently through the portal. It could be today, tomorrow or even a week or two. I'm writing about things that are still to happen in your time but are long time ago in mine.

Do you like the picture of Jason Doyle? Is he anything like you imagined? I hope the photographs we took with the camera come out well. You will have to let me see them. I want to have one of the photographs of you and me to keep. I'd like you to send one with me on to a newspaper so that I can look it up in the future and prove I travelled back in time. Wouldn't that be great?

Please keep safe. I wish I could do something to change things, but I can't. Remember to tell your granfer not to let the Corporation take your railings; they'll only end up in a dump or out at sea. Tell them to take all the bloody shrapnel instead!

Trust me <u>there won't be any gas bombs.</u>

*This is just in case I **CAN'T** come back again:*

Now the other things I've left you. My torch, I want you to keep hold of that. I don't know if you have the same batteries in your time as in mine, but if it runs out it needs a 'double A' sized battery. You'll be able to buy them in the future, so keep hold of it for your children.

The pens, use them for doing code work and please keep at it. It will make for a great career when you get older – I promise! The small oblong card – that won't make any sense to you and won't for many years to come, probably not until you're quite old. Keep it safe as it

248

is a very important link to the future. It is probably the most important thing I have given you —it tells you how I got here, but I'm not saying anything more on that. I'm sure if you keep up the code work you will eventually work it out.

Your special friend,

Joel

Will studied the picture of Jason Doyle, he was nothing like he imagined and at the same time just like he had imagined. The picture was in colour and the detail amazing. It was like looking at something in real life, but in miniature. It was his leathers that stood out the most though. They were blue, black, white and gold and had all sorts of writing on them. He wore a funny peaked hat with 'Nice' written on it. Was that his nickname? Was it because he was good and everyone liked him? He certainly looked a happy sort. Joel had never mentioned him having a nickname and 'Nice Doyle' didn't really have a ring to it; to be honest it sounded quite silly. But, it was from the future and maybe some nicknames would be different then; descriptive of a person's looks or personality – such as Cheery Gillespie or Smiler Graham.

His race jacket wasn't like the ones they wore in Will's time either, it had strange lettering on it rather than a team logo. It had 'Kjaergaard' written on it and underneath another code 'www.kia.dk' – maybe this was what Joel was on about; codes being so important in the future. He also had on the number 69; which seemed strange, as there were only seven riders in a team. Maybe these strange letters and numbers were Jason Doyle's code. The 'D and A' thing Joel mentioned? The future was certainly strange.

Will decided he should try out Jason's codes on his code wheels and see if he could decipher anything from them. Maybe he could work out what Jason Doyle's code was.

He then examined the piece of card – it was small, probably two by three inches in size and with a waxy feel to it. It had a funny brown stripe on the back and on the front two orange stripes, top and bottom and lots of lettering, numbers; again, all code. Will wondered how people coped in the future with all these codes.

"What you doing boy eh?" It was Uncle Des. He pointed to Will's treasure box. Will quickly shoved the letter, card and photograph back into the envelope and box underneath his newspaper cutting and other paraphernalia.

When Joel woke up it was quarter past eight in the evening and starting to get dark.

"No, no, not the shelter!" he wailed.

Grandad was shaking his shoulder. "Time, you woke up and had some supper. You've been asleep for over four hours."

Joel was disorientated, he didn't at first realise where he was. He thought he was still dreaming and asked where Will was and if the house was badly damaged. Gran and Grandad gave each other a funny look.

"You're over tired, likely too much sun. Probably dehydrated," said Gran; although he didn't actually look as though he had caught any sun at all. "You left your phone behind. I tried ringing you but then I heard it ringing upstairs." Gran tutted. "You never know when you might need your phone in an emergency. What if something had happened to you?"

Joel sat there, fighting between sleep, trying to wake up and listening to what Gran was saying.

"A phone would be of no use to me if something had happened to me where I was Gran." Joel pictured himself in the Anderson shelter, moving around in the cramped space trying to get a signal on his phone. Kneeling on the top bunk in the only spot where there was a signal and shouting into the phone. 'Police and Ambulance please, we have incendiaries and bombs falling all around us.'

Gran looked at him puzzled, he wasn't making much sense. "No signal Gran. You know what Cornwall's like."

Gran had to agree, there were a lot of places in Cornwall where there was no phone signal at all. Still, he could have written a text and it would then have sent when his phone had eventually picked up a signal.

"Your mum rang earlier, she said your dad is coming down around lunchtime tomorrow to pick you up. He's got the day off, it's a Bank Holiday, so he said he'll come and pick you up then rather than you having to get a train back on Tuesday. I know it's a day early, but I'm sure you'll be looking forward to going home." Gran chuckled, "I'm sure you'll be relieved to get away from us oldies and back to your friends."

Joel hadn't really thought much about his friends in Exmouth. It was his friends in 1941 he was more concerned about. But whilst he was in 2017 there was nothing he could do as life in the war no longer existed, it had happened; it was over and had been for over seventy years. That thought gave him some comfort. Will and all his family would likely be long dead; cousins Pauline, Deidre, Alfie, Sylvie. The little girl in the air raid shelter in town. Andy Gray, Malcom and Alec. It all sort of felt like a dream; maybe it had all been just a dream?

His mind began to wander; he pictured a young girl of about eight years old, wearing a pink summer dress and with blond pigtails either side of her head. In the near distance behind her a small sapling tree. He watched as she and the tree behind began to grow and change; its leaves sprouting and shedding in quick succession. Her life flitted by so rapidly that within no time at all she had grown, shrunk and then disappeared in a puff of dust. The tree on the other hand had grown and its thick sturdy trunk dominated the scene. That was pretty much how he felt Will's life had been in his time, Joel's time. What was time anyway, apart from a measure of putting dates on moments, fixing the durations of events, and specifying which events happen before other events. The longer the space of time between events, the less time specific needed to be.

"What's up dear?" asked Gran, looking concerned. Joel seemed distant, distracted.

"Just still half asleep," he said and dragged himself from the sofa and to the bathroom.

"That boy worries me you know Jim," said Gran. "He just sleeps, eats and is off in a world of his own most of the time."

Grandad who was watching television, let out a harsh laugh. "That's what all boys his age do. Can't you remember our Darren when he was that age?"

"But he was put playing football and sport," replied Gran. "Joel and this Will boy, just seem to do nothing but talk about the war."

".....and go on adventures and walk for miles." Grandad butted in. "You remember that catapult his friend made him. The walks down by the river he talks about and how he often comes back grubby." Gran did nod in agreement but thought it odd that Will had never come knocking for him; he'd always had to go to Will's house. She had a slight fear that Will wasn't quite who Joel said he was.

"I think that pal of his has brought him alive if anything," said Grandad. "Joel's always been a bit of dreamer, but this Will lad has certainly got him away from playing on his mobile phone all the time like most kids today do. Have you noticed, he never takes it out with him. I've seen him in the evenings on my laptop, researching science pages and history stuff; not like other boys his age. They just do some home from school, have their tea and then talk to their mates online until it's time for bed; then, when they wake up in the morning, its straight back on their phones talking to their mates again, updating their social media profiles and posting selfies."

It had been only hours ago, but also so very long ago. Joel lay in bed recounting his adventures. He pictured Will finding his letter and seeing Jason Doyle for the very first time. He was determined in the morning to go back again and try and find Will, hopefully get one of the photographs; if he'd manged to get them developed. He'd be able to say goodbye properly and promise to come back again as soon as he could.

He awoke to the familiar sound of cars and lorries trundling along the road behind Gran's house. He looked at the clock – it said 8.20 a.m. – he'd slept much longer than he'd expected. He got up and hurried downstairs.

"Morning, I didn't want to wake you." Gran was sitting on the sofa in her dressing gown, drinking tea and watching television. "You seemed so tired last night, even after your long nap. Your dad phoned and said he should be along about eleven. Do you want some breakfast?"

Gran got up to go to the kitchen, but Joel told her he wasn't hungry. He wanted to go and say goodbye to Will. He dashed back upstairs and threw on some clothes, not bothering to wash or clean his teeth. He hurried out the door saying he wouldn't be long. Gran called after him saying it was still very early, but he didn't reply. He ran up the road, across the bridge and slowed down as he walked towards Will's house, or Mrs Stanfield's as it was in 2017. He opened the gate quietly and stepped inside. As he did so he caught Mrs Stanfield looking out of her front room window; she had seen him and was now going to come to and open the front door.

The rubble had been moved and the front door boarded up, as were the windows. There was quite a lot of superficial damage to the property, but it would be repaired in time. The neighbouring properties were in a similar state, as were a few others dotted along the street. He stood there for a few seconds wondering what to do. He could go to Ellen and Des's house – but not without 'holding on to the past' as he now called it. He wanted to step back out of the gate and in again, knowing some time would have passed in 1941 – but in 2017, it would only have been a matter of seconds and Mrs Stanfield would likely be standing at the door in astonishment, wondering where he had disappeared to. He couldn't just re-appear in front of her. He waited for a while, hoping someone would come past, someone he knew.

Mrs Stanfield looked up and down the street, and in next doors porch. There was no one there. Surely, he wasn't playing silly games and hiding behind one of the cars? Maybe she was mistaken. She knew she'd seen a boy; he looked rather like Anna's grandson Joel. She went back indoors and accepted it was likely someone going into next doors gate, not her own.

Joel waited and waited. A small boy aged about four, from a few doors along came and chatted. Joel asked if he knew Will, but he said he didn't, he wasn't allowed to play with big boys. He was soon called back by his mother, who gave Joel a suspicious look. He called along to her and asked if she knew where the Robert's had moved to. She responded that he'd need to go and ask Ellen at 34; she'd be able to tell him.

As much as he wanted too, Joel knew it was impossible. As soon as he stepped forward he would be back in 2017.

He then heard a voice calling him. He looked around and caught sight an older gentleman over the road waving to him. He was dressed rather like Mr Robert's; with a waistcoat, fob watch and chain and a collarless shirt. He also smoked a pipe.

"'Ere bey," he gestured Joel to cross the road. Joel called out to him, asking what he wanted, but the old man insisted he come over.

"I can't, I have to wait here," Joel shouted back. His cries drowned out by a passing truck. The old gentleman was sitting on a stool by his open front door. He got up and leaning on his gate called over again. "What you up to bey eh? I seen you comin' an' goin' – disappearin' an reappearin'.

What you at, eh bey? I sit 'ere all day an' I see what goes on. You a magician or summat?"

Joel didn't know what say. He'd never thought about someone watching him; seeing him disappear from one time period to another.

"Go on, do it again!" The old man began laughing. Joel stepped forward; it was 2017 again. He stepped back immediately; the old man was still there but reading a newspaper.

"Oi mister!" called Joel, as he waved his hands in the air. The old man looked up and began chuckling. He got up from his stool, tucked the newspaper under his arm and began to make his way towards Joel, out of the gate and across the road. Joel panicked and quickly stepped forward into 2017.

The door opened behind him.

"I thought it was you," said Mrs Stanfield. "Has your Gran sent you round?" She beckoned Joel indoors. He slipped the glass lens from his pocket and pretended to fasten his shoe, placing it on the path and praying no-one came along and stood on it or worse, took it. He followed Mrs Stanfield into the house – Will's house. It looked very different to how the Robert's had it decorated; though the ceiling rose was still the same, as were the built-in cupboards and the picture rail. They'd been painted green in Will's house, but now were white. A fitted carpet lay where the Robert's had a lovely patterned rug. It all seemed so strange. He had been in that very room yesterday; seventy-five years before.

He told Mrs Stanfield that he'd been to visit his friend Will, but he hadn't been home. She asked where Will lived and Joel said, "down the road." She offered him a drink of juice and some biscuits, to which he agreed, as he wanted to see more of Will's house. He asked to use the bathroom even though he didn't need it. He found it not outside, but in what had been Will's bedroom; which was strange but funny at the same time. He noticed the door handle was still the same and he held it for a while longer than necessary when opening the door.

After fifteen minutes or so of chatting to Mrs Stanfield about Will and some of their more sedate adventures, excluding all details of bombs and incendiaries, he made his excuses to leave; picking up the glass lens from the path on his way out. Joel felt sad that he hadn't managed to see Will again, but it was somehow cathartic that he had finally visited the house in his own time.

He made his way slowly back to Gran's; he certainly couldn't make another attempt to go back and see Will. He reflected on the differences in the Will's house from when he lived there until now. He couldn't wait to tell him…. and then he remembered that he couldn't tell him. Not for a very long time yet anyway; a longer time in Will's time than in his own.

When he arrived back at his gran's house, he found her fussing around, checking that he had everything that he had come with, as well as the items he had acquired whilst visiting; including the shrapnel and catapult, not that she thought his parents would approve of it. She filled a carrier bag with items that wouldn't fit into his backpack. She flicked through his code books and the strange cardboard wheels with writing on. The temptation to throw them in the bin was over-ridden by the fact they looked as though a lot of work had gone into making them.

His dad arrived sooner than expected. It was good to see him again. "Roads were quieter than expected," he said, as he wandered into the courtyard to inspect Gran's pots and troughs of plants. He took his time looking at each one in turn. Darren was no expert gardener but enjoyed the beauty of a summer garden. "I remember when we were kid's and me and Jane and Martha would plant sunflower seeds. It was a competition every year to see whose grew that tallest."

Gran put the kettle on and offered Darren something to eat.

"Just a cup of tea Mum," he said. "I've promised Jenny we'd take the kids swimming and for a burger this afternoon. Spend some family time with them." Darren then slumped down on the sofa and began telling his mum about a meeting he'd had with Carl Spooner, who apparently was a right dick-head and no one liked him. He always had huge sweat patches under his arm pits and had a habit of always saying "How the devil are you? - good good." Without waiting for an answer, as he ushered visitors into his office. He also had a loud guffawing fake laugh that annoyed Darren just as much as his repetitive greeting.

Joel decided to go upstairs and re-pack his belongings. He was relieved to see his phone charger, it was still plugged into the wall socket. He then sat on the bed and looked out of the bedroom window. He looked at Will's old house and pictured the pair of them reading in his bedroom and playing the electric speedway game. Taking out his phone, he took a photograph of the back of the house, and Will's old room. He wanted some memories to hold onto.

Darren soon called him down and said they needed to be making tracks. Joel placed his belongings in the boot of the car and gave Gran a hug goodbye and promised he would see her again soon. He turned to his dad and asked if he could come and stay with Gran and Grandad again soon. His dad laughed and said "We'll see, maybe at half term."

"But that's ages away!" moaned Joel. He clambered into the back of the car and fastened his seatbelt. He then slipped his headphones on and made himself comfortable. Dad and Gran stood talking for a while and eventually Darren got into the driver's seat and put his key into the ignition. He turned the key and checked his rear-view mirror before putting the car into gear. "Thanks again for having him Mum, just hope he wasn't too much trouble."

"No trouble at all," said Gran as she waved to Joel. "It was a pleasure."

Joel waved back. Darren indicated away from the kerb and the car slowly pulled away.

'I'll be going back at school soon,' thought Joel. 'Back to normality, back to Marley, Ben and Jez.' He wondered what they would say when he told them all about his adventures in war torn Plymouth? That he had met the King and Queen – yes, the King and Queen of old. Not the Queen and Prince Philip, but the Queen's ACTUAL parents! How he and Will had run through the streets as bombs were falling? He'd tell them about Mr Roberts and his smelly old pipe. The glass lens, the time portal. He'd show them the catapult Will had made him and the shrapnel they'd picked up in the street – some of it still hot.... and then he knew he couldn't tell them, not the whole truth anyway. He had told Marley about some of his adventures in his text messages and occasional calls. At first, Marley seemed interested, and then he stopped responding to the texts about the war and just messaged about ordinary stuff. Joel has sent him a couple of the photograph's he'd taken as 'evidence' – but they didn't really mean anything. They were just people's legs and feet in a street. The footwear wasn't that standout different. Marley had agreed with him that no one in the pictures was wearing trainers, but that didn't mean anything. Joel had to admit it was grasping at straws. What both of them had omitted to notice was the white stripes painted on the kerb stones, in the far left-hand corner of one of the pictures.

Joel closed his eyes; he imagined the music playing through his headphones was instead coming from Heart FM, the radio station Jason had tuned into, in his van. The Swindon Robin's had a home fixture against the Somerset Rebels that evening and Jason had called Joel, virtually begging him; "Come and give 'us a hand mate? Me mechanic, Johno, he's got a dodgy belly."

How could he refuse?

Joel and Jason were now heading to the Abbey Stadium. Joel had his feet propped up on the dashboard and was wearing one of Jason's snapbacks that he'd found lying in the back of the van. He recounted various stories to Jason about Ken Le Breton, Bluey Wilkinson and Lionel Van Praag, that his Grandad had shared with him. Jason said they sounded like 'awesome guys,' and gave Joel a high five.

Will was grateful for the speed at which the workmen had repaired their damaged house. It was now late-June, and even after the extensive wave of bombings only a few weeks previously, that had devastated the city even more than they had in March; they were now ready to move back into number 52. Staying with Ellen and Des had been a squeeze, though they had only been there three nights before being offered temporary accommodation in a flat a few streets away. The April blitz damaged that house and they had been on the move again, this time to a shared house with two other families. It was a large house though, and everyone had managed to get along well enough. Grandad had struggled with being so far away from his A.R.P post and his allotment garden.

The house still needed some redecorating and minor cosmetic repairs. All the major work had been carried out to an acceptable standard. So many families had been made homeless that the Corporation and the Army had put extra men to work to help repair the damaged properties. Those that were beyond repair or in need or extensive repair work, were left to be dealt with at a later date. So far there hadn't been any air raids this month and things were beginning to return to normal; although what normal could ever be again was debatable, after the whole city had just about been destroyed. Nerves were shattered and families separated – there never was going to be such a thing as normal again.

Will had started smoking occasionally, his pal Eddie had been smoking for ages. He said it was a good way to relax and calm the nerves. It also had the added bonus of being a way of chatting up girls. "Go up and ask one for a light," he said. "Then ask them if they want to go to the cinema or maybe for a walk. All the film stars smoke."

There were of course the cigarette cards to collect too.

Will had started work; an apprentice draughtsman in the dockyard. How he'd managed to get through his school exams, he didn't know. Everyone was in the same boat though - it was accepted that huge chunks of children's education had been left out.

He sat on his bed and opened the Kodak envelope with the photographs he'd collected from the photographer's. He hadn't dared take the film to be developed any sooner due to the fact there were so many other priorities across the city. Developing a film of photographs was very low on that list of priorities. There had also been of course the risk that the developing studio could have gotten bombed and the pictures lost forever.

Will laughed at the 'selfie' as Joel called it. Joel holding the camera out and trying to take a picture of them both together. The picture had them pictured from the nose up, cutting off the lower part of their faces. He especially liked the one of them all together Mum, Gran, and Granfer in his A.R.P helmet and uniform; taken just before they set off down the road to see the King and Queen. Joel had told them to say 'sausages' and everyone was laughing as the picture was taken. It also brought a tear to his eye. Granfer had been in hospital over two weeks now; a stroke brought on by stress. They'd been told he would never fully recover. He was paralysed down the left-hand side, and his speech and his vision badly affected. Will was the man of the house now.

The next picture was of Vi and Mum, standing by the Anderson shelter in the garden linking arms.

The pictures with the King and Queen in the background had turned out quite well, though on the one with Joel in the foreground you couldn't see the King's face as Granfer's helmet was in the way. The picture of him with the King and Queen in the background was good, as the King was looking directly into the camera.

When would Joel return he wondered? Every day he looked out for him, every knock at the door….. He promised he'd come back again in his letter.

Will put all the photograph's in his treasure box, except one. Vi had offered to take a snap of him and Joel together. They were standing by the front gate and Will had his arm around Joel's shoulder. They looked as though they didn't have a care in the world. Joel was wearing one of his strange tops with writing on it. He had momentarily side glanced at Will as Vi had clicked the shutter, so she was only able to capture part of his face, but even so they were both smiling; they looked so carefree and happy.

He put it on his bedside table - he would keep it there until Joel returned.

To be continued.

95033137R00157

Made in the USA
Columbia, SC
03 May 2018